High Praise for
Christopher Fowler
and the Bryant & May
Mysteries

THE WATER ROOM

"The author's black humor evokes Peter Lovesey's
Peter Diamond series, and his successful revival of
the impossible-crime genre is reminiscent of John
Sladek's superb Thackeray Phin novels.... Fowler
should win a whole new set of readers with these
fair-play puzzlers."—*Publishers Weekly*

"A clever twist on the traditional police
procedural ... Genuinely fresh."—*Booklist*

"Humorous [and] engaging."—*Kirkus Reviews*

"They're old, they're cranky, and their chaotic work
habits inevitably lead to disaster. But life always
seems livelier whenever Arthur Bryant and John
May are on a case."—*New York Times Book Review*

"The team of John May and Arthur Bryant,
both far, far past retirement age, have the title
'Coolest Old Men' in a lock.... I'd follow these two
guys anywhere, just to hear them think out loud."
—*New Orleans Times-Picayune*

"[A] most unusual and impressive detecting duo ...
Fowler's wit and visual acuity combine for
entertaining and thrilling results."—*Chicago Tribune*

"[A] circuitous, entertaining and utterly satisfying ride."—*I Love a Mystery*

"There are generous dollops of quirky humor and a cast of memorable characters in this impossible-crime mystery by a new master of the classical detective story."—*Denver Post*

"An absolute gem."
—*Booknews* from The Poisoned Pen

"Unlike any police procedural I have ever read ... A wild tale full of odd facts and fascinating lore ... The author is busy writing up the third chronicle—definitely something to look forward to!"
—*Mystery News*

"Who would believe that the 'lost' rivers flowing under London could make for such an interesting mystery? Fans of Christopher Fowler, perhaps ... Fowler laces his novel with humor, as well as a particularly chilling killer. The reader will hope his two detectives postpone retirement much longer."
—*Richmond Times-Dispatch*

"More down to earth than [Jasper] Fforde but just as delightfully quirky ... Witty, erudite, and full of beans, these aging detectives contemplate their own mortality while investigating several deaths on a quiet street.... This book is stuffed with more amazing information than you ever thought possible about, among other topics, London's intricate and messy underground waterways."—*Seattle Times*

SEVENTY-SEVEN CLOCKS

"Compelling ... A twisty thriller, full of action and plot surprises." —*Publishers Weekly*

"Fowler magnificently presents the traditional mystery in a fresh light. The standard police procedural gets a unique interpretation thanks to an unusual, unpredictable plot and the somewhat unconventional investigative techniques of Bryant and May. Setting and characters are brought to life by Fowler's graceful, elegant writing and flow with ease through a taut, engrossing tale. This is an outstanding read in every respect." —*Romantic Times*

"Bryant and May are much younger in this volume than in the previous two, and readers will find that it offers a fresh look at the comedic relationship with one another, as well as highlighting their personal foibles and perceptions. I enjoyed reading this text [and] was surprised at the ending." —*Fresh Fiction*

"Swell!" —*Seattle Times*

FULL DARK HOUSE

"Atmospheric, hugely beguiling and as filled with tricks and sleights of hand as a magician's sleeve."
—Joanne Harris, author of *Chocolat*

"A most promising series ... [by an] energetic and imaginative author." —*Chicago Tribune*

"A delightful and unusual series."
—*Mystery Lovers Bookshop News*

"A madcap mystery that's completely crazy and great fun for it ... Invulnerable, genial and crafty, Bryant and May wend their perky way through hazards, pitfalls and false trails and finally run the culpables to ground.... Those who enjoy this intermittently hilarious charade should be many."—*Los Angeles Times*

"This darkly atmospheric first mystery introduces two most unusual detectives and nicely sets the Grand Guignol terror of a *Phantom of the Opera*–like plot against the dramatic backdrop of a city devastated by war."—*Library Journal*

"Unusual and absorbing ... Life in wartime London is beautifully drawn here, as are the behind-the-scenes theatrical shenanigans."—*Seattle Times*

"This is a rip-roaring start to what promises to be a wonderfully colorful, character-driven series that combines humor with marvelous setting detail and clever plot twists."—*I Love a Mystery Newsletter*

"Thrilling, exciting, edgy, and realistic—*Full Dark House* is easily all that and more."
—*Curled Up with a Good Book*

"Fowler skillfully moves back and forth between the two investigations, creating for the reader a particularly realistic portrayal of London during the Blitz.... This book left me wanting more of Bryant and May's in-between cases."—*Mystery News*

"Highly original debut of an unusual detective duo ... Witty and ironic, the time lines of this story weave seamlessly and take the reader back to Britain and its most perilous—and finest—hour."—*Calgary Herald*

"A first-rate debut that will keep you engrossed to the end."—*Anniston Star*

"Fowler manipulates the twists of his plot skillfully while creating unforgettable characters and delivering it all with a twig-snappingly dry wit."
—*Victoria (BC) Times-Colonist*

"What a unique way to start a new series ... Fowler may have struck gold with this unusual twosome. He promises there are more stories to follow."
—*Chronicle Herald*

"Eccentric characters and a fine sense of the period coupled with a touch of occultism and an edgy sense of humor make *Full Dark House* a 'smashing' read. Having once made the acquaintance of Bryant and May, you'll find yourself among the rapidly expanding ranks of Fowler's admirers."
—*Register-Pajaronian* online

"The witty dialogue and often gothic atmosphere will keep most turning the pages. Overall, this is a quirky, oddball mystery for those who like something a little different."—*Deadly Pleasures*

"The novel has all the essential ingredients: A labyrinthine theater makes a fine setting for a mystery; the dialogue is enjoyable; characters provide drama and comic relief; and there is much to flatter thespians and please Anglophiles."
—*Winston-Salem Journal*

ALSO BY CHRISTOPHER FOWLER

FULL DARK HOUSE
SEVENTY-SEVEN CLOCKS

And coming soon in hardcover from Bantam:

TEN SECOND STAIRCASE

THE WATER ROOM

CHRISTOPHER FOWLER

BANTAM BOOKS

THE WATER ROOM
A Bantam Book

PUBLISHING HISTORY
Doubleday UK hardcover edition published 2004
Bantam hardcover edition / July 2005
Bantam mass market edition / April 2006

Published by Bantam Dell
A Division of Random House, Inc.
New York, New York

ISBN-10: 0-553-58716-1
ISBN-13: 978-0-553-58716-6
Printed in the United States of America
Published simultaneously in Canada

www.bantamdell.com

OPM 10 9 8 7 6 5 4 3 2 1

To Kath
WAAF conscript, greyhound-stadium cashier, legal secretary, debt collector, charity worker, critic, mother, friend—because everyone has a story

ACKNOWLEDGEMENTS

The most bizarre facts in this book are the truest, but listing them all here would perhaps arm you with too much knowledge for the story ahead. They can, however, be readily found and substantiated by anyone interested in such arcane matters.

I would especially like to thank my fearless agent Mandy Little for providing so much support, encouragement and enthusiasm. Huge thanks also to my editor Simon Taylor, truly a gentleman and a man of his word, and to the whole Transworld team for ensuring the safe return of Bryant and May.

Thanks, Richard, for a million things, especially being funny and finding time, to Jim for always coming up with brilliant solutions, to Sally for organizing my life and to everyone brave enough to attend the atmospheric but occasionally insalubrious venues where I read, especially Maggie, Simon, Mike, Sarah, Andrew, Martin, Graham, Michelle, Poppy, Amber.

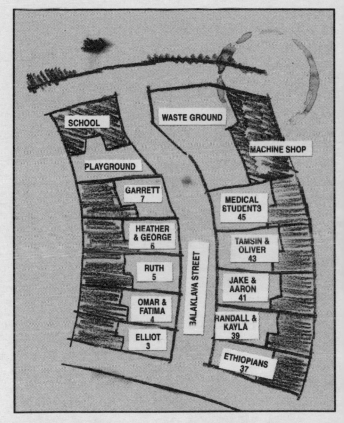

Mr Bryant's highly unscientific map of the afflicted area.

'Home is a name, a word, it is a strong one; stronger
than magician ever spoke, or spirit ever answered to,
in the strongest conjuration'

Charles Dickens

'A little water clears us of this deed'

Macbeth

I

A CHANGE IN THE WEATHER

Arthur Bryant looked out over London and remembered.

Fierce sunlight swathed Tower Bridge beyond the rockeries of smouldering bomb-sites. A Thames sailing barge was arriving in the Pool of London with a cargo of palm kernels. Its dusty red sails sagged in the afternoon heat as it drifted past Broadway Dock at Limehouse, like a felucca on the Nile. Dairy horses trotted along the deserted Embankment, empty milk cans chiming behind them. Children swam from the wharves below St Paul's, while carping mothers fanned away stale air from the river steps. He could smell horse dung and tobacco, meadow grass, the river. The world had once moved forward in single paces.

The vision wavered and vanished, displaced by sun-flares from the sealed glass corridors of the new city.

The old man in the unravelling sepia scarf waited for the rest of the party to gather around him. It was a Saturday afternoon at the start of October, and London's thirteen-week heatwave was about to end with a vengeance. Already, the wind had changed direction, stippling the surface of the river with grey goose-pimples. Above the spire of St Paul's, patulous white clouds deepened to a shade reminiscent of overwashed socks. The enervating swelter was giving way to a cool breeze, sharp in the shadows. The change had undermined his group's stamina, reducing their numbers to a handful, although four polite but puzzled Japanese boys had joined thinking they were on the Jack the Ripper tour. Once everyone had settled, the elderly guide began the last section of his talk.

'Ladies and gentlemen ...' He gave them the benefit of the doubt. 'If you would care to gather a little closer.' Arthur Bryant raised his voice as a red wall of buses rumbled past. 'We are now standing on Blackfriars—formerly Pitt—Bridge.' *Remember to use the hands,* he told himself. *Keep their interest.* 'Bridges are causeways across great divides, in this case the rich city on the north side'—*hand usage to indicate north*—'and the more impoverished south side. Does anyone have a Euro note in their pocket? Take it out and you'll find a bridge, the universal symbol for something that unites and strengthens.' He paused, less for effect than to catch his breath. Bryant really had no need to freelance as a city tour guide. His detective duties at the London Peculiar Crimes Unit would have kept a man half his age working late. But he enjoyed contact with the innocent public; most of the civilians he met in his day job were under criminal suspicion. Explaining the city to strangers calmed him down, even helped him to understand himself.

He pulled his ancient scarf tighter and abandoned his set text. What the hell, they were the last group of the season, and had proven pretty unresponsive. 'According to Disraeli,' he announced, ' "London is a nation, not a city." "That great cesspool into which all the loungers of the Empire are irresistibly drained," said Conan Doyle. "No duller spectacle on earth than London on a rainy Sunday afternoon," according to De Quincey, so take your pick. One of the planet's great crossing-points, it has more languages, religions and newspapers than any other place on earth. We divide into tribes according to age, wealth, class, race, religion, taste and personality, and this diversity breeds respect.' Two members of the group nodded and repeated the word 'diversity', like an Oxford Street language class. *God, this lot's hard work,* thought Bryant. *I'm gasping for a cup of tea.*

'London's main characteristic is an absence of form. Its thirty-three boroughs have busy districts running through them like veins, with no visible hierarchy, and neighbourhood ties remain inexplicably close. Because Londoners have a strongly pronounced sense of home, where you live counts more than who you are.' Bryant mostly lived inside his head. *Remember the facts,* he told himself, *they like facts.*

'We have six royal parks, 160 theatres, 8,600 restaurants, 300 museums and around 30,000 shops. Over 3,500 criminal offences are reported every day. Poverty and wealth exist side by side, often in the same street. Bombings caused slum clearance and social housing, rupturing centuries-old barriers of class, turning the concept into something mysterious and ever-shifting. London is truly unknowable.'

Bryant looked past his under-dressed audience to the swirling brown river. The Japanese boys were bored and cold, and had started taking pictures of litter bins. One of them was listening to music. 'A city of cruelty and kindness, stupidity and excess, extremes and paradoxes,' he told them, raising his voice. 'Almost half of all journeys through the metropolis are made on foot. A city of glass, steel, water and flesh that no longer smells of beer and brick, but piss and engines.'

He lifted his silver-capped walking stick to the sky. 'The arches of London's Palladian architecture lift and curve in secular harmonies. Walls of glass reflect wet pavements in euphonious cascades of rain.' He was no longer addressing the group, but voicing his thoughts. 'We're heading for winter, when a caul of sluggishness deepens into *thanatomimesis*, the state of being mistaken for death. But the city never dies; it just lies low. Its breath grows shallow in the cold river air while housebound tenants, flu-ridden and fractious with the perpetual motion of indoor activity, recover and grow strong once more. London and its people are parasites trapped in an ever-evolving symbiosis. At night the residents lose their carapace of gentility, bragging and brawling through the streets. The old London emerges, dancing drunk skeletons leaving graveyard suburbs to terrify the faint of heart.'

Now even the hardiest listeners looked confused. They spoke to each other in whispers and shook their heads. Their guide seemed to be straying from his topic: 'A Historic Thameside Walk'. The Japanese boys gave up and wandered off. Someone said, rather loudly, 'This tour was much better last time. There was a café.'

Bryant carried on, regardless.

'London no longer suffers from the weight of its

past. Now only the faintest resonance of legendary events remains. Oh, I can show you balustrades, pillars and scrollwork, point out sites of religious and political interest, streets that have witnessed great events, but to be honest there's bugger all to see. It's impossible to imagine the lives of those who came before us. Our visible history has been rubbed to a trace, like graffiti scrubbed from Portland stone. London has reinvented itself more completely than ever. And whoever grows up here becomes a part of its human history.'

He had completely lost his listeners. They were complaining to each other in dissatisfaction and disarray. 'That concludes the tour for today,' he added hastily. 'I think we'll skip question time, you've been a truly dreadful audience.' He decided not to bother with his tip box as the mystified, grumbling group was forced to disperse across the windy bridge.

Bryant looked toward the jumble of outsized apartment buildings being constructed at the edge of the Thames, the yellow steel cranes clustered around them like praying mantises. After so many years in the service, he was quick to sense approaching change. Another wave of executives was colonizing the riverbank, creating a new underclass. He wondered how soon the invasion would provoke fresh forms of violence.

It's metabolizing quickly, he thought. *How long before it becomes unrecognizable? How can I hope to understand it for much longer?*

He turned up his collar as he passed the urban surfers of the South Bank car park. The clatter of their skateboards bounced between the concrete arcades like the noise of shunting trains. Kids always found ways to occupy ignored spaces. He emerged into daylight and paced at the river rail, studying the evolving skyline of the Thames.

Hardly anything left of my childhood memories.

The Savoy, St Paul's, the spire of St Bride's, a few low monuments palisaded by international banks as anonymous as cigarette boxes. A city in an apostasy of everything but money. Even the river had altered. The ships and barges, no longer commercially viable, had left behind an aorta of bare brown water. Eventually only vast hotels, identical from Chicago to Bangkok, would remain.

As ever, Londoners had found ways of cutting grand new structures down to human size. The 'Blade of Light' connecting St Paul's to Bankside had become known as 'The Wobbly Bridge'. The Swiss Re building had been rechristened 'The Erotic Gherkin' long before its completion. Names were a sign of affection, to be worn like guild colours. The old marks of London, from its financial institutes to its market buildings, were fading from view like vanishing coats of arms.

I've been walking this route for over half a century, Bryant thought, stepping aside for a wave of shrieking children. A Mexican band was playing in the foyer of the Festival Hall. People were queueing for an art event involving tall multi-coloured flags. He remembered walking through the black empty streets after the War, and feeling completely alone. It was hard to feel alone here now. He missed the sensation.

His fingers closed around the keys in his pocket. Sergeant Longbright had mentioned she might go into the unit today in order to get things straight for

Monday. He preferred to work out of hours, when the phonelines were closed and he could leave papers all over the floor without complaint. He could join Janice, collect his thoughts, smoke his pipe, prepare himself for a fresh start. For a woman who had recently retired, Longbright showed an alarming enthusiasm for returning.

For the past month, the Peculiar Crimes Unit—or rather, what was left of it—had been shunted into two sloping rooms above Sid Smith's barbershop in Camden Town, while its old offices were being rebuilt. The relocation had been forced by a disastrous explosion that had destroyed the interior of the building and years of case files. The ensuing chaos had badly affected Bryant, whose office was virtually his home. He had lost his entire collection of rare books and artefacts in the blaze. Worse than that, he had yet to recover his dignity. The sheer embarrassment of being presumed dead! At least they had uncovered a long-dormant murderer, even if their methodology had proven highly abnormal.

But of course, nothing at the PCU had ever been normal. Founded as an experimental unit during the War to handle the cases no one else understood, let alone wanted, the detectives had built a reputation for defusing politically sensitive and socially embarrassing situations, using unorthodox and controversial methods. Some of the more rule-bound Met officers hated their guts, but most of the force's foot soldiers regarded them as living legends, if only because they had repeatedly refused promotion to keep their status as ordinary detectives.

Bryant climbed the trash-stickered steps to Waterloo Bridge and hailed a taxi. Thirteen weeks of airless summer heat had passed without rain, but now the warmth was fading from the yellow London brick, and there was moisture in the rising breeze. The autumn chill stealing up the river would bring rheumatism and new strains of influenza. Already he could feel his joints starting to ache. The only thing that would take his mind off the problems of old age was hard work.

He dug into a pocket and found his pewter flask, granting himself a small nip of cherry brandy. When he was alone he thought too much. John May was the only person who could bring calm to his sense of escalating panic. Their fifty-year-plus partnership had the familiarity of an old radio show. The bald head gave a little shake within its yards of musty scarf; Bryant told himself he would never consider retiring again. The thought of doing so made him feel ill. When the unit reopened in its rightful office on Monday morning, he would return to his desk beside John and Janice, and stay in harness until the day he died. After all, it was where he was needed most. It would be important to show he could still do the job. And he had nothing else without it.

2

THE FIRST DEATH OF AUTUMN

'I came to you, Mr Bryant,' said Benjamin Singh, 'because you have such an incredible capacity to be annoying.'

'I can't imagine what you mean,' said Bryant, stuffing his bentwood pipe with a mixture of Old Holborn and eucalyptus leaves.

'I mean you can get things done by badgering people. I don't trust the regular police. They're distracted and complacent. I'm glad you are still here. I thought you would have retired by now. You are so very, very far past retirement age.'

Bryant fixed his visitor with an evil eye. Mr Singh dabbed his cheeks with a paper handkerchief. He hadn't been crying; it was a gesture of respect for the dead. He paused to take stock of his surroundings. 'I'm sorry, have you been burgled?' he asked.

'Oh, no.' Bryant fanned out his match and sucked noisily on the pipe. 'The unit burned down. Well, it blew up and burned down. They're still rebuilding it and we haven't had time to unpack anything yet. We don't officially reopen for business until ten o'clock this morning. It's only nine, you know. It'll be a nightmare around here later because we've got painters, carpenters and IT bods turning up. There's no floor in the toilet. Health and Safety said they wouldn't be responsible if we moved in, but we couldn't stay above a barbershop. It doesn't help that I'm also in the middle of moving house, and appear to have mislaid all my socks. Sorry, do please go on.'

'Perhaps we should go and see Mr Singh's sister,' ventured Sergeant Longbright.

'No one will move her body until I tell them to, Janice.' Bryant shot her a look.

Longbright knew better than to argue with Arthur's working methods. The inability of the Peculiar Crimes Unit to conduct its affairs in a conventional manner was embarrassingly well documented. Having abandoned attempts to make it properly accountable, the Home Office had now separated the unit from Metropolitan Police jurisdiction and placed it under the nebulous security services of MI7. There would be certain advantages: the detectives would no longer have to pay exorbitant charges for equipment usage or fight the Met for their annual budget, and the old demarcation lines would finally be resolved, but they would now be accountable to passing governments, where personal resentments ran deep. Bryant and his partner John May had been given six months to make the revised unit successful or train up their own replacements, for they were—as everyone seemed so keen to point out—both far beyond the statutory retirement age. There had been talk of closing the place down altogether, and yet it seemed a guardian angel existed in the labyrinth of Whitehall, because eleventh-hour reprieves continued to appear with the regularity of rainbows.

'I didn't have time to change.' Benjamin Singh indicated his clothes, clearly feeling disrespectful for wearing a stripy tank-top, brown trousers and a purple shirt. 'I visit my sister Ruth every Monday morning to clean the house for her,' he explained. 'She's very old and can't lift the vacuum cleaner. The moment I opened the front door, I knew something was wrong. She was sitting on a chair in the basement, dressed for the shops, which was strange because she knows I always go for her. Ruth just makes out the list. She was cold to the touch.'

'Forgive me, but I don't understand why you didn't immediately call for an ambulance.' Bryant remembered that the new office had a smoking ban, and tamped out his pipe before Longbright had a chance to complain.

'She was dead, Arthur, not sick. Kentish Town police station is only three streets away from her house, so I walked around there and saw the duty sergeant, but I didn't like his attitude— he told me to call an ambulance as well—so I came here.'

'You know we don't take cases off the street any more, Ben,' Bryant explained. 'They have to come to us through proper channels now.'

'But when I found her, my first thought was to—'

'You're supposed to be recording this conversation, Arthur,' Longbright interrupted. 'From now on we have to stick to the rulebook.'

Bryant poked about in the cardboard box at his feet and pulled out a battered dictaphone. 'Here,' he offered, 'you have a go. It doesn't seem to let me record, for some reason. Perhaps I'm doing something wrong.' The patented helpless look suggested innocence but didn't wash with Longbright, who was familiar with her boss's ability to cause malfunctions in the simplest equipment. Bryant was no longer allowed to touch the computers owing to the odd demagnetizing effect he had on delicate technology. His application to attend an IT course had been turned down six times by those who feared he would cause a national meltdown if let loose near PITO, the Police Information Technology Organization. His facility for picking up old broadcasts of *Sunday Night at the London Palladium* on his Sky dish had been documented with fascination but no hope of explanation by the *Fortean Times*.

'All right, let's go and have a look at your sister.' Bryant clambered wearily to his feet. Tortoise-like, scarf-wrapped, argumentative to the point of rudeness, myopic and decrepit, Bryant appeared even more dishevelled than usual, owing to the current upheavals in his life. A waft of white hair rose in a horseshoe above his ears, as if he'd been touching static globes at the Science Museum. Behind his watery sapphire eyes, though, was a spirit as robust and spiky as winter earth. He had been described as 'independent to the point of vexation and individual to the level of eccentricity', which seemed accurate enough. John May, his dapper partner, was younger by three years, an attractive senior of considerable charisma, modern in outlook and gregarious by nature. Bryant was a loner, literate and secretive, with a sidelong, crafty mind that operated in opposition to May's level-headed thinking.

'Janice, when John finally deigns to turn up, would you send him around to join us? Where are we going?'

'Number 5, Balaklava Street,' said Mr Singh. 'It's between Inkerman Road and Alma Street.'

'Ah, your sister's house was built in the 1850s, then. The roads are all named after battles of the Crimean War. Victorian town councils were fond of such gestures.' Bryant knew historical facts like that. It was a pity he couldn't remember anything that had happened in the last twenty years. Recent events were his partner's speciality. John May remembered everyone's birthdays. Bryant barely recalled anyone's names. May exhibited a natural charm that disarmed the toughest opponents. Bryant could make a nun bristle. May had girlfriends and relatives, parties and friends. Bryant had his work. May would smile in blossoming sunlight. Bryant would frown and step back into darkness. Each corresponding jag and trough in their characters was a further indication of the symbiosis they had developed over the years. They fitted together like old jigsaw pieces.

Longbright waited for Bryant to leave the office, then opened all the windows to clear the overpowering smell of paint. She set about unpacking the new computers, thankful that the old man could occupy his mind with the unit's activities once more; he had been driving everyone mad for the past month, acting like a housebound child on a rainy day.

Arthur's sudden decision to move house had been uncharacteristic. Furthermore, he had chosen to leave behind his landlady, the woman who had tolerated his dreadful behaviour for more than forty years. Alma Sorrowbridge had been shocked and hurt by her tenant's determination to abandon her in Battersea as he moved alone to the workshop of a converted false-teeth factory in Chalk Farm. As she unbattened boxes and uncoiled cables, Longbright wondered at his motive. Perhaps Arthur felt that time was running short, and was preparing to distance himself from those closest to him. Perversely, his morbidity always increased when he was removed from death. Proximity to a fresh tragedy concentrated his mind wonderfully. Truly ghastly events took years off him.

Longbright caught herself humming as she worked, and realized that she was happy again.

'So you and Mr May still have the Peculiar Crimes Unit.' Mr Singh made conversation as he drove his little blue Nissan from Mornington Crescent to Kentish Town. Bryant had given the unit his Mini Cooper, a sixties relic with a history of rust and electrical faults, and as it was away being repaired he was forced to rely on getting lifts, which at least allowed the pedestrian population of north London to breathe a collective sigh of relief.

'Yes, but we've had a change of brief since the days when you worked with us,' said Bryant. 'Now it's problem homicides, low-profile investigations, cases with the potential to spark social panic, general unrest and malaise. We get the jobs that don't lead anywhere and don't suit Met's wide-boys. They're too busy number-crunching; the last thing they want is the kind of investigation that hangs around for months without producing quantifiable results. They have league tables now.'

'So you're meant to free up the regular police.'

'I suppose that's how they see it. We've had a few successes, but of course the cases that pay off are never the ones you expect.' He wasn't complaining.

While everyone else was streamlining operations to board the law-enforcement superhighway, the PCU remained an unreliable but essential branch line no one dared to close down, and that was how he liked it. 'I'm sorry you were the one who had to find your sister.'

'It's not her dying, you understand, I've been expecting that. But something is wrong, you'll see.'

'What are you doing these days?'

'Both my daughters finally married. I said to them, "Don't wed Indian boys, they'll make you have babies instead of careers," but they wouldn't listen to me, so I fear there will be no more academics bearing my name. I retired from the British Library when it moved to King's Cross, but I'm still lecturing on pagan cults.' Benjamin had once provided the unit with information allowing them to locate a Cornish devil cult. 'You know, I had asked Ruth to move in with me, but she was too independent. We never got on well with each other. I wanted her to wear one of those things around her neck, a beeper, you know? She refused. Now look where it's got her.' This time, Bryant noticed, Mr Singh's tissue came away damp.

The little Nissan turned a corner and came to a stop.

Balaklava Street was a surprise. It was cobbled, for a start; few such thoroughfares had survived the most recent invasion of property developers, and only an EEC ruling had prevented London's councils from ripping up the remaining streets. The pavement consisted of velvety flagstones, the kind that were pleasurable to roller-skate over, and ran in a dog-leg that provided the road with the appearance of a cul-de-sac. Commuters rarely used it as a rat-run and

casual pedestrians were infrequent, so a peculiar calm
had settled across the roof slates, and it was quiet in
the way that London backstreets could often be, with
the traffic fading to a distant hum and the rustling
of high plane trees foregrounded by birdsong. Deep
underground, passing Tube trains could be faintly detected, and only the proliferation of parked cars suggested modern times.

Bryant opened the car door and eased himself out
with the help of the hated walking stick that May had
bought for his last birthday. He noted that the frame-
work of the street's original gas lamps still stood, although they had been rewired for electric light. There
were ten terraced yellow-brick houses, five on each
side, before the road skirted a Victorian school that
had been converted into an adult-education centre.
Opposite, at the end of the road, a parched patch of
waste ground was backed by the car park of a kitchen
centre and a chaotic wood joinery, the triangle forming a dark corner where youths could play football by
day and buy drugs at night.

At this end of the street, beyond the terraces,
someone had dumped an old sofa, a dead television
and some fractured chairs against a wall, creating an
al fresco lounge. The walls of the school had been
daubed with luxuriant graffiti and stencilled slander,
marked with the initials IDST ('If Destroyed, Still
True'). Around the next corner was a van-repair centre, a hostel and a block of spacious loft apartments.
Different worlds abutted without touching.

Mr Singh slipped a disability permit on to the dashboard. 'I have to use this,' he explained, 'Camden has
zoned all the streets and they'll tow me away otherwise, the greedy cash-grabbing bastards. They've no

respect for a decent educated man. What are their qualifications, I'd like to know?'

Bryant smiled to himself. Benjamin was still confusing culture and commerce, even though it was twenty years since they had last met. 'Number 5, you say?' He waved his stick at the littered front garden. Although it appeared relatively prosperous, the street had obviously seen better times. The houses had been amended with white porches, sills and railings, probably Edwardian additions, but these had started to corrode, and were not being replaced. Each house had two floors above the road, one floor below. It was starting to spit with rain, and the front steps looked slippery. At Bryant's age, you noticed things like that.

Mr Singh had trouble with the keys. He seemed understandably nervous about going back into his sister's house. Bryant could detect a sour trace of damp in the dark hall. 'Don't touch anything,' he warned. 'I shouldn't really let you lead the way, but— well, we still do things differently at the PCU.' He tried the lights, but nothing happened.

'They disconnected Ruth after she refused to pay the bill,' Mr Singh explained. 'She was getting—I wouldn't say crazy; difficult, perhaps. Of course, we were raised by oil-light, because our grandmother retained fond memories of her home in India. But the basement here is always dark, and the stairs can be treacherous. Wait, there are candles.' He rattled a box and lit a pair.

Bryant saw Mr Singh's point as they descended. 'You found her down here?' he asked.

'This is the puzzle, as you will see.' Mr Singh entered a shadowed doorway to the left of a small kitchen. The size of the bathroom took Bryant by surprise; it was disproportionately large, taking up more than half of the basement. The old lady was tiny, as dry and skeletal as a long-dead sparrow. She was seated on a large oak chair, her booted feet barely reaching the floor, her head tilted back on a single embroidered cushion draped over the top rail, her hands in her lap, touching with their palms up. The position looked comfortable enough, as though she had simply dropped back her head and died, but Bryant felt this was not a place where one would naturally choose to sit. There was no table or stool, nowhere to place a light, nor were there any proper windows to look out of. The chair was a piece of furniture on to which you would throw your clothes. Ruth Singh was dressed for going outside. She was even wearing a scarf.

'You see, this is all wrong,' said her brother, turning uncomfortably in the doorway. 'It doesn't seem at all natural to me. It's not like her.'

'Perhaps she came down to get something, felt a pain in her chest and sat down for a moment to regain her breath.'

'Of course not. Ruth had absolutely nothing wrong with her heart.'

That's why you came to see me, thought Bryant. *You can't accept that she might just have sat down and died.* 'You'd be surprised,' he said gently. 'People often pass away in such small, unready moments.' He approached the old woman's body and noted her swollen, livid ankles. Ruth Singh's blood had already settled. She had been seated there for some hours, probably overnight. 'Doesn't seem to be any heat in here.'

'It's been hot for so long. There's a storage heater for the winter. Oh dear.'

Bryant watched his old colleague. 'Go to the back door and take a deep breath. I think it will be better if you wait outside while I take a quick look at her. It isn't really my job, you know. I'll only get told off for interfering.'

The room was cool enough to have slowed Mrs Singh's body processes down. Bryant knew he would have to bring in Giles Kershaw, the unit's new forensic officer, for an accurate time of death. The rug beneath the old woman's boots looked wet.

'There's no one else left now, just us,' murmured Mr Singh, reluctant to leave. 'Ruth never married, she could have had her pick of the boys but she waited too long. She shamed her parents, being so English. All her life she was fussy and independent. My sister was a headstrong woman, my daughters are not. It seems the generations can no longer teach each other. Everything is out of place.' He shook his head sadly, pulling the door shut behind him.

The room was so still. It felt as if even the dust in the air had ceased to circulate. Bryant drew a breath and gently exhaled, turning his head. Watery light filtered in from an opaque narrow window near the ceiling, at the pavement level of the bathroom. Perhaps it had opened once for ventilation, but layers of paint had sealed it shut.

Ruth Singh looked as if she could have died watching television, were it not for being in the wrong room, and for the odd position of her legs. She had not suffered a heart attack and simply sat down, because her hands were carefully folded in her lap. Something wasn't right. Bryant absently stroked the base of his skull, leaving the nimbus of his white hair in tufted disorder. With a sigh, he removed a slim pack from his pocket and separated a pair of plastic anti-static gloves. He performed the obvious checks without thinking: observe, touch, palpate, listen. No cardiac movement, no femoral or carotid pulse, bilateral dilation in the clouded eyes. The skin of her arm did not blanch when he applied pressure; it was cold but not yet clammy. Setting the candle closer, he slipped his hand behind her neck and gently tried to raise her head. The stiffness in the body was noticeable, but not complete. At a rough guess she had been dead between eight and twelve hours, so she would have passed away between five-thirty p.m. and nine-thirty p.m. on Sunday night. Kershaw would be able to narrow it down.

When he tried to remove his hand, he was forced to raise the body, but the cushion slipped and Ruth rolled sideways. *Next time I'll leave this to a medic,* he thought, trying to upright her, but before he had a chance to do so, she spat on him. Or rather, a significant quantity of water emptied from her mouth on to his overcoat.

Bryant wiped himself down, then gently prised her lips apart. Two gold teeth, no dental plate and a healthy tongue, but her throat appeared to be filled with a brownish liquid. As he moved his hand, it ran from the corner of her lower lip. He had assumed that the wetness of the rug had been caused by the incontinence of dying. Her clothes were dry. He checked on either side of the chair, then under it. There was no sign of a dropped glass, or any external water source. Passing to the bathroom cabinet, he found a toothbrush mug and placed it beneath her chin, collecting as much of the liquid as he could. He studied her mouth and nostrils for tell-tale marks left by fine pale foam, usually created by the mixture of water, air and mucus churned in a suffocating victim's air passages. The wavering light made it hard to see clearly.

'You're going mad,' he muttered to himself. 'She dresses, she drowns, she sits down and dies, all in the comfort of her own home.' He rose unsteadily to his feet, dreading the thought of having to warn Benjamin about a post-mortem.

Standing in the centre of the front room, he tried to see into Ruth Singh's life. No conspicuous wealth, only simple comforts. A maroon Axminster rug, a cabinet of small brass ornaments, two lurid reproductions of Indian landscapes, some chintzy machine-coloured photographs of its imperial past, a bad Constable reproduction, a set of Wedgwood china that had never been used, pottery clowns, Princess Diana gift plates—a magpie collection of items from two cultures. Bryant vaguely recalled Benjamin telling him that his family had never been to India. Ruth Singh was two or three years older; perhaps she kept a trace-memory of her birth country alive through the pictures. It was important to feel settled at home. How had that comfort been disrupted? *Not a violent death*, he told himself, *but an unnatural one, all the same.*

Outside, summer died quickly, and the rising wind bore a dark fleet of rainclouds.

3

BUSINESS AS USUAL

By Monday afternoon it was as if the hiatus of the last month had never occurred. Ten crates unloading, nine boxes opened, eight phones ringing, seven staff complaining, six desks in various states of assembly, five damaged chairs, four cases pending, three workmen hammering, two computers crashing and a cat locked in a filing cabinet with no key. Arthur Bryant was sitting back at his desk, beaming amidst the chaos, looking for all the world as if he had never left.

'It's very simple, Janice,' he explained to the confused and exasperated sergeant. 'At the base of the unit's new structure I've appointed two detective constables, an enormous, accident-prone innocent with a positively Homeric attitude to groundwork named Colin Bimsley, and I've found him a partner, DC Meera Mangeshkar, whose experiences in various south London hell-holes have apparently equipped her with the twin rapid-response mechanisms of cynicism and sarcasm. Blame John, he gave me their CVs. They'll be occupying the room next door.'

'Right, got that.' Longbright was having to make

notes with a blue eyeliner pencil because she was unable to locate any pens.

'Now, above these two are another new pair, a vulpine young officer named Dan Banbury, who's joining us as a hyphenate crime-scene manager and IT expert, and the nervous twit Giles Kershaw, with whom I've already had an argument this morning, who has been forced upon us as a replacement for our ancient coroner, Oswald Finch. He'll be, I quote, our "forensic pathologist slash Social Sciences Liaison Officer", whatever that means, although I shall insist on using Oswald for certain specialized duties. I can't believe John still hasn't turned up yet. He sat in on the interviews with me, he knows all about this.'

'He'll be here, don't worry.'

'The unit's fifth member is of course your good self, supposedly retired but now freelance, whom I have agreed to take back on a renewable three-month contract which will allow you to continue working with your oldest and dearest friends, viz John and myself, the sixth and seventh members of the unit.'

'Thank you, much appreciated,' said Longbright with just a hint of sarcasm.

'Naturally, you will continue to enjoy our inexcusable favouritism, not just because you remind us of Ava Gardner or because you make a proper cabbie's mug of tea, but because you're the only one capable of keeping this place in a semblance of order. The eighth and final member of this workforce will continue to be the terminally indecisive Raymond Land, our acid-stomached acting head, who has been forced to return for another season until he can effect a transfer to traffic control or a small-crimes division, preferably on a Caribbean island where the pressures will be fewer and the weather warmer. I make that six men and two women, employed to tackle the cases that no one else in London wants to touch with a stick. Not much of a team, I know, but we can draw on outside forces if necessary.'

Longbright knew what that meant: a motley collection of disbarred academics, crackpot historians, alternative therapists, necromancers, anarchists, spirit healers, nightclub doormen, psychics, clairvoyants and street mountebanks, many of whom consorted with known criminals, drafted in on a promise of cash in hand. They were unreliable, expensive and occasionally indispensable.

Kershaw stuck his head around the unpainted door-jamb. 'The remains of two bodies were taken to Bayham Street Mortuary while you were out,' he explained in a high, plummy voice that Bryant had grown to hate in less than an hour. 'One non-caucasian male approximately forty-five to fifty years old, multiple stab wounds to the stomach, the other a caucasian pre-operative transsexual, male to female, approximately nineteen years of age, throat contusions indicative of strangulation, quite chatty in the ambulance but DOA at A&E. Camden Met wants nothing to do with them.'

'They're not our cases, surely?' John May picked up on the conversation as he sauntered in with a folded newspaper under his arm.

'Where on earth have you been?' Bryant demanded to know.

Kershaw shrugged. 'Right here.'

'Not you. Him.' Bryant pointed at his partner, who was unfolding the paper and scanning the arts pages as he slipped behind his desk.

'Anyway, you're supposed to knock before entering,' Bryant told Kershaw testily.

'Not possible, old chap, you haven't got a door. Do you want to hear about this or not?'

'I suppose so, and I'm Mr Bryant to you, chum. John, you remember Giles Kershaw, the forensic wallah you promoted for candidature in our happy circle? Does no one introduce themselves properly any more? The French permit themselves the extravagance of kissing one another, surely a simple English handshake is common decency. Where *have* you been?'

'Personal business, tell you later,' smiled May, which meant he had stayed over with a woman, a habit Bryant felt was ridiculous and probably dangerous at his age.

'They were picked up at around five o'clock this morning in Camden Town, according to the duty sheet,' explained Kershaw. 'D'you ever wonder why there are so many murder cases involving transsexuals?'

'No, why?' asked Bryant, pulling out desk drawers and rummaging through them noisily.

'Oh, I don't know, I just wondered if you'd wondered.'

'Visible victim status encourages domination and attracts sexual sadists, read your Krafft-Ebing, it's not brain surgery. These ones were most likely victims of a drunken fight. North London Met is overloaded so they couldn't wait for a chance to start palming us off with the extra, even though they're no longer entitled to do so. I'm not working on common fatal assaults, it's degrading. The key must be around here somewhere.'

'What have you lost?' May asked Longbright.

'Mr Bryant's rescued another cat.' She rolled her thickly painted eyes. 'He was taking it to the vet.'

'We've got to get him free before he runs out of air.' Bryant turned a drawer over the desk, cascading rubbish everywhere. 'I've christened him Crippen, because we had that ginger tom named Lucan who disappeared after killing a bird.'

'You're not good with animals, Arthur. Look what happened to your parrot. That poor carpet-layer was distraught, hammering it flat in the underlay after you told him you couldn't find your tobacco pouch. How on earth did the cat get shut in a filing cabinet?'

'I thought he'd be safe there while I went out. I didn't know the drawer was self-locking.'

'Raymond's still in the next room.' Longbright pointed at the door. Raymond Land was allergic to cats. He had also tripped over Crippen's litter tray and nearly fallen down the stairs, and had now begun to suspect that the others were hiding something.

'If he starts sneezing I'll tell him it's the fresh paint,' Bryant promised. He had discovered the tiny black and white stray dumped inside a bin-bag on Camden's Chalcot Road at the weekend, and had brought it to work inside his jacket with the intention of overcoming its apprehensions about the cruelty of humans. Unfortunately, Crippen's worst fears had now been confirmed. To add to the confusion, two men had arrived with a photocopier, and had started unpacking it in the middle of the floor, trapping everyone at the edges of the room, and now they were all getting wet paint on their clothes. From inside Bryant's filing cabinet came a high feline whine.

'Any tea going?' asked John May, throwing his

overcoat into a corner. 'Did your doctor give you the all-clear after that crack on the nut?'

Bryant had sustained a head injury during the unit's last investigation. 'He made me read a couple of eye charts. I passed with flying colours.'

'Really? You can't usually see a hole in a ladder.'

'I had crib sheets. See.' Bryant held up miniature copies of the charts.

'And you got away with it?'

'No, he saw me looking up my sleeve and prescribed new reading glasses. Look.' He donned the spectacles, his eyes swimming up like great blue moons.

'My God, they make you look like Reginald Christie. Is that who I mean, the murderer who gassed his victims? Except you're older, of course. Why is it so cold in here? What happened to summer? It's going to pelt down any minute.'

'We haven't got any heaters yet, we can't shut the windows because of the smell, and until this year summer in London only existed as a tentative concept. You should know, you've lived here for about a hundred years yourself.' Bryant accepted a hot mug from Longbright, stirred it with the end of a paper-knife and passed it to his partner. 'I'm afraid it's bags until we can buy some decent stuff. The toilet doesn't appear to have a door, we're missing a couple of desks and part of a ceiling. Oh, and the electrics keep shorting out. It wasn't me; I haven't touched anything. It's nearly half past three. Were you really all this time with a woman? You could have got so much done.'

'Actually, I had a medical at lunchtime and was sent for a chest X-ray. Had to wait for ages. I tried calling you when I got out, but your mobile wasn't answering.'

'No, it wouldn't. It got wet, so I tried to dry it out in Janice's sandwich toaster. The toaster and the phone sort of—*melded*—into a single appliance, scientifically interesting as a new mechanical life-form but utterly useless for communication. Kershaw, you can bugger off now, there's a chap, we'll be fine.'

'What do I tell Bayham Street?' asked Kershaw with a faint air of desperation.

'Tell them you'll take a wander over with Mr Banbury after you've visited the crime scene, give them the kind of report they love—yards of statistics, no opinions. Not that you'll find anything at the site after Camden's gormless plods have trampled around in their size tens. And be careful near Finch, he bites.'

May looked up from his newspaper. 'Do you know that's the third mobile you've destroyed this year, not counting the one you lost when the unit blew up?'

'Surely not. I quite fancy one of those videophones. I'm surprised no one's created a collective noun for them yet, or even any decent short-form generic terminology. I thought we were supposed to be an ingenious race, but I fear America has the edge on us when it comes to branding. Have we got any biscuits, Janice? Not Hobnobs, they get under my plate.'

The streets around Mornington Crescent station were quiet for a Monday afternoon. If you had been walking past, and had looked up at the arched first-floor windows above the Tube entrance, rebuilt in their original maroon tiles, you would have seen Arthur Bryant and John May in silhouette against the opaque grey glass beneath the station logo, Bryant seated under an 'N', May tilting his chair below the 'S', as sharply delineated as Balinese puppets.

'Tell John about your old lady,' Longbright suggested.

'What old lady?' asked May. 'Have I missed something interesting?'

'Do you remember a fellow called Benjamin Singh? Ah.' Bryant found the keys and released a traumatized Crippen from his cabinet. A less appropriately named kitten was hard to visualize. 'Expert on English occult literature and pagan mythology. I used him as a consultant a few times in the eighties. His sister died this morning, and he came here.'

There was a bang as DC Bimsley nearly went through the window with a box of stackable files. Everyone flinched except Bryant, whose deafness was highly selective.

'He wanted her to be seen by someone he trusted, so I went round there and took a look.' Bryant patted his pockets for a match. 'She was in her late seventies. Body was in the basement on a very hard upright chair, and there was water in her throat. I've given Banbury the sample, and I'm waiting for a quick confirmation from the child Kershaw, but it would appear to have been a dry drowning.'

'What's a dry drowning?' asked DC Bimsley, listening in.

'No water in the lungs, death as a result of laryngospasm—constriction of the windpipe. Quite rare, but not unheard-of,' May explained without thinking.

'The problem is, it's an unprovable method of death. Most drownings are accidental, often because the victim is pissed. A deep breath is taken in shock, and the lungs inflate like balloons. There was a small contusion on the back of her head, might have been an old mark but I'm inclined not to think so.' Bryant, ignoring the newly installed No Smoking signs, poked about in his coat and produced his pipe. He started to light it but Longbright snatched it out of his mouth with a tut. 'I got Oswald in to take a quick look at her.'

'No wonder Kershaw's upset with you,' said May. 'Oswald Finch is retired, you can't just call him in over the new boy's head.'

'I can do what I like,' Bryant reminded him. 'I don't trust someone whose surname sounds like a sneeze. I was going to use him, but Finch is an expert on drowning. You know how instinctive he is about such deaths. He reckons there's no mucus in her air passages, nothing agitated by an attempt to breathe, no real distension in the lungs, no broken blood vessels in the nostrils. He's opening her up tonight but doesn't think he'll find diatomic particles in the heart ventricles because she went into spasm almost at once.'

'Could she have drowned at her sink?'

'It's possible, except that we found her bone-dry and fully dressed for going out, seated in a chair. She could have drowned in half an inch of water if she'd been unable to get up, but not in a chair.'

'Did she have swollen ankles, bare feet?' asked May suddenly.

'Not bare—old-lady bootees, the non-slip kind—but swollen.'

'I was thinking footbath. You know what old ladies are like. Was the floor wet?'

'Yes, a little. There's a rug over parquet.'

'You didn't ask the brother if he'd moved anything?'

'I'm losing my touch, John, forgive me, I'll call him right now.' He turned to Longbright. 'Why is everyone else's phone connected except mine?'

'Forgive me for pointing this out,' said Longbright, 'but Mrs Singh's case hardly falls within our official jurisdiction.'

'I do recall the tenet under which this unit was set up, Janice. "*Taking pressure off the Metropolitan service by dealing with those cases deemed too problematic or sensitive for traditional channels*"—they'll hardly have time to give something like this more than a cursory glance, will they? Besides, I have no other work at the present time. I don't count eviscerated drunks.'

Bryant had an offensive way of dismissing what he called 'ordinary crime'. He looked from one face to the other with such an air of childish enthusiasm that both Longbright and May wanted to slap him, even though they realized that he was simply happy to be back. Today he was alive with a restless excitement. For decades, he and his partner had divided their workload along the lines of their personalities. May followed the ingrained rules of Metropolitan Police detection, handling the groundwork, chasing up the most obvious and logical leads, interviewing family members, appealing for witnesses, covering tracks, proud of being thorough. His skills were technical because he enjoyed working with new technology, and observational because he liked people. Arthur had never exhibited sociability. He preferred to be left alone, taking off at tangents, following lateral hunches and sensations, enjoying the jolt of unlikely synaptic responses. Bryant did the heavy thinking, May did the heavy lifting. 'Come on,' he nudged. 'Aren't you even a little curious?'

'Well, yes,' May admitted. 'But it can't take precedence over the caseload Raymond's handing us.'

Bryant knew he had won. 'Fine. I thought I might work late tonight. My new kitchen's not connected up and the plumber's behaving like the last of the Romanovs, refusing to visit until Wednesday. You're the only one with a dependent, Janice, you should go home. There's nothing more you can do until tomorrow.' Most of the new computers had yet to have their software installed, and the only items to survive the blast undamaged were still packed in boxes.

'Ian's going to leave me if I go back on regular shifts,' the detective sergeant agreed. 'But I should make myself useful. Now that you're both here, perhaps I'll stay a little while longer, just to get things shipshape.' She looked around the partially painted room. 'I must say it's good to be back.'

'Excellent, you can give me a hand unpacking my reference books. I don't do manual work with my back.' Bryant slapped his hands on the desk. 'Lend me your phone. I won't break it.'

'Yes you will. I thought you lost all your books.' Longbright examined the flyleaf of *Witchcraft through the Ages*. 'You've stolen these from the library.'

'Incoming email marked urgent,' warned Meera Mangeshkar, getting wet paint down her sleeve as she looked in. 'Do you know anything about a Christian Right minister from Alabama whose legs were found in a bin-bag behind Camden Stables?'

'Is his name Butterworth?' asked Bryant.

Mangeshkar ducked back and checked her screen. 'No, Henderson.'

'Wait, I'm thinking of a Baptist, torso in a bin-bag behind Sainsbury's.'

'Home Office wants a unit representative to go up there this evening. Angry Republicans placing phone calls to Westminster, doesn't look good.'

'Ah, Arthur, John.' Raymond Land squeezed past Mangeshkar and hailed them with patently false bon-homie, which faded as he tried to climb around the partially assembled photocopier. 'I'm glad you're both here. The Home Secretary would like to see you for a brief chat tomorrow. He's very upset that you've been rude to his brother-in-law.'

'I have no idea what you're talking about,' Bryant told him. 'Who the hell is his brother-in-law?'

'Your new chap, Giles Kershaw. Apparently you're refusing to use him.'

'His *brother-in-law*? You're joking. What a total Quisling. I didn't like the cut of his jib the moment I saw him. *Quel crapaud.*'

'Well, no doubt you'll use your legendary diplo-matic skills to sort the whole mess out,' Land smirked. 'I mustn't keep you, I'm sure you have plenty of work to do.' He turned to leave, and stood on the cat's tail. One of the workmen putting a parti-tion across the office dropped his circular saw. It shot across the floor, making everyone scream.

The Peculiar Crimes Unit at Mornington Crescent was open for business once more.

4

OPENING DOORS

By Tuesday morning, the irradiation of the long dry summer had already faded to a memory as the temperature tumbled and a translucent caul of rain returned the city to silvered shadows. Cracked earth softened between paving stones. Pale London dust was rinsed from leaves and car roofs. Back gardens lost their parched grey aridity, returning to rich moist greens and browns. The air humidified as wood stretched and mortar relaxed, the city's houses pleasurably settling into their natural damp state. Rain seeped through split tarmac, down into uneven beds of London clay, through gravel and pebbles and Thanet sand, through an immense depth of chalk, to the flinted core and layers of fossils that crusted the depression formed by the city's six great hills.

London's workforce barely registered this mantic transformation. It certainly didn't take long for DC Bimsley and DS Longbright to cover the ten houses in Balaklava Street and the properties backing on to Mrs Singh's house. Longbright came along because her flatpacked desk was still being assembled—too few dowelling pieces had been provided. While her

colleagues bickered amiably, she armed herself with
May's newly programmed electronic interview-pad
and headed for the street. She still liked footwork because meeting the public kept her connected, and it
did her good to get out. The rain was scouring the
acidic urban air, making it fresh once more.

She had worked with the bull-necked Bimsley before, and enjoyed his company. He was an extremely
able officer, but also one of the clumsiest, lacking coordination and spatial awareness while retaining the
grace of a falling tree. It had seemed an endearing
trait the first few times they had met. His baseball cap
usually covered a bruise.

It occurred to Longbright that everyone who
ended up working with Bryant and May had some
kind of physical or mental flaw that prevented them
from functioning normally with fellow officers. Oswald
Finch, for example, had been the unit's pathologist
since its foundation. He was a man not given to dele-
gation. He trusted his instincts, was rational and
cautious and prone to calm understatement, but
everybody hated dealing with him except Bryant, because he looked like a Victorian mourner and reeked
of cheap aftershave, which he used to cover up the
cloying smell of death.

'That last woman, Colin, was it really necessary to
listen to her talking about shopping trips?' asked
Longbright, who had never known the pleasure of
spending because she was always broke. Most of the
clothes she owned had been bought at thrift shops
and dated back to the 1960s, lending her the air of a
disreputable Rank starlet. She was smart and tough,
and scared men with a kind of carnality that she had
never learned to turn off.

'You have to listen to them, Sarge. Mr Bryant taught me that. You get more out of them after they think you've stopped taking notes.'

'All right, but I'll do this one, speed things up a bit.' She ticked off the ninth house and climbed the steps to the next on the list. May's notepad translated her handwriting to text and emailed it to his terminal for appraisal.

'I like this street, sort of cosy and old-fashioned,' said Bimsley, tipping rain from the collar of his jacket. 'Like my grandma's old house in Deptford before they pulled it down. Council said it was a slum just 'cause it had an outside lav, but she was happier there. Odd the way the numbers are laid out, though. Thirties and forties on one side, three to seven on the other.'

'One side probably continued the numbers in the street joining it. The other side was built at a later date and had to start over. You see it all the time.' Longbright rang the doorbell of number 43. 'How many are we missing?'

'Only three not at home so far, that's pretty good.'

'They're starter-plus-ones, that's why.'

'What do you mean?'

'Your first purchased home is probably a flat, right? These are the houses you buy after selling your first place—something with a garden to remind you of childhood, but the rooms are small, best for a couple with one young child, husband's on the career ladder so the mum's usually at home. Next stop after this is something bigger, a bit further out, where your family can grow.'

'You don't think the wife's out working as well?' Bimsley asked.

'Depends. The area's Irish Catholic, they're not much given to childminders.'

'I don't know where you get your facts from, Janice.'

'Knowing the terrain. Call yourself a detective.'

The door opened, and an orderly blond woman in her late twenties smiled coldly at them. She wiped her hands dry on faded jeans, waiting for an explanation. In the background a loud television cartoon was keeping a child amused.

Longbright pointed to the plastic-laminated ID card on her jacket. 'I'm sorry to disturb you. We're checking the street to see if anybody knew the elderly lady who died at number 5, Mrs Ruth Singh.'

'I didn't know she'd passed away.'

'Perhaps I can take your name, for elimination purposes?'

'Mrs Wilton—Tamsin. My husband is Oliver Wilton. When did she die?'

'Sunday evening. Were you at home?'

'Yes, but I didn't hear or see anything.'

Longbright made a dismissive mental note. This was the type of woman who recognized her neighbours but never spoke to them. An implicit class barrier, faint but quite implacable, would prevent her from getting involved.

'No unusual vehicles in the street, no one hanging around outside the house between the hours of eight and ten?'

'Not to my knowledge.'

'Perhaps you could ask your husband.'

'I don't see that he would be able to—'

Longbright checked her pad. 'He was doing something to his car last night, wasn't he?'

Mrs Wilton looked affronted. 'Actually, it's my car. And he was just cleaning off some leaves and emptying the boot.'

'Is he at home today?'

'No, it's a workday, he's at his office.' Mrs Wilton stared at Longbright as though amazed by her stupidity. If the look was intended to intimidate, it didn't wash. Like so many of the old movie stars she admired, the detective sergeant's glamorous aura was constructed over the epidermis of a rhinoceros. She handed over the unit's contact card. 'You can freephone me at this number, or email us if either of you think of anything.'

'Did Mr Bryant do door-to-doors when he was younger?' asked Bimsley as they walked away.

'He still does occasionally, although he's supposed to use his cane for distances. John bought him a beautiful silver-topped stick from James Smith & Sons in New Oxford Street, and he's finally been forced to use it. He's very good at doorstep interviews because he has so much local knowledge. Although of course he's appallingly rude to people, but witnesses put up with it because he's elderly. He doesn't mean to be so vile, it just comes out that way. Politeness used to be one of law enforcement's greatest tools. We just outsmiled the opposition. Now it's liable to get you shot at. Let's do the other next-door neighbour.'

They had called at number 4 and introduced themselves to a shy Egyptian woman, Fatima Karneshi, who lived with her husband Omar, a railway guard currently posted at Archway Tube station. It seemed that Fatima had brought the traditions of her country to England; her reluctance to leave the house during the day prevented her from bumping into her neighbour, and chores kept her from socializing. She had seen Mrs Singh once or twice in the garden, but they had not spoken. Longbright had wondered if her husband was the kind of man who liked his women subservient. She readily acknowledged the importance of domesticity in the hierarchy of Egyptian marriage, but dealing with so many different cultures made her job more demanding.

The door on the other side, number 6, was opened by a woman in a lime-green face-pack and towel-turban. 'I'm sorry, this is absolutely the only thing that helps a hangover,' the woman explained in a muscular, penetrating voice. 'You're the police, aren't you? You've been going door to door and you don't look like Jehovah's Witnesses. If you come in, are you going to get water everywhere? I'm waiting for a little man to come and revarnish the hall floor, and it does stain. I'm Heather Allen.' She offered her hand and withdrew it, blowing on her nails as she beckoned them in. 'Your polish is a wonderful colour, I don't think I've seen that shade before.'

'They stopped making it in the 1950s,' Longbright admitted, hiding her hands. 'I have to get it mixed at a theatrical suppliers.' No one had ever noticed before.

'How unusual. Can I get you anything? Presumably you don't drink alcohol on duty, and this lad doesn't look as if he's old enough.' Now it was Bimsley's turn to be embarrassed. 'I didn't really know the old lady—it *is* the old lady you're asking about? But I did run a few errands for her. She couldn't get out. Her brother had bought her one of those little motorized cart-things, but she wouldn't use it. I can't imagine why, they only do about eight miles an hour.' The tinge of hysteria in her prattle bothered Longbright, who made another mental note: *this one spends too much time alone, and needs to impress upon others that everything is fine.*

'When did you last run an errand for her?'

Heather Allen tucked a glazed lock of auburn hair beneath the towel as she thought. 'Before the weekend, it must have been Friday, she told me she needed some bread.'

'How?'

'What do you mean?' Mrs Allen looked alarmed.

'How did she tell you? Did you call on her?'

'Oh no, nothing like that. It was a beautiful day, she was standing at the back door and we spoke.'

'She didn't say anything else? Other than asking you to get her some shopping?'

'No, well—no, I mean. No. I'm sure she didn't.'

Longbright sensed something. 'For example, she didn't say she was worried about anything? Didn't seem to have anything pressing on her mind?'

'Well, that sort of depends.' Mrs Allen appeared to have been manoeuvred to the lounge wall. Longbright stepped back, wary of her tendency to be aggressive.

'On what?' she asked.

'I mean, there had been the letters. I presume you've been told about those.'

'Perhaps you should tell me.'

'It's really none of my business.' Mrs Allen's voice rose as her sense of panic increased.

'Anything you say will be treated with the utmost confidence,' assured Bimsley.

'It seemed so childish—not to her, obviously— some racist notes had been put through her letterbox. It's not the sort of thing you expect any more.'

'How do you know about it?'

'I've no idea. I suppose she must have told me, or maybe one of the neighbours, but I can't remember when. I never saw them.'

'She didn't know who'd sent them?'

'I don't suppose so. I mean, she didn't know anyone.'

'Perhaps you would inform us if any other details come to you.' Longbright produced another business card, but knew that the unit was unlikely to receive a call. Some people had an instinctive distrust of the police that no amount of goodwill could alter. She enjoyed seeing in people's homes, though. The décor in this one was far too cool and impersonal, especially for a woman who favoured leopardskin.

'Come on, you,' she told Bimsley as they headed out into the rain. 'Let's get back. Notes and impressions.'

'I don't do impressions. And I thought you took the notes.'

'Mr Bryant wants to see what you can do.'

'Nobody can read my writing,' Bimsley protested, narrowly missing a tree.

'James Joyce had the same problem. You'll manage.'

Arthur Bryant knew far too much about London.

It had been his specialist subject since he was a small boy, because it represented a convergence of so many appealingly arcane topics. Over the years he had become a repository of useless information. He remembered what had happened in the Blind Beggar (Ronnie Kray shot Big George Cornell three times in the head) and where balding Jack 'The Hat' McVitie had been left dead in his Ford Zephyr (St Marychurch Street, Rotherhithe), how a Marks & Spencer tycoon had survived being shot by Carlos the Jackal in Queen's Grove (the bullet bounced off his teeth), and where you could get a decent treacle tart (the Orangery, Kensington Palace). He knew that Mahatma Gandhi had stayed in Bow, Karl Marx in Dean Street, Ford Madox Brown in Kentish Town, that Oswald Mosley had been attacked in Ridley Road before it became a market, that Notting Hill had once housed a racecourse, that the London Dolphinarium had existed in Oxford Street in the seventies, and that Tubby Isaacs' seafood stall was still open for business in Aldgate. For some reason, he also recalled that John Steed's mews flat in *The Avengers* was actually in Duchess Mews, W1. Not that any of this knowledge did him much good. Quite the reverse, really; the sheer weight of it wore him out.

But Bryant wasn't tired, even though it was nearly midnight. He sometimes took a short nap in the afternoon but hardly ever slept before two in the morning, and always rose at six. Sleeplessness had come with age; fear of dying without lasting achievement kept him awake.

Longbright had printed out the Balaklava Street interviews from her Internet-gizmo and had thoughtfully left a hard copy on his desk, knowing that he would work into the night. In return, he had left a pink rose—her favourite, named after the fifties singer Alma Cogan—on her newly erected desk for the morning.

He studied the names before him and rubbed at the bags beneath his eyes. Seven residents interviewed out of ten in the street, two more from the gardens beyond the house, a statement from the brother, no strangers or unusual occurrences seen on Sunday night, all a bit of a dead end. The old lady had no friends, and apparently no enemies beyond the writer of the racist notes only Mrs Allen seemed to have heard about. Finch had been over the body and found nothing except the skull contusion, too small to have caused any damage, and a throat full of dirty water, not from a clean London tap but some other murkier source, hopefully to be pinpointed when the sample had returned from analysis. What other source could there be? Something ingested against her will? Rainwater? It made no sense. He lit his pipe, almost feeling guilty that the No Smoking sign had been pointedly re-pinned above his desk, and tried to imagine what had happened.

Suppose . . .

Suppose Benjamin Singh had found his sister drowned in her bath? It happened to small children with depressing regularity, and the elderly could often behave like children. The bathroom was downstairs, along with the kitchen and dining room, below the road at the front, but level with the garden at the back. What if Benjamin had come down the stairs calling for her, had panicked upon seeing her body and pulled her out, dressing her and leaving her in her chair? Shock and grief caused strange behaviour. He might be too embarrassed to admit what he had done. But no, there would have been wrinkling in the skin. Suppose she had been upstairs, soaking her swollen feet, and had gone down to empty the foot-spa—she could have slipped, hitting her head on the stairs, and, in an admittedly awkward fall, drowned in the little bath. Her brother wouldn't have wanted her to be seen like that. He could have taken the bath away and emptied it before tidying it up.

Perhaps he hadn't mentioned it because he knew he would be in trouble for moving the body.

It was an unlikely explanation, and yet it vaguely made sense. Because, acting on May's suggestion, Bimsley had found such a foot-spa downstairs, stowed in a cupboard. Finch had already suggested that the case wouldn't go to jury, who were limited to three verdicts: accidental death, unlawful killing or an open verdict.

He thought about calling May for advice but decided against it. *You rely too heavily on John,* he told himself. *He's younger than you, the man still has a life outside of the unit—you don't. You're getting too old to do the work, you're just refusing to give it up.* But retirement meant sitting at home as the world passed by his window, creeping to the high street and forcing conversations on uninterested teenaged shop-helpers, or—God forbid—listening to litanies of illness from his peers. He had no children, no family to speak of, no savings, nothing left except his job. The women he had loved were dead. Nathalie, the fiancée he had worshipped and lost, long gone. He admired the enthusiasm of the young, their energy and freedom, but the young rarely reciprocated with friendship. They exercised an unconscious ageism that had been placed upon them by the world's all-conquering emphasis on youth. The elderly embarrassed them, bored them, failed to match the frenetic pace of their own lives. Elders weren't respected in English-speaking countries, they were merely taking up room.

Bryant had a feeling that the answer to discovering satisfaction in his late years was connected with doing good, perhaps teaching—but how could you teach instinct? Instinct told him that something terrible had befallen Mrs Singh, but there was no proof, and until he had that there was no case. This evening, a racial-harassment officer from Camden Council had checked in with Mr Singh. She wanted to know if his sister had really been sent anonymous letters, or if she had been subjected to any kind of racial abuse. Benjamin had called Bryant in a state of mortification. If such letters had existed, Ruth would have burned them out of shame. Camden Council should never have been told; didn't he realize that some matters were private? They had lived their entire lives in England, this was their home, why on earth would anyone even think they were different?

Bryant's renowned insensitivity to the anguish of crime victims had created an enduring reputation for rudeness, but he could exercise restraint, even finesse, when required to do so. They had chatted for half an hour, two men of similar ages and opinions, and Bryant had closed by promising to take Benjamin to a lecture on Wiccan literature at the new British Library next week. What remained unspoken between them was any resolution concerning Ruth Singh's inexplicable demise.

The thought nagged at Bryant: the old lady hardly ever went outside, so why had she been dressed for an expedition? And if she had voluntarily ingested some foreign matter, how would Benjamin react to being told that his closest surviving relative had committed suicide?

The front doors were tightly closed on Balaklava Street. His job would be to prise them open.

5

OPPORTUNITY

Their third fight in three days.

She knew why it was happening, but was powerless to prevent it. Kallie Owen pulled another plastic carrier bag from the tines of the checkout bay and piled in the last of the groceries, carefully placing the eggs on top. In the doorway of Somerfield, Paul fumed and paced, cigarette smoke curling from beneath the raised hood of his parka. He was a placid man, but the situation was getting them both down.

After living together in the cramped Swiss Cottage flat for eight months, they had fallen out with the landlord over rising rent and his inability to carry out essential repairs. Exercising their rights as tenants, they had asked the council to mediate, and the situation had been resolved in their favour. As a consequence, the landlord, an otherwise affable Greek Cypriot with a string of properties in Green Lanes, wanted them out, and had given them notice to quit within a month, citing his decision to subdivide and renovate the building. Paul was refusing to pay rent, claiming a breach of the tenants' agreement. Kallie just wanted to leave. The latest argument was about where they would go, and if they would even go together.

Paul flicked his cigarette into the road and came in to help her with the bags. He became claustrophobic and sulky in busy supermarkets, and had returned only to make a point. 'You know if we move any nearer, she'll come around every five minutes to check on you,' he warned. 'It's bad enough at the moment, all that business about "I was just passing." She doesn't know anyone who lives near us.'

Kallie's mother lived in a small flat behind the Holloway Road. She didn't approve of her daughter living with a man like Paul, who kept odd hours and had a job she didn't understand. She visited Kallie less to check on her welfare than to assuage her own loneliness.

'I'm not getting drawn into this again, Paul. We need to buy a place and put down some roots. I'm fed up with moving around. Three flats in four years, it's got to the point where I hardly bother to unpack the boxes. And the King's Cross idea—'

'King's Cross would have gone up in value.'

'Meanwhile we'd have been stepping over crackheads to get to our front door.'

'Come on, Kallie, buying somewhere decent around here would take more money than we've got. You know we'd have to move further out.'

This is the point where you don't mention his lack of commitment, she told herself. *This is where you change the subject to looking for a bus.*

'You hate the idea of settling down,' she heard herself say. 'You think you'll never have a chance to do all the things you planned to do when you were eighteen.'

'That's bullshit. We're going to have a baby, that's commitment, isn't it?'

The baby thing. Kallie coloured and ducked her head. She knew that at some point she would have to own up to the truth. Why had she told him she was pregnant? What part of that particular overstatement could have turned in her favour? True, her period had been late, they had been out for a rare dinner, she'd drunk too much wine, and Paul had talked about his father with such admiration in his voice that she had taken it as a coded message about parenthood. In the euphoria of the moment, she had told him that her home test was positive. She was ready to have a baby, they would make one a few days later and she really would be pregnant. The desire was there on both sides, all she had needed to do was make it happen. Sensing that he was ready, even if he hadn't said as much, she stopped her contraception and calculated the right time. She planned the best sexual position for maximum fertilization, and their lovemaking had taken on an intriguing edge of urgency.

But nothing had happened. Now she was stuck with a lie, and time was passing fast. She had never expected to welcome his insensitivity to gynaecological matters. Luckily, he couldn't tell the difference between a uterus and a U-bend. It was all just plumbing. He already had her pegged as a dreamer, a fantasist. Now he would be able to call her a liar.

'Great, that's all we need.' Paul set down the bags and tipped up the hood of his jacket as it began to rain hard. 'Look at the bus queue. I hate this bloody country—the rain, the roadworks, the sheer bloody incompetence, everyone looking so miserable all the time, rattling between the shops and the pub as if they were on rails, and now the summer's gone, there's just months of bloody rain to look forward to.'

She nearly said *then you should have travelled when you had the chance,* but this time she caught the words before they could escape her lips. She knew he regretted working through his gap year, not going around the world as his brother had, and now the baby story was backfiring on her, trapping him, pushing them further away from each other.

When they arrived back at their third-floor flat, they found that the front-door lock had been changed. Paul went downstairs to see the landlord and lost his temper, while Kallie sat on the gloomy landing surrounded by her shopping bags, trying to stay calm. As the shouting continued, the police were called.

She didn't understand how it could have all gone wrong so quickly. She had been modelling and making a decent living, but after her twenty-fifth birthday the work was harder to come by, and she found herself being downgraded from style magazines to catalogue jobs as the unsubtle ageism of her career made itself felt. Paul worked in the A&R department of a record company that was going through a rough patch. The era of superclubs and celebrity DJs was over, and there was a possibility that he would be made redundant. Nothing was quite as easy as it had been when they first met, and she hated the effect it was having on them, a gentle but persistent dragging at the edges of their life that robbed them of small pleasures, making laughter less easy to come by. Paul was two years younger, and had developed the annoying habit of treating her like an older woman, expecting her to sort out his problems.

On the evening of the Sunday they were locked

out of their flat, they went to stay with Paul's brother in Edgware, and after two weeks of sleeping on his expensive and uncomfortable designer leather couch, with Paul sinking into a kind of stupefied silence, Kallie decided to take matters into her own hands before something irreparable occurred between them. She went to see her former schoolfriend for advice. Heather Allen was nuts, everyone knew that, but she was ambitious and decisive and always had answers. She owned a nice house and had made a successful marriage; there were worse people to ask.

'Who died?' Kallie asked as Heather ushered her into the hall of number 6, Balaklava Street.

'Oh, the funeral car. Not many flowers, are there?' Heather peered out of the front door. 'Shame. I wondered what the noise was. The old lady next door passed away. We hardly ever saw her, to be honest. She couldn't go out. Her brother always came around with her groceries, and he's no spring chicken. Come into the kitchen. I've been baking.'

Kallie found it hard to imagine her former classmate tackling anything domestic, but followed her.

'Well, I was attempting to bake because of all these bloody cookery programmes you see on telly, but I couldn't keep up with the recipe. Some cockney superchef was rushing all over the kitchen tipping things into measuring jugs, and I didn't have half the ingredients I was supposed to have, so I started making substitutions, then he was going "Lovely jubbly" and waving saucepans over high flames and I totally lost track. God, he's annoying. Nice arse, though. You can try a piece, but I wouldn't.' She shoved the tray of flattened, blackened chocolate sponge to one side and tore open a Waitrose cheesecake. 'Don't sit there, use the stool, otherwise you'll get cat hairs all over you. Cleo somehow manages to get white hairs on dark items and vice versa, it's the only talent she has. A legacy from George. My God, you're so thin. Is that a diet or bulimia? I take it you're still modelling.'

'I was supposed to be working today, but I threw a sickie,' Kallie admitted. 'I don't do it very often, God knows we need the money, but things were getting on top of me, and I wasn't in the mood to stand around in thermal underwear smiling like an idiot for five hours. They said I could pick up again on Monday. We've been kicked out of Swiss Cottage.'

'That awful little flat? A blessing, surely?' Heather never appeared to think before she spoke. She reboiled the kettle, grabbed milk and, more oddly, sugar from the fridge, and started rinsing cups. Whenever Kallie thought of her friend, she imagined her doing three or four things at once. The kitchen was so immaculately tidy that it looked like a studio set. Heather possessed the kind of nervous energy that made everyone else feel tired. There was too much unused power inside her. She was competitive in a way that only women who were never taken seriously could be. Consequently, her enthusiasm was ferocious and slightly unnerving.

'I only agreed to rent the place with Paul because it was near his office. Unfortunately the landlord had other ideas. We're sleeping in Neil's lounge, and I think I'm really starting to bug his girlfriend. She comes in first thing in the morning and slams about in the kitchen, sighing a lot. Plus I don't like the way Neil looks at me when I'm in my pants.'

'Well, *Paul*.' Heather tapped crimson nails on the breakfast counter while she waited for the kettle. 'It's admirable that you've stuck by him, of course. He's never really been able to hold down a job very long, has he? Not much of an attention span. Funny how women always see the long term, while men struggle to concentrate on the next twenty-four hours.' Heather and Paul had a history of antipathy toward one another. It was the main reason why Kallie hadn't seen anything of her in the last two years.

'If you're determined to make it work with him, I don't know why you don't buy somewhere and have done with it.' Heather poured tea, dispensed biscuits, laid out coasters, cleaned the sink. 'It was the best thing George and I ever did, getting this place.'

'How is he?'

'Oh,' she waved the thought away, 'working all the hours God sends, making an absolute fortune, but still travelling too much to enjoy it, and it's no fun for me, pottering about with female pals. You get too well known at Harvey Nicks and the staff start to look at you with pity. I suppose it could be worse, I could be a golf widow.'

'Where is George now?'

'In Vancouver for a week. He asked if I wanted him to bring anything back. I said Vancouver, don't bother. We mostly communicate by email these days. Listen, you'll get another place together and things will calm down between you. Moving is stressful, particularly when you do it as often—'

'I told him I was pregnant.'

If Heather was surprised, she didn't show it. 'And you're not?'

'No, we'd talked about it, and then we went out to the Italian place in Kentish Town—'

'*Pane e Vino*? The lovely one with all the garlic?'

'And I had a bottle of Soave and got a bit carried away. I thought we really might go for it later, but he ate too much and just wanted to sleep. I left it too long to tell him the truth and now he's expecting me to start traipsing to the doctor. He doesn't really want a baby—he says he does but now I can see it in his eyes. He thinks it'll tie him down and he'll never go travelling like Neil did, and he'll have to be a grown-up for ever, and I don't know, it's all getting screwed up.'

'You can't work out your life when you're sleeping on someone's couch,' said Heather. 'That's the first thing you have to change.'

'You were so lucky, getting this house. A cobbled street, it's like something out of a fifties black and white film.'

'I know. It's all a bit *faux*-shabby, but we really do have a milkman, a paperboy, a knife-grinder, a rag-and-bone man, ice-cream vans in the summer. Men take their shirts off and mend their cars in the street, as if they're reliving their childhoods. The woman opposite still washes her front step. Some mornings you half expect Norman Wisdom to walk past with a ladder. We even have our own tramp, a proper old rambly one with a limp and a beard, not a Lithuanian with a sleeping bag. And you'd be surprised how cheap it still is around here. Urban chic, you see, much more bang for your buck than any *pied-à-terre* in Kensington, and we still have the cottage in

Norfolk—not that I'll go there alone, because who wants to be surrounded by nothing but scenery? There's only so many times you can go for a walk. Here, we're sandwiched between two dreadful council estates, and of course there are no decent schools, not that I'll ever have children. But it's quiet and we all have gardens. Not quite Eden, given the number of stabbings you get near the Tube.'

Heather lowered her mug. 'You know, you should go after the old lady's place. You've always wanted a garden. I suppose it will be put on the market now, and some developer will snap it up. She's been there for years, so it would probably need a lot of work, which is good because the asking price will be lower.'

'Won't her brother want to live there now?'

'I don't suppose he'd be happy about climbing the stairs. These houses are quite small, but they're arranged on three floors.'

Kallie refused to allow herself the indulgence of such a fantasy. 'There's no point in dreaming, I wouldn't be able to afford it.'

'You'll never know if you don't ask.' Heather had that determined and slightly crazy look in her eyes that Kallie remembered from their school days. It always used to envelop her whenever she decided to adopt someone else's problem as a challenge. 'Tell you what, I'll ask for you. I do know the brother, after all. Let's see if he's there right now.'

'Heather, he's burying his sister. You can't badger someone on a day like this.'

'Opportunity is not a lengthy visitor, ever hear that? If we don't ask, someone else will. Come on, don't be such a wuss.'

'I can't, it's her funeral. It's wrong.'

'Look, I'll just pay my condolences and ask if he's going to move in—stay here until I get back.'

As usual, Heather led the way. She always had, since they were eleven and nine. Heather, in trouble for stealing from the art-supplies cupboard, Kallie, the shy one who took the blame and never told. Heather, charging across roads and walking along the railway lines, Kallie stranded imploringly at the kerb or beside the track, waiting with clenched lips and downcast eyes. Heather with the lies of a demon, playing terrible games with older boys, Kallie with the heart of an angel, being terribly earnest. Men and money had driven them apart, but perhaps it was time to be friends again.

She sat in the kitchen and waited. The house was extraordinarily quiet. Walking to the window, she saw that the street was deserted but for a man and a woman from the funeral parlour, standing rigid and dormant beside the car, dressed in neat black suits and ribboned top hats, like a pair of chess-pieces. Having witnessed a thousand moments of sadness, their studied melancholia, so at odds with the urban world, appeared unfashionably graceful.

It was so very calm and still. Even the dingy clouds above the rooftops appeared to have stopped moving. They were, what, less than three miles from Piccadilly Circus? She could see the Telecom Tower through rain-spackled glass, although the top was hidden within low cloud. You forgot that there were still postwar pockets like this. Dark little houses. Cool still rooms. Ticking clocks. Settling dust. Polished wood. Time stretched back to the boredom of childhood. The houses were charming but slightly bothersome, as though they were waiting to dust down some half-buried memory and expose it to the light. Something here was comforting, yet best forgotten, a temporal paradox only serving to prove that you couldn't go back.

Kallie let the curtain fall. The front door opened and quickly closed. Heather came in with a smug smile on her face.

'If you don't ask, you don't get.' She grabbed Kallie's arm. 'His name's Ben Singh. Sounds like a character from *Treasure Island,* doesn't it? But he's her only surviving relative and he's going to let the place go. He's not doing it up to make money—he wants a very fast sale, even if it means going below the market price.' She gave a muted scream of excitement. 'I'm sure you could get in there, Kallie. The house could be yours. You'd finally have independence. You'd have somewhere you could call home.'

Kallie thought of the dark windows and doors behind which a woman had died, and smiled back uncertainly.

6

TAKING THE PLUNGE

'I don't understand how you got my mobile number.'

Paul Farrow set his beer back on the bar and studied the two men perched on stools before him. They had announced themselves as Garrett and Moss, sounding like an old music-hall act, but were involved in property. They represented a matched pair, a modern-day version of Victorian Toby jugs, with their grey suits, sclerotic cheeks and thinning fair hair, pink ties knotted loosely, stomachs forcing gaps between the buttons of identical blue-striped shirts. The heavier jug, Garrett, wore rings made from gold coins. As a plea for credibility, the look was singularly unsuccessful. Paul wore torn Diesel jeans and a black sweater, the regalia of the media man, regarded with disdain by men in cufflinks. They were doomed to be enemies before anyone had opened their mouth.

'I've been in touch with Mr Singh on a number of previous occasions,' said Garrett. 'Obviously, properties like the house belonging to Mr Singh's sister are highly prized in this area because of their proximity to the new King's Cross rail link. We have a lot of European interest.'

'So Mr Singh came to you for a sale.' Paul fingered the beaded sandalwood strap on his wrist as he studied the two men, taking a fantastic dislike to them.

'Not exactly.' Garrett fidgeted atop his stool while he sought a way to shift the facts into a better light. 'I've been trying to impress on him the importance of achieving the maximum financial benefit from his inheritance, and heard you were in touch—'

'Bit aggressive, these selling tactics, aren't they?'

'Pro-activity in the marketplace, pal.'

Paul sipped his free pint, knowing that he was about to discover its price. 'He doesn't want to sell to you, does he?'

Moss stepped in. He appeared to be sweating, even though the bar of the Pineapple pub on Leverton Street was cold. Theresa, the barmaid, was keeping a watchful eye on them; spotting fights before they happened was a talent that came with her job.

'Listen, sonny, we're in the middle of delicate negotiations with Mr Singh and the last thing any of us needs is you coming along and upsetting them.'

'Sorry, I missed what it is you do,' said Paul sharply, waving his forefinger between them. 'You're not part of this guy's agency but you're working with him—how does that operate?'

'I'm the property developer.' Moss had meant this as a declaration of pride; he might have announced that he was a child molester. 'Mr Singh stands to make a lot of money by selling at the right time to the right person.'

'Which you think is you. And you plan to divide his sister's property into how many flats?'

'We haven't decided yet. They'll be for executives, you know—beech floors, slate kitchen counters, dormer windows. King's Cross in ten minutes, Europe in a couple of hours. Camden Council is buying up everything it can get its hands on. It's a gold rush. There's big money to be made.'

'But Mr Singh doesn't want to sell to you. Am I missing something?'

Garrett realigned his matches on top of his cigarette box, next to his pint. 'He'll sell. He's going to Australia.'

'What's that got to do with it?'

'His oldest girl lives in Brisbane. He wants to be with her family because they're expecting twins any day now, so he has to make a fast sale.'

'So what's the problem?'

'He'll suffer a substantial loss by letting the house go in its present state.'

The conversation was starting to bore Paul. He watched a shoal of curled oak leaves tumbling past the pub window, battered by rain and wind. Somewhere the air was warm and scented with the sea, but not in this hemisphere. 'I think I'm beginning to understand. The market's stagnant at the moment and the King's Cross interchange won't be finished for years, but if you buy the property now, you can get your pal here to carve it up, chuck in recessed lighting and en-suite bathrooms, and be ready to make a killing when executives flood in from Europe.'

'We'll hardly make a killing on one property, Mr Farrow. It's a toe in the water until we're ready to take on larger conversions in the surrounding area. But we're keen to see whether it will work. Number 5 Balaklava can become a template for other properties in the neighbourhood.'

'Listen, the question is academic, because the Singh guy has already agreed to sell to my girlfriend. He likes her.'

'But there's nothing in writing between you,' smiled Garrett. 'I think the game is still open. I would be in a position to compensate you for the inconvenience of switching your attention to another property—'

'From your own books, the asking price of which you'd mark up by the size of your bribe.'

Garrett removed a white envelope from his briefcase and placed it on the bar between them. 'Listen, lad, we're businessmen, not comedy gangsters, and this is just a reimbursement cheque, standard business practice, something you probably don't understand. Think of it as payment for having done our groundwork.'

'I haven't done anything.'

'Your girlfriend spoke with Mr Singh and talked up the idea of selling. She's paved the way. So in effect, you've been freelancing for us, and we'd like to repay you for your efforts. All you have to do is let us put the property in our name.'

'You guys are amazing.' Paul shook his head in wonder. 'Take a look around you.' He ran his hand over the polished counter. 'How old would you say this pub is?'

Garrett looked at Moss, puzzled. 'I don't know. The fittings are original, maybe 1870?'

'A couple of years ago, a property company tried to tear the pub down and turn it into offices. The street's residents put up a fight until the council was forced to list the bar, and the company backed off. Now it's the most popular local in these parts.

They're on to people like you around here. I'm surprised you got through the door without setting off the Scumbag Alarm.'

'You won't be able to go to the council on this one, Mr Farrow.' Garrett's smile faded as he took back the envelope. 'Balaklava Street has nothing worth listing, the place is filthy and the floors are rotten. You'll need new electrics, new plumbing, a new roof, damp courses. It'll cost you a fortune to do up. It's only good for pulling down and starting again, and you'll never get the planning permission without throwing a lot of cash at Camden. You just missed the gravy train.'

'Then why are you looking so miserable about it?' Paul rose to leave. He needed some fresh air, but for now the streets of north London would have to do. 'Thanks for the drink.'

'River water,' said Oswald Finch testily. 'Which word don't you understand?'

'She was sitting in a chair, not fished out of the Thames,' replied Bryant. 'How can it be river water?'

'Do you know what the most popular murder weapon is in Britain? A screwdriver. Have you *ever* brought me a screwdriver victim? No, I get human sacrifices, torsos in bin-bags and curare poisonings. Just once you could bring me an open-and-shut job. A nice simple confession on the statement—*He came toward me so I hit him.* Common assault not good enough for you?'

Bryant looked around at the depressing green walls of the Bayham Street Mortuary. The fierce overhead strip-lighting buzzed like the faint memory of a head injury. The police building had been converted from a Victorian school, and had so far defied all attempts at modernization. Rumbling steel extractor ducts had been set into the ceiling to alleviate the emetic smell of chemicals, but it still looked like a place where Death would choose to sit and read a paper. Finch's countenance, peering over a plastic sheet at him like a doleful hatchet, added an extra layer of gloom to the proceedings.

'Which river did it come from?' asked Bryant. 'When will the sample be back?'

'It's already back. Your lad Kershaw brought it over a few minutes ago. I rather like him. He seems to know what he's doing, which makes a pleasant change in your place.'

'That's odd, you never like anyone. Have you noticed how fruit gums don't have any taste since they stopped putting artificial flavours in them?' Bryant proffered the tube. 'I shouldn't eat them, they stick to my plate. I don't see the old lady anywhere.'

'I've put Mrs Singh away. She's to be spared the indignity of any further exposure in this room. Look at the lights they've put in, it's like McDonald's.'

'Smells like it as well. Have you been cooking meat?'

'I caught my assistant eating a doner kebab in here last night. I warned him that his dietary habits could legally invalidate us. This is supposed to be a sterile zone, although I've lost count of the number of times I've found your cough drops in a body bag. My toxicology database makes no provision for boiled sweets. Ah, here's your Mr Kershaw now.'

Bryant was amazed. Oswald Finch was clearly taken with the new recruit. Perhaps he knew about

Kershaw's powerful political connections, although at his advanced age he couldn't be hoping for promotion. Kershaw was wide-eyed, bespectacled, blond and unironed, with a cowlick of gravity-defying hair, as tall and thin as a sparkler, a later edition of Finch. He tapped at a plastic-coated analysis data-sheet and grinned, reminding Bryant of himself in his early twenties. 'Well, it's not actually a poison,' he told them, 'but there's enough muck in it to have given her a nasty stomach ache, if it had managed to travel that far. Traces of mercury and lead, various harmful nitrates and plenty of interesting bacteria, the kind of cryptosporidia that lurks about in dead water, only prevented from proliferation by low temperatures. I think we've got ourselves some Monster Soup.' He slipped the page to Finch, who read the bar graphs.

'What do you mean?' Finch asked over the top of his glasses.

Bryant smiled knowingly. 'I think Mr Kershaw is referring to the title of a famous satirical print published in 1828, dedicated to the London water companies. It shows a horrified woman dropping her tea as she examines a drop of London water and finds it full of disgusting creatures. People drank from the Thames, which was incredibly polluted by faeces and rotting animal carcasses.'

'Just so,' Kershaw agreed, nodding vigorously.

'You're saying this is Thames water?' asked Finch.

'Exactly.' Bryant found himself concurring with the new boy.

'The kind of bacteria you find in dead water?'

'That's right.'

'But the Thames isn't dead. Far from it.'

'Sorry, perhaps I didn't make myself clear. It's Thames water, all right, but extremely stagnated.'

'Does it taste bad?'

'Really,' Finch complained, 'how would he know a thing like that?'

'Oh, absolutely vile,' said Kershaw, happy to answer the question. He turned to Finch. 'Naturally I did a taste test to see if she could possibly have ingested it by mistake, but I think it's highly unlikely.' He shoved his glasses back up his nose. 'I checked with Mr Banbury about the contents of her kettle—I had an odd thought she might somehow have filled it from an unclean source, but no, pure London ring-main water from her kitchen tap, fewer trace elements than many bottled designer waters.'

'Then I can't imagine what it was doing in her mouth.' Bryant offered Kershaw a fruit gum.

'That's your job to find out, isn't it?' snapped Finch, annoyed by the shifting loyalties around him. 'Meanwhile, I can tell you we're heading for an open verdict.'

'Why, what's the cause of death?'

'Heart stopped beating.'

'Yes, I know that—' Bryant began.

'No, I mean it just stopped beating. No reason.'

'There has to be a reason.'

'No, there doesn't,' Finch replied stubbornly. 'Sudden death can happen to anyone at any time, although one is more vulnerable at particular ages, especially in infancy and dotage.' The pathologist narrowed his eyes at Bryant. 'So you'd better watch out.'

'She was in some kind of stressful situation,' said Bryant, chewing ruminatively. 'She must have been, with the water in her mouth. It would be easy for us to make the biggest mistake of all.'

'What's that?' asked Kershaw.

'Insist on a logical explanation.' Bryant jammed his shapeless hat back over his ears. 'She might simply have lost her wits. We only have hearsay on her mental health. The Royal Free appears to have mislaid her hospital notes.'

She looked beautiful tonight, seated with the shining water at her back, her dark-blond hair bobbed to the jawline above pale bare shoulders. 'I don't get it,' said Paul, guiltily taking his seat at the table. 'We never come to restaurants like this.' The great glass wall of the Oxo Tower revealed a segment of the restless river. Beyond its bank, sharp pinpoints of blue-white light scratched and sparked as welders worked late into the night. A new city of steel and glass was rising.

'We do when we can afford it,' she told him, 'and when we've got things to celebrate.'

He raised his eyebrows. 'Things? You have a list?'

She ticked her fingers. 'First, you saw off the wicked, moustache-twirling property barons, and now they've officially renounced interest in the house.'

'How do you know this?'

'Mr Singh called me this afternoon. He had an argument with either Garrett or Moss, I forget which. They appear to have decided that it's too much trouble, and are washing their hands of the whole business. Second ...'

'What, they gave up just like that?'

'Maybe you made them feel guilty. Maybe they've found another sick old lady sitting on a goldmine nearer the terminus. More importantly, I've got the money and I'm buying the house for us.'

'How can you do that?'

'Ah, this is one of those little things we've never actually talked about.' Kallie sat back with a secret smile as the waiter poured wine. 'I don't often say it, but thank God for having a stage mother. I was going on shoots for baby clothes before I could even walk. I carried on with catalogue work right through school. My mother called it rainy-day money. I think it's raining now, don't you?'

'Yes, but—'

'It's finally time to use it for something useful. Can you believe old Hoppit and Toad wanted to flatten the place and squeeze not two but *four* flats on to the site? Apparently they were talking about bunging some councillors to let them build another floor, but they only wanted to pay Mr Singh once the planning permission came through. Obviously, he doesn't intend to wait for months while they screw around with architects and builders. He just wants to see his daughter and his grandchildren. Besides, he has another reason for wanting to divest himself of the house. It hurts him to have it, Paul, his sister died there. He says she received hate mail, racist stuff, and it upset her badly. He doesn't ever want to set foot inside the place again. Can you blame him? I can deal with his solicitor, and that way he can go as soon as he likes. I've got enough ready cash for the deposit and I can just about raise the mortgage on my own, but I'll need you to kick in with money for the work that needs doing. We can do it, Paul.'

'I haven't even seen the place. And my job's risky

at the moment. I could be out of work any day now—'

'It's got a spare room and a garden.'

He misunderstood her. 'You're right, we'll need somewhere for the baby.' He raised his glass. 'That's another reason to celebrate, isn't it?'

'Yes, that's a reason to celebrate.'

'Then let's have a toast.' He studied her carefully. 'To the baby.'

'The baby.' Kallie raised her glass, and tried not to catch his eye.

'You're not pregnant, are you?'

Her eyes held his. 'No.'

'Why did you tell me you were?'

He didn't seem angry, and she found herself resenting his obvious relief. 'I don't—I wasn't trying to—' The words dried in her mouth.

'It doesn't matter.' He reached across the table and cupped her hands in his. He seemed to have finally made up his mind about something. 'Do you understand? It doesn't matter.'

'Paul—'

The waiter had arrived with the starter, but discreetly stood to one side. The other diners watched them kiss, but being British, pretended not to notice. Outside, the first heavy squalls of rain prickled the river.

7

HOME AND DRY

'You don't understand what it's like, and I have no way of explaining to you,' said April. Hands trembling faintly, she relit her cigarette. Her purloined Michelin ashtray had filled with Silk Cut in the last half-hour. It was the only untidied thing in a room filled with carefully arranged mementoes from a happier life. 'I know Arthur meant well, but I just can't do it.'

'I'm trying to understand,' said John May. 'Please, let me help you.'

She shook out her hair as though the idea was preposterous. 'How? What can you do? You have no idea.' Her pale fringe fell forward, hiding her face. She appeared healthier than he had expected, but the off-kilter body language that had so long hinted at some unspecified disquiet had become habit, so that she appeared hunched. She had been living in the shadow of the past for so long that it seemed any emergence into daylight might melt her away.

'April, I've been in the police force all my life, I've dealt with every kind of situation imaginable. In my experience—'

'That's the problem, this isn't in your experience.

It's not something that can be cured by making an arrest.' Her voice was as thin and cracked as spring ice. 'You've had a lifetime of good health, you think you're invincible, you come from a generation that doesn't understand why people can't just pull themselves together, but it's not that simple.'

'I know it's been tough for you—'

'Why do you talk as if it's in the past? It's still tough for me. I want to work. I want to stand outside, beneath a vast blue sky. I want to be able to pass a stranger in the street without feeling terrified. But I open the front door and the world comes in like a tidal wave.' She hid her eyes behind her hand. He recalled the fierce methylene blue of her irises as a child. It seemed that the colour had faded from them since.

Agoraphobia was the latest spectre to haunt April in her battle to cope with her mother's death. John May's granddaughter had grown ill soon after Elizabeth died. Years of therapy had made little difference to her. John loved her with the desperation of someone who had seen too many others fall, but saw a damaging blankness inside her heart that no one could fill. Lost siblings, dead parents, the whispered cruelties of children drawn too close— May's family had been so unlucky that it was hard not to believe that some dark star trailed them, bringing harm and hardship in its wake.

Three months earlier, following signs of improvement and a positive report from her doctor, Arthur Bryant had put April forward as a candidate for a new law-enforcement training initiative. The Chief Association of Police Officers had invited non-professionals to train alongside detectives in an exercise designed to bridge the widening gulf between police and public. It had seemed an ideal opportunity to protect April while allowing her to rediscover some independence, but now she had suffered a relapse, retreating further back into the shadows of her bleakly pristine flat.

'You know none of us like you living here by yourself, April.' The Holloway Road was a railed-off corridor of run-down pubs and short-lease shops selling a curious mixture of plastic bins and mobile-phone covers, an area where too many lives were lived at discount rates.

'I'm not earning, Granddad—I can't afford to move anywhere else.'

'You need a place you can call home, somewhere safe and light. I told you I'd help you financially—and could you not call me that?'

'You think you're going to stay young for ever, just because Arthur is three years older and acts his age. You have such *conviction*. You always knew who you wanted to be. I never had the faintest idea.' She stubbed out the cigarette and thought for a moment. 'I'm starting to wonder if I exist beyond the walls of this flat. I could go out into the open air and vanish.'

Observation is a habit officers find hard to turn off. May could see how the apartment reflected April's state of mind, with its numbingly neat compositions of disinfected crockery and cutlery, forks all set in the same direction in their drying rack. Here, she could control her environment. Outside was only the stomach-churning panic of disorder. May's granddaughter was twenty-three, but already the damage ran so deep that he feared she might never find a way to restore her spirit. As a child she had been untamed and tomboyish, a noisy, messy, natural force. Looking at the polished shelves of paperbacks coordinated by their spines, the towels and rugs stiff with overwashing, he could find no trace of the wild girl he'd loved. The problem was exacerbated by the fact that it could never be discussed. Her mother's death was a sealed subject; to speak of it would require an acknowledgement of guilt that would destroy the little faith April had left in him. Perhaps there would come a time when an honest exploration of the past would prove healing. Until then, they would have to step warily around the events of the terrible night that lay between them like an open mineshaft.

'Arthur reckons you'd be a good liaison officer with the unit. He thinks you're a very perceptive young woman. He believes there are skills that can't be taught. He wouldn't have proposed you if he thought you couldn't handle it.'

She raised her eyes as if seeing him for the first time, and for a moment it seemed he might win her over. 'Uncle Arthur.' The hint of a smile appeared. 'I remember the smell of his pipe. Everything was scented with eucalyptus for days after he'd visited. He used to leave sweets under my pillow.'

Bryant had always believed in her, even during her darkest moments. He had insisted on taking April to visit one of his oldest friends, Maggie Armitage, leader of the Coven of St James the Elder, who was as much a student of human nature as she was of white witchcraft. Maggie had pressed her hands over April's and told him that her subject feared loss of control, that she quickly needed to regain her sense of identity. When people lose confidence in themselves, Maggie had warned, they can be overwhelmed by powerful forces, possibly satanic in origin. Maggie had at least hit the button psychologically, so the detectives conspired to bring their favourite grand-daughter back into the embrace of the world.

'Will you at least consider it? We could take things slowly. Some part-time work, then if things pan out, you could join us on a more permanent basis. You'd start making new friends.'

'Let's talk about something else.' She tapped out another cigarette. 'Janice told me you have a murder case.'

May was relieved by the change of subject. 'It may not be murder, that's the trouble. Arthur took the job to help out an old pal, and I wish he hadn't. We've no motive, no cause of death, no leads, no prints, nothing.'

April's interest was piqued. 'You've always told me that every murderer leaves something behind.'

'Yes, but unfortunately the house is thick with dust. I was hoping we could collate microfibres from a laser-scan of the floor, but the chance of finding anything has to be weighed against the expense of running tests. If Raymond Land discovers what Arthur is up to, doing favours for friends, he'll blow a gasket. At least it's good to be back in our own building.'

April smiled. 'Perhaps you're a little agoraphobic, too. It's a very English habit, the preference for familiar surroundings. The victim lived in Kentish Town, yes? Did you know it now has an official gangsta name, K-Town? Because kids are shooting tickets in the high street. The dealers are selling wraps of powdered ketamine folded inside lottery tickets. Kids can snort it straight from the palm of the hand without being noticed. It's referred to locally as Cat Valium.'

'How do you know that? You never go out.'

'No, but I have friends who do.'

'You see how good you'd be at the job? Arthur and I are completely out of touch. He still uses his network of street misfits and fringe-dwellers, but I don't think someone who reads psychic auras from bins and paving stones is a very reliable informant. Just think about the job, April, that's all we're asking.'

'I understand that. And I'll try, I promise.' Her eye had been taken by some white silk roses on the window ledge. She was unable to resist realigning them until they stood as regimented as pencils in a box, and barely acknowledged her grandfather's silent departure.

'She's right, it *is* a very English habit, not going out much,' said Bryant, hanging his Bangkok spirit-beater behind his half-buried desk. 'My father wore his unadventurous spirit like a badge *"Take your jacket off, you won't feel the benefit when you go back out." "I could never live in a country where you can't buy Marmite." "Looks like rain, we'd better not chance it."* If it hadn't been for the War, he'd never have met people from other countries, although of course he had to kill them. Before 1940, the average English family had travelled less than nine miles from their home. Many never got beyond the end of their street. Now look at us—we can't stay in one place for more than two minutes. April will come around in her own time, you'll see. You can't force these things.'

He pulled an old Sharp's toffee hammer from his drawer and nailed an effigy of a Tasmanian dog-demon beside his knotted whaler's rope made from human hair. On the mantelpiece he had placed the silver-chased Tibetan skull, with moonstones for eyeballs that looked like drum-polished cataracts. Beside it were several leatherbound copies of *The East Anglian Book Of Civil Magicke,* the collected essays of G. K. Chesterton and a privately circulated volume entitled *Gardening Secrets of Curates' Wives.* His office was brand spanking new, but had already begun to look like some kind of esoteric rural museum.

'A nation of shopkeepers.' Bryant dragged a letter off his desk with a derisive snort. 'Greedy little proprietors.'

'What now?' May looked up from his computer screen, only mildly interested. Bryant's background monologues formed the soundtrack of his office life.

'Those property bods, Garrett and Moss. They're at it again. They moved in for a quick kill in Balaklava Street, and now they're hounding some poor old dear in the next road. In the absence of any other suspects in the Singh case, I ran a quick check into their past history. Lots of local complaints, a couple of lawsuits that even reached the courts, but no actual prosecutions.'

'You didn't touch my computer?' May asked hesitantly.

'It may surprise you to know that there are other methods of accessing information apart from the Internet. I talked to a couple of their past victims.' Bryant dropped back into his chair. Despite the scorching air from the fan heater blasting his legs, he had layered his clothes more heavily than ever. *Shirt, sweater, two coats and the disgusting scarf he refuses to throw away,* May marvelled. *Alma knitted it for*

him, and he can't bear to part with it. The poor landlady was distraught about her dismissal, but he hadn't
yet summoned the nerve to raise the subject with
Arthur.

'Of course, London's always been full of that
type,' Bryant continued. 'It's a very selfish city. For
centuries, ships bearing treasures from all over the
world sailed into the Thames, but two-thirds of their
cargoes never made it any further than the docks. For
all of our much-vaunted honesty, we're a nation of
blasted thieves. I remember hearing stories of factory
owners who delayed sending their staff down to the
shelters during the Blitz in order to maintain produc-
tivity levels. They refused to sound their sirens until
the last possible moment, said they were concerned
for the city's economic survival, if you please.'

'Your naivety is touching, Arthur. Garrett and
Moss are required to be opportunists by the nature of
their employment. You can't paint everyone with the
same brush.' Although the detectives were in public
service, May's sensibilities veered toward industry,
while Bryant's favoured the artist. It was a mark of
their respect for each other that the division actually
improved their relationship. 'Look at your Mr Singh,
he kept his promise and sold to the young lady, didn't
he? Didn't you say he's even going to let her move in
prior to completion?'

'He feels sorry for her having to sleep on a couch.
Benjamin is a gentleman of the old school. He acted
against my advice, but he knows a hawk from a
handsaw. He recognizes honesty when he sees it, and
it's lucky for her that he does. These days, the innocent are routinely victimized by the rapacious.'

'She succeeded in getting the property where

Garrett and Moss failed,' remarked May. 'Perhaps the girl isn't as innocent as she makes out.'

'Well, there are no tidy moral lines any more,' Bryant grumped. 'Everything is so tainted now. The best you can do is follow a personal code of practice.'

'I will never understand how someone as open-minded as you can be such a closet Victorian, Arthur. If it was left to you, the police would still be walking about in their Number Ones.' Metropolitan police officers had been required to keep a Number One uniform for ceremonial duties, consisting of a high-necked tunic, heavy belt and cape. The Victorian out-fit had only been phased out in 1971.

'Not at all. Victorians were ghastly hypocrites, but there was an appealing sense of order.'

'Remember you're from working-class stock. You'd have been a boot-black.'

'God, it's freezing in here. I've got two T-shirts on,' Bryant complained. 'Look.' He unbuttoned his coat and cardigan to reveal a logo that read TRUST NO ONE UNDER SEVENTY. 'I've always had thin blood. Where do I have to go for a smoke?'

'I keep telling you, out on the fire escape. But I wouldn't—it's pouring.'

'I need to think. The verdict on Ruth Singh is bothering me.'

Since the investigation of Mrs Singh had ended with the pathologist's open verdict on her death, there was no just cause for further analysis, and the file had been discreetly closed. Leaving the final arrangements of the property transfer in the hands of his lawyer, Benjamin Singh was preparing to head for Brisbane in order to be with his daughter's family.

'You'll have to let it go some time. You heard what

Kershaw said.' The young forensic scientist had come up with an ingenious solution to the water found in Mrs Singh's mouth. He had speculated on the possibility that she might have inhaled dust containing dried residue from the river, reconstituted into a thin fluid by the mucus in her lungs brought about by a coughing fit. It seemed no less likely than any of their other scenarios, except that the solution had been found in quantity, and lacked the necessary viscosity.

'Well, it's bloody odd that I've never come across anything like it in fifty years. I knew about London getting blasts of Sahara sand under certain weather conditions, and I had a boring conversation with Banbury about the creation of dust patterns in urban environments, but I've never heard of anyone accidentally inhaling a river bed.'

'You can't make a mystery out of everything, Arthur. Death by natural causes can be strange. Sometimes the heart just stops beating for no apparent reason. Look at SDS.' No one had yet discovered what caused Sudden Death Syndrome, or why it so often affected young males in perfect health.

'So you're saying I should just accept some things as inexplicable.'

'Nothing's cut and dried these days, you said so yourself.'

'Fine.' Bryant returned to his case-files, only to look over the tops of his reading glasses at May. 'So I should let it go.'

'Oh, for God's sake.' May looked up in annoyance. 'According to Janice, nobody saw anything, nobody came or went, nobody visited the house the night before, she was in there alone. It's all in the notes, and you know exactly who's been there since the body was discovered, because I showed you the Scene Log, OK?'

'Then you clearly don't know that a man called at her front door on Sunday night,' said Bryant triumphantly. 'Medium height, dressed in some kind of peculiar old-fashioned coat. He was seen speaking to Ruth Singh on her step.'

'Who told you this? Have you done something you're not supposed to?'

'I merely sent Colin Bimsley back to pick up the remaining interviews. I'm entitled to do that. Besides, we need to occupy the staff in order to keep them out of the Met's claws. This so-called "Camden Bin-bag Murderer" is operating a little too close to Westminster. Why else would Scotland Yard be giving television briefings every five minutes? Land will be under pressure to rent us out, and you know how easily he gives in. We fought long and hard to hire staff, and once we lose them, we won't be able to get them back. Remember, we don't answer to the Met any more, so if you and I can keep the unit on late shifts and full time-sheets, they won't be able to poach us.'

'What else did Bimsley find out?'

'That's pretty much all. One of his interviewees was a television producer called Avery. He spotted the pair of them talking in the doorway of number 5 as he was coming back from a takeaway outlet in the high street.'

'Perhaps it was just another neighbour.'

'Possibly—Avery couldn't tell. He had no reason to be looking in the first place.'

'God, Arthur, it's not much to go on, is it? An anonymous visitor with rotten dress sense. Why did he recall the coat?'

'He remembered thinking it didn't fit properly. The weather broke on Sunday evening,' Bryant reminded him. 'It rained solidly for several hours. Avery was on the other side of the road and didn't get a good look—you know how it's difficult to concentrate when you're carrying a box of fried chicken— but he can at least place the time close to Ruth Singh's death.'

'So the verdict's been settled, and *now* you have a possible suspect. You do realize that we can't go any further beyond this point.'

'Understood,' Bryant agreed. 'Absolutely against the rules, not worth the risk, we're publicly accountable, God knows what would happen if Raymond Land found out.' He patted various pockets for his pipe, his shredded winter-mixture and his matches. 'Don't worry, I fully appreciate that the case is now "officially" off limits.'

May heard the parenthesis in his partner's voice and bridled. 'Arthur, wait! You come back here!' But Bryant's selective deafness had muffled everything except a song from the first act of *The Gondoliers*, which he hummed as he set off for the freedom of the fire escape.

May walked to the window and wiped a clear arc through the condensation, looking down into the glistening street. He needed to think of another way to keep the unit fully occupied until the Met's senior officers stopped eyeing up his bright new team. Luckily, it didn't take him long to think of a solution.

8

RISING VAPOURS

'Oh God, this is *so* disgusting.'

Meera Mangeshkar found herself holding a pair of paisley-pattern Y-fronts as large as a shopping bag. 'What kind of man chucks his pants in the dustbin? Is this the best job May could find to keep us out of circulation?' Rooting carefully within the bin, she pulled out the remains of a Marks & Spencer family fruit pie, some haddock heads, a broken pink dental plate and a brassiere, the cups of which were filled with sponge cake. 'I haven't been given rubbish duty for years.'

She and Bimsley were on their knees in the back garden of a house in Belsize Park, sifting through half a dozen binliners. Under normal circumstances, the bags would have been removed and examined at a secure site because of the danger from contaminated sharp waste, but Banbury's steel micromesh gloves were proving a success, even though they were cold to wear. It was nearly one a.m., and the hours they spent here would be added to the next shift's timesheet, protecting them further from requisition.

'Pass me your torch—mine's fading.' Bimsley held

up an empty jar and sniffed it. 'Foie gras—goose, not duck. There was a magnum of Veuve Cliquot earlier. He's been living well.'

Meera narrowed her eyes at him. 'You know Arthur Bryant only made you finish the doorstepping in Balaklava Street because the victim's brother is a mate of his. He's granting preferential treatment to his pals.'

'Let it go, Meera. I don't know what you're so angry about. There was no one else around to do them, and besides, I don't mind if it reduces duty like this. I got interviews with all three remaining residents, and one of them told me Ruth Singh had received a visitor that night. So it was worth going back. Information that could lead to an arrest, as they say.'

'Yeah, right, that'll happen.'

'Well done, Meera, a triple positive to make an emphatic negative—nice use of English.'

'What are you, my grammar coach? Nobody likes a smart-arse.' Meera sat back on her haunches and raised the white polystyrene mask from her mouth. She made a sour moue as she tipped the last of the bag's reeking contents on to the grass. 'I'm beginning to wonder if I made the wrong decision in transferring.'

'Bryant thinks this sort of work is character-building,' Bimsley assured her. 'When he gets his teeth into something, he won't let go. Even when the cases are cold and closed, he'll go back in and find something new. They say he and May never officially accepted senior titles because they didn't want to become separated from groundwork.'

'Well I'm used to a proper hierarchy, teams and

briefings, method stuff without too many nasty surprises. Instead, I'm on my knees searching through garbage. I'm not even sure what we're meant to be looking for.'

'You heard Mr May. One of his academic colleagues from the Museum of London has come into dodgy money. He must have reasons for thinking there's something illegal going on. Academics are usually broke, so how come he's dining on foie gras?'

'So the bloke's doing a bit of untaxed freelance. Workers in the grey economy don't keep documentation. What does May think we're going to find? Receipts?'

Bimsley rocked on his heels and looked at her. 'You came up from Greenwich, didn't you?'

'Yeah, I've done Greenwich, New Cross, Deptford, Peckham, all over south London. Great catchment areas if you like arguing with drug squads and dealing with complicated social structures involving "respect" in all its gruesome manifestations, but not if you're interested in anything more sophisticated than gunshot and knife wounds.'

'What made you come in for the PCU position?'

'I wanted to work on crimes with causes, not club stabbings where the motive is always "He gave me a funny look." I heard some of the local lads talking about this unit, slagging it off. Thought it sounded interesting.'

'Bryant and May know a lot of people. They've made plenty of enemies, and some loyal friends. John's great, but Arthur can be dangerous.'

'In what way?'

Bimsley thought for a moment. 'They spent twenty years looking for some lunatic who called himself the Leicester Square Vampire. Bryant pushed the case too hard. The story goes that he persuaded John to use his own daughter as a decoy. Something went wrong, and the daughter died.'

'Christ. How come they don't hate each other?'

'I don't know. Nobody seems to know the full story. Longbright must, but she's not talking.' Bimsley slapped his mitts together. 'Come on, it looks like it's going to rain again, let's wrap this up.'

They worked in silence as the night deepened and a diaphanous mist began to dampen their hair and clothes, settling on the grass like threads of silk.

'Your interview result isn't enough to keep the Ruth Singh file open after its verdict, is it?' asked Meera. 'No conclusive forensic evidence, no real suspects, all friends, relatives and neighbours accounted for on the night in question.'

'Yeah. Bryant must be disappointed.'

'Why?'

Bimsley dug deeper, shining his torch into the bottom of the last bag. 'Oh, he wants the answers to life's mysteries. Why people die, what makes them evil, how corruption takes root. It's a hiding to nothing, because you never truly find out, do you? You don't get to the source. May doesn't look for meanings all the time, he just accepts what he sees and deals with it.'

'And which do you think is best?' asked Meera.

Bimsley shrugged. 'We're the law, aren't we? You've got to accept it all on face value or it'll drive you bleeding mad.'

'Nietzsche said, "There are no facts, only interpretations." If you believe that justice can be meted via a simple binary system, you're cleared from any moral responsibility.' Meera's sharp brown eyes were steady and unforgiving.

'Look, I know what's right and wrong, but I'm not going to go around with a chip on my shoulder about it, pissed off at never getting closure.'

'It's human nature to try and understand your environment, even if it only leads to more questions. Nietzsche also said, "Every word is a prejudice." '

'Oh really?' Bimsley was starting to get annoyed. 'What does Nietzsche have to say about the chances of you and I not killing each other?'

'He said that for a man and a woman to stay friends they have to find each other unattractive. So we should be great pals.'

'You and Bryant are going to get on like a house on fire. Sorry, bad choice of words, seeing he managed to burn the unit down.'

'How did he do that?'

'Long story. Be thankful they didn't close the place permanently.'

When Meera looked up, her face widened with an unexpected smile. 'You think there are no answers? Here's one.' She dangled a sodden piece of paper before him.

'You're going to kill yourself if you don't get down from there,' warned Alma Sorrowbridge. The Antiguan landlady had been as plump and lush as a breadfruit in her golden days, but now appeared to be shrinking. She flattened her grey curls and folded her arms and watched in annoyance as Bryant balanced at the top of the steps, batting his stick into the back of the shelf units.

'I know it's up here,' Bryant called. 'You wouldn't understand. If you had an ounce of kindness you'd help me get it back.'

'I don't do steps at my age,' Alma told him. 'I'm a landlady, not a trapeze artist. And I'm not your keeper any more, since you decided I'm not good enough to come with you to your fancy new apartment.'

'You wouldn't like it, Alma. It's hardly fancy. I needed a place to think, something as bare and ascetic as a monk's cell.'

'You mean you got no ornaments?' asked Alma, appalled. 'What have you done with them all?'

'They're *objets d'art*, thank you, and I've taken them to my office to replace the ones that were destroyed.'

'Poor John. I don't even know what it is you're looking for, or why you had to put it in such an awkward place.'

'Agh.' Bryant pulled down the doll and wiped it with his sleeve. 'Help me down.' Alma held the steps while he descended. He was carrying a miniature representative of himself, made out of cloth and accurate in detail down to the missing button on his tweed overcoat. 'It's my *achi* doll. It was made by one of my enemies and sent to me. I had to keep it up there, out of the way, to prevent anything from happening to it. It contains part of my soul, and if it gets damaged, so do I.'

Alma made a noise of disgust. 'You don't really believe things like that, Mr Bryant.'

'Well, of course not, but he was a nasty customer and my evidence got him convicted, so I'm not taking any chances. I'm putting this in my new office safe. If you had helped me to move, I wouldn't have forgotten it in the first place.'

Bryant's ingratitude never ceased to amaze her. She had devoted a large part of her life to making him comfortable. She had even stood by as he uprooted himself from her beloved Battersea apartment, where the river sunlight wavered across her kitchen ceiling, and moved to his shabby, gloomy conversion in Chalk Farm, where, according to John May, the shadows never left the rooms and the bedroom windows were brushed by the decayed fingers of dead plane trees. It was love of a sort that had allowed her to put up with his abuse, even now. If anyone else dared to speak to her in the same way . . .

'Go on, take a good look at it.' Bryant bared his ridiculous false teeth in a rictus as he passed her the doll.

Alma grimaced, but accepted the offering. 'Why did he give it to you? Why didn't he just tear its head off?'

'Oh, he didn't mean to *harm* me,' Bryant explained airily. 'He was planning to petition the medical board for parole at the earliest opportunity, and as I was the only person fully conversant with the facts of his case, he was providing himself with some insurance—these things are as much about the prevention of misfortune as the reverse.'

'It's a good job John doesn't believe in all this rubbish.' Alma gingerly handed back the doll.

'I've been meaning to ask you for years.' Bryant stepped from the ladder and stood before her. 'Why don't you ever call me by my Christian name? You always have done with John.'

Alma sighed. It was a matter of respect, but she

wasn't prepared to tell him that. 'There's nothing Christian about you, Mr Bryant. If there was, you wouldn't spend all your time trying to find out things that don't concern decent people. You could come with me to church.'

'Thank you, Alma, but I think it's a little late for my redemption, don't you?'

'Our pastor says it's never too late.' She eyed him doubtfully. 'Although in your case I think he would have met his match.'

'You must come and visit me in Chalk Farm,' he offered.

'No, thank you.' She refolded her arms, determined not to show her true feelings. 'I'm just getting used to not seeing you.'

He sat down on the brow of Primrose Hill, between the globe lights that illuminated pools of glittering emerald grass, and faced the conjurings of his mind. 'Something is rising to the surface,' he told May, hunching his shoulders and burying his mittens deep in his pockets. 'Unhealthy vapours. You know how I get these feelings. Death is so powerful that its presence can be felt whenever someone sensitive is in close proximity.'

'You're a miserable sod. Birth is powerful, too— why don't you feel babies being born? Always the morbid mind. These presentiments—you must know by now that they don't always mean harm will fall. We can stop things happening.'

'Not this time, John,' said Bryant, pulling his ratty russet raincoat a little tighter.

'Well, thanks for that warning from Doom Central. What's prompted this?'

'I'm not sure. The weather forecast, perhaps. There are storms on the way. Traditionally, harmful events in London are associated with prolonged bouts of low pressure and high moisture content in the air.'

'You're making that up.'

'I promise you I'm not.'

'Then it's time to stop believing in evil omens,' May decided, climbing to his feet. 'Come on, I'll buy you a pint of bitter at the Queen's Head and Artichoke. Perhaps, just this once, there will be nothing bad for you to enjoy.'

9

RUNNING WATER

Nothing in London ever lies in the direction that you expect it to be. The Thames constantly appears to turn the wrong way. The London Eye seems to move around on its own accord. The tower at Canary Wharf wavers laterally like the point of a compass. Buildings north of the river suddenly appear to the south, and vice versa. Walking the streets, London shakes and rearranges itself like an amoeba. Kallie was thrilled at finally being able to get her bearings. She felt like placing a pin on a map. Balanced in the V of the roof, she studied the horizon. 'The house faces east–west,' she called down.

'Is that good?' Paul was framed in the window of the narrow attic, struggling into a sweater.

'It means the front gets the morning sun, and the rear bedroom gets the sunset.'

'How are the slates?'

She looked around her feet. 'A few are broken. And there's a busted gutter.'

'It looks as though the rain comes in. She couldn't have done anything to the place in thirty years. We could have had a survey done if you hadn't been in such a rush.'

'We'll put it right bit by bit.' She had a hard time explaining why the house meant so much to her. Paul had fantasized so often about being free to travel, it seemed odd that her instinct now was to put down roots. 'We're all packed in so closely together.'

'What's that?'

'You can see rows and rows of Victorian terraces from up here. You'd think we would know more about each other. How do we all manage to live such separate lives?'

'Come on down, the van's here.'

Paul's brother had brought over their clothes. Kallie had been shocked to see how easily her world could be packed into a few boxes. She suspected that Paul thought it was rather cool. He didn't like the idea of becoming encumbered by belongings. She had agreed at the time, but being here changed everything. There was something about the house that made you want to draw the curtains and never go out.

She loved being up on the roof, feeling the first spackles of evening rain on her face, looking down at the ten gardens, five from the houses on her side of Balaklava Street, five more from the road beyond, grouped together like a densely cultivated park, divided by strips of fence and low brick walls. She counted rowans, wild cherry trees, a small-leafed lime, holly, crab apples, London plane trees, hornbeams, several ponds, sheds, clothes lines, a conspiracy of gnomes. The gardens harboured the interior life of the neighbourhood. Kids didn't play on the streets any more, but the gardens were still safe, protected by terraced fortresses. She knew she would come up here often on summer nights, the way a cat climbs a tree to better survey its territory.

'It smells damp,' Neil sniffed. 'Needs a lot of work.' He picked at a corner of wallpaper in the hall and lifted it, running his finger across the powdery grey plaster. 'All this will have to come off.'

'It's fine for now,' Kallie told him, protectively smoothing the paper back in place. Neil worked for a mobile-phone company in the city, and wanted to be twenty-five for ever, even though he was in his early thirties. He treated his girlfriends like his cars, replacing them with more roadworthy models whenever they showed signs of mileage.

'That's the last box out,' he told her. 'There wasn't much to unload. How are you going to fill the rooms?'

'Self-assembly stuff, until we can afford something better.'

'It'll have to be flatpack to go down this hall.' Neil had a warehouse apartment with porterage, but the open-plan design had made it virtually impossible for anyone to stay without being in the way.

Paul went off with his brother to buy him a thank-you beer, so Kallie spent her first evening in the house alone. The carpets were filthy. She vacuumed them as best as she could, then set about washing out the kitchen cupboards. Plastic buckets filled with hot soapy water and disinfectant began to make the place more inhabitable. The old lady hadn't intentionally kept a dirty house, but she had clearly been unable to manage by herself. At least the electricity was back on, although it didn't extend to all parts of the house; the ancient wiring needed replacing.

There were odd noises outside: a ceanothus rattling with fresh rain in the garden, dead laburnum leaves dropping on to the yellowed roof of the leaking lean-to conservatory. Inside, too, the pilot light of the central-heating system flared up with a pop that made her jump, pipes ticked as steadily as grandfather clocks, floorboards creaked like the decks of a galleon. The basement light switches didn't work, and it wasn't worth trying to clean by torchlight.

A dead woman's house—worn cups and saucers, a drawer full of odd items of cutlery, another filled with string, bags, three-pin plugs and out-of-date discount vouchers, perished rubber teatowel holders from the seventies. Alien smells in the cupboards—packets of cardamom, juniper, custard powder, spills that were bitter and blackly sticky. Brown L-shaped marks on old linoleum where something heavy and ferrous had once stood and overflowed.

At ten-thirty she sat down in the ground-floor lounge to unpack linen and the handful of chipped china ornaments that had belonged to her grandmother. The street was preternaturally quiet, but now she could hear something. Setting down an armful of sheets, she rose and listened.

The sound of running water.

A steady susurration of rain, cataracts rushing through gutters, swirling into zinc funnels, precipitating through plastic pipes, racing across the bars of a drain. The crepitation was steadily rising to a crescendo.

She climbed the stairs to the floor above and walked into the second bedroom: no light bulb in here. The damp wood of the window frame had swollen so much that she couldn't budge it. The sound was softer beneath the roof, so it couldn't be loose guttering. Collecting her torch from the hall, she clicked it on and ventured into the basement. They would take out the non-supporting walls, she decided, repair the conservatory and bring more light in from the raised garden. The bathroom was absurdly large for the house. She supposed a parlour had been converted, yet it seemed odd to have had a parlour with only a single tiny window, high and crossed with bars, little more than a skylight looking out at street level.

Now she heard the sound quite clearly, running—no, *rushing* water. It seemed to be coming from the right-hand adjoining wall. She hadn't met the people on that side. Heather had told her that their names were Omar and Fatima. What could they be doing that would make such a noise? It wasn't a tap, more like a set of them, all turned on at once. The sound had volume and depth. Coupled with the noise of the heavily falling rain, the sense of precipitation seemed to enclose the house entirely.

She shone the torch around the bathroom, and wished she hadn't. The fittings were cheap, a bilious shade of avocado that had been popular in the seventies. Only the bath was white enamel, and there was a good chance that it had feet, those French ball-and-claws that could look nice if they were cleaned up. Unfortunately, the whole thing had been boxed in with corrugated hardboard. She thought of her parents' house and remembered the craze for boarding over bannisters, sinks, door panels, any decoration that smacked of Victoriana. The house had probably had a dozen makeovers, each according to the prevailing taste of the times, each leaving a residue of personality in a crust of paint.

The Swiss army knife she had used on the packing cases was still in her back pocket. Cross-legged on the cold parquet floor, she unscrewed the six chrome-topped pins holding the bath's front hardboard panel, then dug the tip of the blade under its base. The board groaned as she flexed it, then split and came loose. She bent back the sheet until it lifted free, and was horrified to find that she had released hundreds of tiny brown spiders from their penumbral home. They scattered in every direction, over her legs, across the floor, up the walls, fleeing the torchlight. She leapt to her feet and shook out her hands in revulsion, dusting them from her clothes, feeling the tickle of legs everywhere, imagining more than she could see.

Jumping out of her jeans was the best idea, but scattering the spiders with bright light would have been better. She headed for the safety of the bare bulbs in the hall, leaving behind the churning noise of water. *This,* she thought, *is what owning a house is all about. It's going to take some getting used to.*

10

THE UNDERGROUND MAN

May could hear something odd. It sounded like 'We are the Ovaltinies, happy girls and boys ...' But of course it couldn't be; that radio jingle had surely vanished before the Second World War. He glanced at the new mobile phone on Bryant's desk and realized that the music was emanating from the earpiece. Arthur was even humming along as he fussily rearranged books on the mantelpiece. After all these years, he still had the ability to make May feel as if he was going mad. How the hell did he do it? More to the point, how did he bend radio waves from the past to transmit them through modern technology?

'Can you hear anything unusual?' he asked tentatively.

'I was thinking,' replied Bryant, failing, as usual, to answer a simple question. 'This fellow, this friend of yours, he's simply selling his services, no?' He poked longingly at the bowl of his pipe and eyed the No Smoking notice above his partner's head, reluctantly returning the briar to his top pocket. 'Academic information is a valuable commodity. I don't suppose the Museum of London pays very much. You can't begrudge him earning a little freelance.'

'My dear chap, I don't begrudge him anything. Far from it,' said May, as Longbright cleared a space on the desk and set down two mugs of strong Indian tea. 'The city wouldn't survive without its grey economy. I don't even like him. He's an arrogant bore. I just want to know what he's up to.'

'Even someone as stupid as Raymond Land will notice that a lecturer coming into a chunk of money hardly warrants sending two new recruits to sift through his rubbish bins. He could have won a bet on a horse, or have taken on a second job as a minicab driver.'

'Raymond's in the building,' warned Longbright. 'His golf's been cancelled because of the rain. Don't let him hear you call him stupid again.'

May waited until the sergeant had returned to her office. 'You don't understand, Arthur.'

'Then explain it to me.'

'I've known Gareth Greenwood for years. I'm surprised you haven't run across him, because he does guided walks too—the Late Victorians on alternate Friday evenings, Port of London first Sunday morning of the month. Surely you must cross over each other.'

'There are hundreds of guides, half of them unofficial,' said Bryant testily. 'I don't know them all. Do go on.'

'Greenwood is a brilliant academic with a Master's degree in early modern history. It's his wife who's worried about him. Monica called me a few days ago to tell me he'd taken an assignment through someone he met at the museum. He's being paid a considerable amount of money to perform some kind of illegal task, half up-front, half when it's completed. It's dangerous, too; he made out a will last week.'

'How does she know all this?'

'He's an archetypical academic, vague and rather remote—you could fire a gun while he's reading and he wouldn't notice. She dropped him off at the Barbican last Friday and realized he'd left some papers in the car, so she went after him. He was being met by some dodgy-looking character who was handing him wads of used notes and giving him instructions about what he had to do. Gareth's been in trouble before, you see. It wasn't his fault the first time, he was just a little naive. A friend of one of the museum's patrons offered him a rare piece of London sculpture. Greenwood didn't check its provenance or he would have known it was stolen. Outdoor statuary was never registered very strictly. It's only in recent times that the collectors' black market for large items has opened. The statue was one of a pair of Graces that had stood on Haverstock Hill for over a century. Greenwood had walked past it every day on his way to the Tube, but didn't recognize it when it was offered to the museum. His colleagues were sympathetic, and did what they could. Well-meaning academics have a history of unwitting involvement with fraud, blackmail and robbery. Whatever one might think of him as a person, Greenwood's one of the finest experts we have in this city—I'd hate him to make another mistake. He refuses point-blank to discuss this new business with his wife, and she's very worried.'

'So you asked Meera and Colin to go through his bins. Really, John, you're giving Raymond Land ammunition to take back to the Home Office. Couldn't you just have had a quiet word with him?'

'No, that wouldn't be possible,' said May uncomfortably. 'We were sort of rivals, and he's still a bit, you know, angry with me.'

'No, I don't know. What sort of rivals?'

'Well—the lady he married. I sort of met her first, and meant to break it off when she met Gareth, but neither of us got around to telling him, and then it sort of came out at a bad time.'

'Wait a minute, all this is about a woman?' Bryant fought hard to stop himself from laughing. 'What is it with you and married women? How long ago was this?'

'June 1978.'

He tried to prevent it, but the laugh escaped. 'That's over twenty-five years ago. You're not telling me he still bears a grudge.'

'Academics are capable of bearing grudges until the day they die. Obsession is in their nature. Anyway, we're not exactly being worked off our feet here, Arthur. I want to keep Mangeshkar and Bimsley busy. You know that if no work gets sent our way, the Met will end up using us on their cases by default, and when that happens the unit will be closed down for good.'

'They wouldn't do that. They approved the rebuilding programme in record time.'

'It would have happened anyway, because this site is valuable police property. Have you heard talk about a new style of police shop for the Camden area?'

'What do you mean?'

'It's one of the Home Office's pet ideas, a drop-in

community centre staffed by casually dressed officers who liaise with local community leaders. And it'll sell products licensed to the Metropolitan Police, to interest the kiddies. That's what they're saying this place is going to become, some kind of Disney police store, just as soon as they've got us out.'

'Raymond wasn't happy about my involvement with Ruth Singh,' reminded Bryant, 'so we can hardly afford to have your lecturer—'

'It took them just a few minutes, Arthur. Meera found something. Look.' He flattened out the crumpled receipts. 'Greenwood just spent several hundred pounds on climbing equipment— high-tech stuff.'

'Perhaps he's taken up mountaineering.'

'Don't be daft, he's in his sixties and has a bronchial condition.'

'Well, I don't know. Is it really any business of yours?'

'He has some specialist classified knowledge. The kind of knowledge that could be open to abuse.'

'I thought he taught history.'

'I was thinking of his particular field of interest. Rivers. Specifically, the underground rivers of London.'

Bryant's interest was aroused. 'That's different. The culverts still run through very sensitive areas. Under Buckingham Palace, for example, and virtually under the Houses of Parliament.'

'Really? I thought they had all dried up long ago.'

'Not at all. The entire subject is open to misinterpretation, of course. It's a murky area of London interest; not only are the size, geography and number of the city's rivers up for dispute, but there is very little left to see, and no accurate way of comparing the present with the past. Consequently, one ends up tracking filthy dribbles of water between drains and across patches of waste ground.'

'Then why bother studying them at all?'

'Because just as the old hedgerows shaped our roads, so did the river beds. They created the form of London itself. They are the arteries from which its flesh grew.'

'Since when were you an expert?' asked May, surprised.

'I was going to do an overground guide tour tracing the route of Counter's Creek. That one's followed by a mainline railway line all the way from Kensal Green to Olympia, Earl's Court and the Thames. We studied quite a few, but abandoned the idea because of the difficulty of getting groups around the obstructions. The Westbourne river still surfaces as the Serpentine, you know. Many of the original river beds are mixed in with the Victorian sewer system now. There's something undeniably magical about the unseen parts of the city, don't you think? The roofs and sewers and sealed public buildings, the idea that a different map might emerge to chart previously unimagined landscapes.'

'I agree up to a point. But if there's nothing left of these rogue rivers, I don't see why someone would pay my old rival for information about them.'

'I didn't say there was nothing left. Most of them were bricked in. The best-known missing river is the Fleet, which starts on Hampstead Heath, going down through Kentish Town, diverting past us to St Pancras, then to Clerkenwell and Holborn, and out to the Thames just past Bridewell. It was also known as the Holebourne, or the stream in the hollow. They used to say it was a river that turned into a brook, a ditch and finally a drain. The Smithfield butchers chucked cow carcasses into it, and it was used as a toilet and communal rubbish dump for centuries, so it kept silting up and becoming a public health hazard. I think it was finally bricked over in the mid 1800s, but that's the point—most of the rivers ducked underground at various locations and were provided with brick tunnels, but that doesn't mean they dried up. Look at the Tach Brook, for example. It's still there, running underneath car parks and public buildings in Westminster. When I was a nipper, I used to climb down the viaduct and muck about beside the water that flowed out into the Thames from Millbank. Underground engineers still have to be wary of such channels, because they know their excavations could be destroyed by them.'

May pulled some papers from his drawer and threw them across the desk. 'Monica gave me this. Apparently, Greenwood is our top underground man. He's mapped them all out in his time, and that's only a partial list.'

Bryant scanned the list of evocative names. The Westbourne, Parr's Creek, the Roding, the Slade, the Tyburn, Mayes Brook, Hogsmill, the Crane, the Peck, the Ravensbourne, Hackney Brook, the Falcon, the Effra, the Neckinger, the Walbrook, the Wandle, dozens of other smaller tributaries.

'They run from Hampstead to Acton to Bromley to Barking,' May added.

'What do you expect? The city's in a basin and the water drains down.' Bryant spelled it out as if talking to a particularly inattentive child. 'River beds crisscross the whole of London in a grid, around and underneath and sometimes even through some of the most sensitive buildings in the city. Some of them are connected to the sewers, which means they tap directly beneath government properties.'

'Here's the list of stuff Greenwood's purchased so far. Monica found it in his jacket.'

Bryant dug out his reading glasses and examined the sheets. 'This equipment is for climbing down, not up. Look at these items: high-powered torches, thighboots, pipe-clamps, hardly any ropes. This other receipt is a pharmaceutical treatment for rat bites. Looks like someone's hired him to get into the remains of an underground river for some dubious purpose, possibly to enter private property.'

'You think they might be planning to tunnel into the Bank of England, something like that? Wouldn't it be rather an outmoded notion in these days of computerized security?'

'Just because it hasn't been attempted for a few years doesn't mean it's outmoded, John. Think about it; someone has searched out an expert in the field who has a blotted copybook, and is proposing a venture that involves purchasing safety harnesses and weighted boots. I'm not saying that your cuckold has any knowledge of his client's real intentions, but he's refusing to tell his wife because he doesn't want to compromise her safety, which suggests he knows something.'

'I was planning to confront him with the evidence and warn him off, you know, as a friend,' said May.

'You said yourself he's not a friend, so why should he take your advice? Besides, I have a better solution.'

'What might that be?' asked May, dreading the answer.

'We can find out what he's up to, and stop him

from doing it. It's a clear security issue. Raymond would have no option but to sanction the case.'

'Arthur, please don't do anything that would get us into trouble. We don't need it right now. We have to start playing by the book.'

Bryant's rheumy blue eyes widened in innocent indignation. 'I'm surprised at you, John. When have I ever got us into trouble?'

11

THE HEART BENEATH

Kallie sanded and undercoated the front door before applying a rich indigo gloss to the wood. She had repainted the bedroom and put up some cheap curtains, working her way down a list of chores, but felt as if she had barely scratched the surface. She hadn't lived in a house since her parents were together. She was crouched in the hall, trying to thump the lid back on the paint tin without crescenting her palms, when Heather walked past laden with shopping bags.

'How are you getting on?' she asked, peering in. 'Isn't Paul giving you a hand?'

'He's been called up to Manchester,' Kallie explained. 'He's still waiting to find out if he has a job. I thought I'd get this done before it started raining again. I don't like the look of the sky.'

'I don't suppose he'd be much help anyway. He's never been very practical, has he?' Heather wore full make-up and was dressed in a smart black suit and heels, hardly shopping attire. She was never casual, or even relaxed. 'Still, it's very good of you, doing all this yourself. I wouldn't know where to begin.'

'It's a case of having to. I used up my savings

securing the house. There's hardly anything left over for fixtures and fittings, and nothing for renovations. God knows what will happen if Paul is made redundant.'

'It's still better to invest in property, darling. Look at what's happening to pensions. George lost a fortune in Lloyds, but luckily he has his own business these days. Has anybody told you about the party tomorrow night?'

'I got a note through the letterbox yesterday from the couple who live at number 43.' She straightened her back with a grimace. 'They're not holding it just for us, are they?'

'No, it's their son's tenth birthday, and Tamsin thought it would be nice for you to meet the neighbours, get to know a few people.'

'What are they like?'

'Oh, public school and a bit dim, but friendly enough and well-meaning. They communicate almost entirely through the boy, dote on him a bit too much, really, but she can't have any more children so he's become very precious to them. Actually, they always take our milk in when we're away so I can't complain. The child's called Brewer—an extraordinary choice, but it seems everyone has to come up with a novelty name these days.'

'I haven't seen George around.'

'He's gone on to Montreal. I hate it when he does the Canada office; he always brings me back scarf-and-jumper sets. That's if he remembers; otherwise it's an airport headscarf. Who wears those things? He's back on Friday, but three days after that there's a trade fair in New York. Never marry a successful man if you hate spending time alone. Come over for dinner if you like, I'm just doing venison sausages and grain-mustard mash with onion gravy.'

Kallie pushed back the bandanna on her forehead and left a smear of blue paint. 'Thanks, but I want to finish washing the lounge walls tonight. We've still only got lights in three rooms. I need to find a decent inexpensive electrician.'

'You're in luck. We've got one in the street, at number 3, our rough diamond Elliot Copeland. Actually he's a builder, but he'll turn his hand to anything. He'll probably be at Oliver and Tamsin's tomorrow night. Pour him a couple of drinks and you'll be able to beat a decent price out of him.'

'I guess I have to come, then.' Kallie rose and wrapped her paintbrushes in a cloth. 'I just hope Paul's back in time.'

Heather started to leave, but returned. 'You haven't seen Cleo in your garden, by any chance? She's not allowed out of the front door. Her food bowl hasn't been touched all day.'

'No, but I'll keep an eye out for her.' She had seen Heather's cat picking its way through the foliage of the back gardens.

After cleaning the brushes in the basement's butler sink and thrashing them dry on newspaper, Kallie made some tea and decided to get clean. She had soaked the ancient copper shower-head in descaling fluid, but it had made no difference to the years of stony accretion caused by London's infamously hard water. She stripped and padded across the cold parquet, setting the torch beam at the ceiling. The steep curve of the bath made standing up treacherous, but she had never enjoyed soaking in tepid water. Paul could lie there for hours, but she—

She could hear it again.

Not coming from the right-hand wall of the bathroom this time, but seemingly from under the floor itself. She had assumed that the foundations were solid concrete, so it had to be an acoustic trick of some kind. Copies of the house plans had still not turned up, probably because of a delay in locating the originals. Although the bathroom was below street level, there didn't seem to be any actual damp, but the noise was worrying.

She pressed her palms against the cold plaster of the adjoining wall and tried to sense the arrhythmia of liquid life within the bricks. She could hear it clearly now, a channel of rushing water, pounding and rebounding before it was constricted within some kind of man-made sluice. She could trace its faint pulse in her cold fingertips, a vein pumping waste in freezing peristalsis from the city's hidden heart.

Crouching lower, her eyes drew level with the underside of the bath. Although she had sprayed the dark space with disinfectant, several hairy brown bowls of spider-nests remained beneath the shadowed legs.

The tops of her feet were prickled with pimples that itched when she touched them. They had appeared when she'd discovered the spiders, and now she wondered if they were bites, or even tiny stings.

She told herself that the room would be transformed with fresh plaster and paint, and lights that worked, but resolved to keep her showers short until then.

*   *   *

'Floorboards creak, pipes expand and contract—you've never lived in such an old house before. You have what doctors used to refer to as an overactive imagination; it comes from being too creative, and of course Paul's away ...' Her mother managed to hang sentences filled with insinuations of mental instability and general uselessness in the air like embarrassing items of washing. Helen Owen loved her daughter, but not enough to stop herself from being cruel.

'I'm coping brilliantly,' Kallie rallied. 'And before you say it, I know it wasn't the best time to take on something like this, but it was a lucky opportunity. Nobody knew she was going to die so suddenly.'

'That's simply not true, darling. There's a lot we can do to maximize our health and reduce stress, and I think you have to ask yourself if Paul has your interests at heart. He seems barely employable, he has trouble controlling his temper, and then he leaves you with all the stress of moving, into a house that sounds entirely unfit for habitation—'

'I have to go, Mum. I'll call you later.' Kallie knew better than to talk with her mother when she was like this; Helen was alone and angry and probably drinking.

There was still much to do before going to bed. She pulled on her jeans and ventured out into the garden. The sodden bushes hung like overcooked spinach, or foliage in a drained fishtank. The steps to the small patch of grass were so overgrown that she had to cut her way through with a kitchen knife. She heard the cat's peculiarly human cry before she got to the top. Somewhere inside the tangles of bindweed, she could see Cleo's piebald torso flexing and twisting in an effort to free itself.

Cutting through the bindweed was slow work. When she was finally able to reach in and grab the cat, it slipped away with a whimper of pain. Her foot caught on a broken plastic drain lid, and she tipped over into a wet bed of weeds. Withdrawing her left hand, she was surprised to find her fingers covered in blood. The cat had stopped wriggling now, and was lying on its side under a bush. Even in the watery cloudlight of late afternoon, she could see that its fur had been parted by a number of short, deep cuts that looked like knife slashes.

'Come on, baby, let me help you.' Kallie reached out her hands and gently lifted it up. As the cat feebly batted her with its paws, she could see that its back left leg had been almost severed. Torn sinews gleamed with pearlized whiteness. There were more cuts across the creature's face.

As she sought to regain a foothold in the dark snarls of weed, she knew that the poor thing was dying. She wondered if foxes could do something like this. They had been drawn into the city to scavenge on junk food, but did they also prey on cats? Cleo was covered in mud and blood. It was as if something had clawed its way up through the moist earth to attack her.

By the time she was able to gently lift it free, the cat was dead. Kallie glanced back at the little terraced house, its interior darkened, its brickwork retreating from sight under cover of rainfall, as if the property was disassociating itself from her palpable distress.

12

FOLLOWING THE RIVER

'Are you sure you can keep up?' asked May, concerned. His partner was breathing hard and had paused to lean against the railings.

Bryant waved aside the concern for his health. 'I'm fine, don't worry about me. I've been much better since I started remembering to take my blue pills.'

'Why, what do they do?'

'They alleviate the side effects of my yellow pills. I don't think he's got this right. I expected the river Lea, something over Romford way.'

The detectives were following Gareth Greenwood down Farringdon Road, rather too closely for comfort, but at least the heavy rain was reducing their visibility. The Quality Chop House still advocated working-class catering on its steamy windows, but now most of the shops reflected a neighbourhood filled with single professionals in converted loft apartments. Ahead, where Farringdon Lane branched away, stood the slim wedge of a public house, the Betsy Trotwood. They sheltered in its lee and watched as Greenwood closed his umbrella, striding off in the direction of Clerkenwell Tube station.

'The Fleet is still the best known of all the London rivers,' said Bryant as they stepped back into the rain. 'But its remains don't go near any of the city's financial institutions, so we can assume he's not out to rob a bank. I've been doing a bit of research into the subject of lost waterways, and it's fascinating stuff. Various tributaries fed into the Fleet as it flowed south, the largest junction comprising the two that flowed either side of Parliament Hill Fields, to meet in Camden Town. Beyond the junction, it was reported to be sixty-five feet wide when in flood. By the time it got to Holborn Viaduct it was wide enough to float boats on. He's not carrying any equipment. You're sure he made the appointment for this morning?'

'That's what he told Monica. She rang me last night as soon as he went to the pub.'

Greenwood had alighted from a bus in Rosebery Avenue, passing so close to the detectives that they were obliged to hide themselves behind their umbrellas. The academic was short and stout, with a mane of yellow-grey hair that would have allowed him to pass as a dinosaur rocker, especially as he was wearing brown boots with jeans tucked into them. He strode briskly along wet pavements, but mercifully stopped to admire something in the window of a furniture shop, which gave his pursuers the chance to gain ground.

'There were plenty of wells bored along the valley line of the Fleet in medieval times,' Bryant continued. 'Holy Well, Bagnigge Wells, Clerk's Well, St Clement's Well—they formed spa resorts or the sites of nunneries, and some of the water sources are still active. You can buy bottled water from the Sadler's Wells. It's got a bit of an undertaste but it's quite nice. Listen to this—' He pulled a bedraggled scrap from his pocket. ' "Come prithee make it up, Miss, and be as lovers be, We'll go to Bagnigge Wells, Miss, and there we'll have some tea." *The Apprentice Song*.'

'So you're saying that the Fleet still flows?' asked May. 'I thought you said it had silted up and been covered over.'

'Yes, but apparently not all of it—the wells are there, and water always finds a way. We build dams of brick, and rivers simply flow around them. The Fleet was thirty feet under street level in places. It flowed beneath the Regent's Canal, which is only shallow.'

'You talk about it in the past tense.'

'Perhaps I shouldn't. The London water table is rising fast, you know. Gardens are becoming marshy once more. It's inevitable that some of the old rivers will make a reappearance at such a time. They have before. The Fleet would be with us now if the butchers of Eastcheap hadn't emptied entrails into it for centuries. They were called "pudding", you know, animal guts. That's what Pudding Lane—where the Great Fire started—refers to. People imagine plum cakes, but it's reeking entrails. Can you still see Greenwood?'

'He's heading toward Turnmill Street.'

'You see, "Turnmill". There were a number of water mills here. Dickens often used this area. Saffron Hill was the home of Fagin and his lost boys.'

'Wait, he's stopped. He's looking for something.'

Their quarry appeared to be consulting a piece of paper. After a moment, he folded it away and set off again.

'You know, we're very close to the Fleet Ditch

now,' said Bryant, stabbing his stick in the direction of the drains. 'The Fleet was covered from Holborn Bridge to the Punch Tavern. Today it's a sewer that you can supposedly still reach from the arched tunnel entrance past St Bride's, but it just empties into the Thames. What can he possibly want with it at this point?'

Greenwood had stopped again. Now he stood in a curious stretch of the street between fashionable restaurants and derelict houses, looking along the pavement. The figure who stepped down from the shelter of the bookshop doorway looked familiar to May. He was tall and slender, long-necked, elegantly dressed, possibly of Ethiopian extraction. The pair spoke briefly, and when they made their move it was so fast that the detectives nearly missed them. They had passed through a door cut into the wooden frame covering an alley no wider than a man's arm.

May reached it first, but the door had already been closed. He put his ear to the wood and listened, then deftly picked the Yale lock. The alley beyond was filled with beer crates and empty catering drums of ghee. The brick walls were green with mossy weeds. 'Look,' Bryant pointed, 'river damp. You can smell it. Brackish. Old mud.'

Greenwood and his accomplice must have passed to the end of the alley; the only other door had boxes and coils of wire stacked in front of it. The corridor opened into a small dingy square with the Edwardian stone arch of a former stable, now overgrown and litter-filled, the signs of lost utility and urban misuse. Ahead was the rear of a Romanesque building, solidly built, small windows, probably a warehouse.

A wide wooden door and two narrow, filthy wire-glass panes were set in the wall, but here May's lock-picking skills defeated him, and he was unable to gain entrance. The windows were each divided into twelve small panels. Breaking them would be too noisy and time-consuming. May looked back and saw that his partner was having trouble clambering between some rusted lengths of iron. He led Bryant away.

'Come on, Arthur, they've gone for now. Let's see if we can identify our mystery man.'

'How?' asked Bryant, extricating his overcoat from a length of wire fencing. 'I'm getting holes in my good astrakhan.'

'I fired off a good half-dozen shots on my phone with a reasonably decent zoom,' May explained. 'They've already gone to my computer. I'll tell Bimsley to download them and start enhancing the images.'

'Dear God, it's technology gone mad.'

'Not if it helps us save a colleague from ruining his career,' May replied, linking his arm with Bryant's. 'Let's go back.'

Heather Allen shed a few dutiful tears and quickly composed herself, agreeing to let Kallie bury the tiny cat in her garden. She couldn't have it buried in her own, because George had laid decking.

'I don't understand. Who would do such a grotesque thing to a harmless animal?' She stood hugging her arms in a passable imitation of pet bereavement, watching as Kallie took the shovel and cleared a space in what once had been a flower-bed.

Kallie wanted to believe that Heather had been fond of the cat. Her schoolfriend had produced a credible monologue on the subject, explaining how she had rescued it from a feral existence living off scraps in Camden Parkway, how it had taken her months to gain the feline's trust, and how she had taken it with her to the useless PR job she had managed to hold for nearly a year, nestled inside her cardigan, where it could feel the beating of her heart. But the story rang false. As far as Kallie knew, Heather had never worn anything as homely as a cardigan.

As she finished digging the hole it started to rain, a light-leeching mizzle that darkened the surrounding terrace walls and bowed the branches of neighbours' trees. By the time she had filled the grave, they were both soaked. She could hardly have left the cat in a bin-liner until the weather improved, and could not imagine Heather with a shovel in her manicured hands. Heather loved the idea of organizing others, but hadn't a practical bone in her body. She explained that the last time she had lost her mobile, her entire life had come to a standstill.

Kallie had just pulled the last of the bindweed from the area surrounding the little grave when she saw the creature lying beside the drain. It was jointed and cream-coloured, and looked like a large deformed lobster. 'Jesus, what the hell is this?' She jumped back, nearly tripping in the tangle of weed.

Heather leaned over for a look, then gave a squeal of horror. 'It's covered in blood. What is it?'

'Wait, I saw some gardening gloves.' Kallie returned with them and reached down, lifting the thing by its segmented tail. 'I think it's some kind of crayfish, but it looks too big.' They stared uneasily at the creature, half expecting it to come back to life.

'It's typical that George should be away when there's a problem,' Heather angrily announced. 'He's never around when he's needed. I have to do everything by myself, and now this.'

'Heather, there's nothing for you to do.' Kallie tried to be gentle with her, because that was how you had to be with women like Heather. 'Look at the size of its claws, they're enormous. You think it had some kind of territorial battle with the cat?'

'It looks that way,' said Heather. 'But what on earth was it doing here in the first place?'

'You're right, it is a crayfish,' Giles Kershaw agreed. Kallie had made use of the number on the card that Longbright had left, and had been told to bring in her find.

Kershaw turned over the carcass and matched it to the images on his screen. 'I don't normally deal with non-humans, so bear with me. It looks like there are over a hundred species on my database, but this—' he scrolled down, searching, 'is probably a Turkish crayfish. They're extremely aggressive. They live in the canals around London. Hm.'

Kallie peered over his shoulder, trying to read.

'They've been forcing out the weaker British crayfish, usurping their breeding grounds. I imagine the pale pigmentation is due to lack of sunlight, toxins and a lack of nutrients in the water. It's bigger than it should be. Unusual for one to take on a cat, I'd imagine. Perhaps it had been driven from its home.'

'It was a very small cat, and she probably attacked first,' Kallie explained. 'There could have been more than one, couldn't there? How did it get into the garden?'

'Oh, they can cross land when they have to. Domestic turtles will do the same. They'll foul ponds until they're uninhabitable, then move on until they find a fresh garden with water—but I'd say you have a canal near your house. Quite a few of the tributaries to the Regent's Canal are connected to domestic drainage systems via old sewer pipes.'

'You're telling me this came up out of the drain?'

'That's the most likely explanation.'

Kallie recalled the drain's dislodged plastic lid. *First spiders, now invertebrates,* she thought. *What next?*

'Glad you brought it in,' said Kershaw breezily. 'I can't imagine it has any connection with the old lady's death, but this is just the sort of oddity old Bryant and May like to stick in their investigations. They'll probably work out that Mrs Singh was nibbled to death by lobsters. I'll show them this as soon as they're back. If you find any more, don't be tempted to smother them with mayonnaise—they're highly poisonous.'

What an odd man, she thought as she walked back from the station, puzzled by the little police department above the entrance to Mornington Crescent Tube. But then they had all seemed odd: the female police sergeant who looked like an old-time movie star, various startled and excitable juniors with slept-on hair and slept-in clothes, the spectacular disorder of the place, the back-room experiments and half-laid floors. Could the PCU really be a legitimately sanctioned branch of the law?

By the time she reached the underlit alley connecting Alma Street to Balaklava Street, she realized how comfortable and familiar her new neighbourhood was starting to appear. She was used to gangs of rowdy kids setting off alarm bells and encouraging her to cross the road, but here was nothing to be nervous of—except that the unbroken arrangement of house-backs made it impossible not to feel as if one was being scrutinized.

As she emerged from the alley, she glimpsed a man—no more than a ragged dark shape—passing on the opposite pavement, as if he had been startled into flight. She stopped for a moment to take stock: a row of terraced houses with flaking white paint, worn front steps and defunct chimney pots like orange milk churns; black spear railings; hydrangeas and bay hedges and windowsills with green plastic tubs of dead chrysanthemums; the back of the Catholic primary school; saffron lamps shining through the branches of mangy plane trees. She saw him again, standing like a statue in the recessed doorway of the end house, watching as she passed, and couldn't bring herself to continue without stopping.

'Are you all right?' she asked. 'Do you need help?' As she spoke, he stepped forward, dropping down the steps toward her, and she glimpsed brown eyes above a filthy white beard. Then he was gone, hobbling with fast, truncated steps toward the alleyway, and she remembered Heather's words: 'We even have our own tramp, a proper old rambly one with a limp and a beard, not a Lithuanian with a sleeping bag.' The idea didn't bother her, but she wondered what went through his mind as he stood in the doorway watching the street.

* * *

'I suppose I should feel relieved.' Paul opened a bottle of Beck's and sank back on the sofa to drink it. 'At least I know where I stand.' He had been given two months' pay and notice to quit. The company in which he had been promised such a wonderful career was heading for liquidation.

Kallie had wanted to raise the subject of paying for the house to be rewired, but knew it was time to hold off. 'What do you want to do?' she asked softly.

'What I don't understand is this, right—they hired me to look for innovative music, and the moment things get tight they fall back on old material, repackaged compilations, safe stuff they can hawk around to advertising agencies. The superclubs are dead, the bands are crap and the industry is heading down the toilet. Everyone's downloading, who needs to buy CDs? If we're going to stay here, I'll have to make a complete career change.'

'What do you mean, if we stay here?' she asked. 'I've put every penny I have into this house. We made the decision jointly—where else can we go?'

The ensuing silence worried her more than any answer. She knew he had viewed the move as a way of giving up his old life rather than starting a new one.

The television had no aerial and reception was lousy, but Paul sat before it anyway, opening his third beer while she went downstairs and tackled the painting of the built-in cupboards. She had set up a battery-powered lamp in the bathroom now, making the room a little more cheerful, and further dousings of disinfectant beneath the bathtub had taken care of the spiders. The room still seemed abnormally large compared to the kitchen, and she disliked the fact that it was below street level, but Benjamin Singh had explained that part of the basement was once a coal cellar. Kallie tried to imagine the rumble of coal in the chute, the stone-floored scullery and outside plumbing, but the history of the house had been erased by successive owners.

She remained unbothered by the idea of Mrs Singh dying at home in unexplained circumstances. She considered herself practical, rarely given to overactive flights of imagination. And yet there was something . . .

Kallie was moving the lamp when she saw the damp patch on the far wall, beneath the tiny window, a creeping sepia stain roughly the shape of Africa. Perhaps it had been there all along, but this was the first time she had noticed it. Her fingers brushed the brickwork and found it dry to the touch. Could coal dust have permeated the walls to the extent that it returned, spreading through paint and plaster like asbestos powder silently accreting within the lungs?

Perhaps she had taken on too much. Paul was unhappy and unhelpful. Later, as she lay in the cool, darkened bedroom nursing a headache, she wondered if they had really done the right thing. The property anchored them more firmly than any child. Certainly, Ruth Singh had never stirred from the house. Kallie couldn't let it have the same effect on them.

13

EVERYONE IN THE STREET

'We've got a match on Greenwood's client.' May came through the hole where the door should have been with an air of triumph.

Bryant was taking tea with two of the workmen who had set up a primus stove in the hall to make their own refreshments. 'Ah, so what's the score with your cuckold?' he asked. The carpenters looked at May with fresh interest. They clearly enjoyed chatting with Bryant, and had settled in so comfortably that May suspected they were hoping to drag out the work until Christmas.

'I do wish you wouldn't call him that,' snapped May, uncomfortable at having to discuss his private affairs in front of strangers. Such openness never bothered Bryant, who always behaved as if there was no one else in the room.

'I'm sorry, the situation intrigues me, that's all. You know how unlucky I've been in my own romantic affairs.'

'Oh, come on, it hasn't been all bad. There was that girl in 1968.'

'*Exactly*. The only person in London who didn't

have sex in 1968 was my Uncle Walter, and that was because he was in an iron lung. The trouble is, I've spent too much time on my own. I suspect I've started to behave abnormally.'

'Not at all. You've always been horrible to people.'

'That's very hurtful,' Bryant complained, attempting an empathetic response. 'Do you have any idea how alone you can feel when you think differently from everyone else? You can be as alone as—that cat.' He pointed to Crippen, who was sitting with his back to them, staring intently at a spot on the skirting board. 'Look at it. There's nothing happening in its head at all except for a vague idea about fish and radiators. It's probably been neutered and has lost the will to live. No wonder we relate. Don't talk to me about romance. Let's see what your gizmos have managed to come up with.'

May waited until the listless workmen had taken their leave, then called in Dan Banbury to explain the process to his partner.

'OK, the Bluetooth images are fairly low-res, given the poor light,' Banbury pointed out, tapping his computer screen. 'But the unique thing about the phone is that it takes micro-sequential shots from three separate angles. Of course the electronic images are constructed of code translated into pixels, so they can be translated back using a different program that fills in perception gaps. From here it's a simple matter to wire-frame a 3-D image, plugging the missing pixels with similar textures and colours taken from surrounding surfaces to give a fully fleshed shape. This means that the chances of finding a file match are multiplied a hundred times over, because we can run database checks from almost any angle.'

'I have no idea what you're talking about,' warned Bryant, 'but go on, it's terribly interesting.'

'I ran the shots against everyone entered in the system with a visual reference—that includes Index Offenders, people who have been put into the mental-health system, as well as standard AMIP files, SPECRIM reports and central Met database convictions. The problem with the system—'

'I knew there had to be one,' Bryant grumbled.

'—is that we're only dealing with priors, naturally,' Banbury continued. 'The software hasn't been invented yet that can finger someone before they've committed a crime. I'm not Cassandra.' He gave a shrill laugh. Bryant looked at him as if he was mad. Banbury coughed awkwardly, then punched up a file on his screen. 'But we did come up with a match. Here's your man. Jackson Ubeda, aged fifty-one, three priors for fraud and intent to deceive, couple of B and Es, one grievous bodily harm, likes thumping people and rather fond of bankruptcy, usually disappears owing a small fortune to investors. No reason why your academic—'

'Gareth Greenwood.'

'—Greenwood, would know any of this, although a couple of the financial papers have run steer-clears on him in the past.'

'So what does this fellow want with an expert on underground rivers?' Bryant wondered, shifting closer to the computer.

'That's our job to find out.' May steered Bryant's hovering hand away from the keyboard.

'It's OK, Mr May,' Banbury smiled. 'The equipment is drool-proof.'

'How dare you,' said Bryant, affronted.

'He means even you can't damage it,' May explained. 'Longbright is keeping the Met off our backs by helping them with the Camden bin-bag killer, which means that Bimsley and I are free to go back to the Clerkenwell site this evening for a nose around. We're waiting for a premises code, but the fire officers can argue that the blocked alley is a health hazard if we have to sort it out quickly.'

'Not like you to steam in without a Section 8,' Bryant sniffed. 'I suppose you think I'd be holding you back. That's fine, take Bimsley, because I have something to do tonight anyway. And it's business.'

'What are you up to?' May asked suspiciously.

'I've been invited out,' said Bryant. 'I'm going to a cocktail party.'

The gathering was uncomfortable. The hosts were nervous, the guests suspicious and argumentative. From Bryant's point of view this made it interesting, as the bad atmosphere encouraged people to make mistakes. They had gathered in the knocked-through ground-floor rooms of number 43 Balaklava Street, home of Tamsin, Oliver and Brewer Wilton, ostensibly to celebrate their son's birthday and to welcome Kallie to the street—but as no details of Ruth Singh's death had been made public, everyone was anxious to know what the police thought.

'And this is Mr Bryant,' said Mr Singh. 'Tonight I am saying farewell to my old friend.' If Benjamin was upset with the outcome of the investigation into his sister's death, he managed not to show it as he introduced the police officer to the assembly.

'So you're the detective—how exciting,' said

Lauren Kane, a thickly painted blonde who appeared to have designed her own clothes by removing strategic buttons. 'This is my partner, Mark.'

A bulbous thirty-five-year-old in a straining blue-striped shirt reached over and shook Bryant's hand vigorously. Arthur hated physical contact of this nature, and found himself surreptitiously wiping his fingers on his jacket. 'Mark Garrett,' said the estate agent. 'I'm at number 7, the one on the end. The houses get larger as they go up the street because the shape of the plots is dictated by the line of the alley behind them. Dunno why. It's the way the property was parcelled back in the 1850s.'

'Take no notice of him—that's shop talk, he's in real estate,' Lauren explained. 'Mark's idea of fun is to spend the weekend poring over an ordnance survey map, looking for bits of land to buy. He knows everything there is to know about this area.' She didn't make it sound like a good thing.

'When are you deserting us, Benjamin?' asked Garrett. There was no politeness in his voice, and since the sale of number 5, no love lost between them.

'Tomorrow, and I am not sorry to go,' replied Mr Singh. 'There is nothing left for me in this city.'

'Please spare us your this-country's-gone-to-the-dogs speech again,' said Garrett, looking to his girl friend for approval and failing to find it. 'We know what you think of the people around here.'

'It's not safe any more, Mr Garrett. You know that. You sell properties in the area but you never tell anyone how dangerous it is.' His voice overrode the agent's protestation. 'Six brutal killings in as many weeks in the borough of Camden—this is why they are calling the High Street "Murder Mile".'

'Only the tabloids call it that, Ben, and the murders are mostly teenagers invading each other's territories.'

'So that makes it all right, I suppose? The police are too busy with these gang wars, they have no time to deal with muggings and burglaries. Yet there are flats being built on every piece of waste ground. You and your friends in the council, encouraging so many people to live on top of each other. Things will keep getting worse. Why not build a park or plant some trees?'

'What's the use of parks?' Garrett demanded to know. 'Look, I'm not personally responsible for the neighbourhood. I'm making a living, and if I didn't try to increase my turnover I wouldn't be very good at my job, would I?'

'My sister stayed in her house for fear of going outside,' said Mr Singh. 'Somebody was sending her—'

'Look, nobody ever saw these so-called racist notes she received.'

'That's because I burned them, as any decent person would have done.'

'I'm sorry she died, but it's nothing to do with any of us, all right?'

The evidence had been destroyed, and so it was an argument no one would win. Bryant dropped back from the group and found himself beside strangers. He had never possessed a facility for small talk, but having been unable to settle Ruth Singh's death comfortably in his mind, regarded this evening's gathering as a chance to meet the few people who may have known more about her than they were telling. He was studying the guests, his sharp crow eyes searching for detail, when a balding cherub dressed in black tapped him on the shoulder.

'You think there was something odd about Mrs Singh's death, is that it?' he asked, holding out a ringed hand, so that Bryant was forced to shake it. 'I mean, why else would a detective be here?'

'We do occasionally come off duty, Mr—'

'Avery. Call me Jake. This is my partner, Aaron.'

Does he mean business partner or *partner,* Bryant asked himself, taking a slight fastidiousness of manner into account and deciding on the latter.

'Forgive me, I suppose it's like teachers,' Jake apologized. 'You know how surprised you are to see a teacher in the supermarket when you're a kid, and you have to reconsider them as a human being. Aaron teaches—he's at the primary school in the next street.'

'That's handy for you,' said Bryant to Aaron. 'Tell me, how do you find children these days?'

'People always ask me that,' Aaron replied, 'as if they should suddenly have undergone transformations, but I don't suppose they're much different at the age I teach. They still play games and form alliances and elect leaders, and hero-worship and bully and get picked on. My classes are pretty young, so I don't have the kind of trouble teachers face with older age-groups. You wouldn't catch me teaching over-tens. The little ones watch too much TV, of course. They remember every character they see on their favourite shows, but won't recall the names of people they meet in the street.'

'Perhaps they don't know the difference.'

'Oh, they know the difference, all right,' said

Aaron. 'It simply isn't in their interests to bother re-membering. Children are merciless that way, almost entirely lacking in sentiment. I'm sure it's one part that hasn't changed at all. As soon as they hit ten some kind of switch turns on. They suddenly learn at-titude and duplicity. It's a survival mechanism, of course, probably an essential weapon when you're forced to walk around the neighbourhood with no money in your pockets.'

Bryant found Aaron's honesty encouraging. 'Do you teach any of the children in this street?' he asked, wondering if it was worth interviewing them. He had no fondness for modern children; their motives were sinister and obscure. They became blanker and more alien with each passing generation, probably because they saw him as impossibly decrepit.

'We're a working-class Catholic primary, Mr Bryant. The houses around here were constructed to provide homes for the Irish labourers who built the railways, and many of them are still lived in by their descendants. The area is split into original working-class inhabitants and new arrivals from the middle classes.'

'And how do you tell them apart?' asked Bryant.

'The middle-class couples never have a granny liv-ing in the next street. They'd hate to be thought of as economic migrants, but that's what they are, nesting in the upcoming neighbourhoods, quietly waiting to turn a profit, moaning about the lack of organic shops in the high street.'

'Do you teach the Wiltons' son?'

'No, Brewer goes to a private school in Belsize Park. That family over there—' he pointed out a West Indian couple with two Sunday-dressed children

'—send their kids to a Church of England school with a three-year waiting list. Among the working-class Catholic families, religion still plays a part in choice of education.'

'You surprise me,' Bryant admitted. He made a mental note, ticking the family off against Longbright's interview register: *Randall and Kayla Ayson, children Cassidy and Madison.* Randall looked fidgety and keen to leave. His children appeared hypnotized with boredom.

Paul had recognized the estate agent as soon as he entered the room, and suddenly understood how Garrett had got in on the deal for number 5 so early—he lived in the same street. No wonder he'd been annoyed by his failure to secure the house. He knew so much about the value of the property, it was almost like insider trading. 'That fat bastard is the one who tried to warn us off the place,' he whispered to Kallie. 'Where do estate agents buy their shirts? There must be a special store that caters for them.'

Mr Singh was refusing to drop his argument with Garrett. 'I heard that you are trying to purchase the waste ground in front of the builders' merchant. Don't tell me you're planning to squeeze another house on to the site.'

'I've never announced any intention to buy the land.' Garrett crushed a beer can and set it down, an act of vulgarity that did not pass unnoticed by the hosts. 'Nobody even knows who owns it.'

'You know the old man who lives there,' Mr Singh accused.

'Which old man is this?' asked Bryant. Tonight he was wearing a hearing aid, not because he needed to, but because it amplified all sounds equally, so that he was able to catch several conversations at once.

'There's a tramp—he uses the waste ground to sleep on sometimes,' said a large Egyptian man who was listening in. 'Omar Karneshi. My wife Fatima and I live at number 4.' Bryant received another damp handshake. 'If you buy the land, he'll have nowhere to live.'

'Bloody hell, why is everyone having a go at me?' Garrett complained to his discomfited girlfriend. 'How come I'm the bloody villain? Look, pal, no one can put in a bid for the land because the builders are planning to expand, so get off my back and give them a hard time instead.' Lauren quickly placed a fresh beer in his hand.

Tamsin mouthed 'Mingle and replenish!' across the room at her husband, pointing to various low-levelled glasses. She knew they should have hired someone to do the canapés, but had been worried that it would seem pretentious in a property of this size. They would save caterers for the house in Norfolk, a Christmas party perhaps, where waitresses could glide in unnoticed from the kitchen. Tamsin would never admit it aloud, but she hated spending her weekdays surrounded by Greeks and Africans and Irish Catholics, and groups of black teenagers who shouted and laughed in incomprehensible argot. Oliver had adopted the role of betrayed socialist, re-fusing to buy a place in Islington because Tony Blair had lived there. Kentish Town, he felt, was 'more real', although he was forever telling people how he could reach Norfolk in two hours on a Friday night.

'Everyone seems to be having a go at Mr Garrett,' Bryant observed, hoping to stir things up further.

'I think he has a chip on his shoulder about being uneducated,' said Tamsin waspishly, something she would never have done if she hadn't drunk quite so many glasses of nerve-steadying Lambrusco before the party started.

Bryant was not famous for his socializing skills, but recognized when a woman was dying to talk. He tried to imagine what May would say in order to encourage her. 'I suppose you've got the dirt on everyone here,' he said clumsily.

'It's a very cosmopolitan area,' Tamsin replied, giving no indication of having heard him. 'We've Elliot the builder at number 3—he's divorced, drinks rather too heavily, you can always find him in the George around the corner—and there's Barbara and Charlie, they used to live at number 37, which is now Ethiopians. He drives a van and has been inside—for bigamy, if you please. She's a nurse at the Royal Free. They moved out to Edgware, but we couldn't *not* invite them because she looked after Brewer when he had pneumonia—'

'You really do know everyone,' Bryant goaded.

Tamsin ticked the houses off on her hand. 'Oh yes, there's the squat at number 45—that's full of medical students. They're very polite and keep to themselves, and they can juggle, which is nice, although we do have to talk to them about their music sometimes, not so much the volume as the *lyrics,* and everyone else is an English professional or foreign, which is always so much harder to gauge, I find. There are mixed blessings at number 4, Omar and Fatima; she's terribly sweet, he's—well, *taciturn* is too kind a word. The Ethiopians at 37 seem pleasant enough but never talk to anyone; the women wear headscarves and

produce unusual cooking smells in the summer. The
Aysons are at number 39, but they don't talk to their
neighbours, Jake and Aaron, because they're devout
Christians and don't approve of the boys' lifestyle.
Kallie and Paul are our new arrivals, then there's
Heather Allen, over there in the Chanel suit, but we
don't see much of George, her husband, because he's
often away on business. Apparently she cries a lot
when he's abroad—Lauren can hear her through the
grate in the party wall—they're very much in love,
but heaven knows what he gets up to in Ottawa or
wherever it is. She used to be in PR but got fired for
taking a backhander, thinks nobody knows.'

'Was anyone friendly with Ruth Singh?' asked
Bryant.

'Nobody saw anything of her because she never
went out. I suppose we're all a little to blame.' Mrs
Wilton adjusted her frills and looked suddenly tired.
'I do want everyone to mix,' she confided, 'but Jake
and Elliot have been huddled in the corner discussing
something for the last twenty minutes, which is odd
because they normally can't stand each other. Jake
won't speak to Mark Garrett because the estate agent
apparently made some derogatory remarks about gay
people to his girlfriend, who promptly told Aaron,
because they go to the same gym. Omar sold us our
kitchen, but the drawers stick and Oliver can't bring
himself to complain because they're friends. My husband doesn't like to make a fuss. Mark Garrett bought
Omar's family store, and promised he'd be careful
who he sold it to, but he allowed a betting shop to
take over the lease. We already have four bookmak-
ers and two saunas in the high street and there's still

no patisserie, so I had to invest in a bread-maker. It's all so difficult. I need a drink.'

Brewer wandered in clutching a Gameboy, the headphones still in his ears. Oliver attempted to remove the device as guests made soothing sounds around them.

'Fat, ginger and private school,' said Garrett behind his back, 'poor little bugger.'

'You must be Kallie and Paul,' Tamsin smiled. 'That's Brewer, and he says he's very pleased to meet you.'

Let the kid speak for himself, thought Paul. *He's ten today.*

'I hope you're settling into our little street. Oliver tells me you have your work cut out, getting the house back in order.'

'He's right,' Kallie agreed. 'We just don't have the finances to do it for a while.'

Tamsin tried not to flinch at the mention of impecuniosity. 'Ah well, these things take time,' she offered vaguely in retreat. 'Do try the brioches, they're Oliver's favourite. We had to go miles to get them.'

'How quickly they all appear when there's drink on the table,' said Benjamin Singh. 'Incredible, isn't it, Arthur? There was no one around when my sister needed help. Ruth rarely saw her next-door neighbours, that's why she didn't talk to them. The Allen woman was overbearing, the Egyptian lady was all but invisible. People in this country complain about how wrong it is for a caste system still to exist in India, but they should look at their own behaviour.'

Bryant regarded the assembly, squashed into the lounge pretending to enjoy themselves, with a misanthropic eye. *How little they have in common,* he thought, *except the desire for upward mobility, an eagerness to turn their little corner of the city into some kind of urban village. They're waiting for delicatessens and designer opticians, praying for the local tyre factory to be turned into lofts. Then they'll know the corner has been turned, and won't be ashamed of their postal address any more. Fifty years ago the streets were filled with smog and working men wasted away from chest diseases. People dismiss their good fortune and instead become more restless than ever ...*

The rivers of conversation ebbing back and forth across the room were filled with dark undercurrents, the swirl of old rivalries, the scent of bad feelings. Benjamin was right; none of the conversation seemed to involve Ruth Singh. It was as if she had never existed.

Perhaps you've made too much of the matter, Bryant told himself. *This is the last time you're going to see Ben. He's leaving it all behind. It's time you did as well.*

14

EGYPTIANS

What bothered John May more than anything was the location of the building.

As a teenager he had been warned away from the soot-coated pubs and rough-houses crammed into the roads off the embankment. The area between the river and the railways was traditionally fringed with the poorest homes; here had lived the workers who built the tunnels and arches and laid the tracks, the Thames lightermen, the coalboys and dockers, their women in laundries and sweatshops. Too much poverty, too many people crammed together to survive a Saturday night without drunken fighting. The poor lived in lowlands, the rich on hills; a rule that applied to so many of the world's major cities. London sloped up from the Thames, to Shooter's Hill and Crystal Palace in the south, to Hampstead Heath and Alexandra Palace in the north. Crime drifted down to the base, gravity-drawn like the cloacal water sucked into London's lost rivers.

He nearly called the whole thing off after Bimsley fell over his second dustbin. The boy was a hard-working officer, but had clearly inherited his father's

strange lack of coordination. The PCU had a long
history of apprenticeship: Janice Longbright's mother
had worked there, as had Bimsley Senior. When there
were fewer rules to follow, you had to work with people you could trust.

May's trick with the Yale lock failed in the jaun-
diced gloom that passed for London night, and they
were forced to climb over the wall, an exercise for
which May showed surprising aptitude. Although it
was after ten there were still plenty of people on the
streets, but no one seemed interested in what they
were doing. The light pollution reflecting from the
low cloud-base enabled them to see as they picked
their way through the rubbish.

At the end of the passage, they crossed the small
square and edged down between a mulberry-tiled gap
in the buildings, coming out on to a brick-strewn
floor inside the two remaining walls of a warehouse.

'That answers Arthur's question,' said May. 'He
told me that every foot of the Fleet had been mapped
and explored, that there was nothing left to see. But
according to his maps, the buildings around here are
at least a hundred and fifty years old. If they're demolishing this one, they're clearing a path back to the
Fleet that hasn't been accessible for at least that long.'

'So what are we looking for?' asked Bimsley, backing around a stack of bricks from which a rat had just
dashed.

'I don't know. Maybe we should listen out for the
sound of running water.'

'All I can hear is the traffic in Farringdon Road.'

'Follow me.' May picked his way to the edge of
the interior wall, which had been painted an institutional shade of railway green at some time in the

1930s. Between the back wall and the start of the next building was a narrow gap. 'Want to go first?' May offered.

'I'm not sure I'd fit down there,' warned Bimsley. He wasn't nervous of what he might find, but some of the tiles were broken and he was wearing a decent jacket, having arranged to see some friends later in a West End pub.

'We need evidence of what Greenwood has been hired to do,' May told him. 'Don't think of it as a favour to Arthur so much as trying to close the reaction gap between us and the law-breakers.'

'Oh, very funny,' said Bimsley, squeezing into the space. Reaction-gap reduction was a training initiative long touted by the Met to its forces, and was consequently the butt of many jokes. The idea of crime anticipation and prevention was hardly new and not overly successful, but it was well suited to the PCU. *At least,* thought May, *we should be able to manage an arising situation between a convicted fraudster and an easily duped academic.*

'Do you think I can get an advance on my wages?' asked Bimsley. 'I'm broke.'

'You're supposed to be,' replied May. 'You're a junior.'

'Yeah, but I'm working overtime.'

'I'll give you one if you find something.' May shone the torch ahead. The tiles were covered in the kind of calcified slime he associated with river walls at low tide. 'It looks like you can get all the way down there,' he encouraged. 'Take my Valiant.'

Bimsley accepted the torch. 'If I ruin my clothes, I'm going to put in a chit.' He tried to avoid touching the walls, but couldn't help it after something sleek and squeaking ran across his boots. His palm came away green.

'What's that on your right?' called May. 'Down by your boot.'

Bimsley lowered the Valiant. 'I can't see anything,' he called back.

May had spotted the pale keystone of an arch, and a stone known as a *voussoir*, part of a curving cornice, mostly obscured by rubble. 'Pull some of that rubbish away, can you?'

Grimacing, Bimsley plunged his hands into the pile and dragged back a rotted mattress. It took him several minutes to remove the panels of wood and piles of brick that had silted up against the top of the underground arch, which he saw was staked with iron bars at six-inch intervals. He shone his torch inside. 'Looks like it goes a long way back,' he called. 'No way of getting in there without cutters.'

'If we can't gain entrance, that means Greenwood hasn't been able to get inside, either. They've probably only just taken the warehouse wall down. That means we're still in time.'

'Yeah, but in time for what?' Bimsley pressed his face against the rusted bars, lowering the torch.

'Nothing at all?'

'Nope.'

'Let's go.' May began stepping back through the debris.

'Hang on.' Bimsley crouched as low as the gap permitted. 'Stinks down here. I think I can see ...'

He turned around, flashing his torch along the gap, but May had already disappeared from view. Shining the beam through the bars, he could make out a curving brick wall with weeds protruding from it. At the bottom, below a deep ridge, was a thread of glittering silver.

'I think there's water, if that's what you're—Mr May?' The circle of light dropped lower, picking up another reflection. Bimsley pushed himself closer and found one of the bars loose. It jiggled in its concrete setting, then dropped down several inches. After a minute or so of further bullying, he was able to remove it completely. The resulting hole was wide enough to ease his head and shoulder through. He raised the torch again.

He nearly overlooked it because it failed to reflect the beam, but the light picked up something against the wall, a coil of tiny wooden beads fastened together with a strip of leather. Pushing his bulk flat against the bars, he was just able to raise the strand in his fingers.

But now there were two reflections of light above the bracelet, like small gold coins, bright and flat. It took him a moment to work out that they were eyes, and by that time he had heard the throaty rumble of a growl.

The dog attacked before he could unwedge himself. It leapt at him, spraying spittle, its jaws desperately snapping shut on his shoulder, biting down hard, its teeth clamping together through the generous padding. Bimsley cried out and fell back as the material tore, and the rottweiler launched itself into the gap. It got halfway through and stuck, wriggling back and forth with its hind legs off the ground until it twisted sideways, falling back into the cavernous cellar.

He could hear it trying to breach the space again, barking frantically, maddened by its imprisonment, as he stumbled over the chinking bricks toward the alley and the exit.

Back on the street, Bimsley examined the damage to his jacket. 'Bloody dog—must be another way in.' He poked the torn material back in place, then remembered the bracelet. 'Here, this qualify me for an advance?'

'I don't know—let me see.' May raised it to the light and gingerly sniffed. Sandalwood, he thought, *santalum album,* a popular item of cheap jewellery for those on the hippie trail; the cloying smell stayed for years. A flat bone medallion hung in the centre, an intricate design he couldn't decipher without his reading glasses, which were back at the unit. He slipped the bracelet into his pocket as Bimsley limped along behind him before departing for the West End, still complaining about his ruined clothes.

'He was shaken, but fine,' May told his partner the following morning. 'The dog's teeth just grazed his skin, but I sent him for a tetanus shot all the same, and he's going to charge us for the jacket. You think Greenwood put the dog in there? I can get the RSPCA down now.'

'No, don't do that.' Bryant was sitting on a pile of encyclopedias, taping together a set of surveyor's maps. 'I don't want anything to alert him. Look at this.' He waved the tape roll over the far side of the map. 'That blue line I've marked out is the Fleet. It discharges into the river via a bricked tunnel beneath Blackfriars Bridge, at the very point where Roberto Calvi's body was found on 17 June 1982. He was a senior banker, if you recall, a member of the Italian

Masonic lodge P-2. He was discovered hanging there, just about the most unlikely suicide London has ever seen. He'd lost a fortune as the chairman of the Banco Ambrosiano, owing something like 1.2 billion dollars. The money had been siphoned off and hidden from the IOR, the Vatican bank. Blackfriars Bridge has historic connections with the Freemasons, and it looked as though his assassins were deliberately leaving a warning to others, although the official verdict was still suicide. After continuing pressure to reopen the case, the body was exhumed in '92 and was found to exhibit clear evidence of murder. Five years later, prosecutors in Rome indicted four Mafia members. They belonged to the *Banda della Magliana,* not the kind of people you want to mess around with. The inference that the Vatican hired hitmen to punish their embezzler is unthinkable to the devout, but not beyond the realms of possibility to the rest of us.'

'You amaze me,' May marvelled. 'Considering you can't remember your PIN number or where you've left your glasses.'

'This is work,' Bryant retorted, adjusting his spectacles. 'Oh, and I've read up some more on underground rivers. Did you know that in 1909 the Hippodrome Music Hall in Charing Cross Road staged a water spectacle called "The Arctic"? They built icebergs and placed fifteen polar bears in a giant tank. Guess where they got the water for the display? The Cranbourne, the ancient river that runs right underneath the building. And of course we know that there's an artesian well beneath the Palace Theatre, because you nearly fell down it once. It seems there are entrances and exits to rivers all over London.

Listen to this.' He raised a leatherbound book and adjusted his reading glasses. ' "Until 1960, the garden of 20, Queen Square, Bloomsbury, WC1 contained a trapdoor and steps leading to the stone tunnels of a stream known as the Devil's Conduit." And there are dozens of other examples. No wonder Ubeda needs to employ an expert like Greenwood as a tracker.'

'I have something to show you.' May rummaged in his pocket and produced the broken sandalwood bracelet. 'Bimsley found it. I thought you'd like to see.'

Bryant wrinkled his nose and held it away. 'Probably came from Camden Market. Where did you get it?'

'Our intrepid DC found it inside the sewer inlet, just before the dog attacked him. There's another way in, but we couldn't find it. I took your advice and let Bimsley handle the dangerous part.'

'Good. You know you're not supposed to do anything too strenuous,' Bryant admonished. 'Sooner or later you'll have to start acting your age.'

'If I did that, I'd never get out of a chair again. It may be nothing, but I thought I might send it to Banbury, see what he can get out of it.'

'Let me take a good look first.' Bryant's desk-lamp revealed a little more information about the panel on the bracelet, but he needed a spotlight to see it properly. Dragging an illuminated magnifying stand from beneath his desk, he set the bracelet underneath and studied it through the distorting glass.

'Oh, I think there's a penis.'

May looked surprised. 'I don't see that. Are you sure?'

'Quite sure. It's rather faint.' Bryant slid the bone panel under a sheet of paper and ran a pencil back and forth across the top. 'See it now?' He held up the rubbed sheet. 'It isn't just any penis, either. I've seen this before.' He had that knowing smile on his face that May had come to dread, the one that said, *I know something you don't.*

'Go on, then. You're dying to tell me.'

'Look at the base. It's a penis that's not attached to a body. It's got wings—you can just make out the traces. See these tall flowers in the background—they're lotus leaves. And the other ones intertwined—that's papyrus.'

'What does that mean?'

'The lotus flower and the papyrus reed are the symbols of Lower and Upper Egypt. When they're tied together like this, a new meaning is created, an indication of unity and strength. These are very common symbols, especially when used in conjunction with river glyphs. Rivers feature strongly in Egyptian mythology because life springs from the waters of the Nile. But the penis ...' He scratched thoughtfully at his unshaven chin. 'According to Plutarch, Osiris was killed by his evil brother Seth, who tricked him into climbing inside a coffin which he then cast into the sea. He later ripped the corpse into fourteen pieces and threw them into the Nile. Isis and her sister Nephthys found all the pieces except the phallus, which had been swallowed by a crocodile, and buried them. They gave new life to Osiris, who stayed in the underworld as its judge and ruler. The penis of Osiris is therefore a potent symbol of fertility and rebirth.'

'Very interesting. But does it have anything to do with Greenwood?'

'It's an Osiris bracelet representing death as a male and rebirth as a woman. It could simply mean the loss of the sun and the arrival of the moon, or any other great change. The flight symbolism is interesting. A winged penis was a Tudor icon used by the prostitutes of south London, specifically the ones working near the river between Blackfriars and Lambeth.'

'Is the bracelet old?'

'No, it's probably quite recent. Things like this are still sold all over the Upper Nile. The symbolism is clearly connected with the site of its discovery. The bracelet cord and clasp are unbroken; it didn't fall off someone's wrist.'

'I wonder why it was left there.'

'I think we can work that out, John. Old beliefs never die. There's hardly a building or thoroughfare in London that doesn't contain a token somewhere in or under its construction. A more interesting question is *who* left it. We should congratulate Bimsley on his discovery.' Bryant pinned the bracelet on the wall behind his desk. 'While you were out in the field, Meera and I did a bit of research. The demolished building you entered was once the headquarters of Carolson Watchmakers, who bought it from a violin manufacturer. We know that violins were first produced from this address in 1835, which would lead me to believe that the building would be listed, despite being invisible from the road. But Meera checked with the council and it appears to be a legal demolition. The site has recently been purchased by a development company, and if Jackson Ubeda is involved, his name certainly doesn't appear on the company register. All we can really do is wait for Greenwood to return to the spot.'

'Let's suppose he has a way of getting into the re-maining Fleet tunnel,' May suggested. 'You said it doesn't pass beneath any important buildings on its way to the river, but you may be wrong. There's a dis-creet bank behind Ludgate Circus, a new one with smoked-glass windows and ram-raid-prevention bars, that deals with fund transfers from the Upper Nile. I think your first idea wasn't so barmy after all, Arthur. Jackson Ubeda was born in Tennessee, but according to his file he's of Egyptian extraction.'

'You think he's about to drop in on an old friend?'

'Or an enemy.' He helped Bryant gather up the maps. 'There's not a jot of evidence, of course, which means we'll have to hope that Greenwood decides to go spelunking while we can still afford to keep an eye on him.'

'I have a better idea,' said Bryant. 'Janice, would you step in here a moment?'

'You won't be able to bellow at me when they fi-nally put a door on your office,' Longbright warned. 'What do you want?'

'Tell me, do you own any valuable jewellery?'

'On my salary? Don't be ridiculous.'

'Well, could we perhaps borrow some for a couple of hours?'

'You nearly got me fired the last time we raided the evidence room. Why?'

'I want you to become a wealthy Egyptian woman for about half an hour.'

Sergeant Longbright straightened her skirt and wondered if she had overdone the eye make-up. She knew that older married women in Cairo sported the look one saw all around the Mediterranean, gold sunglasses and bright boxy jackets, but she felt like a cross between Cleopatra and Dalida. She was wearing an ostentatious emerald necklace which Bryant had borrowed from a sealed evidence bag, much to Kershaw's horror. The waiting room of the Upper Nile Financial Services Group was a cool marble sarcophagus. Longbright seated herself between arrangements of dried flowers on plinths, like a bereaved relative waiting to view a corpse.

She had booked an appointment with the manager, Monsieur Edouard Assaad, explaining that she wished to transfer money from a town near the Sudanese border to an account in London, trusting that he would prefer to speak English rather than French or Arabic. To enter the building, she had been required to pass through a metal detector and have her bag examined, in line with the requirements of banking in Cairo. May specifically wanted to know about the building's vault, and she was considering how to angle the conversation when M. Assaad arrived.

He had agreed to meet with Longbright to reassure her that Upper Nile FSG was the secure and sensible choice for a woman of means. Small and almost absurdly neat, from his waxed black tonsure to his freshly polished Oxford toecaps, he shook her hand warmly and ushered her to a side-room lined with crimson tapestries and low cushions.

'I may also wish to deposit a number of valuable items with you,' Longbright explained as a small silver tray of mint tea arrived. 'Would that be possible?'

'It can certainly be arranged,' promised M. Assaad, supervising the ritual of pouring.

'I was given to understand that you have a vault here on the premises.'

'I'm afraid you have been misinformed, Madam. We primarily deal with electronic transactions, but if you wish, we will contact an affiliated company where space in a secure vault may be set aside for you.'

'Thank you.' She wondered if she had failed to observe the rules of formal hospitality, moving too quickly into the discussion of business. Like Bryant, Longbright had never been adept at small talk. 'I was recommended to you by an old friend of mine, Mr Jackson Ubeda. I assume he is a client of yours?'

'I am sure you would be the first to appreciate that we are unable to divulge the identities of our clients.' M. Assaad's gracious demeanour shifted slightly. Longbright could tell that she had made him suspicious. Or perhaps the mention of Ubeda's name had bothered him.

She decided to press on. 'Surely you do have some kind of underground storage facilities?'

'Alas, no. The lower-ground floors were filled in many years ago. There were apparently some problems with damp undermining the building.'

'That's right, an old river runs near your property.'

'So I have been told.' M. Assaad was clearly losing patience. 'Perhaps you would care to see our chief clerk, who will supply you with the appropriate documentation for your account.' He punched out a number, covering the mouthpiece while he waited for a reply. 'We have a great many friends and clients in Aswan—I am sure you will find our services invaluable.'

* * *

Well, that was bloody embarrassing, she thought as she waited for a bus in Farringdon Street. *I know he saw right through me.* More problematic was the idea that the bank had no basement. It meant that Bryant's line of inquiry was misdirected, and as the matter was not an officially sanctioned case for the unit, it could not go much further. As soon as the Met's claim on the unit had ended, Raymond Land would be waiting to approve a number of new investigations for them, so there would be no more time to spend on pet projects.

First Ruth Singh and now this, she thought. *The pair of them have only been back at work for a couple of weeks and they've already managed to set everyone's teeth on edge.* She would defend Bryant and May against anyone, of course; that was what you did with old friends, no matter how annoying they became across the years. Still, she wondered how long they could continue to follow their own meandering path at the unit without being held accountable. The Home Office demanded results, and they would all have to face the consequences of failure.

15

RIVERWATCHING

Kallie was growing quite used to it now.

As she turned off the hot tap, the sound of running water continued, gurgling and churning somewhere under the floor. She tried to work out if it ran from the back of the house to the front, but there was no telling if what she could hear was a metre away, or ten. She had tackled Elliot Copeland at the party, telling him about her problems with the basement wiring. He had offered to take a look for her, but had so far failed to make good on the offer, forcing her to make do with the battery lamp. Paul had gone to the pub with Jake Avery, the TV producer from across the road, hoping to find out about job opportunities, while she had been left to do the laundry in Ruth Singh's decrepit washer-dryer.

And the house was starting to bother her.

The omnipresent sound of water, the damp patch growing in the wall and the return of the seemingly invincible spiders were minor causes for concern. She could manage without electricity until someone reliable could be found to repair the system. Even having to bury Heather's cat in her back garden had not fazed her—there was something far less tangible at work within these bricks. The attic echoed with rain, the pipes ticked and tapped with the passage of water, the floorboards stretched and bowed like the deck of a ship. Window frames, dry for so long, now expanded in the wet weather and refused to open or close.

Sometimes it felt as if a stranger's eyes were at her back, watching in silence as she moved about the basement. The sensation didn't occur in the front room or the bedrooms, even though they were the only ones which were overlooked. Something felt wrong inside the building: dead air displaced, events rearranged. It was nothing more than a vague sensation, but she had learned not to overlook such presentiments. She couldn't explain the feeling to herself, or articulate it to Paul, who had a habit of dismissing such ideas with an impatient wave of his hand. According to him she was simply not used to owning a house. More insultingly, he implied that using a room in which a woman had recently died would always be the source of some kind of female hysteria.

Then there was what she had come to think of as the Presence. After returning from the party two nights earlier, she'd felt sure that someone had been in the house. Nothing had been conspicuously moved, but the arrangement of items left out in the kitchen looked wrong to her, as though she was viewing them from a slightly altered perspective, as though the miasmic air within the closed rooms had kaleidoscoped, allowing the dust to drift gently and realign itself in alien patterns, like reordered synapses.

There had been another argument over money,

this time because Paul had spent part of his redundancy pay on a laptop computer, when they had agreed to pool their earnings toward the refurbishment of the house. They had never fought this violently before, even when they were sleeping on Neil's sofa. It felt as though the house was siphoning off their happiness, allowing it to stream away beneath the cold bathroom floor.

At twenty past eleven she heard the front door open, and found Paul fighting to free himself from his jacket in the hall. 'I thought you'd be asleep by now,' he said, with the faint struggle for clarity in his voice that marked him as a man who had drunk more than his limit. 'Come and sit in the front room.'

He tugged at her until she sat beside him on the couch. 'I've been wanting to talk to you.'

'You're drunk, Paul.'

'Only a bit. I've just had a chance to think about you, and I can tell you're not happy.'

'Let's discuss this in the morning.'

'Suppose—' he raised his voice, 'suppose we had money in the bank, I mean a decent amount, enough to buy a new place.'

'What are you talking about?'

'I was in the pub with whatsname—Jake—he goes hang-gliding in France—'

'What's this about money? Did he offer you a job?'

Paul pressed the heel of his hand into his eye, concentrating. 'Jake hasn't got anything suitable at his company. He wants me to go hang-gliding with him, you remember I used to—'

'You can't make money from hang-gliding,' she told him. 'Come on, I'll get you to bed.'

'I can manage.' He rose unsteadily. 'Look at this place. We can do better—Jake was talking to the other guy, at the party—'

She challenged him on the upstairs landing, folding her arms across her chest. 'I'm not with you. Which other guy?'

'Wait, I have to get this right in my head. Let me get undressed.' She waited patiently until he was installed on his side of the sloping bed they had borrowed from her mother. 'The builder guy—Elliot—he knows how we can make some money, but there's someone else who knows—' The rest of his thought drained into the pillow.

'Someone else knows what, Paul? You're not making any sense.' She knew how he behaved after a few beers. He would fade fast and not remember the conversation in the morning.

'We have to leave the street, Kal,' he mumbled as sleep started to claim him. 'It's not safe to stay ...'

Kallie watched the bronzed droplets brushing the windows, and wondered what she was supposed to do. Paul was already snoring lightly, leaving her alone and all too aware that although nothing was really wrong, nothing was quite right.

'What do you think he's doing?' May peered through the rain-spotted windscreen, trying to see if any lamplights were showing across the road, but the low branches of the plane tree obscured his view. Bryant had insisted on backing the car into the underbrush surrounding the car park because he didn't want Greenwood spotting them.

'He's checking out another underground river.'

'What makes you say that? Don't tell me you're developing a psychic link with him.'

'Oh, I don't think so.' Bryant unglued a sherbet lemon, popped it in his mouth and sank down into the shell of his protective overcoat. 'I'm basing my assumptions on concrete evidence, right here.' He withdrew a folded section of map from his overcoat and tapped it.

May was rattled. 'I don't get this. It's the first time in years that you haven't tried to drag palmists, mediums, witches, druids or any one of your fringe specialists into a case to prove a point. I thought we'd at least end up with a dowser. But you seem quite happy to sit here and wait for the worst to happen.'

'A dowser's not a bad idea. I thought you preferred me like this, calm and rational.' The boiled sweet clattered against his false teeth.

'Yes, I do, but it's starting to bother me.'

'I don't have much choice in the matter. At first I presumed that your pal was a total innocent, duped into something nefarious by a dodgy speculator or some kind of burglar. But now I'm starting to think that he's ready to go beyond the law in order to provide some kind of illegal service.'

'How do you know he's even breaking the law?' asked May.

'According to Meera, he's not requested permission to enter premises, and he hasn't petitioned the London Water Authority, who have to be officially notified of right-of-way access in the case of underground waterways. You told me that Mr Greenwood was an ordinary penniless academic until his first brush with criminals. My guess is that he's in some kind of transitional phase. Who knows what he'll decide to be next? People drift away into all kinds of dark worlds, and sometimes nothing can bring them back.'

'Hm.' May shrugged. They had seen Greenwood, wearing a yellow hardhat and wrapped in a coil of rope, heading across a piece of waste ground with the Egyptian in tow. The pair of them had vanished inside a boarded-up railway arch.

'Look around you. Know where you are?'

May scanned the landscape. 'South of Vauxhall Bridge. The kind of place tourists never see. No Man's Land.'

' "Those green retreats where fair Vauxhall bedecks her sylvan seats." That's this concreted-over hell-hole. The Vauxhall Gardens were right here, all around us, until 1860. For around two hundred years the area was filled with birds and fragrant flowers, a public garden available to everyone. There were spectacular fountains and illuminations, ornate Italian colonnades, a Chinese pavilion, balloon ascents. In the middle of it all was a sumptuously tiered orchestra house, with groves of multicoloured lamps undulating in the trees.' The sherbet lemon cracked between Bryant's teeth like a pistol shot.

May watched the Nine Elms lorries spraying and shaking around the one-way system. 'You're joking.'

'Hogarth drew "The Four Times of the Day" here. Walpole and Dickens, princes, ambassadors and cabinet ministers ate in elegant supper boxes over there. Two centuries of pleasure and happiness.' Bryant sighed. 'Eventually the popularity of the gardens created disruptive behaviour, and wardens were posted on the walkways. The admission fee fell as the grounds became run down, the punch was watered, the food dropped in quality. Fights broke out, thieves moved in. The orchestra house fell to bits. Soon it was gone for ever. Now look at it. Why does the blacker side of human nature eventually swamp the good? Why should beautiful things always have to die? Look at those pernicious monstrosities for the soulless rich, the dozens of riverside tower blocks crowding in along the Thames like futuristic slums.'

'You can't change any of it, Arthur. Wealth attracts wealth. You have to maintain a sense of humorous resignation about the things you can't change.'

'What a dreadfully woolly piece of advice.' Bryant had always shown appreciation toward the joys of the past, just as May was attracted by the prospect of the future. 'I'll tell you what he's up to. He's following the path of the Effra.'

'The Effra?'

'Another of London's so-called "lost" rivers. He's just entered a building that was built over the top of it before the start of the twentieth century.'

'First the Fleet, now this. What's the connection?'

'You might well ask. Perhaps something caused him to give up on the Fleet. Here.' He unfolded the map and laid it across the dashboard of the steamed-up Mini Cooper. 'Obviously, the underground rivers of London drain down into the Thames, so this one flows south to north, from Norwood through Herne Hill to Brixton, Stockwell, Kennington and finally here, to Vauxhall. It's referred to as a stream in the history books, but was apparently wide enough for both King Canute and Queen Elizabeth I to sail on. Considering they lived half a millennium apart, the river obviously had a strong source that kept it flowing. Elizabeth used it to visit Sir Walter Raleigh. Like most of the other rivers, it now exists in a handful of small disgusting ponds, the odd muddy dribble and a few bricked-over sewers. The interesting thing is that Greenwood has gone to the mouths of both rivers, where there would still be Victorian pipework in existence.'

'So if he's not looking to rob a bank,' asked May, 'what the hell is he after? Could it be something in the tunnel itself?'

'Buggered if I know. Let's go for a beer.'

'I'm starving,' May complained. 'Couldn't we eat?'

'I'm not indulging your fetish for fried-chicken outlets. We can go to the upstairs bar of the Union Jack for a curry and some decent bitter. We'll be able to keep an eye on Greenwood from there.'

'What if Raymond Land calls?' worried May. 'He'll want to know where we are.'

'Oh, I can run rings round Raymond,' Bryant assured him. 'His father was a jellied-eel merchant from Cable Street, don't tell me he's sophisticated enough to see through one of my ruses.'

'All right—but we drop everything if Greenwood comes back out. And if he's carrying something he didn't have when he went in, I'm going to arrest him.'

'Absolutely, good idea,' agreed Bryant, who knew exactly how to get his own way.

16

PHANTOMS

Someone had been in the house. Kallie was sure she had shut the door of the front room before going out. Unnerved, she waited in the shadowed hall, staring at the inch-wide gap between jamb and frame.

'Hello?'

No answer. What did she expect? That a burglar would announce himself? In the last few days a bitter smell of damp had begun to hang in the air, as though the rain-mist from the grey cobbled street had found a way to invade the house. But now it had been replaced by the odour of male sweat. She entered the other rooms one by one, and found that both the attic skylight and the basement garden door were still locked. No windows broken, no other way in or out.

Checking the bathroom, she noticed that the strange brown patch in the wall had dried and vanished overnight. None of it made sense. She returned to the front room and gingerly pushed at the door, letting it swing wide. Inside, nothing was disturbed. The stripes left on the carpet by her vacuum cleaner were unmarred by footprints.

She decided that a stray draught must have pulled

open the internal door, but it didn't explain the smell of sweat. New things were beginning to bother her. The turn in the basement stairs, permanently in shadow. The back window, against which the branches of a dead wisteria tree tapped and scratched like something from a children's book of witches. Worst of all was the great bathroom that seemed impervious to warmth or light, that bred hairless brown arachnids in its moist recesses and became stained with impossible patches of mildew that spread like cancer, only to recede and disappear before she could prove to anyone that she had not imagined such a thing.

Since the rain had begun to fall virtually without a break, the house had become wet. Sheets and blankets felt damp to the touch. The floorboards and window frames flaked varnish. Plaster felt soft and crumbly beneath the peeling wallpaper. It was quite obvious that Paul didn't believe her, and nor did Heather, who had begun breezing in for coffee, expecting to be waited on. She had taken Heather to the basement to hear the sound of rushing water, but her neighbour had insisted she could hear nothing, and even went so far as to suggest Kallie's mind might be playing tricks on her.

She wanted to rent industrial dryers and paint everything white, to let in sun and heat, but they were too short of money to do anything that would make a difference. The monthly mortgage repayment would keep things tight, and according to the papers it was likely to rise soon. Perhaps she shouldn't have taken Heather's advice. Even at school, her friend had never been without money. She had rented her first flat in a square just off the King's Road, and had met her future husband at a polo match, for God's sake. She and George ate in expensive restaurants, spent their weekends in Paris and Rome, never felt the need to check their bank balances ...

A white towel lay crumpled in the centre of the bathroom floor. It had definitely been folded on the rack beside the bath, she was sure of it. Paul was away in Manchester again. He'd told her he was going to argue his case for compensation, but had already started spending his redundancy. She wanted to talk, but his mobile had been switched off for hours. Why, what was he doing? Whenever they spent more than three days in close company they quarrelled, but she missed his absurdly inappropriate enthusiasms, his innocent longing for the freedom of youth. The house was less forgiving without him, as if it would only seek to press its peculiar aura when his insouciance was not there to temper it.

The bathroom tap shuddered and clanked when she twisted it. She was about to start washing her hair when the front-door knocker boomed through the house.

Jake Avery was immediately apologetic when he saw her dressing-gown. 'I'm always getting people out of the bath,' he told her. 'I should have called first, but I don't have your phone number.'

'Then I'll give it to you,' she promised, ushering him in. 'I was only going to wash my hair because there's nothing on TV. I'll make us some tea.'

He seated himself awkwardly on one of the mismatched kitchen stools and looked around. 'It's coming along nicely in here.'

'Thanks. I'm doing it by myself—Paul's hopeless with DIY.'

'You should get Elliot in from number 3. He's good

as long as you keep him off the booze. He painted and rewired our place, and now he's laying the front yard for the builders' merchant at the end of the street. You know, the piece of waste ground old Garrett was trying to get his hands on? It's going to be a car park.'

'I don't think Mr Copeland is interested in the job. I'd like to take a couple of walls out and stop the rooms looking quite so Victorian.'

'Yeah, Paul told me your plans.'

'Did he?' *I wish he'd tell me,* she thought. 'You two had a bit of a boozing session the other night.'

'Yeah, we got a bit pissed. Sorry about that.' He didn't sound contrite. 'I realize now that I don't talk often enough to my neighbours. We all work so hard that we've no time left for social niceties when we get home. I mean, I give money in the street to professional charities I've never even heard of, and yet I'm too tired to bother with the people who live next door. That's not right, is it? Paul told me how you two met. It sounded kind of romantic.'

'Paul has a way of sexing up every story. You have to take him with a pinch of salt.'

They had spent twenty minutes together inside a ghost-train car that had broken down in Blackheath funfair. She had been sitting with her girlfriend Daniella, debating whether to leave the car and risk walking through the cuprous gloom, when Paul had loomed out from a graveyard tableau and made them both scream. The happiness of that memory had been undermined by the fact that Daniella had died a month later, hit by a delivery van while riding her bike home late one night. No one had ever traced the driver. You could fill every square of the city's map grid with the stains of hidden tragedies.

'What did you guys find to talk about for so long?'

'Oh, you know, men in pubs can stretch any subject until closing time.' Jake accepted the tea. *Unusual to meet a gay man who's overweight,* she thought idly. *Pleasant face, obviously comfortable dealing with people in his job.*

'It's just that Paul mentioned something about hang-gliding.'

'Oh, *that*. It was nothing. I told him that Aaron and I had been hang-gliding in France, and he suggested coming along with us some time.'

'How long have you two been together?'

'Eleven years, believe it or not.'

'That's longer than most of my friends.'

'We have a deal. I told him if he ever leaves me I'll kill him, which pretty much sorted the whole thing out.'

'So,' she tried to sound casual, 'what was the part about making some money?'

'Oh, nothing really, not even first-hand information, just something I'd been told.' He suddenly looked like a small boy who had been caught stealing sweets. 'I wouldn't demean either of us by recounting another half-drunk conversation. But I did offer to lend him some money. He told me you were a bit strapped for cash right now.'

She bridled at the idea that her finances had been discussed with a virtual stranger. 'We'll be fine. It's just that there's a lot to do here. The electrics, the plumbing, the basement needs to be damp-proofed and re-plastered, the roof needs repairing. And I don't know how long I can live with this seventies wallpaper.' She indicated the mauve paisley print behind them.

'I can see what you mean. It's unfashionable without being fabulous.'

'Do you have any problems with water?'

'What kind of problems?'

'Surges in the plumbing.'

'No, but I've got rising damp. I think we're still Victorians at heart. We spend so much time trying to keep the rain out, but it always finds a way of getting in.' Jake drained his cup and rose to leave. 'Look, I have to get back. There's something I need to do.' He seemed undecided about explaining himself, but gave in after a brief moment of hesitation. 'It's about Ruth Singh. When the police came and did the interviews, I told a bit of a lie. I didn't want to get anyone into trouble, but it's started to bother me.'

'What did you tell them?' asked Kallie.

'It was about Ruth's visitor, the night before she died. I stopped to dig out my keys and saw someone ring the doorbell to number 5. Ruth definitely recognized her visitor, but I couldn't hear what they were saying. I told the constable I didn't know who it was. But there was this hat and a long black leather raincoat, not the kind of outfit you'd miss. At work I'm used to checking wardrobe continuity all the time, so I notice these things. Then I saw the coat lying in one of the bedrooms at Oliver and Tamsin's party.'

'You mean it belonged to Oliver?'

'No, to one of the guests.' He looked pained. 'It doesn't mean they know anything about Ruth's death, does it?'

'Who are we talking about?'

'Well—Mark Garrett. The coat was odd, not the sort of thing I'd imagine him wearing, and the sleeves were empty. It looked as if it had been draped over the shoulders, you know, so you could run out into the rain.'

'How do you know it was Garrett's?'

'Because I was so surprised to see it in the Wiltons' bedroom that I checked the label. His name was sewn inside the collar—who sews their name inside their clothes any more? I suppose there could be more than one coat like that, but there was something very odd about the length of it, and the one in the bedroom was identical. I reckon the police have a right to know, even if I'm proven wrong.'

'It'll make you feel better to tell someone,' she replied, thinking, *Oh my God, Garrett was desperate to buy the house, and he went to see the owner the night before she died.*

When Longbright called on him the next day, Garrett complained indignantly, balancing in the doorway like a man interrupted during the football results. 'I don't know what you're talking about. I haven't been running around with a raincoat over me. What are you implying?'

'Perhaps you borrowed it from your girlfriend,' the detective sergeant suggested, 'to put the rubbish out or something. It was raining hard. Maybe you've forgotten—'

'I'm not bloody stupid, woman. I run a very successful business—I didn't get that way by suffering mental lapses. I know where I've been, and I didn't visit Mrs Singh before she died, not for any bloody reason.'

'Then perhaps you could have a look in your girlfriend's wardrobe for us. Maybe she's put the coat in there by mistake.'

'And maybe someone wants me to take the blame for the old cow's death.' Garrett's face reddened as he raised his voice, hoping somehow that the neighbours would hear. 'People should learn to mind their own bloody business in this street. Tell me, why should I even care who she was? These damned people—Indian, Chinese, African—the liberals tell us we have to be one big community, we have to integrate, but why the hell should I? What do they do for me? Absolutely bugger all. I am English and this is my home, and it's nothing to do with any other bastard.'

One of them is either mistaken or lying, thought Longbright, turning away as the door was slammed in her face. She couldn't insist on searching the house without first applying for a warrant, and knew that one was unlikely to be granted. No one remembered seeing Garrett at the party with the coat, so it was Avery's word against the estate agent's, and because people knew they disliked each other, it could be argued that Avery was trying to make trouble for Garrett. *There's nothing that anyone can do about it now. Let's hope Arthur finds something more constructive to do with his time.*

She turned up her collar and began walking toward the Tube station. She adored working for the detectives, just as her mother had done before her. They had been there for her in the most difficult circumstances, but it was time to face the fact that they were getting old. She knew it was only work that kept them both from dotage, but if Raymond Land failed to get the unit assigned to high-profile cases, it would be closed down, and that would be the end of them all.

Something will turn up soon, she thought, peering up into the scudding black world above the high-street rooftops. *Something has to.*

17

INFIDELITIES

She would always remember how strangely the day had begun.

A Krakatoa dawn, intense and viridescent, had been obliterated by dim silhouettes of cloud, great grey cargo ships bearing fresh supplies of rain. By noon it had grown so dark that she had been forced to switch on the hall lights, and, not knowing what to do for the best, waited for the call.

She had known it would be George before the second ring. They had established the pattern of communication whenever he travelled, to fit around the time differences. If he was further west, he never rang before one. Further east, and he would call just as she was having breakfast. He never grew tired of waiting in airport lounges or dining late in half-empty hotels. He seemed to have deliberately chosen work that would deny him the comforts of home life. He was meeting factory representatives in company branches around the world, but she often wondered if he could have delegated these tasks and requested an administrative position in London. Perhaps, like Kallie's partner, it was something to do with never having taken a

gap year; perhaps he too imagined that beneath the
jacket and tie he was a backpacker, free to watch
dawn from mountaintops and follow the contours of
the shorelines. Except that his journeys took him to
places no student would choose to visit. And on that
day the call came at the wrong time, the pattern disrupted. He was only in Paris—no distance at all—but
something was wrong.

According to the readout on her receiver, he
stayed on the line for no longer than four minutes.
Barely time to boil an egg; certainly not long enough
to discuss a divorce. She had been half-expecting him
to raise the subject for almost a year. When she added
up the days they had spent together, the total came to
little more than three months in twelve, but it was
still a bitter shock. He recited the guilty man's litany:
*It's me, not you ... You've done nothing wrong ... I
need to rethink my life ... I'm holding you back ... I
can't expect you to wait for me.* But it rang so false
that she knew there was someone else involved, that
there would be a younger version of herself, probably
living in Paris, where so many trips had taken him
lately. He wouldn't rethink his life, merely repeat it
with someone more naive. She resented the fact that
he had reached the decision without her involvement.
*Let someone else deal with his intermittent sex drive
now,* she thought. *Let someone else feel the weight of
his damp flesh on top of her. I hope it's worth it.*

From an early age, Heather had worked hard to
have the life presented in style magazines; but it
hadn't turned out like that. She had hated the kind of
women who hung out at sports events with an
agenda for searching out the right class of man, yet
she had done exactly the same, attending fixtures in

the season's calendar, frequenting the fashionable
Kensington restaurants and bars until meeting George.
Her desire to establish such a specific lifestyle had
separated her from Kallie, whose honesty and sim-
plicity were quite uncalculating.

He had promised her the London house; he would
sign it over tomorrow, but there would be nothing
else. She was sure he would move his base of operations to Paris and live with his younger-Heather
clone, this year's more desirable model. Heather
would join the ranks of embittered divorcees who
prowled the cafés of the King's Road, sipping their
lattes and stalking certain designer stores because the
staff were cute, dining with women in similar situations, discussing shoes and spas and drinking a little
too much wine over lunch. And the worst part about
being cast into this tastefully appointed limbo was
that she only had herself to blame. She had made a
single, humiliating mistake that would taunt her for
the rest of her life.

'Come through to the studio. It's better that you're
here while my husband's still out. You look absurdly
well.'

Monica Greenwood led the way through the
cramped apartment occupying the top half of the
house in Belsize Park. Every spare inch of space had
been filled with books and canvases. When shelves
had overflowed, paperbacks had been stacked in pre-
carious piles along the already narrow hallway, beside jam jars of turpentine and linseed oil. Monica
looked much as he'd remembered. Although her hair
was now more studiedly blond, it was still carelessly

tied back, kept from her face while she worked on her paintings. Her figure was fuller, subject to the natural effects of a miraculous maturity. She looked sumptuous in jeans and an acrylic-stained sweatshirt, comfortable in this stage of her life. Too much time had passed for John May to remember if he had truly been in love with her, but he had certainly been bewitched at some point during the national miners' strike.

She carried mugs of coffee into a narrow conservatory coated in peeling whitewash. 'I'm glad to see you still paint,' said May. 'I've been looking out for exhibitions featuring your work.'

'You won't have found any,' she warned, pulling the cloth from a large canvas. 'I'm off the radar of popularity these days. I switched from figurative stuff to rather fierce abstracts; I think you often do as you mature and become interested in states of mind rather than accurate depictions of people and buildings.'

May examined the painting, an arrangement of curling cerulean lines that drifted to a dark horizon. 'I like that. Is it sold?'

She blew an errant lock of hair from her eye. 'Please don't humour me, John. There have been no takers so far. I'll let you have it if you can sort out this problem with Gareth. I'm glad you're still in the force.'

'That's just it, I'm not really. The unit has been separated from the Met, but we still handle cases in the public domain.'

'Whatever happened to that funny little man who was rude to everyone?' she asked. 'The one with the foul-smelling pipe?'

'Arthur's very well, touch wood,' said May apologetically. 'I'm still partnered with him.'

'You two have lasted longer than most marriages. Doesn't he drive you mad?'

'I don't know, I can't tell any more. Do you still call yourself Mona?'

'God no, nobody's called me that in years. Gareth hates contractions. I had to become respectable in every way when I married an academic. All those formal dinners with elderly men. Tell them you paint and they look at you with condescension, another bored housewife looking for hobbies to fill the evenings while her husband is working on something important. I lost my husband to them after he made his mistake about that bloody statue, the Nereid. He needed to regain their respect, and they made a pact with him; they would allow him back into their exalted circle if he devoted all his time to their various causes. So Gareth behaved himself, joined the right committees and worked late every night, and we were grudgingly re-admitted.'

'If things got back to normal, why do you think he's in trouble again now?'

'We're short of money, of course. I'm not allowed to work, so we survive on his pitiful salary. But I think it's more than that. This "client" has appealed to his vanity by insisting that no one but Gareth can work for him. He's the best in the field, there's nobody else who could handle the job, it's the opportunity of a lifetime, a chance to make some real money, etcetera. You should see him when he comes off the phone, as excited as a schoolboy.'

'What made you think he was planning something illegal?'

'He won't talk about what he's been asked to do, and I know what he's like. He thinks that if I find out, I'll have a go at him for being so stupid.' She lit a cigarette. 'Do you still smoke?'

'No, I gave up years ago—doctor's orders.'

'Any idea what he's up to?'

'I can tell you a little,' May admitted. 'He's exploring the remains of London's lost rivers. We've tracked him at the sites of three so far—the Fleet, the Effra and the Walbrook. He seems particularly interested in the point where their tunnels widen and open to the Thames.'

'Why? I know it's his area of expertise, but surely that sort of exploration is all above board.'

'We checked out the most obvious reasons. I thought the various councils involved might have failed to grant access, but no requests to explore closed sections of the rivers have been received at all. Thames Water occasionally issues permits for non-professionals to enter the system with a team, but they've told us they know nothing about this. Besides, the recent rainfall has made conditions so hazardous that only experienced workers are entering for essential repairs. The rivers run through and under various parcels of private property, so we've made discreet inquiries with landlords and developers. But we've turned up nothing there, either. Which means that your husband is acting without permission, on behalf of a private client. He's been photographed at all of these sites.'

'You're talking about breaking and entering, trespass at the very least. It'll get back to the museum, these things always do. He'll be thrown out again. Can't you do something to stop him?'

'Arthur wants to find out what he's up to. The idea is to step in before he commits himself to anything serious, and hopefully avoid the trespass charge by getting something on his client.'

Monica ran a hand through her hair. 'I can't take much more of this life, John. I'm not very good at being a sidekick. I don't want to just be supportive. I was seriously thinking of leaving him when this came along, like some kind of a test. I know it wasn't fair to involve you, but I didn't have anyone else to turn to. The academic wives don't want anything to do with me, and my old friends have all moved on. I thought you might remember me fondly.'

May smiled. 'You know how I felt about you.'

'Then why did you let me go?'

'What can I say?' The subject embarrassed him even now. 'They were the disco years. Nobody acted their age, nobody settled down.'

'That's the lamest excuse I ever heard.' Her laugh was unchanged. 'You were married when I met you. What happened?'

'Oh, it was all a long time ago,' said May evasively as he rose and examined the canvases.

'So it didn't last.'

'No, Jane and I divorced. She was—there were health problems. She became ill. Not physically, you understand, just—' He couldn't bring himself to say it. He saw little point in resurrecting the past, at least not while the pain of those years remained.

'You don't have to tell me, John.'

'That's just the problem—I haven't talked about it in a long while. I rarely discuss my marriage with Arthur because—well, he has very particular views on these things.'

'You're talking about mental illness, aren't you?'

'We didn't know what we were dealing with back then.'

'But you had children.'

'Yes, two. Alex was born first, then Elizabeth came along four years later. Now there's only Alex.'

Monica rose and came to his side, resting her hand lightly on his shoulder. 'What happened to your daughter?'

He turned aside, barely able to voice his thoughts. 'She died, and it was my fault. I was more ambitious in those days, perhaps too much so. Alex is married and lives in Canada now, but wants nothing to do with me. Elizabeth—she gave birth to a baby girl. April reminds me so much of her mother. She lives here in London, and will be fine one day soon, I'm sure. She still has problems, but we're learning to overcome them.'

'Poor John, you haven't had the things you deserve.'

He tried to make light of it. 'I don't know, I suppose it's still better to have raised a family than to be like Arthur, even if I eventually lost it.'

'You never lost me,' said Monica, raising her hands to his face.

'You're telling me you slept with her? Somebody from our own neighbourhood?' Kayla Ayson yelled.

'What the hell has that got to do with it?' Randall shouted back. The front bedroom of number 39 was small, and Randall was sure that the neighbours could hear every word. 'What does it matter anyway? It was two years before I met you.'

'Then why wait until now to tell me? Wait a minute.' Kayla raised a hand to her forehead. 'You were the one who liked this house so much, even though I thought it was too small for the children. Did you do that just so you could be near her again? Are you still seeing her? Christ, she came to the Wiltons' party. You call yourself a decent Christian but you still want her.'

'Will you listen to yourself? Of course I don't, I'm telling you because it's bound to come out sooner or later. I didn't even know she lived in this street until I saw her that evening. She came over and spoke to me when I went to get a drink in the kitchen. What could I do?'

'You could have told her that you're happily married.'

'Of course I did that, but she's the kind of woman—I just thought you should know.'

'She's probably told half the neighbourhood. How do you think that makes me feel, knowing that they're laughing behind my back?'

'I wanted to be honest with you,' Randall pleaded. 'I wish I hadn't told you.'

'Was she married? Did you commit the sin of adultery?'

'No, she was single, working in a plant nursery in Camden. I was just as shocked to see her as she was me. And she won't have told anyone, it would only cause more trouble.'

'But you had to tell me. And now she lives with that awful estate agent in the house opposite. What a convenient coincidence.'

'We had a few dates, Kayla, that's all. Lauren

means nothing to me. Do you think I'd have told you about her if she did?'

Behind them, their daughter began to cry, awoken by the discordance in the house. Randall stamped out of the room, slamming the door behind him, leaving his wife in anguish and bewilderment.

Kallie had never been prone to tears, but she found it hard to stop them now.

'I have to do it, Kal. They're not going to pay me a penny more. I don't have a job. I don't have any savings. I can't get work here. What else can I do?' Paul was pacing before her in his unravelling turquoise sweater, more angry and confused than she'd ever seen him.

'There must be something. What about Neil, doesn't he have any connections?'

'He sells vases and candle-holders to retailers, for God's sake. Even if he could find me something, how long do you think I'd last? I've always been in the music business. I survived the price-fixing scandals, the Britpop explosion, I made it through hip-hop and the boy bands, but the only growth area is acoustic stuff and I know nothing about that.'

'Couldn't you learn?'

'I detest acoustic sets. I don't want to earn a living doing something I hate. I know it's selfish, but if I don't take the chance now, I'll always be thinking about what might have been. You're covered, you've got this house and your modelling work, your friends, all your other interests. Besides, it may turn out to be good for both of us. It's not going to be for ever.'

He wanted to take off. Paul had already decided to fulfil his dream and travel around the world. He explained he would be back in six months, nine at the most. Paris, Nice, Amsterdam, Prague, Greece, Russia, Thailand, Vietnam, Japan—he had already described the itinerary in detail. She wondered how long the idea had been forming in his head. She wanted to argue that he was running away from his problems, that if he couldn't make it here and now, building a new home with her, then she was not about to wait around for him. But the words dried in her mouth.

'I could go with you.' She hadn't meant to suggest it, because she knew what he would say.

'I'll be doing bar and DJ work to pay my way. What would you do? You're happy in your own home, it's what you always wanted.'

She had promised herself that she would discuss the matter rationally, but now a crackling cloud of panic settled on her. 'I don't know. There's something wrong here and I don't understand—while you were away I became so nervous, it's not like me, I kept hearing water, and it felt as though someone had been in the house behind my back, my stuff was moved around—'

'You're just over-sensitive to the fact that the old lady died here, Kal. And there are pipes running under the bathroom floor. How do you think the water drains away?'

'There was that awful thing, the crayfish, in the garden. It's like we're living at the coast instead of being in the centre of town.'

'But you love it, and I know you'll settle. You took a year off and got the travel bug out of your system.

Can't you see how unhappy I am? If I wait any longer, I'll grow old and die under these fucking grey skies without ever having experienced the world.' He untangled her reluctant hands from his. 'I have to, Kal, this place is killing what we have. I don't feel at home here. I have to go.'

She found it hard to believe this was the same man who had said he would never leave. Something deep within him had changed. Paul's determination to be free of her finally made her cry. She sobbed because now there was no going back to what they had shared, because he had not answered his mobile, and because she had seen the faint crescent of the lovebite on his neck.

18

THE HOUSE IN BRICK LANE

Arthur Bryant wedged his crowbar under the lid of the mildewed pine storage crate and prised it off, scattering rusty nails all over the floor of the office at Mornington Crescent. The box had been kept under a railway arch in a lock-up at King's Cross, but construction companies were tearing down the arches, and he had been forced to find a new home for his collection. It had been May's idea to bring his partner's memorabilia into the unit, because he felt sorry that Bryant had lost so much in the blaze, even though it had been his own fault.

Bryant knew that he was being provided with a displacement activity, something to quell his overactive imagination until Raymond Land sanctioned a new case. Inside the musty container were relics of his greatest successes. He carefully eased out Rothschild, his mange-riddled Abyssinian cat, and set it on the shelf above his desk. He had replaced its missing eyes with a pair of coloured marbles, but there was no substitute for the back leg that had fallen off some years ago. The stuffed feline had once been the familiar of Edna Wagstaff, the renowned Deptford medium, who had now sadly passed to the Other Side herself, to join Squadron Leader Smethwick and Evening Echo, her informants from beyond. Most of Bryant's books had been destroyed in the fire, but reaching into the box he was pleased to discover battered copies of *Malleus Maleficarum*, *The Oxford Handbook of Criminology* (first edition), Mayhew's *London Characters and Crooks*, J. R. Hanslet's *All of Them Witches*, Deitleff's *Psychic Experience in the Weimar Republic*, *Fifty Thrifty Cheese Recipes* and Brackleson's *Stoat-Breeding for Intermediates*. Further down were items that stirred long-dormant memories: a programme from the Palace Theatre for *Orphée aux Enfers*, the scene of their first case; the claw of a Bengal tiger found pacing about a west London bedroom; a monarch butterfly that had acted as a vital clue in stemming a Soho drug epidemic; a runic alphabet used to solve a bizarre suicide in the city. He had begun to write up each case as a chapter in the unit's memoirs, and knowing that they could not be published in his lifetime, made them as scurrilous and slander-packed as possible, a cathartic exercise that temporarily expunged the bitterness he felt at being held back by idiots.

As happy as a child in a dressing-up box, he fished out each item and carefully wiped it, looking at his shelves with pride. Satisfied that he had made the room homelier, he took down his copy of *The Luddite's Guide to the Internet* and decided to tackle May's new Macintosh laptop.

Half an hour later, May arrived and noticed that the building had become ominously quiet. He went to check on his partner.

'Ah, there you are. What do you know about Hot

Dutch Interspecies Love?' Bryant looked up from the computer. 'Specifically, how to get rid of it?'

'What have you done?' asked May, dreading the answer. 'You know you're never supposed to touch my things.' He cleared a patch in the chaotic landscape of Bryant's spreading paperwork to set down his Starbucks cup. The last time Bryant had accessed police files via the Internet, he had somehow hacked into the Moscow State Weather Bureau and put it on red alert for an incoming high-pressure weather system. The Politburo had been mobilized and seven flights re-routed before the error was spotted and rectified.

'I was trying to find the address of the Amsterdam Spiritualist Society. I had to give these people my credit details for some reason, and then the screen filled up with the most disgusting pictures of ladies in barnyards. When I tried to cancel my American Express card, I somehow went through to the Parker Meridien Hotel in New York, specifically their internal telephone system. I followed the recorded instructions about entering a code, then everything went dead and a man started threatening me with a lawsuit. He says I've crashed their switchboard, and now all these horrible animal pictures are popping up again. I hope I haven't broken the Internet.'

'Don't *ever* give anyone your credit-card details.' John turned the keyboard around and began closing his files. 'You just have to accept that there are some things you shouldn't attempt. Let me do it for you.'

'I think I caused electrical interference somehow. I didn't want to bother you.' Some aspects of Bryant's ageing process had begun to mutate into characteristics more commonly associated with troublesome babies.

'It bothers me a lot more when your experiments

in the digital domain start to produce global effects. I don't want you messing around with my laptop. It's bad enough that I can't receive email at home any more.' Bryant had somehow managed to get his partner blacklisted by every server in the country. May had explained the principles of the Internet dozens of times, but always ended up being sidetracked into the kind of arcane discussions Bryant enjoyed having, like how the Macintosh apple symbol represented Alan Turing's method of suicide, or how Karl Marx had once run up Tottenham Court Road (where May purchased his computer equipment) drunkenly smashing streetlamps.

'What are you still doing here, anyway?' May asked. The division's promised casework had been delayed pending the arrival of new equipment that had so far failed to materialize. Wyman, the mistily evasive Home Office liaison officer, was full of excuses. At a time when terrorist splinter groups had been caught attempting to blast London targets with American-made Stinger missiles, tentatively experimental divisions like the Peculiar Crimes Unit were the first to feel the financial pinch.

Bryant thrust his hands into his pockets and swung around on his swivel chair. 'My legs are killing me tonight, so to take my mind off them I thought I'd go through the Permanently Open files, see if there'd been any recent sightings of the Leicester Square Vampire.'

'And have there been?'

'Nothing for months. He's never disappeared for such a long period before.' The elderly detective had a duty to continue checking. Even though the trail had long gone cold, he owed it to May to track down the man who had indirectly destroyed his family. Pulling the lid from his partner's coffee, he poured in a shot of brandy from his hip flask. 'This stuff is undrinkable unless you do something to it.'

'It's mine, actually,' said May.

'I've been thinking about this business with your academic. How did you get on with the wife?' Bryant poured a second shot of brandy in, ignoring him.

'Er, OK,' stalled May. 'She called me this morning. Apparently, Gareth's at home studying the Water Board's survey maps.'

'Why don't we go and visit Jackson Ubeda's office?'

'And say what, exactly? That we know he's employed someone to break into buildings built over the estuaries of forgotten rivers?'

'I don't mean to visit him when he's *there*. I have his business address.' Bryant could see his partner wavering. 'He's based in Spitalfields. I called his number. According to the telephone message, the office is closed until tomorrow. We can take my old skeleton keys.'

'Arthur, they don't work with modern deadbolts. Besides, he might have an alarm system. Although Banbury reckons he has something to get around the basic models.'

Bryant knew he would get his partner to agree. Neither of them enjoyed having time on their hands.

'Where is everyone, by the way?' May looked about.

'I sent them home so that the painters could finish up. They're laying the floor in the lavatory overnight. I suppose you heard that they caught the Camden bin-bag killer? Positive ID, evidence matches, witnesses, the lot. That means it's make-or-break time for us; Raymond will either find us fresh work or have us closed down. He's ordered Meera and Colin to seal the remaining files under Longbright's supervision tonight. They'll be working through until it's done, so Janice has gone to KFC for a bargain bucket. They're dining *al desko*.'

'What you mean is, we don't have much time left to discover what Ubeda is up to,' said May, throwing Bryant his hat. 'Then let's go before anyone sees us.'

Bryant stood back in the street and looked up at the redbrick terrace. 'It's a shed,' he announced.

'What do you mean?'

'Look at the sign. J.U. Imports Ltd, fifth floor. That must be the tin hut on the roof. How very Dickensian. Perhaps he keeps chickens in it.'

They were standing in the middle of Brick Lane, umbrellas raised against the spattering of broken gutters. Beside them, two Indian boys were attempting to manoeuvre a rack of red leather jackets into their crowded ground-floor outlet. Back in the sixteenth century, tiles and bricks had been kiln-blasted in the area. The reek of the tile kilns had permeated the buildings, but now the air was sweet with the scent of cardamom and curry. Not even the steady rainfall could dispel it. One end of the street was dominated by the Truman brewery, formerly the Black Eagle, now an art gallery, but the overall sense was of a seamlessly transplanted Indian community, which had replaced the Methodists, French Protestants and Jews who had occupied the area in succession. Signs of previous tenancies still existed: a packed 24-hour bagel store, a battered chapel; but mostly there were Muslims and Hindus, taxi-drivers and restaurants, cafés, leather-goods shops—and people, people every-where, even in the pelting rain, dashing across the street with shirts in plastic liners, splashing through puddles with yellow polystyrene takeaway boxes and armfuls of hangers, even at this late hour.

'Cover for me, old chap. This only works on mor-tise locks, so keep your fingers crossed that it's not a cylinder.' May slipped a titanium loop through the gap in the narrow brown door and lowered it over the latch bolt. He felt the latch lever raise against the bolt follower, and the door swung back with a faint click, admitting them into the dark hall corridor.

'Hang about, I've got a light.' Neither of the detec-tives owned firearms, but both were particular about their torches. May removed a large cinema flashlight from his overcoat. He had been given the red-tipped Valiant by an usherette at the ABC Blackheath in 1968. All he could remember about her was that she had slapped his face halfway through *They Came to Rob Las Vegas*.

The beam illuminated a corridor as twisted as a funhouse walkway. The damp brown stair carpet covered rotten wood; an acrid smell of mould filled their nostrils. The building had hardly changed since the arrival into the area of Huguenot silk-weavers. As they crossed the sloped landing, rainwater cas-caded down the window, seeping through its cracked frame in tobacco-coloured streams.

'It doesn't have the smell of a man with money,' said Bryant. 'I wonder how he can afford to pay Greenwood?'

'Perhaps we should let Janice know where we are. I left my mobile in the car. Have you got yours?'

'I'm not sure when I had it last.' Bryant studied the

cracked ceiling as he tried to think of a way to explain that he had mislaid it. By way of diverting attention and taking a breather on the gloomy stairs, he paused to unscrew the cap from his engraved pewter flask. 'That coffee gave me the taste. Here, have a tot of this—buck you up.'

May took a swig and choked. 'What on earth are you drinking?'

'Greek Cherry brandy goes surprisingly well with fish,' said Bryant, taking back the flask. 'Confiscated from an unlicensed Cypriot restaurant with asbestos ceilings in the Holloway Road. They were mixing it in a tub at the back of the shop.'

'Your sense of taste never ceases to amaze me.'

As they continued climbing, the stairs grew darker. 'Careful—there's a broken floorboard here,' warned May.

'Hang on.' His partner had paused on the landing to regain his breath. *This is embarrassing,* Bryant thought, fighting to catch the air that seared in his chest. *An investigation called off because the poor old bugger can't handle five floors without resting on every landing.* He gripped the bannister once more and followed May up the next flight. He wasn't about to admit defeat.

Because his mind was so active, May sometimes forgot that his partner's body was failing. Arthur's heart attack had occurred eight years ago, in the middle of an exhausting investigation. His doctor had warned him to cut back on his office hours, but he seemed to be spending more time than ever at work. The truth was, he hated the lack of structure that came with being alone. Having toiled with no holiday longer than a fortnight since he was eighteen, he found it impossible to break the habit of putting in punishing shifts.

'Don't worry, there's no need for both of us to go up,' said May gently. 'If there's anything special you want me to look for—'

'Don't patronize me, I just need a minute.' They waited together, listening to the crackling rain. Something scurried on tiny feet across the floor above.

'Wonderful, rats as well. I wouldn't let you go up there alone, John.' Bryant reached the top of the steps as the unhealthy warmth spread from his sternum to his shoulder. Sam Peltz, the unit's doctor, had tried to put him on a treadmill once a week, but had given up with him after Bryant dropped pipe tobacco into the mechanism, jamming it.

Pressing a palm over his ribs, Bryant detected the muscles of his heart flexing with considerable violence. Strangely, the problem only occurred in overheated rooms. Placed in a cold wet environment, he developed the stamina of a salmon in a stream. The irony of it was that he always felt cold, and, being forced to wrap up, risked further health problems. The elderly, he decided, thought too much about illness. Weak health accompanied seniority, and debilitated further by being dwelt upon. Still, he was glad when the floor levelled out before them into a short corridor.

There were just two doors, neither locked. The first opened into a cluttered office that appeared, with the exception of an elderly computer, not to have been modernized since the 1950s.

'Looks like Mr Ubeda is bankrupt,' said May, shining his torch into the top drawer of a grey filing cabinet. 'These are all unpaid bills, threatening letters, legal warnings. He's just shoved them into folders, as if he doesn't care.'

'He's relying on the outcome of his venture with Greenwood to bail him out.'

'What's in the other room?'

'It's just the toilet,' called Bryant. 'How do we get up to the shed?'

'Hang on.' May checked the landing ceiling. 'It's a pull-down ladder. There should be a pole around somewhere.' He found it leaning in a corner, and hooked the end through the brass ring in the trapdoor above him. The hatch opened, and a set of steel steps telescoped down.

'I won't be following you up there with my legs, I'm afraid,' said Bryant.

'All right, I'll report back.'

May climbed up and vanished. 'My God,' he called down. 'You won't believe this.' Then an uncomfortable moment of silence.

'What is it?' asked Bryant impatiently.

'Some kind of shrine. There are statues everywhere—all the same figure, but all different sizes. I wish you'd come up.'

'I wouldn't get back down.'

'You'd make more of this than me. I recognize the image.'

'Can you show me one?'

'Here.' May reappeared in the hole, smothered in chalk dust. He shifted the torchbeam on a foot-high plaster figure, broken at the neck. In his other hand he held the head of a jackal.

'Well, that's Anubis,' said Bryant. 'Ancient Egyptian

god of the underworld, protector of the dead and the embalmers, guardian of the necropolis.'

'There must be thirty or forty identical statues up here. They're all broken, every single one of them.'

'Let me see that one in your hand.'

May passed it down to his partner.

Bryant ran a finger across the figure's snout and around its long pointed ears. 'It's a cheap replica of a genuine artefact,' he sniffed dismissively. 'The paint-work is far too vivid. Very few of the real article still have this kind of dense black colouring. What a pity. And they're all broken? It's easy to find replicas in one piece. How odd.' He handed it back. 'The Egyptians gave their god the head of a jackal because so many of the animals wandered about their grave-yards. Priests would wear jackal masks during the mummification process. He's inspired all kinds of worshippers. Perhaps our Mr Ubeda belongs to some kind of a cult.'

'This is giving me the creeps,' said May. 'I don't like dealing with obsessives, they're unpredictable and dangerous. These things are on the floor, on shelves, everywhere. There are some on the walls, too, painted on papyruses. There's even what looks like a mummified dog up here. Its head is severed from its body as well. What's the point of collecting this sort of stuff if it's damaged and worthless?'

Bryant had walked back into the office, and was trying the cupboard doors. 'I think we'd better go before he returns,' he called.

'Why?' asked May. 'Is there a problem?'

'Let's just say I agree with you about obsessives.' Bryant was looking at the gun on the cupboard shelf.

19

FEET OF CLAY

It had taken Elliot Copeland all day to get the front yard of the builders' merchant broken up and loaded on to his truck. Beneath the concrete slabs, the earth was as wet and heavy as a Christmas pudding. He had found fragments of horse bone buried deep in the brown London clay, remnants from the time when the Green Street Races were held in Kentish Town. Dozens of delicately curved white pipes poked out of the mud like bird ribs; each lay discarded where it had been smoked. The soil held more secrets than anyone could know. The roads traced the jigsaw patterns of ancient settlements, following their hedgerows and tributaries, titled after their landlords and hunting grounds, their mistresses and battles. Nothing was as arbitrary as it appeared. Even the public houses were still imprisoned by their nomenclature, despite numerous name-changes and makeovers.

. His arms and back ached. He badly needed another drink, but had finished the quart of scotch he kept in the cab. At least the men in the builders' machine shop were decent local types, not like the street's new arrivals, who were incapable of painting a wall without calling for help. Somewhere along the line he had got the reputation of being cheap, and now it had proven impossible to raise his prices without them all complaining. He could have done with a work-mate today, but couldn't afford to pay one. Was this, he wondered, what his life had boiled down to? He'd left art college with big ideas, but unfortunately so had everyone else. After the time of the Hornsey riots, everyone had wanted to be a rebellious art student, but what all that rebellion and popularity meant was that there were no jobs at the other end.

He was forty-six, the divorced father of a child he was no longer allowed to visit, because his inarticulate anger arose in drunkenness. And all people saw when they looked at him was an overweight loser with a screwdriver and a paintbrush. He had thought this was all life could offer now, loss and disappointment—but you never knew what fate held in store, and a short while ago he had been given his chance. The trick was knowing when to act upon his knowledge—but soon, he was sure, people would look at him with new-found respect. He shouldn't have talked to Jake Avery at the party, though. It didn't pay for too many people to be involved. The drink always made him gabby. He backed the truck up to the muddy pit and clambered down from the cab, thinking about what to do.

Before he went to the police, he would have some fun with the yuppie scum. He was the longest-remaining resident in the street, had lived here when kids still played in the road and mothers sat in deckchairs on their front steps, when there had still been a corner pub and a shellfish stall, long before all the estate-agent boards had appeared and the dry-as-dust middle-class couples had transformed the street's loud, crowded family rooms into havens of hushed elegance. Now the road was lined with pristine cars and the houses were inhabited by invisible people who came home late and sat in their gardens drinking wine in the summer, hankering for a kind of village life that only existed in their collective imagination, because community spirit, the real spirit of the streets, meant brawling and shouting and getting your hands dirty.

He'd been invited to their party out of politeness; no one had intended him to take the invitation seriously and actually turn up. But he had a secret that would surprise them all, and perhaps it was time to do something with it.

Kallie closed the windows in the front bedroom because the rain was soaking the carpet. It seemed impossible to keep water out of the house. She could hardly believe that Paul had gone. The drawers in his side of the flimsy flatpack wardrobe were empty. This morning at dawn he had thrown some pants and T-shirts into a brand-new nylon backpack, and had taken off. It did not matter who he had slept with in Manchester, only that he had done it at all. The thought allowed her to release him. If he was ever to go, let it be now.

He had tried to write her a note; she found several unfinished attempts in the kitchen bin. It struck her as odd that in order for a man to find himself, he first had to shake off the attentions of those who truly cared for him. She sat on the bed and listened to the rain in the gullies, wondering whether she had smothered too much, pushing him too quickly into setting up house. He had craved spontaneity and she had acted accordingly, but apparently it had been the wrong type of spontaneity.

She shopped and bought a paper, leaving the dripping umbrella to form a puddle on the bare boards in the hall. She painted a dresser pale-blue, and attempted to strip some of the maroon lincrusta wallpaper in the lounge, but cut her hand on the scraper. Finally, she went to see Heather.

Kallie had not been looking for a shoulder to cry on. Compassion ill-suited her neighbour. Heather was far too self-interested to express concern for anyone else's misfortune. However, when she opened the door, she was an alarming sight. Heather was seething with misplaced energy, Kallie could almost see sparks arcing in aberrant neural connections. *What's wrong with her?* she thought. *Is she ill?* She had expected to be faced with Heather's patented brand of nervy bravado. Instead she found a borderline hysteric, as distracted as any Ophelia. Heather had flung back the door and walked away into the kitchen, where she paced beside the counter.

'He's planning to divorce me,' she explained, 'taking everything and giving it all to her. What is it about Paris that makes middle-aged men do this?'

'Wait, back up,' begged Kallie. 'George is having an affair?'

'He's screwing some dark-eyed child in the City of Light, and he'll spend all his money on her, the money that should be coming to me because *I'm* the one that sits and waits, the one who gets older waiting for him to come home, while she's bought bracelets and dinners in discreet hotels.'

It was hardly earth-shattering news. George had never put his feet on the ground for fear of taking root in this dank city, and Heather clearly did not have the kind of attitude that could encourage him to stay.

'He'll leave me with nothing.' Her pacing and turning seemed overwrought and theatrical.

'But you'll keep the house?'

'Oh, the *house,* yes. This place, that's just great, wonderful, a terrace of redbrick that comes with rising damp and a resale value slightly lower than we paid. I can't wait to see how the rest of my life pans out based on this.'

Kallie cleared her throat. 'Well, we seem to be in the same boat,' she admitted. 'Paul's gone.'

Heather stopped in her tracks. For a moment, Kallie thought she might break into a smile. The misfortunes of friends had always cheered her up. 'What do you mean, he's gone?'

'You know how he's been since he lost his job. He never had the chance to travel. He started work the day after he left school. He wants to see the world, and I can't go because I've bought this place and I'm still working.'

'Is that how he convinced you? Christ, Kallie, how gullible can you be? That's what men say when they feel the noose tightening. Thank God you didn't marry him. How do you know he's really gone travelling? For all you know he might have met someone else. It could be just a pack of lies.'

Kallie thought of the purple crescent on the back of Paul's neck. It was so fresh that he probably hadn't even spotted it himself. 'No,' she heard herself lie, 'he needed a break. Actually, I encouraged him to go. He works hard and he's never had any time to himself. We both thought it was a good idea.'

'You're lying.' It was amazing how quickly her old friend had brightened. Suddenly she was almost enjoying herself. 'Aren't we a pair? Dumped in our prime, although I'm older, so you haven't even reached yours. God, we need a drink.' She yanked open the kitchen cupboards and slammed them. 'There's nothing here because his bloody wine club didn't deliver. Now that he knows he's going, I don't suppose he'll pay any of the bills.'

'I have a bottle of gin,' Kallie offered.

'God no, mother's ruin, we'll end up sobbing on each other's shoulders. This calls for some decent vodka. I'll go to the offie.' She strode through to the front room and yanked up the roller blind. 'Christ, it's coming down stair-rods out there.'

Kallie joined her and peered out. The other side of the street was half-hidden behind a canescent veil, and yet there was someone standing near the corner, working on the waste ground in front of the builders' yard. 'Who is that?' she asked.

'My glasses are upstairs, but it must be Elliot—that's his truck.' She watched for a minute in silence, suddenly subdued. 'Wait, there's a man with him. It looks like—'

Kallie wiped her palm through the condensation. She saw a figure, faint and dark, hunched behind the builder, covertly watching as he worked. 'I have no idea who that is. Look, I can go to the off-licence. I've got an umbrella, it'll only take me a few minutes.'

'Then let me at least give you some money.'

Heather was still peering through the streaked glass. Kallie had forgotten how much her old friend thrived on the misfortunes of others. It seemed an odd trait in someone who could be so generous. Everything about Heather was schizophrenic. Her unpredictable behaviour had probably helped frighten poor old George into a belated bachelorhood.

'Could you get a decent French dry white? I think we're going to need chasers. And plain Pringles.'

Some things never change, thought Kallie as she grabbed her coat and headed out into the downpour. *She always manages to get away without lifting a finger, and does it so sweetly.*

Heather returned to the window of her front room, and gazed through the rain to make sense of what was happening across the road.

The soil had an elastic quality that pulled it from his shovel, and now the rain was turning the ground to mud. Distant thunder sounded, an industrial cacophony that tumbled about the buildings, trapped in whorls of pneumonic cloud. So far, Elliot's labours had turned up a cache of tough yellow Victorian housebricks, as good today as the moment they had cooled in the mould. They were highly prized by developers offering properties constructed from reclaimed materials, and would fetch a good price. There were old floorboards, too, leached of their oils and twisted with perpetual damp, but still ripe for resale. He was stacking them in the cabin of the truck when he felt the man's eyes on him, a prickling of his back that told him someone was watching.

It was almost dark now, and the light on the corner had still not been replaced. Looking up, all he could see was the empty street, the figure of a young woman—Kallie, the pretty new neighbour who had purchased number 5—vanishing into the next road, and the tall rustling bushes that bordered the waste ground. He moved behind the truck to dig again, just for five more minutes. It was hard to stop, knowing that there might be some other treasure waiting to be unearthed. The pit left by the bricks had already filled with dense brown liquid, as if fed by some unseen river. He wanted to jump down and continue digging, but was worried about losing his work boots in the mire. The back wall of the hole was already collapsing as the water took it, undermined from below.

He stopped and glanced back at the bushes just in time to see the branches close. It wouldn't be kids, they couldn't be torn from their terminals on sunny days, let alone on wretched nights like this. Something in the water surfaced for a moment, just long enough to give him hope. There was no way of avoiding it; he had to lower himself into the cavity and use his hands to search. There was nothing harmful in London soil, just soot and stones kept long from the light.

He didn't see it, but he would have heard, if only thunder hadn't bellowed the air once more. The first stone fell into the churning water with a plop, not enough to draw him from the task of finding what he'd seen. He groped deeper, feeling some small metal item slip from his fingers. He bent and reached again, his fingers closing over something that pricked him. A child's badge: *I Am 10*. He tossed it back into the water in disgust. Moments later, the thick dank earth cascaded about him in a quicksilver torrent, pouring from above as if the world had collapsed upon itself, the pickaxe-broken concrete slabs skimming on plumes of soil as they slid from the diagonal bed of the truck, gathering lethal speed in their fall. One sizeable piece fractured his neck from behind, sending him face-down into the shallow swamp. He gasped in shock, drawing only the slippery loam-clouds of the ditch into his throat as earth and stones surged down with a terrible stifling weight, pulling him over, choking out his life in a grotesquely mechanized premature burial.

In his final moments, the thought flew by that he might be preserved in the city's compacted dust and clay, to lie for ever in the fields beneath, truly a man of the soil.

20

SEEING AND BELIEVING

Arthur Bryant stood at the edge of the waste ground in his sagging hat and baggy black mackintosh, looking like a cross between a collapsed umbrella and an extremely decrepit vampire. 'Have you found anything?' he called.

'Insofar as I have no idea what I'm searching for,' said Giles Kershaw, 'not a dicky bird.' The young forensic expert's exquisitely enunciated English grated on Bryant, who was taking perverse pleasure in having him stand thigh-deep in a water-filled ditch in the pouring rain.

'Why don't we let him come back when things have dried out a little?' John May suggested.

'Because there'll be nothing left by that time. Look around you.'

Bryant was right. A steady torrent of rainwater was passing over the waste ground, carrying detritus down the slope of the street toward a blocked-up drain, swirling it into scummy pools. The area in front of the builders' merchant formed a rough triangle at the junction of the road. Elliot had succeeded in breaking up the surface concrete and tarmac, and had dug down below layers of compacted brick to rich fulvous earth, removing entire sections which he had loaded on to his truck. It must have taken him all day to do so; the truck had been half-full when it had shed its load.

'Mind you, according to Blake, everything exists for ever,' said Bryant. 'Matter is like experience, it accumulates and remains, albeit in unrecognizable forms.'

'That's not much help right now, old chap,' replied Kershaw, ladling another shovelful of muck on to the bank. 'There's been so much rebuilding around here that there's only rubble near the surface. The actual topsoil doesn't start until about three feet down.'

'It's good-quality stuff, though,' said May. 'My gardener says London soil is very rich.'

'That's because it's full of shit,' called Kershaw. 'Manure from horses, pets, cows, chickens, sheep, and rotted vegetables that have passed through human digestive tracts. This whole city is built on shit.' He dragged a brick out of the hole and threw it to the side. 'And it's coming in over the tops of my waders.'

'There's more rubble under Kentish Town than there is in places like Hampstead or Chelsea,' Bryant told them. 'Poor areas get knocked about, while wealthy boroughs are preserved. The amount of social upheaval around here ensures an almost continual disturbance of the ground. You can come out now, Kershaw. I don't suppose you'll find anything in there.' They gave him a hand up.

Elliot's body had been zipped and loaded, ready for a trip to the Camden morgue, but the instrument of his death remained at the site, its rear offside wheel wedged half over the inundated water pit in which the builder had been discovered. Bryant checked that his plastic overshoes were still in place, and approached the front of the vehicle. The driver's door was wide open. The truck had tilted slightly, but surely not enough to disgorge its entire load. Housebricks lay all over the churned ground.

'Pawprints,' warned Kershaw. 'Don't touch the handle.'

'I'm not an idiot.' Bryant hooked it with the end of his walking stick and peered inside. 'What a mess. There's mud everywhere. Bricks on the floor.'

Kershaw joined them. 'Looks like he got them from the site. They're covered in the same earth.'

'Worth something, decent bricks?'

'I suppose so.' Kershaw climbed carefully into the passenger seat. 'There's an awful lot of mud in here.'

'How did this happen?' asked May, examining the truck's dirt-caked tyres. 'He was working in the pit, the rear bank gave way behind his back, undermining the stability of the truck, it shifted to the left and shed half a ton of earth and bricks.'

Bryant's derisive snort was enough to suggest that he did not agree.

'What, then?'

'Even if the very small shift in this vehicle's stability had been enough to send earth cascading out of its back, it would surely have occurred at a slow enough speed for this fellow to get out of its way. And besides, look at this.' He led the others to the rear of the small lorry and thumped his stick against the back flap. 'Do you see that swinging back and forth? No, because it's on a safety catch. It can't swing open just because the vehicle's at an angle, otherwise it would do so climbing every steep hill. The catch had to be taken off, and to do that you have to raise the flatbed.'

He returned to the cabin. 'Look at that.' He pointed to the fat red punch-button on the dashboard. 'Even if he had left the lorry with its engine running, someone would have needed to push that in order to raise the bed and release the rear panel. You've seen how loads slip. The mound would have stuck for a while as the floor tipped, then it would have poured out in one grand slide. Imagine: Elliot is shin-deep in the hole, pulling out his precious bricks. He's bending down or simply resting over his shovel. The rain and thunder are cacophonous, more than enough to drown out the noise of the rising flatbed. A more familiar rumble makes him look up. The mud is sucking at his boots, hindering his escape. The concrete and brick comes down in a deadly wall. Mudslides kill people all the time. Did you see the size of the wound on the back of his head? Let's hope it was quick.'

'You realize what you're saying?' May said. 'That someone climbed into the cabin and punched the button.'

'Yes,' said Bryant.

'It probably has to be held in while the flatbed ascends, as a safety measure. You take your hand off and the pistons go back down. I bet it makes a warning beep, too.'

'Try it,' Bryant suggested.

'Let me do it, I won't smear the prints.' Kershaw reached in and gently twisted the truck's ignition key. With the engine running, he tried raising the flatbed pistons. 'No warning beep,' he called back. 'Might have been once. Don't suppose this crate has passed a legal MOT in years.' The empty scotch bottle on the floor of the cabin caught his attention.

'What was so important that he had to work in the middle of a storm?' asked May. But his partner was already stumping off into the rain, his coat flapping about him like a trapped bat.

Heather's leather sofa was as cold and slippery as a frog-pond. The two women sat beside each other listening to Mr May's questions. It was nearly midnight. Heather worried a nail and glanced out of the window, as if expecting to witness the whole thing again.

'I'd like to get some accurate times on this,' said May. 'Miss Owen, you came over to visit Mrs Allen at what time this evening?'

'It must have been around seven p.m. I don't call on people between seven-thirty and eight because of *Coronation Street*.'

'I watch the soaps too, I'm ashamed to say,' Heather admitted.

'We decided to have a drink, but there was nothing in the house, so I volunteered to go to the off-licence.'

'You did this as soon as you arrived, or a little later?'

'Later. I should think it was around seven-twenty.' Kallie was intrigued. She'd seen detectives barking at witnesses on TV, and was almost disappointed to be treated with such casual civility.

'You didn't know that Mr Copeland was working over the road?'

'I think he might have been working there yesterday,' replied Heather. 'I'm only vaguely aware of it because there's always something going on over at the Bondinis.'

'That's right, I'd seen him too,' agreed Kallie.

'I'm sorry—the Bondinis?'

'The brothers who own the builders' merchants,' Heather explained. 'I looked out of the window and made some comment about him working in the rain.'

'And there was someone with him,' added Kallie.

'Did you recognize them?' asked May.

'It was hard to see clearly,' said Heather. 'It was definitely a man, though. They sort of looked like they were arguing.'

'How could you tell that?'

'I don't know—maybe they were just talking, but it was something to do with the way they were standing.'

'Then what happened?'

'I went out to the shop,' said Kallie.

'Did you pass Mr Copeland?'

'No, I walked on the other side of the road. His side was partially flooded. The drains were blocked.'

'And you didn't look back at him?'

'I don't remember doing so. It took me another couple of minutes to reach the main road.'

'Where did you have to go?'

'Just to the supermarket on the corner. There was a bit of a queue, so I waited there, paid and came back.'

'How much time would you say elapsed between when you set out and when you returned?'

Kallie thought about choosing the wine and the

vodka. 'Maybe ten minutes. But as soon as I came around the corner I knew something was different.'

'How?'

'Because where Elliot had been digging, there was now a mound of earth and rubble. I thought he must have quickly filled in the hole, but it seemed unlikely, because why would he have dug it out? I remember thinking it was more likely that he was removing the earth to ready for pouring concrete or something, so that the machine shop could extend their property. As I drew alongside, I went a bit nearer. There was mud everywhere and I didn't want to ruin my shoes. That was when I saw the tip of his hand sticking up.'

'I'm sorry, it must have been an awful experience for you.'

'Not really,' Kallie admitted. 'In a funny sort of way it didn't seem real.'

May found such honesty surprising. 'Mrs Allen, you say you saw it happen.'

'I looked back out of the window, but I wasn't watching the whole time. It was raining very hard. There wasn't much to see. Then I noticed that the bed of the truck was tipped up, and that the earth had slid out. I couldn't tell what had happened to Elliot.'

'But you didn't go out there to check?'

'I didn't have any shoes on. Besides, why would I? I suppose I just assumed he had finished and was in the truck, or had gone home out of the rain. I don't know, I didn't think anything.' She kept her face turned toward the window, hardly daring to move. If she caught their eye, they would know she was lying. She had seen it all—the slide of earth cascading down over him, the concrete blocks knocking him to his knees and then on to his face. She should have run but could make no move. The sight of the fast-filling hole was appalling, fascinating.

She had heard Kallie push open the front door, concerned and calling for help. How could she ever tell them the truth?

'And Miss Owen, you came back to the house,' prompted May.

'I almost ran—it was belting down.'

May noted that the front-room carpet was still damp and spotted with traces of mud. 'Let's go back to this man you saw arguing with the deceased,' he requested, watching as the two women shifted uncomfortably. 'We're not normal policemen, you know. You can say what you like. I'm not taking verbatim notes.'

'I didn't see him clearly,' Heather explained.

'But you have an idea who it might have been?'

No answer. Neither of them wanted to place anyone under suspicion, but it was obvious to May that an idea had formed in their minds.

'Look, we're not going to rush off and arrest someone based on what you think you saw, Mrs Allen. Nor will anyone accuse you of having made a mistake. This is about a process of elimination. At the moment we have no proof of how this gentleman lost his life, and that will make it very hard to get to the truth. The rain has effectively destroyed the crime scene. If there's anything you can tell us, I promise you the information will be treated with the utmost respect.'

Silence. He sighed. 'This is how most murder cases are solved, by talking to people. Not by analysing DNA or finding stray fibres, that's just corroborative detail. So perhaps you could tell me who you think you saw.'

Heather chewed her nail for a while, and finally removed it from her mouth. 'I think it was Randall Ayson,' she admitted, looking to Kallie for confirmation.

Outside in the street, the elements appeared to be in collusion, taking turns to demonstrate their power, for as the rain started to abate, a howling wind began to rise.

21

MURKY DEPTHS

'There's only one word for present driving conditions: atrociously bad,' squeaked Hilary, the Sky One weather lady. 'Flood warnings have been posted across Kent and Sussex, and there's another belt of low pressure sweeping in from the south west. The AA is offering this advice: if you're going out, don't.' She suddenly folded in half and vanished as the cable signal popped from the tiny wall-mounted television. Oswald Finch threw the TV remote on to his dissection table with disgust. 'Stupid woman. I can't believe the rain in England always makes the headlines.'

'I can't believe you're still here,' called Bryant, checking his watch.

'Nor me. I was supposed to retire fifteen years ago.' The ancient pathologist creaked up from his chair and shook Bryant's hand. 'I could be seeing out my retirement in a fisherman's cottage overlooking the Channel. It's all bought and paid for, but it'll fall into the sea before I get there. I'm stuck here, and it's your bloody fault.'

'I don't know what you mean.'

'You know very well that the Home Office won't

pay the going rate for newly trained technicians because they can't afford to buy them more up-to-date equipment, and most kids can't work with antiques, so I'm being blackmailed to stay on.'

'All right to smoke in here?' asked Bryant, dragging his pipe from his top pocket.

'No, it is not. You're the one who requested my services in the middle of the bloody night. You know they'll only agree to supplement my pension if I do two days a week for you. So instead of fresh sea air I get formaldehyde poisoning and rheumatism from sitting in a damp Camden basement twice a week.'

'I thought you were getting a new building.' Bryant looked about with distaste.

'We are,' sniffed Finch. 'Not in my lifetime, however. It might have helped if you hadn't incurred everyone's wrath by blowing up your office.' This part of the morgue had been housed in the old school gymnasium. Where once the youth of Camden had come to stretch their muscles, there were now only departed souls waiting to have their sinews sliced open and examined.

'Come on, you old misery, I'll give you a game of basketball.' Bryant pointed at the steel hoop still attached to the far wall.

'At my age the effort of getting up from a chair becomes an Olympic event in itself.' He looked at the hoop longingly. 'The only thing I can still dunk is a doughnut. I used to go ballroom dancing, you know. Now I can't even get the shoes on.'

'I hope this infirmity hasn't spread to your brain,' said Bryant rather rudely.

Finch ignored him. 'I suppose you're here about Mr Copeland.'

'That him over in the corner?' asked Bryant cheer-fully.

Finch led the way to a shiny metal container shaped like an overgrown takeaway box. 'This is what your bosses are providing for me instead of a sterile laboratory. They're meant for use in the field, and they're bloody awkward. I have to stand on a stool in order to get my arms over the sides, and they're sharp, too. Take a look.'

Bryant climbed up beside the pathologist and peered into the tray. He found himself staring at a fleshy white male, face-down. Lilac bruises had blos-somed across his lower back like pressed flowers. In the folds of his neck, a black contusion erupted in torn crimson petals.

'I wanted to get the back of his head open before you arrived,' Finch complained, 'but the caterers up-stairs keep borrowing my tools. They used my cra-nium chisel to take the top off a jar of piccalilli yesterday. I'm not meant to be alone in here. I've got a part-time technician and no exhibits officer. No notes, no video, nothing. I'm having to share the pho-tographer and police witness with the Met, and all this after promises of increased personnel.' He gave the corpse a desultory flick with his forefinger. 'Jack the Ripper's pathologist had more technical expertise at his disposal. I have to tell you, Arthur, I've lost a lot of faith in the system in the past few years. We define a few addled souls as being worthy of removal from society, and everyone's under such pressure that we consider the job done when we're lucky enough to find a court that will shut them away. You know, doc-tors look for five main signs of mental disturbance in prisoners: personality disorder, psychosis, neurosis, drug dependence and alcohol misuse, and less than one in ten inmates is clean of all five. The prison population stands somewhere above 70,000, which means that over 5,000 of them are functionally psychotic. And all you do, every time you catch someone, is add to the problem.'

'You're right, Oswald, we should just leave them out on the street to slaughter each other. Have you seen the headline of this week's *Camden New Journal*? "YARDIES TORCH TOT." I'm surprised mothers don't do the school run in armoured cars.'

'There's no need for sarcasm.' With a quick slip of the scalpel, Finch exposed the back of Elliot Copeland's neck to reveal damage at the base of his skull. 'Take a look at that. A nasty crack, wouldn't you say? It's a large area. First and second cervical vertebrae have copped it, anterior and posterior tubercles crushed, so it came at him from the left side. Plenty of myofibril rupture, pretty straightforward. Was he hit with a large flat-edged rock?'

'In a way,' Bryant explained. 'It was part of a paving slab, among other things.'

'Hm. I assume the weight of it slammed him forward. Broken nose. You see this sort of thing in industrial accidents, except that there's no bruising to his shins, so he had a soft landing. A manual worker, obviously, judging by the state of his hands. John phoned me and explained about the bruising. At first I thought the single blow had killed him, but that was before I cleaned him up. Mouth and nostrils blocked solid with earth.'

'Hardly surprising. He fell face-down in a mud-filled ditch.'

'Not the point, old fruit. He took a deep breath

after he was hit. Do you remember the Aberfan disaster—ghastly business of the coal tip sliding on to the Welsh school? The nightmarish part of that was the coal dust, very fine. It poured in like water, suffocating those who had survived the collapse of the building. This is the same. Basically earth—fine particles of soot, clay, grit, vegetable matter and non-biodegradable stuff like polystyrene granules, held in a suspension of water—straight down into his throat. He couldn't get up because of the weight on his back, so he choked to death. Nasty way to go, but at least it was fast. I ran a standard internal; judging by the state of his liver he was an alcoholic, which reduced his resistance to blood-vessel rupture. His stomach's full of half-digested pizza, high sodium—heavy drinkers eat salt. What puzzles me is why he's here. You usually only get me out of bed for murders.'

'That's exactly what it was,' said Bryant, looking for something to put in his mouth. He finally located a tube of Love Hearts in his raincoat. 'He was standing behind a truck that shed its load. Do you see anything contradictory to that?'

'No, I suppose not. Except—' He thought for a minute, resting his hand disconcertingly on Elliot's waxy back. 'It's rather an inexact method of execution, isn't it? I mean, ensuring that your target is standing exactly where you want him.'

'I thought that,' Bryant admitted. 'The biggest problem it poses for me is the matter of premeditation. As far as we can tell, he had nothing stolen. Longbright's conducting a search of his house, and has found his wallet. This isn't the sort of crime you plan in advance. Which means it had to be committed by someone waiting to cause him injury.'

'Rough neighbourhood, is it?'

'Not really. The street doesn't get much foot traffic. With the exception of the residents, hardly anyone uses it.'

'Then I would suggest they're your first port of call,' said Finch, wiping his hands and stepping back to admire his handiwork.

The following morning, Balaklava Street was anaemic with mist as May knocked on the Aysons' door.

The front room had been aggressively polished, and was clearly reserved for guests; it was an old-fashioned notion but appropriate to the street, and to the Aysons, a third-generation Caribbean family who honoured the attitudes of their grandparents. Kayla Avson prepared breakfast while her children dextrously thrashed each other in a lurid Nintendo race, ignoring calls to the table. With Randall's entrance, the atmosphere subtly shifted; the children became more subdued, and Kayla found something to occupy her attention in the kitchen. May appreciated that Randall Ayson took a dim view of the detective visiting his house, but he was required to check out witness statements as quickly as possible, and Heather Allen was adamant about having seen him on the edge of the waste ground.

'You think they're connected, don't you?' asked Randall. 'Copeland and the Singh woman.'

'We have no reason to think that, Mr Randall.'

'She was of Indian extraction. Tamsin Wilton told us she'd been receiving offensive notes. You should be looking for a racist, not wasting your time picking on the black man.'

'In case you haven't noticed, Mr Randall, you have an Egyptian lady across the road from you, a large Ethiopian family next door, a same-sex couple on your other side and several South African medical students in the end house. This is an ordinary London street, and I don't appreciate you playing the race card. My visit has nothing to do with your ethnicity. I'm here because a neighbour identified you last night at the crime scene.'

The room was enveloped in a tomb-like silence. May could feel the temperature drop. *Bryant's bluntness is starting to rub off on me,* he warned himself.

'What do you mean, identified me?'

'They say you had an argument, or at least a conversation, with the deceased.'

'That's a lie. I don't have to listen to this. It's that damned estate agent over the road, isn't it? He has no right to tell people—'

'Think about this rationally, Mr Randall, and you'll help me to disprove the possibility. First, forget about who saw you, it doesn't matter. When you take into account the distance and the weather conditions, it's obvious to me that they've made a false assumption. All you have to do is provide me with details of your whereabouts to have the statement discounted.'

When Ayson glanced at his wife, May knew he was in trouble. 'What is it?' he asked.

'I was here.' Another flick of the eyes, as if Ayson was seeking tacit support from his wife. 'But I did talk to him.'

'While he was working in the rain?'

'Well, yes. I was coming home from work and saw

him digging, but we didn't argue. I just asked him why he was working in such lousy weather.'

'What did he say?'

'That the men in the builders' yard were paying him extra to finish quickly.'

The Bondini brothers wore matching blue boiler suits, and looked like Italian acrobats. May half expected one to back-flip on to the other's shoulders with a cry of 'Hop-La!' They came out of the shop wiping their hands on rags in unconscious mimicry of one another.

'Builders' supplies, right?' May shouted above a cacophony of hammering.

'Yeah, and manufacturers.'

'What do you make here?'

Bondini One thrust his hand inside his boiler suit and pulled out a finely marbled fountain pen. 'Traditional craftsmanship, mate. Look at the cap. See the metal ring around the base? We make those.'

'Wrought-iron teapot stands,' bellowed Bondini Two.

'Stained-glass frames. Window boxes. Bathroom pipes. Garden furniture. Lots of stuff. Come inside.'

The machine shop was lethally active. Young apprentices—three or four, it was hard to tell exactly how many because they moved with such agility—hurled themselves in and out of doors, bursting up from traps in the sawdust-hazed cellar and down from hatches in the ceiling, laden with trays of searing metal, razor-sharp shards of steel, huge willowing sheets of glass, splintery pine beams, glinting drills and blades. May edged between the electric saws and tin-stamping equipment, trying to avoid being snagged. A young man, little more than a child, limped past him with blood seeping from a badly bandaged hand.

'We got a lot of rush orders on,' Bondini Two explained. 'Big department stores, very low profit margins but we make it up on bulk. Oi, Darren, mind what you're doing with that.' This last admonition was directed at a youth with bleached and knotted dreadlocks who was bending over a lathe. 'He's always getting his hair caught in it. I've told him 'undred times.' The wood on the lathe had split and fragments were flying off at alarming tangents. Nobody was wearing goggles, or any kind of safety equipment.

'Why were you paying Elliot Copeland extra to finish quickly?' May shouted above the din.

'You seen the state of it out there, all dug up? We got the concrete posts coming Thursday and new die-cutting machinery being delivered two days after that. Where else am I gonna put it all? I told him I'd pay time and a half.'

'You're expanding the premises,' May answered. 'Have you got permission from the council?'

'Don't come the old acid, Granddad, I've got all the documents. Bleeding council is a scam, we already own the property, innit? We're just converting part of the waste ground into off-street parking and extending the machine shed, but we gotta pay the council for the change of use. Bleeding Camden Mafia, the United Bank of Backhand. Don't make me laugh. I'd get a better deal in Palermo. They're all crooks, innit?'

'Did you have any trouble from Mr Copeland? Did he talk to you much?'

'Nah, bloody good worker. His wife had left

him—drank a bit, but blokes like that all hit the bottle, don't they? My brother thinks he was pissed.'

Bondini One spoke up. Behind him, someone threw a sheet of glass into a bin with a smash. 'Stands to reason, you'd have to be pissed to bury yourself under your own rubble, wouldn't you?'

May decided not to bother explaining the logistics that would have prevented Copeland from falling under his own truck load. 'Did he have any friends? Anyone who came around to talk to him?'

'Nah, he was a real loner. Cut up bad about his missus. Never saw him with anyone.' Both brothers shook their heads.

'Well, thanks for your time,' said May. 'I'll call again if I need your help.' He stopped in the doorway. 'Have you met anyone else in the street?'

The brothers conferred as jets of steam blasted around them. 'The Caribbean bloke in the sharp suits,' Bondini One decided. 'He's been coming around a fair bit.'

'What for?'

'He's been buying wood, doing some shelves. And he had some glass cut.'

'Can you remember when he last came around?'

'Day before yesterday, wannit?' More fraternal conferring took place. 'Yeah, Tuesday.'

'Anyone else apart from that?' May breathed the scent of freshly sawn timber. It reminded him of the garden shed where his father had worked before the War.

The brothers exchanged glances, each waiting for the other to speak first. 'There's a bloke called Aaron—Jewish boy,' said Bondini Two finally. 'He lives down the street.'

Jake Avery's partner, May recalled. 'Is he buying wood as well?'

'Nah.'

'Then what?' There was something here that May wasn't picking up on. He looked back at the machine shop and suddenly realized. 'He's got a friend here?'

'Yeah, he comes round to see Marshall sometimes. Oi, Marshall.' Bondini Two clearly did not approve.

May studied the muscular young man who looked up at the mention of his name. *So,* he thought, *the water gets a little murkier.* His mobile rang.

'John, I think you should come back as soon as possible,' said Bryant. 'Your friend Mr Greenwood's on the move again.'

22

DREAMS OF DROWNING

'I hate getting into this vehicle with you,' admitted May, eyeing the rusted yellow Mini Cooper with alarm. 'I don't know why you had to get rid of your old Rover.'

'It was starting to steer itself,' said Bryant mysteriously. 'The man in the garage said he'd never had a car fail every single item on its MOT before. He was quite excited. I had to go back to Victor here.' The Mini had been purchased at the height of flower power, and still bore a painted chain of vermilion daisies around its roof. Its noxious colour-scheme was enough to make it stand out from the other vehicles in the police car park at Mornington Crescent. Bryant unwedged the driver's door with the pronged end of a cheese-knife, which he kept about him for the purpose.

'That's an offensive weapon, you know.'

'What am I going to do with it?' asked Bryant. 'Threaten someone with a slice of dolcelatte?' He held open the car door. 'Come on, it's quite safe.'

'No thanks. You nearly killed us the other day, going around Vauxhall roundabout.'

'They'd changed the one-way system without telling anyone.'

'I seem to recall that you were on the pavement.'

'Sometimes it's hard to tell where the pavement begins these days.'

'It's usually the bit with the shoppers on. No, Arthur. Today we're taking my car.' May bipped his graphite-sleek BMW.

'Wonderful, now we'll look like Camden drug-dealers. I didn't think you ever used your car.'

'Well, I am today. And you're not smoking that inside my vehicle.' He pulled the unlit pipe from Bryant's mouth and reinserted it into his jacket. 'Where are we going this time?'

'Beverly Brook.' Bryant made a theatrical fuss about getting himself settled in the passenger seat.

'Wasn't she a forties singer?'

'It's another underground river. Runs from Cheam and Richmond to Barnes, goes through Raynes Park and around the edge of Wimbledon Common.'

'That's miles away.'

'Spoken like a true townie.'

The detectives hardly ever left London. May's under-furnished modern flat in St John's Wood had the melancholy air of an airport at midnight. Only his computer room showed signs of habitation. In this respect, he lived like a teenager.

After the tumult of the city, Raynes Park seemed not so much depopulated as derelict. The neighbourhood appeared to have been stunned into silence, as if someone had thrown a bucket of dirty water over it. There were only becalmed avenues of redbrick houses, graffiti-covered shops and mangy green verges.

They hadn't intended to drive out this far, but Bryant had misread the road signs. 'Someone's been busy with their lawn-mower,' he observed. 'Look at these gardens. There aren't any neat box hedges like this near me. All we have are scabby old plane trees with plastic bags in their upper branches and front yards full of McDonald's containers.'

'You've never owned a garden.'

'My mother had one in Bethnal Green. We used to keep chickens in the Anderson shelter. We had nasturtiums and a tortoise. That was a proper garden, a place where your dad could take his motorbike to bits. This is different.'

Bryant was right. Even the air felt thinner; for a start, it wasn't vibrating with fluorocarbons. At Wimbledon they found themselves surrounded by jeeps, 4x4s and truck-sized people-carriers, vehicles taken on school runs by high-income nesting families who never travelled further than Tesco or a Devonshire bolthole. Neighbourhood Watch stickers in front windows, no street life away from the superstore, nothing but the odd dog-walker, invariably an elderly lady in a Liquorice-Allsort hat and matching gloves.

'Longbright says people who spend their whole lives in the suburbs have no social graces because they never talk to strangers,' Bryant pointed out.

'That's a bit harsh.'

'I don't know. The Balaklava Street residents clearly have trouble talking to me.'

'Arthur, *everyone* has trouble talking to you. You scare them.'

'Rubbish. I'm much more charming these days. I hardly ever get annoyed with the officers Stanley assigns to us, even slack-jawed drooling neanderthals like Bimsley.'

Detective Chief Superintendent Stanley Marsden acted as a liaison officer between the detectives and the government. He was meant to operate with impartiality, but the Home Office paid his salary. He was known to play billiards with Raymond Land, but he also attended Arsenal matches with Sergeant Carfax, an astonishingly unpleasant Met officer who had been passed over for promotion four times, and who had decided to blame Bryant for his failure to rise through the ranks. There was still some bad feeling about the special status accorded to the PCU, but most situations were calmed by May's tact and inexhaustible patience. Even his enemies liked him. Bryant, on the other hand, had only to raise a telephone receiver to upset everyone within hearing distance.

Bryant map-read under sufferance because he said it hurt his eyes, and they had to keep stopping while May checked their coordinates.

'I've been rewriting your notes.' Bryant dug out a small book bound in orange Venetian leather and passed it to his partner. 'I thought if we have to submit something to Raymond, it should at least be entertaining.'

May waited until they reached red traffic lights, then examined the pages with impatience. 'You can't rewrite these. They're witness statements, not tone poems.' He shot Bryant a look of irritation.

'I just added a few impressions.'

'We've all seen your impressions, thank you.'

'I was just thinking about Balaklava Street. First

the old lady drowns, then a man is buried alive. There's an assonance, isn't there?'

'There may be assonance, Arthur, but there's no motive. Nothing was stolen from either victim. There are unmotivated deaths in every borough, but when two occur in the same street within the same month, I'm tempted to find a causal link. There's a lot of drug-related street crime in the area, but nothing like this. I'd be willing to swallow accidental deaths if I could understand how they happened. What do we really have? In the case of Elliot Copeland we've a witness and a suspect, but neither are much use beyond placing Randall Ayson at the site. I think the Allen woman actually saw Copeland die but didn't do anything to help, and she's too ashamed to admit so. It was left to her friend to discover the body a few minutes later, when she turned back into the street.'

'Perhaps you should talk to the neighbours again. I can't help thinking you've missed something.'

'Where are we now, Arthur?'

'Barnes Common. Nearly there.'

'Why did we go all the way out to Raynes Park?'

'Don't ask me. You're driving.'

'But you're map-reading. Give me that.' May took the A-Z. 'This was printed in 1958. You don't have to keep everything for ever, you know.'

'It's nice to own old things. Better than living in an apartment that looks like a car showroom.' They barely realized they were bickering, but at least the habit provided a form of natural evolution for their opinions.

The BMW purred to a stop beside the river. On the page, May's finger traced the outlet of the brook to the river's edge. He looked out of the window. A low concrete flood-wall had been installed along the river road. 'Well, this looks like the spot, but where's Greenwood?'

'Over there.' Bryant pointed toward the black Jaguar parked beside a low house with boarded-over windows. 'That's Jackson Ubeda's car.' The building was a light industrial unit, an unadorned Victorian box of the type that existed in swathes across the city.

They did not have long to wait. After fifteen minutes, Ubeda appeared in the doorway of the building, followed by Greenwood. Inside the entrance, May could just make out some kind of pumping equipment. Fat flexible pipes lolled across the floor. 'What on earth are they up to?' he wondered aloud.

'Perhaps they're trying to drain the brook,' suggested Bryant.

'But this is the fourth underground river they've visited. They can't be trying to drain the entire system. What do we do?'

'You go and attach your electronic gizmo, and we wait.' Bryant pushed himself down in the passenger seat, his hat sliding forward to meet his collar, so that he seemed almost to disappear. 'I know it's foolish, but I had this image of Ruth's basement flooding, drowning her and suddenly emptying out again. Of course, nothing was wet when we got there, but the idea still troubles me. Images of water are the images of dreams. To dream of a lake is suggestive of a mind at peace with itself. To dream of a rough sea, or drowning, indicates psychological disturbance. According to her brother, Ruth had been disturbed by racist messages, all of which he destroyed. Suppose she discovered a bizarre way to take her own life?'

Bryant often did this, connecting ideas that took

him beyond rational thought. For him, past and present, fact and fantasy were melded together in unfathomable ways, but occasionally connections could be found by following overgrown paths. May was used to dealing with his partner's disordered synaptic responses, but to other detectives it was a little like discovering that witchcraft was still in use.

May relied on his own form of sorcery, in the form of devices passed on to him by a Met R&D team who allowed him to trial-test their technology before it was approved for official use. Nothing in his arsenal could prevent the academic from succumbing to temptation, but a tiny Bluetooth receiver attached to their quarry's vehicle would at least pick up some passing conversation. May waited until the pair had re-entered the factory, then made his way over to the car while his partner kept watch. Half an hour later, they began to pick up dialogue.

'I think it's time for a talk with Mr Ubeda,' said Bryant shortly.

'You think we should go and see him?'

'No, I think Longbright should. A middle-aged man driving a Jaguar will respond more willingly to an attractive woman. Hello, Janice, is that you?' Bryant had a habit of shouting when he used a mobile. 'You don't mind dolling yourself up and pumping someone for information, do you? Well, tonight if possible, because we know where he's going to be. Just get a chap drunk and flirt a bit, could you do that?'

'It's sexism,' Longbright complained, 'and probably counts as entrapment.'

'Rubbish, you never mention sexism when a man takes you out for dinner, do you? You go on about empowerment, but when the bill arrives you suddenly discover your femininity.'

'I very much resent that. I've never been in favour of equal opportunities.'

'No?'

'Of course not. I've always thought women should be in charge.'

'So you'll do it?'

There was a deep sigh on the line. 'Do I get a clothing allowance?'

'All right, but don't go mad.'

'Where's he going to be?'

Bryant checked his notes. 'A lap-dancing club in Tottenham Court Road.'

The first postcard had arrived, franked in Amsterdam. Inevitably, it pictured a hump-backed bridge above a toad-green canal. On the back: 'First stop Holland, heading to Istanbul at the end of the week. I'm doing this for both our sakes. I hope you'll be there when I come back. You can reach me via my hotmail address. Love, Paul.' It felt oddly impersonal, not his style at all. Even the handwriting looked different. She checked that the paint was dry on the mantelpiece, and placed the card there, wondering how many would accrue, how far apart the spaces between them would grow, how long it would be before he stopped writing altogether.

The street was ethereal with rain again. According to the TV weathergirl it was shaping up to be the wettest autumn on record. The Thames barrier had been operated a record number of times in the past week. At least Kallie was working—a press shoot for mobile phones, another for floor cleaner. She noticed that her image was shifting from 'girl-next-door' types to more maternal roles, and decided to have her hair cut. It wasn't hard keeping herself busy between jobs. The house demanded attention. She was teaching herself electrical repair, plumbing and decoration, but knew she would have to call someone in about the split roof tiles. The first and ground floors were now half-painted in cheerful colours that drew light into the rooms, but the basement and rear had yet to be started. Under the stairs she had found a cardboard box filled with items belonging to Ruth Singh, but now that her brother had moved, there was no one to send them to.

Kallie went down to the kitchen and filled a kettle.

Heather had become even more distracted and tense since the night of Elliot Copeland's death. Her failure to act was clearly a source of discomfort; could she have discovered a conscience? Kallie wanted to tell her not to worry, that it shouldn't stand in the way of their friendship. The sight of the buried man had not disturbed her sleep. She was not given to imagination, and had seen death before: her father, a car accident, a dying friend. Heather was more highly strung, and responded to the darkening atmosphere around her. George's decision to leave had made matters much worse. Heather was keen to find parallels in the behaviour of both their partners, but Kallie wasn't ready for the kind of sisterhood session that involved sitting around complaining about male hormones. Perhaps it would be best to allow some space between them for a while.

She stood at the counter vacantly waiting for the kettle to boil, watching the drizzle through the rear window, and turned away to find some biscuits. When she turned back, the face jumped from the glass and made her scream.

How long had he been standing in the garden, watching her? She ran to the back door and searched for the key, fumbling it into the lock, running out and almost sliding over on wet ceanothus leaves. He was pushing his way up the garden, into the big bushes at the end, a figure with a hobbling gait that dropped him from side to side like a sailor crossing a deck. Moments later the bushes stilled, the branches falling back in place. But she had recognized him.

She headed back into the house and began searching for the number John May had given her.

23

A NIGHT OUT FOR SERGEANT LONGBRIGHT

'I recognized his face,' Kallie explained. 'His eyes were so sunken, and yet you could see such pain in them. I felt sorry for him.' She showed Longbright how the man had climbed out of her garden. 'He's the local tramp. He used to sleep over on the waste ground, but I guess when the land was dug up he was forced to move. I don't know where he is now.'

Longbright's shopping trip had been cut short by Kallie's phone call to the unit. As she sounded upset, the sergeant had agreed to cover for May and stop by Balaklava Street. 'There are a couple of hostels in the neighbourhood. I can check those. You don't have a name, or even a nickname?'

'No, but Tamsin Wilton at number 43 would know. She told me to watch out for him. She says he's harmless, and he was only staring at me through the window, but it made me jump.'

'Well, he was on your private property, where he had no right to be, so I'll look into it. The problem with most of the hostels is that they only allow users to stay overnight. It pushes homeless people back on to the streets, and puts them in the way of trouble.'

'I certainly don't want to get anyone into trouble,' said Kallie quickly. 'He's been living rough for a long time. I guess now the workshop is expanding its premises, he's been displaced. He wasn't doing any harm.'

'That won't be how everyone sees it. The average life expectancy of a homeless person is forty-two. Someone dies on the streets of London every five days.'

'Doesn't anyone treat them?'

'The homeless can't be registered by GPs. Most people can stand about a month of sleeping rough before long-term problems set in. They often start as sofa surfers, sleeping on friends' floors prior to becoming homeless.'

'God, I did that just before getting this place,' said Kallie.

'Then you know how easily it can happen. The statistics are depressing. Forty per cent of all homeless women are victims of sexual or physical abuse. Something as simple as a divorce can be enough to force someone into the open air. So let me see what I can turn up on this bloke. He must be pretty nimble if he could scale that wall.'

'He was crippled in some way—his right side, I think, both the arm and the leg. So I don't know how he managed to do it.'

Longbright saw her point; the wall was almost five feet high and covered in dense black bracken. The back gardens fitted together to form an oasis of ponds and bushes, partitioned by brick walls and wavering grey wooden fences. Entrance to one garden could only be gained by crossing several others. The school playground at the end of the street was bordered by a high wall, and there were no rear gates to the overgrown alley behind.

Longbright replaced her notebook in her jacket. She just had time to catch the Oxford Street stores. She was determined to make Bryant pay for sending her to a lap-dancing club.

'There was one other thing,' said Kallie. 'There was talk of Mrs Singh being sent threats, racist stuff. I was clearing out the cupboard under the stairs, and found this.' She dug in her pocket and produced an old audio cassette. 'It's from her answering machine. I played it back. There's only one message, but it's pretty nasty. I thought it might be helpful.'

Tonight, thought Janice Longbright, *you will be Grace Kelly.* She turned to the side and pulled in her stomach, checking the mirror. *OK, Grace Kelly's heavier sister.* Longbright was in her early fifties, and had inherited her mother's love of old movie stars. Off duty she dressed the part, coming out somewhere between Ava Gardner and Jane Russell, and still looked damned good. She had left it too late to train for the stage, and had found herself joining the police instead, just as Gladys had before her. Inside her was the actress who might have made the big time, if only times had been easier.

Janice stared at her stomach and sighed.

She resented being used as some kind of fishing lure on an investigation that was clearly in breach of the unit's case remit, but was perversely starting to enjoy herself. She had purchased a black dress, a distant carbon of the original design—the unit was paying, after all. The high heels made her too tall and prevented her from walking with anything resembling a normal gait, so she abandoned them for something plainer. May had provided her with a photograph of Jackson Ubeda. There was an undeniable urban elegance; darkly complexioned, his shaven head hid the effects of male pattern baldness. He looked as though he would wear cufflinks.

She felt uncomfortable entering the club premises alone, because men were here with one purpose: to behave badly around women. In her mother's day, it had been considered a good thing for a man to place a woman on a pedestal; but this was not what had been intended. The foyer was as garish as a child's drawing, black-light, zebra-skin and pink neon, exuding ersatz sophistication to men who were unfamiliar with the notion of restraint. *I bet the blokes who come here would love to work in tall buildings and drive overpowered cars in town,* she thought, smiling to herself.

Along the industrial-steel runway that protruded into the main room like a late-eighties video set, a pair of unnervingly upbeat latex-thonged girls dropped and flexed before the drinkers. The preference here was for female extremes: big hair, long legs, hard breasts, fat attitude. She had imagined that the audience would be raucous and dangerously playful, overweight schoolboys hiding their sexual discomfort with jibes and dares, but was surprised to find many groups almost ignoring the dancers. Workers huddled in urgent clusters, jacketless, arguing office politics, holding the kind of intense discussions that had been pumped up to nonsense level by chemical stimuli. Private rooms hosted the stag nights, keeping aggressive behaviour out of the main room. She couldn't entirely blame the clientele; the work-hard, play-hard ethic had invaded everywhere.

Longbright knew at once that Ubeda would not be found near the stage. She asked a hostess to check the booking, and was sent to a private bar on the first floor. He was seated alone, drinking something with a lot of leaves sticking out of it. She required a pretext for approaching him without drawing suspicion, but after wracking her brain and failing to come up with anything original, settled on a direct approach.

'Do you have a light?'

He withdrew a slim silver Cartier and flicked it, then looked at her in puzzlement. 'Do you have a cigarette?'

'No, I don't smoke.'

Ubeda did not look happy about having his reverie interrupted. 'Then what do you want?'

'I've seen you before.'

'That's because I'm usually here.' Now he appraised her. Longbright hoped that the softer lighting was working in her favour. 'I've never seen you before.'

'Well, I've definitely noticed you. We share something special in common. Let me buy you a drink.' She summoned the bargirl, pointing to Ubeda's glass. 'Two of whatever he's having. It looks like it has a hedge in it.'

'Two Gold Mojitos.' *All the staff in here are women,* Longbright noted. *There was probably something like this on the same site three hundred years ago.*

'What's in it?' she asked.

'Rum, mint, molasses, but you switch the soda

water for champagne.' *Interesting accent,* she thought. *Possibly Alexandria. Dead eyes. They'd watch someone being hurt without flinching.*

'I do know you,' she persisted. 'You were at the British Museum the other day, in the Egyptian gallery.' Another tip from Greenwood's wife. She hoped it would work.

'I wonder what made you single me out from so many visitors.' His smile revealed matching gold eye teeth, like some Monte Carlo version of a pirate.

'You stand out. Besides, it's mostly grazing tourists. I can spot someone with a real interest in artefacts a mile off.'

'I've been known to look in from time to time,' he conceded. 'What were you doing there?'

The drinks arrived. Longbright took a sip, then another. She was a large woman, and could drink most men under the table, but reminded herself to be careful; she was dealing with a man who carried a firearm. 'I've a friend who works at the museum— Gareth Greenwood,' she said casually. 'I was meeting him for lunch at the Court Restaurant and saw you.'

He was watching her carefully now, choosing his words with deliberation. 'Then it seems we do have someone in common. He is an acquaintance of mine. But I presume you already know that.'

'Actually, no, I didn't.'

He leaned closer, then a little too close for comfort. 'What exactly is your interest in my affairs? I wonder if—oh, I *wonder* ...'

She saw the unveiled accusation in his eyes. He knew that someone had been to his offices, and had connected her with the act of trespass.

'Mr Ubeda, I'll level with you. I know who you

are because you're a familiar face to sellers of antiquities. Your interest in Anubian statuary is common knowledge to us all.'

He sipped his drink and smiled. 'I know all the dealers in London, Paris, New York and Cairo. I don't know you.'

'There's no reason why you would. It's my job to find potential clients before they can find me.'

His impatience with her was burning through to anger. 'You're saying you have something to sell. I'm not some easy mark waiting to be sold a crappy chunk of hieroglyph smuggled from the Valley of the Kings. There's more necrobilia circulating on the black market these days than there is left in those limestone hills. I have friends working on every excavation gang, and you're going to tell me you have something no one's seen.' He stopped to light a cigarette. She remained silently watchful, knowing that he would continue because he was a collector, and collectors needed to transmit their zeal to others.

'The necropolis of the New Kingdom has been steadily robbed for the last three and a half thousand years,' he told her, 'from the interment of Tuthmosis I to the arrival of Howard Carter—sixty-two tombs and there's nothing left. Carter was as big a liar and cheat as the rest of them. Take a look at what remains. Merneptah, Amenhotep, Siptah, Sethnakht, a few chambers filled with pretty little bas-reliefs to amuse the waddling tourists. Relics sell because everyone wants to touch the past, but the past makes no sense if you smash it up to make a quick sale. It's robbed of all purpose and life. It will only mean something if its mythical power remains intact. There's nothing of interest left in Thebes.'

'What about KV5?' she asked quietly. Bryant had briefed her on the most recent developments in Egyptology. In 1994, an American archaeologist named Kent Weeks had discovered the valley's biggest tomb to date, the burial site of the fifty-two sons of Rameses II. Excavation was still continuing.

'It's been over ten years. No treasures have been discovered there.'

'But thousands of artefacts have been recovered from the debris, pieces of great importance.'

The jet eyes remained too still. 'Now... I think you're trying a little too hard.'

She was about to shift her stool back a little, but he was too fast for her. His hand had slipped around her neck, his index finger looping beneath her gold chain. As he twisted, the chain tightened. Anyone glancing at them would think he had embraced her.

'Forget Thebes, tell me about this.'

It had been Arthur's idea to thread the central panel of the sandalwood bracelet on to a neck-chain, in the hope that Ubeda would notice it. 'It has a special meaning for those of us who are prepared to keep searching,' she said, thinking *I deserve an Academy Award for this.*

He let the bracelet panel fall from his fingers. 'The seeds of regeneration springing from ancient waters. How quickly we forget our own creation myths. Look down there.' He nodded to the gyrating dominatrices of the blue-lit stage. 'The artificial pleasures of a civilization in decline.'

'Then why do you come here?'

'I own the place.'

I should have been told that, she thought, wincing inwardly. No wonder he was so deeply in debt. How many thousand square feet did he have to maintain here?

'And you want to sell me an Anubis. Do you have a genuine interest, or are you merely a vendor?'

'I find the myth fascinating.'

'In what way, I wonder.'

'The rituals, mostly—the Opening of the Mouth, the Lake of Offerings, the Weighing of the Heart.' She congratulated herself on remembering that protective ceremonies guided the dead to their afterlives. The Opening of the Mouth allowed for the reawakening of the senses. Anubis weighed the heart against the Feather of Truth. If it was found to be heavier, it was fed to the monster Ammut.

'Well, those rituals have always been popular with a certain kind of buyer,' he said disdainfully. 'There are countless other rituals, less spoken of.'

'Of course. I imagine many still continue, and they all require ceremonial artefacts.' It was like prospecting for oil, testing each area and hoping for a strike, but she saw his eyes betray a faint interest. 'People look in the wrong places. As you say, the key treasures of Thebes have all been disseminated. They could be anywhere, even here.'

He was watching her intently now. That was the wonderful thing about collectors; there was always a way to their hearts.

'Of course, they would have been carefully hidden. Beneath the city, perhaps. In the water.' She had played her last card, and could only wait in silence while he considered her.

'So,' he said at last, 'you know about the five rivers.'

'I may know where to find what you're looking

for.' She was stepping off the script, but the bait had been taken, the reel was turning and he was coming in nice and gently. He opened his mouth to reply, to share a confidence, then looked past her right shoulder and started to rise.

She followed his eyeline and found herself looking at Monsieur Edouard Assaad, manager of the Upper Nile Financial Services Group. *Not now,* she thought. *Not him.* Recognition was already spreading across Assaad's baby-smooth face as he began to speak. 'C'est merveilleux de vous revoir, chère Madame. Je vous croyais repartie en Egypte.' His outstretched hands came toward her.

A glimpse of Ubeda's face was enough to power her up from the stool, but he was fast, and held her wrist with a lightness that surprised her.

'You know M. Assaad,' he said approvingly. 'Your business must pay well.'

While the two men spoke in French, Longbright realized that the manager's appearance could provide proof of her credentials. She sat back down, and waited for a lull in the conversation.

Fifteen minutes later she left the club, walking fast toward the exit, not daring to look back. By the time she hit the pavement outside, she had pulled her pinching heels free and was carrying them in her hand. The cab driver who drew up at her signal looked as if he had time to chat. She thought of hauling him through the passenger door and taking his place at the wheel before Ubeda could appear in the entrance behind her.

The cab pulled out into traffic as the driver flicked off the hire sign. Balancing a pad on her knee she scribbled notes, trying to remember everything that had been said, deciphering their conversation with her schoolbook French. Behind her, the lights changed and a shoal of vehicles swarmed up around them, but her sense of panic did not begin to fade until they had lost sight of the club.

24

___

BREAKING THE SURFACE

Giles Kershaw caught up with Bryant as he was heading to the unit car park. 'Ah, Mr Bryant,' he called, hopping over puddles with long corduroy-clad legs. 'I'm glad I caught you. I tried calling your mobile but got no response.'

'No, you wouldn't,' agreed Bryant, fumbling with his umbrella. 'What do you want?'

'It's about Elliot Copeland's death. I wanted to take the cabin of his truck to pieces in order to recreate a sequence of events, but the Kentish Town constabulary moved it from the site and I haven't been able to requisition—look, have you got a moment?'

'It's Thursday,' Bryant explained. 'I'm late for my evening class. Can't you walk and talk?'

'I made a scale model instead, took your advice about working with the materials at hand, and well, my theory, it was wrong. I had the whole thing pegged as an unfortunate accident. Because of the bricks inside the cabin, you see.'

'No, I don't see,' said Bryant, fighting to get the

rusted door of the Mini Cooper open. 'Jump inside or you'll get soaked.'

Kershaw gratefully concertinaed himself into the tiny car and ran a hand through his blond hair, spiking it. 'He saved the good bricks from the ditch, over thirty of them, stacking them in the cabin. He'd laid a sheet of plastic on the passenger seat to protect it from mud. But he knew he wouldn't be able to stop the whole lot from sliding over if he braked suddenly, which he might well have had to do in the rain, so he held the bricks in place with two pieces of cut plank. He created a sort of makeshift hod. This is just the sort of thing builders do just before they have accidents. When I saw the planks on the floor, I could imagine what had happened. He'd propped the bricks in place, alighted from the cabin and gone back to work. At which point, the truck shifted in the mud, the planks became dislodged and fell forward with the full weight of the bricks behind them. The only thing they could have hit was the dashboard, punching the hydraulic starter and holding it in. I figured it was a freak misfortune, the kind that occurs on building sites all over the world. There are no normal accidents; each one is a particular confluence of circumstances.'

'You're not going to give me a lecture on chaos theory, are you?' asked Bryant. 'I wrote a book on that subject.'

'I'm sure you know about such things, Mr Bryant—'

'No, I mean I really did write a book on the subject. It's behind my desk if you'd like to borrow it.'

'But you see, my instinct was wrong,' Kershaw

admitted. 'I built a cantilever, weighting it proportionately and angling it to match the digital shots we took on the night. Even on my reduced scale, the bricks wouldn't have been responsible for holding in the button because the truck was already inclining backwards, toward the ditch, so I'm pretty certain that gravity would have held the load in place even if you'd taken the planks away.'

'How much of a shove would it have taken to shift the load forward?'

'Exactly what I asked myself. The answer, on my model, was the mere push of an index finger. It's certainly a possibility that they were knocked forward by someone reaching into the truck cabin.'

'They'd have to know the workings of the hydraulic system, wouldn't they?'

'Not as far as I can see. The engine was running, and there's an illuminated white pictogram of the raised truck bed printed across a large red button. A child could have grasped the meaning and pressed it. In fact, it could have been local kids, looking to give him a fright. I talked with Dan—after all, he's in charge of the crime scene, I'm rather treading on his toes with this—but he agreed with me about the likely sequence of events.'

'To prove premeditation you need motive and opportunity, Mr Kershaw, and now it looks as though we have both.'

'You're including Ruth Singh's death, then.'

'I'd say it's part of a grand plan, but "I will be the pattern of all patience; I will say nothing"—Lear.'

'King—'

'—Well, it would hardly be Edward. Too much

theorizing, not enough evidence. Proof is needed to cement the connection.'

'I'm not sure I'm with you—'

'Water, dear boy, water! Rising up from the damned earth to drown the innocent!'

Kershaw barely managed to tumble out of the car before Bryant crashed the gears and jerked away from the car park, into the teeming city night.

Someone in the street knew more than they were telling.

Curtains, doors and thick brick walls, blinds and shutters to exclude light and rain and other people, to keep out warmth and kindness and cold hard truth. Anything to keep lives hidden from view. Was there anything more subtly malicious than the lowland mentality of people in cool climates? England in the rain, wet gardens, chilly rooms, London dinner conversations over pudding served in xanthous light, hushed arguments behind amber supper candles, quietly spreading the poison of rationality.

This won't do, Kallie thought. *I'll go crazy.*

When the letterbox clapped, she picked the postcard from the mat and turned it over. A picture of Cairo at night. The photograph looked old and artificially coloured. Tall hotels reflected in a flat wide river, a sheet of dark light pierced with luminous neon streaks. She could almost have been looking at London after dark, except that there were more boats. On the back, a handful of lines, something about a change of plan. He had the nerve to add that he was missing her. *Then come home,* she almost said aloud, then fought down the plea.

What was wrong with the men she knew? Paul didn't have the guts to stay with her through the settling-in period of their relationship, presumably because it involved some responsibility. His brother barely spoke to his girlfriend unless he wanted sex. Heather's husband was trading her in for someone younger. And the other men in the street: Mark Garrett in a state of belligerent inebriation, Randall Ayson accused by his wife of infidelity (according to Jake, who shared the party wall), Oliver communicating with his wife via their morose son, Elliot lonely and antisocial, coming to an ignominious but probably inevitable end in a mud-filled ditch. It didn't say much for the men of the twenty-first century. Omar and Fatima next door—she didn't know enough about them to be critical, but having seen Fatima in the street, head covered and bowed, mincing invisibly in her husband's shadow, the urge to do so was tempting.

The infinite dark skies made her as fractious as a school-bound child. She wished the walls that separated them all would melt away to reveal their communal lives. Brick, lathe, gypsum, plywood, plaster, paper, dissolving all along the terrace. Ten houses, at least twenty-five people by her reckoning, most interacting more with their computers and televisions than with their neighbours, because there was too little time and too much uncertainty.

And what would others think of her? The new girl at number 5 arrived with hardly any furniture, her boyfriend lost his job and didn't stick around, now she watches the world splash past from her misted lounge window. *This has got to stop,* she told herself, throwing the postcard into the bin, knowing that she would later retrieve it. Pulling a blanket from the sofa, she wrapped herself and, opening the back door, sat on the step to watch the deluge. She had always loved the fulgent clouds, rain-circles in swirling pools, burgeoned leaves releasing droplets, roots drawing sustenance through dense weeds. In London, the ever-present water brought survival and regrowth. The sun only dried and desiccated, making pavements sweat and people uncomfortable.

It seemed as if her trace-memories were entirely filled with water: shops with dripping canopies, passers-by with plastic macs or soaked shoulders, huddled teenagers in bus shelters peering out at the downpour, shiny black umbrellas, children stamping through puddles, buses slooshing past, fishmongers hauling in their displays of sole and plaice and mackerel in brine-filled trays, rainwater boiling across the tines of drains, split gutters with moss hanging like seaweed, the oily sheen of the canals, dripping railway arches, the high-pressure thunder of water escaping through the lock-gates in Camden, fat drops falling from the sheltering oaks in Greenwich Park, rain pummelling the opalescent surfaces of the deserted lidos at Brockwell and Parliament Hill, sheltering swans in Clissold Park; and indoors, green-grey patches of rising damp, spreading through wallpaper like cancers, wet tracksuits drying on radiators, steamed-up windows, water seeping under back doors, faint orange stains on the ceiling that marked a leaking pipe, a distant attic drip like a ticking clock.

She looked through the rain and saw him, a hunched old man with monkey eyes, brown and watchful. According to Sergeant Longbright, the tramp's name was Tate; that was what everyone had always called him. Now here he was again, waiting, keeping guard, willing something to happen.

Call us if he reappears. She didn't like to bother them, but they had insisted on her using the number. She punched out the hotline digits on the Peculiar Crimes Unit card.

Meera Mangeshkar looked up from sixty pages of hardcopy, listening to the call-out. She had been trying to absorb city stats for the last two hours, but hated coursework. *Forty-three police forces. Around 130,000 officers in UK, just one for every 400 civilians. 20,000 women, only 2,500 ethnic.* The Met's five areas were each the size of a complete force elsewhere in the country, but could still barely cope. *Over six million 999 calls a year. 5,000 cars a month stolen in London, figures rising fast. Borough of Camden has the highest suicide rate in London.*

What was the point of familiarizing yourself with the figures when you could do nothing about them? Raise the strike rate, drop kids into the criminal-justice system, watch them re-offend, pick up the pieces, console the latest victims. She had been on the edge of leaving the Met before her transfer, and still hoped that this unit would make a difference to the way she felt. The old guys had made her welcome, and John May, in particular, had gone out of his way to spend time explaining the unit's unorthodox structure, but where were the interesting cases? When the call came through she took it, calling to Colin Bimsley as he was about to go off duty.

'You can handle this, Meera. She's seen the tramp

before—just give him a warning, find out where he's staying and take him back there.'

'I know how to do my job, sonny,' she yelled back. 'I thought you might want to come with me.'

In the next room, Bimsley buttoned his shirt and threw his boots into his locker. 'What, like a date or something?'

'No, not a date, but you could give me a lift on your scooter.'

'Only if we get something to eat afterwards, I'm starving. Look at the weather, it's still pissing down. I could wait for you, then we could grab a takeaway and eat it at my flat . . .'

She could see where he was going with this. 'Forget it, Colin, you're *so* not my type.'

' *"Not my type"*?' he mouthed to himself, amazed. He stuck his head around the door. 'I'm clean-living, kind-hearted and pathetically single. If you're going to pass on this great opportunity, can you at least fix me up with a date?'

'Sure. My sister would like you. She's cute and she might even go out with you. Just say the word and I'll arrange it. But I warn you, she's a Muslim.'

'Would she really? What difference does it make, her being a Muslim?'

'She'll only go out with a Muslim boy, so you'd have to give up the beer,' Meera told him. 'And Muslims are circumcised, so you might need a small operation.'

'Jesus, Meera, you have a sick sense of humour.'

'What's the matter, Colin? Feeling threatened? Now you know how I feel when you pester me.'

'I think you spent too much time roughing it in the south London stations.' Colin kicked his locker door shut. 'Come on then. I'll give you a lift, no strings attached.'

'It's Tate, he's in the garden again,' said Kallie, holding open the front door.

'Does he know you've seen him?' asked Meera, entering.

'I don't know—I don't think so. He hasn't moved for over half an hour, even in this rain.' The lights in the hall had been turned off. 'I could keep an eye on him more easily in the dark,' she explained, leading the way down to the back door. Meera stood in front of her, looking out. She was unusually short for a police officer, but could hold down a man twice her weight.

'OK, I see him.' A figure could be discerned inside a large elder bush. Meera ascended three steps to the small sodden lawn. It was hard to see any detail through the gloom of the overhanging ceanothus. The garden was so enclosed and dense that she could have been stepping into the green underwater murk of a pond.

'I need to talk to you, Mr Tate,' she said briskly, raising her hands in a gesture of friendship. 'Please, come on out.'

His movement was so sudden that she started. The bush shook violently, spraying rainwater as he twisted about and dropped low. The last thing Meera wanted was to plough through wet undergrowth in semi-darkness, but she instinctively shoved her way in between the leaves.

Suddenly he was pushing away fast, bending and cracking the branches. She heard the thud of his

boots hitting the fence, saw him scrambling over with
ease, even though it was clear that he only had the use
of his left arm and leg. He'd either been born with the
affliction or the injury was old: his movements were
practised and agile. She remembered a young heroin
addict on the Peckham North estate who had lost a
leg after passing out in a crouching position down the
side of a club toilet, cutting off his blood supply.
Afterwards, he moved as if the limb was still in place:
Phantom Limb Syndrome. The mind still worked
when the body failed.

Her jacket was caught on rose thorns. She yanked
her sleeve free and ran for the fence, taking it easily,
keeping her eye on his retreating back as he leapt the
next divider, turning the back gardens into a mud-
spattered steeplechase.

This time he swerved and dropped over the low
brick wall at the rear, into the narrow alley that separated Balaklava Street from the road behind. She was
no more than a few feet behind him, vaulting in his
wake, slipping and scrambling to her feet, but the
dim brown corridor of the overgrown path was deserted. There was nowhere he could have gone. She
fought her way to one end, then back to the other.
Nothing in either direction, not even any footprints
in the muddy track.

Meera returned to the bush where the tramp had
been hiding. The centre of the elder had been hol-
lowed out and shielded with branches to form a small
hideaway. The earth inside was trampled flat, and
several squashed cigarette ends lay in the mud at her
feet. A familiar green and gold tin lay on its side. She
picked it up, shining her pocket torch across the
metal surface, and saw the macabre image of a dead

lion with a swarm of bees feeding from its stomach. The label read 'Out of the Strong Came Forth Sweetness.' An emptied can of Tate & Lyle Golden Syrup. At least she now knew how the old man had got his nickname.

She looked back at Kallie shivering in the doorway. *Home is meant to be the one safe place,* she thought. Meera had grown up in the tower blocks behind Archway, and knew what it felt like to lie awake in bed, listening for every small sound.

'I'm in no rush,' she said, taking Kallie's arm and leading her back into the house. 'My colleague's waiting outside. He wanted me to have dinner with him. Let's send him off for a takeaway.'

25

UNDERCURRENTS

Raymond Land straightened his golf-club tie, checking his appearance in the steel plate bolted into the green tiled doorway, then swiped his security card through the slot. As he walked into the partially unveiled entrance of the PCU headquarters, he resolved to put a stop to the rumours circulating the force about his unit. It was said that Bryant and May were already up to their old tricks, that they were sending their staff off on wild-goose chases around the capital, that their bad habits were resurfacing to infect a new generation of staff. What he saw as he entered the unit gave him no cause for encouragement. Detective Sergeant Longbright was packing away an evening dress.

'What the devil do you think you're doing, Longbright?' asked Land.

'I'm still a woman, sir,' Janice snapped. It was the first time she had taken a break since her arrival at eight that morning. She had just wanted to take one last look at the dress before it went back. Bryant had refused to cover the price, demanding that she return it. This attitude was to be expected from a man who had never paid more than ten pounds for a shirt. The black satin slipped beneath her fingers, a mockery of the wedding dress she would never wear. Her long-time partner owed more allegiance to the force than to any mere woman. Ian Hargreave thrived in the undertow of interdepartmental politics, preferring to catch up with her two evenings a week, after work, when they were both tired and irritable. Longbright would sit in his kitchen eating Chinese takeouts direct from the containers. She glared angrily at the acting head, daring him to complain.

Land hastily moved on down the corridor. Amidst the newly purchased equipment in the unit's crime lab, he found Kershaw and Banbury tinkering with an oven tray full of wet sand and a toy truck. 'What on earth are *you* two up to?' he asked.

'Giles is explaining the physical dynamics of accidental death,' Banbury explained, not at all clearly. 'My territory, really, but Giles got there first.'

'So this is your doing.'

'Mr Bryant gave me the idea. It's all right, I've got a job number for it.'

'Why am I not surprised?' Land asked the wall as he passed on. At least Bimsley seemed to be doing something useful, scanning reams of figures on his computer, but Meera Mangeshkar was lying on the floor. She scrambled to her feet as Land entered. 'Sorry, sir, spot of yoga—put my back out last night.'

'On your own time or in the course of duty?'

'Duty, sir. Apprehending a suspicious character.'

'You booked him?'

'No, sir. Vanished into thin air. Literally. Quite impossible, I know, almost as if he flew away, but there you are.'

They're all mad, thought Land. *This is Bryant's doing. He's tainted them with his lunacy. John's marginally more rational. I'll appeal to his common sense.* He headed for the detectives' room.

'We're running on the spot. Or in my case, walking very slowly.' Bryant threw his files down on the desk. 'Land wants me to fill in a unit activity report before lunchtime. If you have any bright ideas about how to take up so much blank space, I'd welcome them. God, it's hard to work with that racket going on outside. What's going on?'

May sauntered to the window and looked down into the street. 'There are a pair of drink-addled skinheads throwing beer cans at each other outside the Tube station,' he remarked off-handedly. 'There's a young woman with a baby, screaming at her boyfriend and slapping him around the head. A couple of men from the council are digging up the pavement with drills. The Water Board's gouging a hole in the middle of the road. Oh, and two van-drivers are having a shouting match at the lights. To which racket were you referring?'

'Why are the urban English so vocal nowadays?' Bryant wondered. 'Go to Paris, Madrid, Berlin, even Rome, you don't get this kind of behaviour. It's Hogarth's picture of Gin Lane all over again.'

'Arthur, you used to sound your age. Now you're sounding several centuries old.'

'What's wrong with that? One of the great pleasures that used to come with senior citizenship was the right to be perfectly vile to everyone. You could say whatever you liked, and people excused you out of respect for your advanced years. But now that everyone is in touch with their emotions and says exactly what they feel, even that pleasure has been taken away. Is there nothing the young haven't usurped?'

May had to listen to this sort of thing at least once a week. He still believed in the redemptive power of the nation's youth, despite his partner's diatribes against them. The contrary thing about Bryant was that, in his own way, he set great store by the capital's younger population. Some of the unit's most useful collaborators were under twenty.

The phone rang. Longbright was warning them of Land's impending visit. 'Raymond has heard that we're still using unit resources to check out your academic adversary,' cautioned Bryant. 'He wants to close up all investigations in which we have a personal interest so he can stick us with the embassy thing.'

'Is that the business I heard him mentioning to Janice?' asked May. 'Some fellow the new Dutch consul was seen chasing across Russell Square at two in the morning? It should be fairly obvious what that was about, even to the Home Office. Says he was after a thief. I suppose that's a tad more believable than the Welsh secretary reckoning Jamaican boys on Clapham Common were asking him out to dinner at midnight. Janice, would you come in here?'

The detective sergeant stuck her head around the door. 'I'm not dressing up again—the frock is going back and I've returned the jewellery. You can do your own undercover work from now on.'

'Are you sure you've told me everything?'

'Sorry, I forgot to mention that it was too tight under the arms.'

'Your sarcasm is unappreciated. What did you say to Raymond?'

'Nothing. He was asking about my time-sheets. I know he's suspicious about our continued surveillance of Ubeda. What are you going to do?'

May had been able to keep the case on their official records because the protection of Greenwood, as a government-think-tank adviser, could conceivably come under the jurisdiction of the unit. However, as the academic didn't appear to be in any danger, and wasn't bringing his colleagues into disrepute by pursuing what appeared to be some kind of esoteric hobby in his spare time, May had no justification for continuing to maintain surveillance.

'Look,' said Bryant, 'I've got Longbright's notes from her conversation with Ubeda, so why don't I follow it up in my spare time?'

May knew all about his partner's offers of help; they came with riders, like insurance contracts. 'What do you want in return?' he asked.

'Keep talking to the residents of Balaklava Street for me, would you? I don't trust them.'

'Which one in particular don't you trust?'

'Any of them. Somebody knows something they're not telling. Ask yourself some questions. Tate, the tramp, why was he watching the girl? I must admit I always found the image on the side of that treacle tin damned odd. After all, the stuff's made from sugar, not honey, so why are the bees there? No one's managed to interview the couple who live right next door to her, Omar and Fatima—I don't seem to have last names for them, and it's not good enough. The medical students, what do they know? That rather smug family, the Wiltons, they must have seen something. And I want photographs of everybody, preferably caught off guard. Even murderers smile when they know they're having their picture taken, and that's no good.'

'I'll do what I can—'

'Land's creeping around the building checking on everyone; it's not very conducive to crime detection. He can't play golf because it's raining, and the last thing he wants to do is go home to a houseful of moaning women, three ghastly daughters and his dreadful wife, so he mooches about making life miserable for everyone else. He's got the charm of a rectal probe, and no social skills to speak of, so nobody wants to go for a drink with him. Let's face it, dogs have more to look forward to in later life—at least they can go to the park and roll in shit.'

'Ah, Raymond, we were just talking about you,' said May hastily.

Land stood in the doorway, fuming. Bryant had decorated the area around his desk exactly as it had been before the fire. Statuettes of Gog and Magog, voodoo dolls, his beloved Tibetan skull, books with reeking singed covers rescued from the conflagration, some odoriferous plants that lay tangled in an earthenware pot—tannis root, probably, marijuana, certainly—an ancient Dansette record player scratching and popping its way through Mendelssohn's 'Elijah', papers and newspaper clippings everywhere, a half-eaten egg-and-beetroot sandwich dripping on to a stack of uncased computer disks.

'I thought we'd agreed to keep the new offices clean and spartan, moving toward a paper-free environment,' said Land weakly. There the senior detectives stood, side by side, working as a team against him, undermining his confidence with knowing looks. 'I thought that having been given all this nearly-new equipment, you'd give a thought to changing your methodology. Instead I find the place more like the set of *Blue Peter* than the offices of a specialist crime unit. Well, it's got to stop. HO is sending us a number of inactive cases it would like cleared up as soon as possible, so I want the decks completely clear by the end of the week.'

'Oh, come on, Raymondo,' smiled Bryant, knocking out his pipe on the side of the waste bin and blowing noisily through it. 'You know we'll sort the outstanding workload in our own time.'

Land's face reddened. 'I think your time's run out. I want you to pack up this business in Kentish Town, for a start. You're probably going to get a verdict of accidental death, you know. You've come up with no useful evidence whatsoever. The case wasn't even assigned to you.'

'Look here, Raymond, if there's going to be a fundamental sea-change in the way we work—the way we've always worked, I might add—' here he nodded conspiratorially at May—'I think you should give us some official guidelines and a bit more warning.'

'You've had about thirty years' warning, Arthur, don't come the old acid. I mean it—closed files and clean desks. Your new regime starts first thing on Monday.' He slammed the door hard as he exited, hoping to leave behind a positive impression.

'We finally get an office door and he tries to knock it off its hinges,' sighed Bryant, packing his pipe with a handful of dried leaves. 'From now on, we're going to have to hide our tracks more carefully.'

'Arthur, you have to explain why you're so convinced there's something going on in Balaklava Street.'

'That's not so easy.' Bryant dropped into his chair and recklessly lit the pipe. 'It's the kind of neighbourhood that looks utterly mundane, but there are undercurrents and subcultures in London that hardly anyone is aware of—people who live entirely outside the law. Who knows who you might meet? Mental patients from St Luke's walk the streets with demons dwelling behind their eyes. I suppose the whole thing interferes with my notions of home. Threaten that and you damage something very fundamental to your well-being. Kallie Owen had no real personal difficulties before she moved in, it's not in her character to attract trouble. She's inherited someone else's bad karma, buying a house from a murdered woman. We're seeing reactions to some buried situation known only to one or two people. This runs much deeper than we can imagine.'

'I hate it when you talk in riddles,' May complained.

'I only do it because I don't fully understand the meanings myself, but it's there in front of me, I know that. Just as I know there will be another attempt on a life. Whoever committed these crimes is more confident now, because we've failed to get close enough to be a threat. You've seen this kind of behaviour before, John, don't pretend you haven't.'

'Like it or not,' May warned, 'we need to repay Raymond's faith in us. We have to start afresh, Arthur, and if we can't do it, then it's time to go. I don't need to spell out what will happen if either of us are forced into retirement.'

Bryant wasn't used to being lectured. He regarded May sceptically through the cloud of illicit smoke that had transformed the office into a Limehouse opium den. 'I suppose you're right. Raymond has been a thorn in my side longer than I can remember, but he's always fought for us. Perhaps we do need to change our approach. If we'd had more staff, I'd have searched the entire area door to door. As for your pal Greenwood, we should have pulled him in and put the fear of God up him, and that would have been the end of that.'

'Then let's have one last try. You find out what Greenwood's up to. I'll talk to the residents of Balaklava Street. And we must keep looking for Tate. Somebody has to know something.' He caught a look of pain crossing Bryant's face. 'What is it?'

'My greatest fear is that we've found something rare—a killer hidden in plain sight.'

'It's the kind of case you would once have dreamed of, Arthur.'

'Not any more,' he told May. 'Death stands too close to me.' Bryant felt a chill in his bones that no amount of warmth could dispel. The time was coming when he would no longer understand the way of the world, and then he would cease to have a purpose. Murders were tests, and solving them was the only way of staying alive. Explaining the murders in Balaklava Street would provide more than a stay of execution; it would extend their life spans, and give them a reason to continue. Although he was tired, Bryant set to work once more.

26

NAVIGATION

There was no other library like it in London.

In place of the usual plaques reading 'Romantic Fiction', 'Self-Help' and 'DIY' were signs for Eleusinian and Orphic Studies, Rosicrucianism and Egyptian Morphology. While the books gathered under its roof were far too esoteric for general public consumption, the collection was too incomplete for scholastic study.

Most of its contents were a bequest from Jebediah Huxley, the great-grandfather of Dorothy Huxley, the library's present and doubtless final custodian. Under the conditions of the bequest, the collection could only be dispersed and the building sold with the approval of the last surviving family member. Dorothy had no living dependants, and was in her eighties. Greenwich Council was itching to get its hands on the small redbrick Edwardian block, tucked in permanent dank shadow beneath the concrete corner of a flyover in the south-eastern corner of the borough. Here, swirling litter and glaring skateboarders warded off all but the hardiest visitors. Rainwater sluiced from the flyover on to the roof of the building, dripping through brickwork, rotting floorboards and spreading mildew into the damp-fattened books with wet fingers of decay.

Dorothy ran the library with her assistant, Frank, who was antisocial and unreliable, but who could afford to work for love of the printed word without being paid, because he had been left some money by an aunt. This was how unfashionable literature had been reduced to surviving: in crumbling repositories, guarded by the very last generation of book-lovers.

'The five rivers of the Underworld,' Bryant read aloud, 'separated the land of the undead from the realm of mortals. Their presence made sure no one could enter or leave unharmed. There should be a picture here.' He fingered the severed edge of paper.

'We've had a problem with thieves cutting out the hand-coloured plates,' Dorothy explained. 'They frame and sell them in antiquarian bookshops. We have no way of making the building secure.'

'I'll try and get you an alarm.' Bryant turned the damaged pages. 'We're talking about Roman mythology, obviously. My contact appears to be interested in Egyptian gods, and yet he mentioned the five rivers.'

'Nothing is clear-cut in pagan mythologies, Arthur. You know that. Rivers are central to ancient-Egyptian worship because of the importance of the Nile, which continues to bring life and prosperity to the barren central plains of the country.'

'Yes, but no one would blur together two entirely separate mythologies, surely.'

'Certainly no one from either of those civilizations ever did,' Dorothy agreed. 'But then, of course, you had the Victorians.'

'Why, what did they do?'

'Having plundered, borrowed and stolen whatever pleased them, they drew on the parts of ancient mythologies that found most correspondence to their own beliefs. They rewrote entire histories, bowdlerizing, adapting, censoring. They weren't the first, but they were the most confident. It wasn't unusual to find statues of Ra and Thoth beside Diana and Venus in the well-to-do Victorian household. You were less likely to find Christian figurines, for that was the presiding active religion. All other beliefs and creation myths were treated largely as naive fairy tales, and their icons had use as decoration. Collectors weren't averse to pairing up different creation gods.'

Bryant came to the page he was seeking. 'So we have five nether-rivers: Cocytus, the river of lamentation; Acheron, the river of woe; Phlegethon, the river of conflagration; Lethe, the river of forgetfulness; Styx, the river of hatred and fatality and unbreakable oaths.'

'That's right. The Styx was an offshoot of Tethys and Oceanus, and flowed nine times around Hades. Like the Lethe, its water could not be stored in any flask or jar that tried to contain it. The Styx corroded all materials, even flesh. Only horses' hooves could survive in its waters.'

'Didn't Thetis dip her son Achilles into the Styx to make him invulnerable? Obviously didn't burn his flesh, then.'

'Mythology is filled with paradox,' Dorothy explained. 'Which river are you particularly interested in?'

'I'm not exactly sure. I suppose the Styx is the most important one.'

'It's certainly the most written about. But the

Lethe is essential because of the belief in reincarnation and the transmigration of souls. Those passing across had to drink from the Lethe to forget their former lives.'

'Cocytus and Acheron sound one and the same.'

'Actually they're not, although both are associated with wailing and misery. Acheron is the river over which Charon ferried the dead to Hades, not the Styx. Corpses not properly buried were doomed to walk the banks of the Cocytus for eternity.'

'I sense myself being drawn into the backwaters, Dorothy. John has warned me about it many times. I have to stick to the central problem of my investigation.'

'Which is?'

'I wonder, is there any modern correspondence of the rivers to something in this city?'

'Victorians were fond of finding explanations for everything. I believe they resurrected the idea that the five rivers of the Underworld matched the five main forgotten rivers of London.'

'They weren't the first to propose the concept, then.'

'Of course not. The Romans made the same suggestion during their occupation of London.'

'Do you have any books on the subject other than this one?'

'Sadly, no,' Dorothy admitted, 'but I know some people who may be able to help you. A group dedicated to rediscovering the lost rivers of the Underworld. I can give you a contact number, but I warn you, they're rather peculiar.'

'Sounds right up my street,' said Bryant with a sly grin.

27

THE MOVEMENT OF WATER

'Darned shame about the weather,' said Oliver Wilton earnestly. 'You've missed seeing the Camden Canal Junior Canoe Club in action.'

John May waited beneath a willow tree while Oliver and his wife buttoned up their yellow plastic cagoules. A pair of tramps were arguing over a can of Special Brew on the bench behind them. Another was eating Spam out of a tin with his fingers. The canal water was studded with chunks of polystyrene, the linings from boxes of stolen stereo units. Even the birds in the trees looked as if they had cancer.

'Your neighbour, Jake Avery, said I'd find you here or at the Christian Fellowship Hall.'

'We like to do our bit at the weekends,' Oliver told him, padlocking the club shelter. 'The local kids haven't really learned how to interact socially with one another, and we find that activities like canoeing, away from the council-estate environment, encourage teamwork.' He looked as if he believed what he was saying.

'Does Brewer enjoy canoeing?' asked May, smiling

at the morose child sitting on his ankles at the water's edge.

'God, we wouldn't let *him* do it, the water's filthy,' Tamsin replied. 'You can get Weil's disease from rat urine.' She grabbed the child's hand protectively. May could see that one day very soon, Brewer would not allow his hand to be taken up so quickly. 'He's saying, "I want to go home, Daddy, I'm tired," aren't you, pet? We usually go to the house in Norfolk at the weekends, but Oliver likes to put something back into the community.' The effort to smile nearly killed her. 'I wanted Brewer to grow up in the countryside, but Oliver insisted we stay in town until it's time to go to big school.' She lowered her voice. 'A nurse was raped on this towpath last month. A *nurse*. Shoved off her bicycle into the bushes. The police won't come down here.' It was difficult to miss the desperation in her eyes. She hated Oliver for imprisoning her in the city. 'I'm from Buckinghamshire originally, and I can tell you, Mr May, this is *not* like home, not what *I* call home.'

She turned and began leading the boy away, so that May was forced to follow. Oliver doggedly fell in behind them, in what May took to be a permanent state of disgrace with his wife. Ahead, several pigeons blocked the path, dining from a spattered pool of sick.

'My work keeps me here,' Oliver explained.

'What do you do?' asked May.

'I thought you knew.' He seemed surprised. 'I'm a senior executive at the Thames Water Board. You have no idea how much water London wastes through leaks each week. My job is to help locate them and replace the damaged pipes. Why did you come and find us?'

'I wanted to ask you about—' He had been about to say 'Elliot Copeland', but something made him change—'Mrs Singh. I know the matter is concluded, as far as the authorities are concerned, but I wondered if you had any personal thoughts.'

'It's funny you should ask. I'd been thinking of what your partner said at our party, about her drowning in her own house. It struck a distant chord, I just couldn't put my finger on it at the time.'

'Oh? In what way?'

'It sounds silly, but—darling, I think Brewer's tired, could you take him home? I'd like to take Mr May to my office and show him something.'

The innocuous steel building on Canal Walk did not look like the headquarters of a water board. Apart from a guard reading the *Sun* in the reception area, the place was empty. 'Oh no, it's not here,' laughed Oliver. 'This is a temporary on-site venue, somewhere we can plug in our laptops and hold meetings. It's a fascinating business. I can give you a potted history, although I don't see how it will help.'

'I don't mind,' said May casually. 'I've a little time to kill.'

Oliver led the way to a bare office of maroon carpet tiles and plan chests. 'Well, it goes back to a chap called Hugh Myddleton who created the New River, which we think was the world's first Build-Own-Operate project, a channel carrying water from springs in Hertfordshire to Islington. It became operational at the start of the seventeenth century; it's still partly in use today.' He pushed over a chair. 'Make yourself comfortable.'

May seated himself. 'So a London water board has been around since then?'

'We were needed from the outset. The huge influx of people from rural areas increased pressure on the water supply, but we had the steam engine and cast-iron piping to improve things. Of course, there was a terrible rise in waste. Indoor plumbing was nonexistent. Chap called Harington invented the first indoor toilet in the 1590s, but it wasn't widely adopted because there was no supply of running water to flush it. Cesspits were an advance, but they weren't emptied very often. Now, I know it's here somewhere.' He pulled out a drawer and began leafing through the plans. 'The Thames was the main source of drinking water for London, and remained pretty clean until around 1800, even supporting a decent fishing industry. You could catch lobsters and salmon in its reaches. Unfortunately, it didn't last because not enough cesspits had been built. Residents started illegally connecting their overflows to surface drains and underground rivers flowing into the Thames. The rising tide of sewage destroyed all life in the water and it began to smell, especially in hot weather. I'm sure you'll have heard of the Great Stink of June 1858, when the stench became so lethal that no one could work inside Parliament. The cholera epidemic killed two thousand Londoners a week until Dr John Snow discovered it was spread in water, and closed the infected pump in Golden Square. The John Snow pub in Broadwick Street is dedicated to him.'

'Didn't Bazalgette come up with a plan to build sewers?'

'Yes; a pity so many people had to die before Disraeli could be convinced to implement the system.

It's an incredible piece of engineering, a series of cascades that race around the city washing everything away. After that came chlorination during the First World War, then double filtration and new steel water mains.'

'What about these days? I mean, where does all the waste go?'

'North London's waste goes to Abbey Mills Pumping Station in Stratford, and an outfall sewer takes it to the treatment plant at Beckton. South London's goes to Deptford, and from there to works at Plumstead.'

'And what happened to the underground rivers?'

'Some were turned into sewage outlets, but most were difficult to drain after centuries of abuse. If you block up a river, the water still collects and has to run off somewhere. Houses are getting wetter again. The water table is rising due to climate changes, and the old rivers are on the move once more. But using them became redundant in 1994, when we opened the capital's underground ring-road, which allows water to circle the streets of London. It's one of the secret wonders of the world.'

'Is it big enough to climb inside?'

'Well, it has a diameter of two and a half metres, but it's pretty full. The Thames is now the cleanest metropolitan river on the planet, and supports 120 species of fish. We're servicing forty-six countries across the world. It's a damned big business. I could tell you about our sludge-incineration programme, but I fear I'd bore you.'

You're right there, thought May. 'Forgive me for asking, Mr Wilton, but what has this to do with Mrs Singh?'

'I'm sorry, I tend to get carried away. Tamsin doesn't like me bringing drains to the table, so when I find a fellow enthusiast ... Ah, I think this is it.' He pulled open another map drawer and tugged at a vast yellow sheet covered in dense, poorly printed lettering. 'This was made in the fifties. It's the last remotely accurate assessment of London's missing tributaries and outlets, produced by the LCC, but parts of it are missing, or the courses have shifted. They need to be tracked because there are so many electrical cables and tunnels under the streets. London doesn't operate on overhead systems. How do you track something that keeps moving? The truth is, we can only measure soil humidity and hope for the best. Look at what happened in Blackheath a couple of years ago—the roads simply caved in without any warning.' He traced his forefinger along the route of the Fleet. 'When rivers change course, strange things happen. If you don't know there's a river underneath, you might be inclined to start believing in ghosts.'

'I'm not at all sure I'm with you.'

'Well, you get sudden localized floods that appear as if from nowhere, and drain away just as quickly. There was a famous case back in the 1920s—some heavy wooden coffins were found moved from their pedestals in a sealed crypt in south London. There had been an unusually high tide that season. The water had seeped in through a tiny crack, lifted the coffins and drained back out. Water can travel fast, in very odd ways. It can be drawn up through a stone wall in dry weather, causing a damp spot ten feet from the ground. And they're saying Mrs Singh was found drowned. When I looked at this, I began to wonder.'

He smoothed out a section of the map centred on the streets where they stood. 'You see this large corner site? It's a gastropub called J.A.'s. Changed its name in the late nineties. Used to be the Jolly Anglers, built on Anglers' Lane. The lane's not marked on this map as a river, but we know from local history that it was a popular bathing spot. The council filled it in some time around 1890. So we draw that in.' He took a blue pen and ran a broken dotted line through the lane. 'The only other Fleet tributary is marked here, two roads further over. But of course it must have connected to Anglers' Lane; the river had to be fed from somewhere. Which only leaves Balaklava Street—or rather, the ginnel running behind the back gardens on the west side of the terrace, where Mrs Singh lived. It then crosses over the road, because it has to get down to its next known point of existence, at Prince of Wales Road. Which means that it flows right underneath Mrs Singh's house.'

'But you said it had dried up.'

'I said that parts of it had, and parts had been bricked up, so that the river has to find ways to re-route itself. You have to remember that the Fleet was once over sixty feet wide here in Camden Town, and flowed to a great basin which is now Ludgate Circus.'

'You're suggesting we had some kind of flash flood, that the water poured into her basement and drained back out, not even leaving a damp spot by the time Bryant and her brother arrived the next morning? It doesn't seem very likely. Where would the water drain to?'

'Here, to the Regent's Canal at Camden. We know the canal is topped up by underground pipes coming from the north. We've never drained enough of the

canal to map what's down there, and half of the
Victorian plans went missing in the sixties—they
made very popular framed prints for a while. We've
had an unusually dry summer, followed by a freak-
ishly wet autumn. I'm wondering if the extreme
weather conditions unblocked some of the pipework.
It might explain how Mr Copeland died as well.
Suppose water suddenly filled that ditch, undermining his truck, then drained away just as suddenly?'

'My partner made a detailed examination of Mrs
Singh's house. He said that apart from one or two
odd patches of damp, it was bone-dry. Yet ten hours
earlier, it was so full of water that a woman drowned
in it? I'm sorry, Mr Wilton, it's an interesting theory,
but a little far-fetched.'

'I knew I wouldn't be able to convince you,' Oliver
sighed, folding away the map. 'But you'd be surprised. I know about these things. The movement of
water far exceeds anything you can imagine.'

28

SPOILS OF THE FLEET

'I'm Mr Bryant. Do you remember me?'

The elderly detective was standing on the Wiltons' front step with rainwater pouring from the brim of his battered brown trilby. May's encounter with Oliver Wilton the day before had given him an idea.

Brewer nodded. 'You came to our party.' The boy spoke at the floor. He had the look of a child who had rarely been allowed outside alone.

'I decided to dig up a little local history, part of an investigation, and thought you might like to come along; if you weren't doing anything. I'd be glad of the company.'

It was hard to tell whether Brewer was flattered or horrified by the idea. He was probably intrigued at the prospect of accompanying a police inspector, but the pleasure was offset by the embarrassment of being seen with an elderly man. Either way, it had to be more fun than watching other kids have battles in canoes.

'You see, Brewer, I'm starting to think there's something very peculiar going on around here, and I could really use a little help. I need someone who

knows the area, someone who's been keeping their
eyes and ears open. I thought that person might be
you.'

'Dad's at work. Mum's out. I'm not allowed to go
anywhere. And she says don't talk to strangers,' said
Brewer uncomfortably.

'Oh, you're not a stranger,' said Bryant airily. 'I
know a little about you. I saw you at the party,
watching everyone. I bet I could tell you something
about yourself.'

'You couldn't.'

'A challenge, eh? I'll make a deal with you. If I
can, you have to give me a hand and put in a full day's
police work with me. I'll clear it with your mum.'
Bryant narrowed his eyes and studied the boy. 'I
know something you probably haven't told anyone.
You really hate your name. You wish you'd been
called something else.'

The boy's continued silence betrayed him.

'In fact, it isn't even your first name.' From the
corner of his eye, Bryant could see the nylon football bag hanging in the hall. The initials printed on it
were D.B.W. Nobody was called Derek any more,
and middle-class parents were unlikely to have opted
for Darren or Dale. Damien had passed the peak of
its popularity. 'Your first name is David,' Bryant told
him, 'which is good enough for David Beckham, but
apparently not for your dad. He wants to move you
to a private school, where they play rugby.' This was
a combination of intuition and common sense. Tamsin
was Oliver's second wife, a fair bit younger and more
of a trophy than his first. Oliver was clearly trying to
pull the boy up a few social rungs to please her. He
held down a decent job, was making money, and had

mentioned the poor quality of the local schools at the party. On the morning of Ruth Singh's death, Bryant had seen the boy leaving his house with football boots slung over his shoulder.

'You've talked to him.'

'Not since your party, and never about you. Grab yourself a coat, David, while I call your mother. I won't come in—I don't want to fill your house with water.'

Brewer hesitated for a moment. Hanging out with a disreputable-looking policeman could prove dangerous, and would probably get him into trouble with his father. The offer was worth accepting for that reason alone. He scampered off down the hall.

It was unorthodox, Bryant knew, but he needed some deeper attachment to the residents of Balaklava Street that went beyond question-and-answer, and looking after the boy was a good way of making friends.

As they splashed off along Balaklava Street a few minutes later, David felt comfortable enough to fall into step beside Bryant. 'Where are we going?' he asked.

'First we're looking up an old colleague of mine who's moved in just a few roads away. She knows all about the area.'

'Is she a teacher?'

'Sort of,' Bryant smiled. 'She's a witch.'

'What do you think of the new place?' asked Maggie Armitage with some pride. The doorway of the small nineteenth-century brick building on Prince of Wales Road was illuminated by a garish red neon sign that read: CHAPEL OF HOPE. 'I got it from the council when the old tenants moved out. Not enough hope in the vicinity, apparently. We've been shifted from our eyrie above the World's End pub in Camden Town.'

'I'm sorry to hear that,' said Bryant. 'Don't tell me the landlords disapproved of your pagan gatherings.'

'They turned a blind eye to our midnight madrigals, but drew the line at our attempts to summon Beelzebub. Now they're planning to build a mall on the site. Have you noticed that every London building eventually becomes a shoe shop? Camden is already the bad-footwear capital of the world. Old gods are no match for new money. But it's nice to be in a real chapel. I had a bash at deconsecrating the area of worship this morning, but I've run out of salt. Spiritual decommissioning isn't a straightforward process. The guidebooks all differ. Some people say you're supposed to return the sanctified altar sheath to a church. Others simply recommend a lick of paint. Wendy, our organist, says you can sing hymns backwards over it, but frankly she has enough trouble playing forwards. I think we've lessened the aura of sanctimonious monotheism, but we can't get rid of the damp. And the local drunks have a habit of weeing in the porch. Is that why Christian temples reek of rot, I wonder? Who's your friend?'

'This is David, honorary junior police officer for today. He lives nearby.'

'Come in.' Maggie took his hand. 'Are you a believer?'

'In what?' asked the boy.

'The darker arts, the lost spirituality of a doomed and wandering humankind.'

David stared at her as if she was mad.

'Do you at least try to keep an open mind?'

'Don't know.'

'That's the best we can expect these days, I suppose. Come through.' She led the way between the oaken pews of the dingy main hall to a small paper-strewn office at the rear. Silver chains, icons and baubles hung from her bosom like miniature wind-chimes. Maggie's eyes closed to crescents when she smiled, which she did often and broadly, revealing strong white teeth. Bedecked in bracelets, with tortoiseshell slides and two pairs of spectacles in her fiery red hair, the diminutive witch was as merry as a Christmas tree.

'What's that extraordinary odour?' asked Bryant, sniffing the air.

'My new herbal incense. Can you smell lavender?'

'No, it's more like burning ants.'

'Oh, *that.* Yes, something's living in the rafters. I've put down poison, but I think it's eating through the wood. If only Crippen hadn't disappeared during the move.'

'How strange. I just found a cat called Crippen. At least, that's what I named it.'

'Small, black and white, male? Piece missing from the left ear? A bit squiffy-eyed?'

'Exactly so.' Bryant was delighted.

'Benign fate! You've found my familiar. That means his aura is intact.'

'Perhaps, but his toilet training leaves much to be desired. I'll bring him round later.'

Maggie handed out some brochures. 'We're on a membership drive. If you know anyone who's interested in the occult and can handle a hod, we need some strong hands to help us restore the place.' A huge bearded man suddenly lurched into the doorway. 'I was just making tea for an old friend of yours.'

'Arthur, dear fellow! How delightfully efficacious!' Raymond Kirkpatrick, English-language professor, gripped Bryant's hand and pumped it hard. Tall and stooped, he appeared at first to be covered in a light shower of grey dust, and on closer inspection, was. 'I'm helping Margaret clear out her reliquary. I thought we might find something of epistolary antiquarian value, but so far all I've found is several dozen copies of *Razzle*, presumably tucked away by the choirboys.'

'Professor Kirkpatrick is one of England's leading experts in semantics and cryptography,' Bryant explained to the dumbfounded boy. 'He likes words.' He decided not to describe the bizarre circumstances that had led Kirkpatrick to be dishonourably discharged from the Met. The professor had once dated a six-foot Zimbabwean girl, who had, to his shame and horror, turned out to be fifteen, false documents having been provided by her parents in an effort to marry her off. The Home Office had branded him a paedophile and arranged his expulsion, and, although the subsequent investigation had exonerated him of everything but poor judgement, Kirkpatrick had become an unemployable outcast. Every time the PCU used him, Bryant logged Kirkpatrick's invoice under an assumed name. He hated seeing a good mind go to waste.

'Mr Bryant usually brings me his palaeographic conundrums for reinterpretation,' Kirkpatrick explained, 'although, alas, I fear his recent reluctance to employ my services suggests that the age of the erudite criminal has passed along with the locked-room mystery, clean public toilets and a quality postal service.'

'I think we have some of the information you're after,' said Maggie, pouring ginger tea for everyone as Bryant snatched a recruitment brochure away from David. 'John told me about the man who died in Balaklava Street, and it doesn't come as a surprise.'

'Oh, really? Why?'

'Because it appears to be a hot spot of psychic activity. There have always been strange stories surrounding the area.'

'What kind of stories?'

'It's long been considered unhealthy to live there because of bad humours rising from the ground. In the fifties, it suffered from sudden mists and smogs that sprang up from the drains and vanished just as quickly. It's in a bit of a dip, you see. A vale. Some are still marked in London, like Maida Vale. Others have been forgotten, like the one in Kentish Town. It's a very old area. Camden was a late arrival in the neighbourhood, 1791 to be exact, and yet they managed to come up with plenty of local legends, ghosts, witches and murderers. You can imagine how many more myths Kentish Town built up in the preceding centuries.'

'The name is derived from *Ken-Ditch*,' Kirkpatrick pointed out, 'meaning the bed of a waterway.'

'The town, combined under its original alias with St Pancras, has been here for well over a thousand years,' Maggie pointed out. 'An entire millennium of harmful atmosphere. Don't forget that it grew up around a rushing river. The water turned mill-blades and provided the lifeblood for its residents. A great many ancient documents refer to the "calm clacking of the mills". Now all we hear is the wail of police sirens. And the river has long been sealed underground.'

'This lad's father works for the water board. He knows a fair bit about it,' said Bryant. 'Part of the Fleet, yes?'

'From the Saxon *fleete* or *fleot*, a flood, or the Anglo-Saxon *fleotan*, to float,' Kirkpatrick intoned.

'It runs down to the Regent's Canal, but nobody's sure exactly where it flows,' added Maggie. 'There's a run-off around here called Fog's Well, for obvious reasons. Long gone now.'

'Did you have any luck with my information?' asked Bryant.

'Your brief was a bit vague.' She checked her notes. 'Around 1840, the land was sold off in neat little plots that followed the rivers and meadow boundaries. Forty years later the plans had changed, with more roads and houses being squeezed on to the original layout. According to my contact at Camden Council, in the 1960s the local authority drew up a new design for the area, a concrete wasteland of tower blocks. Thankfully, it never came to fruition.' She peered over her reading glasses. 'Honestly, we spend so much time attempting to improve ourselves, taking self-help courses, going to the gym, trying to develop more meaningful relationships with one another, and yet we dismiss the other associations we need to support our fragile well-being.'

'What do you mean?'

'Everyone interacts with their location, Arthur. Where we live helps set the level of our happiness and comfort. The English have strongly developed psychological relationships with the landscape. They travelled so little that accents changed from one street to the next. There's a famous *Punch* cartoon showing two locals throwing a brick at a stranger; that's the nineteenth-century English for you—antipathy to outsiders. These days, our relationships with views, buildings, places, objects and strangers are virtually ignored. As a child, you probably had a place that made you happy—nothing special, a small corner of sun-lit grass where you kicked a ball or read a comic. As an adult, you search for an equivalent to that spot. Can you ever truly find it again?'

'I like to take my kite on Parliament Hill,' said David. 'You can feel the wind going round you.'

'There you are.' Maggie ruffled the boy's hair. 'When bureaucrats radically transform an area they remove its markers, damaging scale and ignoring the natural historical landscape. Such an area will quickly become a "no-go" zone, unsafe and disliked by everyone, because we no longer have ways of forming attachments to such a place. When the rivers were covered, we lost something of ourselves. Dreams of lakes and rivers are dreams of calm. No wonder lost rivers hold such mystique. We need to believe that they are still beneath us somewhere, the distant conduits of a forgotten inner peace.'

'She's been getting like this a lot lately,' Kirkpatrick warned. 'Ever since she started her hormone-replacement pills. The rivers are still there, you silly woman, they just built storm drains over the original tunnels. The idea was that the lids could be removed in times of flooding, and water drawn off to prevent it from invading the basements of local houses. I imagine they're all asphalted over now.'

'No,' said David. 'I know where there's one. You can still get the lid off.'

'Would you like to show me?' asked Bryant.

'It's a secret.'

'May I remind you that you're working for the police now?' warned Bryant. The boy's mobile rang. 'It's my mother,' he warned.

'Give her to me.' Bryant waggled his fingers and took the call. 'He's absolutely fine, Mrs Wilton, thoroughly enjoying himself. No, of course not.' He placed his hand over the phone. 'You're not wet, are you?' Then back to the phone; 'No, dry as a bone, I'll have him home in just a few minutes.' He cut her off before she could continue. 'Now, David, let's go and have a look at your storm drain.'

'We're coming with you.' Maggie told him 'Don't tell us we're not allowed.' She knew what Bryant was like. If they were going to poke around sewers, someone needed to keep an eye on them.

The four finished their tea and set off. 'You don't need a dowsing rod to find tell-tale signs of the river's route,' said Maggie. 'Remember how dry it was before this rain started? All the pavement weeds died, but look along here.' She pointed to a ragged row of spindly plants pushing up through the paving stones beside the main road. 'Epiphytes, these are weeds that grow on other plants and live on trapped rainwater. But there wasn't any accumulated water until a few days ago, and where are the plants they grow on? Give me a hand, David, would you?'

Stopping beside a ditch dug out for the Electricity Board, they managed to pull up a loose paving stone.

'Look at that.' The underside of the slab was covered in dark, slippery moss. 'It's a very primitive plant form that feeds on moisture. Something under the street didn't dry out during the drought. All we have to do is follow the weeds. We have a guide to the river right here at our feet. They say you can plot the course of the London rivers by following the paths of diseases, too. Makes sense, when you think about it. Respiratory troubles are brought on by damp air. You get plenty of that around sewers. Ghost sightings, too. There are more of them near water because of high infant mortality, early deaths and drownings.'

'*Sorbus Aucuparia,*' said Kirkpatrick, pointing to the trees that guarded the entrance to the alleyway behind Balaklava Street. 'One usually finds *Tilia Platyphyllos* or *Platanus Hispanica*. But those are a pair of Rowans.'

'Good London trees,' Maggie agreed. 'They are able to withstand high levels of pollution and lousy soil, and birds love their berries. They're strongly associated with witchcraft, of course. Very unlucky to cut one down. There are terrible stories . . .'

'Don't fill the boy's head with—' began Kirkpatrick.

'There's one ghost story in particular that centres on your street,' she interrupted. 'A real ghost story that happened right where you live now.' Maggie's natural flair for the dramatic ensured that the boy's attention was held. 'This would have been long before you were born, in the early 1950s. It seems there was a penniless young man, a student, who lived in a flat somewhere around here. He was in love with a local girl who worked in a bakery behind the high street. Although neither of them had much money, they were very much in love and were soon engaged to be married. The boy was a talented watercolour artist, and told her they would marry as soon as he could sell some pictures. But he painted subjects that were too morbid. No one wanted to buy drawings of ghouls and graveyards. So he was forced to delay his wedding. The third time he did so, his girlfriend gave up on him and married someone else. The student's heart was broken. It was said that he went down to the canal, filled his pockets with rocks and sank into the mud. But his body was never found.

'Some time later, the people in your street started seeing him whenever it rained. He would materialize through the downpour, and walk with his dripping mud-covered head bowed low, mourning his lost love. This continued for some years, until the flood of 1959, when the underground river burst from its tunnel and swamped the street. What do you think happened?'

David shook his head, mesmerized.

'The boy's corpse surfaced through the water. It had been washed up from the canal due to the unusual currents caused by the terrible winter storms. Once his body was properly laid to rest, his ghost was at peace, and it was never seen again.'

'I'm not sure you should be telling the boy this sort of thing,' said Kirkpatrick in some alarm.

'Perhaps we could get back to facts.' Bryant rapped his walking stick on the pavement irritably. 'Where's this drain of yours, lad?'

David stopped in the middle of the alley and kicked at the mud with the heel of his boot. 'It's around here. The rain's washed a lot of earth loose.'

Bryant peered out from under his hat to get his bearings. They were standing at the back of Kallie's garden wall. David was crouching beside an oblong indented iron plate. 'I don't know how it opens.'

'I do,' said Bryant. 'It needs a special instrument, shaped like a T, with a hook at one end.' He thought back to Meera's report about the disappearance of Tate. She had assured him that the tramp had too much difficulty walking to have run the length of the overgrown ginnel. He was small enough to hide inside a bush. Suppose he had hidden inside the drain until the coast was clear? It would mean that the device he'd used to open it must be hidden somewhere in the alley.

The misted rain, drifting in the half-light of the afternoon, obscured the interiors of the brambles that bordered the rear gardens. He pulled out his pocket torch and shone it around their feet. 'David, I wonder if you might reach in there for me and take out that metal rod.'

The boy crouched low and pulled the rusted shaft free. Inserting it into the lid of the drain was a simple matter. One hard push levered the top off. Bryant's torch illuminated a larger hole within, at least four feet square, accessible by an iron-rung ladder set into the wall. One side appeared to lead off to a tunnel.

'I can get down there,' said David. 'Easy.'

'I don't think that's a good idea,' Maggie warned. 'I'm getting uncomfortable vibrations.'

'What does that *mean*, exactly?' asked Kirkpatrick. 'You get vibrations every time a bus goes past.'

Maggie cocked her head on one side and thought for a moment. Rainwater ran in rivulets down her plastic hood. 'I sense nothing evil, just sadness and loss. A great melancholy.'

'It's hardly surprising,' Bryant pointed out. 'Some poor homeless old man having to hide in a drain every time someone spots him in their garden. Can you feel anything else, Margaret?'

Maggie placed her hands on her forehead and began to hum gently.

'Oh, don't encourage her,' Kirkpatrick complained. 'She's going for an Oscar. There must be so many violent vibrations emanating from the London streets, I don't know how she manages to get through the day without imploding.'

When they stopped arguing and looked around, they realized that the boy had gone.

'David!' called Bryant, panicked. 'Where are you?'

'It's all right—I'm down here.'

'Good God, get back up here at once! Your parents will crucify me.' He shone his torch into the hole.

'He's been down here, all right,' the boy called up. 'There's a sort of nest made out of old newspapers, and empty KFC boxes. It's very smelly.'

'Come on out before you catch something,' called Bryant, unable to climb down and follow him.

'Wait, chuck me down your torch.'

It was too late to repair the damage now; the boy was already down there. 'At least give me your other hand so I can hold on to you.' Bryant guiltily passed him the light.

'It looks like the tunnel goes all the way to the end of the street,' David called back. 'And there's another one branching off. I'm going to take a look.'

'You are most certainly not,' snapped Bryant,

struggling down to his knees. 'Come back up at once. This investigation is at an end.'

David's head and shoulders suddenly appeared in the drain. He was smeared with green mud, and highly excited. 'It's fantastic! You can go all the way along, but it looks like there's an iron grille at the end.' Maggie and the professor hitched him under the arms and dragged him up. David grinned at them, suddenly voluble. 'Is this how you normally solve crimes? I thought it was all about asking people for alibis, like on telly, not going down tunnels. I thought you just shouted at suspects in little rooms, but this is great. Can I come out with you again tomorrow?'

'One word about this to your mum and I will put you in a little room and shout at you,' warned Bryant. 'Let's get you cleaned up back at the chapel while I tell Mrs Wilton you're on your way home.'

'I wanted to read you something,' said Maggie, once they were seated in the oak pews of the Chapel of Hope, waiting for David to scrub himself clean. She pulled open a heavy leather-bound book. 'Listen to this: "The word 'Flete' also refers to a special limited place, coined thus by the Templars, who owned land on the Flete at Castle Baynard." The Baynard Castle pub is still there on the spot. The area around it is a sacred place. In 1676, during the widening of the Fleet Ditch, they dug up fifteen feet of rubbish deposited by the residents of Roman London. Silver, copper and brass coins, two brass Lares, one Ceres, one Bacchus, daggers, seals, medals, crosses, busts of gods and a great number of hunting knives, all the same size and shape. It's always been a sacred site, don't you see? For over a thousand years, it was where worshippers went to make offerings to pagan gods.'

'You're talking about some form of sacrifice,' said Bryant, lowering his voice as the boy came back.

'That's right. I'm wondering if they might have practised human sacrifice here.'

'But what bearing could that possibly have on modern-day events?'

Maggie's smile suggested she knew more than she would ever tell. 'Old religions never completely die out, Arthur. They find new ways to stay alive. And sometimes their participants have unwitting parts to play.'

29

MURDERERS

'What on earth were you thinking of?' said John May. 'He's only ten years old, for Heaven's sake.'

'Oh, come on, John, he was thoroughly enjoying himself. Look at the things we used to get up to as kids. It did the boy good to get away from his Playstation for a while. He hardly speaks to his parents.'

'You told his mother you'd be ten minutes, not hours. She's been screaming at us all morning. It's not so much that you took a child with you and allowed him access to a dangerous place—although God knows what would have happened if there had been a flash flood, those drains can fill up in seconds and he could have been swept away—but that you took Kirkpatrick with you.'

'I don't understand,' said Bryant, genuinely puzzled.

'He's registered as a sex offender, Arthur! You took him for a stroll with a child on police duty—are you out of your mind?'

Bryant was genuinely shocked; the thought hadn't even crossed his mind. 'Kirkpatrick had the misfortune to be duped into near-marriage with an under-age girl. The case was thrown out of court. I can't help it if they kept his details on file. I happened to bump into him, and he tagged along with us. Maggie was there too.'

'Oh good, so you had a witch with you as well.' May rubbed his hands across his eyes. He had always known that looking after his partner was a full-time job.

'I made sure I had his mother's permission,' said Bryant plaintively. 'I got the boy home safely.'

'All right, but suppose Raymond had found out? We'd all have been for the bloody high jump.'

'I take your point. I'll be more careful next time.'

'There won't be a next time, Arthur. What will it take to make you act in a responsible manner?'

'Reincarnation?' Bryant noticed the workmen sitting in the corner brewing tea. 'What are they still doing here?'

'Something to do with the computer cables under the floor,' May explained. 'They cut through them with a rotary saw, and now they can't put the boards back down until a technician has repaired the damage.'

He leaned back in his chair and closed his eyes. The few detectives he knew outside the PCU thought he was mad, still working with this crazy old man. Sometimes Bryant's behaviour was positively Victorian. Thank God the investigation hadn't required someone to climb a chimney—he would have sent the boy up first. They could only pray that David Brewer Wilton didn't tell his parents the complete truth about his day, otherwise there would be hell to pay.

At least, he decided, they would be able to close the case by the weekend and start fresh on Monday. He had bent over backwards for Bryant, exploring every avenue and finding nothing, because there was clearly nothing more to find. Sometimes the circumstances surrounding those who died alone encouraged Bryant to hunt for an esoteric cause. Perhaps he felt a need to make their deaths mean something more. Perhaps he was thinking of his own eventual fate. Bryant's irascibility had prevented him from growing close to many people. He had no surviving relatives: Nathalie, his bride-to-be, the love of his life, had died long ago, and he had never been able to bring himself to marry. There weren't many who would miss him—besides, he had already had one funeral in the past year, and his mourners might be reluctant to turn out a second time.

May looked down into the wet street at Mornington Crescent, watching the slow ebb of traffic on the one-way system. At one level, the nature of dying had changed little since the War. Families still gathered at bedsides to say their farewells; few were truly prepared when the time came, but it seemed to him that too many people died alone. The relaxing moral strictures that had freed families could sometimes turn independence into profound and devastating loneliness. Were the young couples out there truly happy with their freedom, or did some part of them secretly long for the ordered lives of their grandparents? *Now you're thinking like an old man,* he told himself. *Offer to buy Arthur a pint and stop being so maudlin.* 'Come on, Arthur—you too, Janice,' he called out, 'we're going to the Pineapple.'

* * *

Kallie saw the three of them across the crowded bar: Bryant in his baggy scarf and squashed trilby, May erect and smartly suited, Longbright with her extraordinary movie-star hair, ledge-like bosom and heavy make-up.

She and Heather Allen had come over to meet Jake Avery for a drink, but he was already a quarter of an hour late. The producer was working on a new BBC sitcom, and had warned them that he might be held up if rehearsals overran.

'Those detectives are back again,' said Heather unenthusiastically. 'What do they expect to find around here?'

'They're locals. They're probably off duty.'

'That type never goes off duty. I don't like being watched all the time. They have no right to treat us like suspects.' Heather was prone to exaggeration when she was upset, and tonight she was as tense as a cat on a wire, chewing her nails and stubbing out half-smoked cigarettes.

'What's the matter?' asked Kallie. 'You're a bundle of nerves.'

'George came back this afternoon and picked a fight with me over the divorce settlement, before heading off to stay with his new girlfriend at the Lanesborough. Do you know how much that place is a night? He's never taken me there. I didn't get married for love, Kallie. I know it's a terrible thing to say, but I wanted security, and now he's pulled that rug from beneath me. What am I supposed to do, just go quietly?' She raised her head and looked around.

'Where the hell is Jake? Why do men think women will always wait for them?'

'The traffic's probably bad. A lot of roads are flooded.'

Heather would not be mollified. 'I'm not going to hang around for him.' She drained her tomato juice. 'I'll go to the gym and run for a while.' She swung her bag on to her shoulder. 'Tell those damned people to stop spying on us.'

Intrigued, Kallie went over to join the detectives.

'We meet again,' said May, 'and in rather more convivial circumstances.'

'Is this your local?'

'Not really, but I like the unusual mix of types you get in here.'

'As opposed to the unusual types you've been interviewing in our street.'

'Oh no, they're fairly usual. You remember Sergeant Longbright and my partner Mr Bryant?'

'Of course.' She shook their hands. 'Thanks for sending your officer round. Did she have any luck?'

'We know the hostels where Tate is registered,' explained Bryant. 'It's just a matter of waiting for him to turn up. We should be able to take him in shortly and have a word with him. I hope you won't be troubled again.'

'I don't think he meant any harm, but it was unnerving, being watched like that.'

'It's not nice for a young woman alone in a house. I mean, with your boyfriend being away.' May shot Bryant a look that silenced him.

'I don't mind being in an empty house,' Kallie admitted, 'but this rain is so depressing. I miss Paul, I wish he'd come home. He sends postcards from all over Europe—I just want him to get the travel bug out of his system and come back to me.' She hadn't meant to mention him, but realized she was with good people who were used to listening, and suddenly needed to talk. There was something so peculiarly old-fashioned and comforting about them, as though they belonged in the crepuscular sooty gloom of King's Cross and St Pancras, between the shunting yards and brown-painted pubs filled with bitter-sipping railwaymen. Sergeant Longbright resembled the photographs of Ava Gardner she had seen in old movie magazines, but was kind and approachable. Bryant was the key, of course, the one who held them together in lopsided camaraderie. You could go to them with a problem. Perhaps this was how all police once were.

'I'm sure he'll come back to you when he's ready,' said Longbright. 'Some men get a fire in them that has to be allowed to burn itself out.'

'We were just discussing forgotten murderers,' said Bryant, in a terrible attempt to change the subject. 'I suggested Tony Mancini, real name Cecil England, unjustly forgotten in my view, very big at the time, though.'

'The Brighton Trunk Mystery,' May explained, a little embarrassed.

'A good example of the dangers of jumping to conclusions,' Bryant forged on. 'His mistress, Violette, was a vaudeville artiste turned prostitute. He sent her body to his house in a trunk. The Crown suggested that he had beaten her to death with a hammer, but it was likely that she fractured her skull falling down the stairs under the influence of morphine. Found not guilty. Yet ten days earlier, another trunk had turned up at Brighton railway station containing a woman's severed torso: victim and murderer never identified. Were the cases connected? If the Peculiar Crimes Unit had existed then, would we have uncovered new evidence?' He gulped his beer, blue eyes glinting above hoppy brown bitter, just a little mad.

'The thirties were a rich time for sensational murder,' May explained. 'The level of moral snobbery was outrageous, but far worse in Victorian times, so I'd have to pick George Joseph Smith, the "Brides in the Bath" murderer. He was born in Bow in 1872—'

'Near me,' interjected Bryant. 'I was a Whitechapel boy.'

'—spent most of his childhood in a reformatory and emerged with that strange emptiness of the soul one still sees in disappointed youths. Proceeded to marry gullible women and steal their savings before deserting them—he ditched one in the National Gallery—then moved on to drowning them in a zinc tub, but his refusal to vary the method of execution led to suspicion and capture.'

'Personally, I always felt for Ruth Ellis,' said Longbright, stirring the lemon in her gin and French. 'If her affair with Blakely had occurred a few years later, neither of them would have acted as they did. If ever a woman was a victim of her time, it was Ellis. She thanked the judge for sentencing her to death, did you know that? Even the gallows seemed preferable to her miserable existence.'

'Oh yes, there have been some interesting deaths in London,' said Bryant with relish. 'Did you know that Peter Pan threw himself under a train at Sloane Square? Peter Llewelyn Davies had been adopted by J. M. Barrie, and was the model for Barrie's fairy-tale hero, but he got sick of fans asking him where Neverland was and chucked himself on to the live rail.'

'Is that true?'

'Absolutely.' Bryant crossed his heart with a finger.

'Aren't there any interesting modern murderers?' Kallie asked.

'Oh, a few,' sniffed Bryant, 'but nothing to write home about. We've handled most of the decent cases. Motivation has changed, of course. Victims still become trapped in the same debilitating circumstances, but now there's so much money swilling around that there are other ways to solve your problems. Get a divorce, have an abortion, take some pills—there's less of a stigma.'

'I suppose it's easier to solve a crime since the discovery of DNA.'

'New technologies will never explain the actions of desperate people,' said Bryant. 'They were using fingerprints to catch murderers in twelfth-century China.'

'How did you become so interested in crime?'

'My grandfather was one of the first constables on the scene when Martha Tabram died,' Bryant explained. 'The previous summer had been the hottest on record. The streets were alive with rats. The following August, all hell broke loose. He used to frighten the life out of us with the story. Tabram was stabbed thirty-nine times. Her body was discovered in George Yard, off Whitechapel High Street. These days she's usually discounted, you see. Mary Ann Nichols is the first universally accepted victim in the canonical order, but the old man didn't believe that. Inspector Abberline himself thought there were six murders. Others in the force reckoned there were as many as nine. Only five are undisputed. Even back then, there were so many Jack the Ripper theories that the case became lost in them. The few surviving files that had been kept in some order by the Met weren't opened until 1976, long after my grandfather died, but he never stopped trying to understand it, and I suppose his curiosity was passed on to me.'

'I can't believe I've known you all these years,' said May with no little indignation, 'and you've never told me that.'

'There are a lot of things you don't know about me,' said Bryant annoyingly. 'Come on, whose round is it?'

They sat in the corner, a group of four at a small circular table with their drinks neatly arranged before them, and talked late into the evening.

30

LETHAL WATERS

Bryant had not walked the length of Hatton Garden in many years. He was pleasantly surprised to find the area still sheltered from the rain by broad-leafed lime trees, resistant hybrids that could withstand destruction by aphids and exhaust fumes. It felt like a street upon which you could loiter and have an interesting conversation. Sheltered by shop canopies, the jewellers, gold and diamond merchants stood proprietorially in their doorways, calling to each other across the street. The windows were filled with loops of gold, spotlit treasure chests of gleaming bullion.

Checking the note in his hand, Bryant searched for street numbers, hoping that Maggie had given him the right address. A scuffed brass plaque on a recessed door read: *The London River Society*.

'Seven to the north, seven to the south,' said a small, attractive Chinese girl, stepping ahead of him to fit her key into the lock and push back the front door. He hadn't heard her approach.

'I beg your pardon?'

'Rivers. Isn't that what you want to know? It's what people *always* want to know, how many major lost rivers there are in London. Don't ask me why, but that's their first question. The easy answer is fourteen—the truth's more complicated. Isn't it always? I'm Rachel Ling. Mrs Huxley told me to expect you, Mr Bryant. Would you like to come in?' She flicked the lights on as she walked through. 'Sorry it's so cold, the central heating hasn't come on yet.'

Bryant hadn't expected to find himself inside a Chinese restaurant. He was surrounded by red silk lanterns, curling dragons stamped from gold plastic, tall-backed ebony chairs set at circular tables.

'I know what you're going to say,' warned Rachel. 'Everyone says the same thing. But we have to find a way to pay the bills. It would be better to have a Jewish restaurant in this area, but my mother's better with noodles than *matzoh* balls, so it's Jewish-Chinese. We do a very good kosher pressed duck. Please, take a seat.' She sat at one of the large circular tables, interlocking her hands to reveal red lacquered nails that complimented the décor. 'Any friend of Dorothy Huxley is a friend of the society. What do you want to know?'

'I'm intrigued,' Bryant admitted. 'What do you do here?'

'We provide study aids and run an educational website about geography, religion and mythology. We're all former teachers who opted out of the traditional education system. We recommend Dorothy's library as a valuable reference resource. Allow me to show you.' She rose and crossed over to a pair of tall lacquered doors, which she rolled back, revealing a large windowless room filled with computers.

'Very impressive.'

'Hardly,' said Rachel. 'It's all obsolete equipment. City firms donate their outmoded computers because they have no resale value. Still, they're fine for our purposes.' She ran her fingers across a keyboard and illuminated the homepage of the society's website, printed over an aerial photograph of the Thames.

'Dorothy said you're researching a theory that five of London's lost rivers correspond to the five mythical Roman rivers,' said Bryant.

'Did she?' Rachel smiled. 'Well, we try not to theorize on our postings. We do, after all, receive grant support from the Ministry of Education, even though it's a minuscule amount, and to meet the funding conditions we're required to be impartial. But there would be no interest without a certain amount of speculation.'

'I like your bracelet.' Bryant pointed to the Osiris panel hanging from Rachel's wrist.

'Thank you. It's a copy of a Victorian design often worn by mud larks. The regeneration symbol is meant to prove lucky when you're searching the river shores.'

'Is it, indeed? That's useful to know.' *So Ubeda is superstitious. What else does he believe?* Bryant wondered.

'How can I help you?'

'Do you get people looking for particular tributaries?'

'Not really. Very few stretches are accessible, and actually it's illegal to do so now under the Prevention of Terrorism Act, because the tunnels pass beneath sensitive property, so you'd be trespassing. Also, there's the risk of disease.'

'I'm particularly interested in the Fleet.'

'Everyone is,' smiled Rachel. 'It's the granddaddy of underground rivers. Once it was crystal clear, but eventually it came to be associated with death, regularly filling with the corpses of animals and babies, not to mention the odd drunk. It's a poet's river; Pope used it as a location for *The Dunciad*.' A light shone in her eyes as she recited the lines from memory: ' "To where Fleet-Ditch with disemboguing streams/ Rolls the large tribute of dead dogs to Thames". And Swift wrote: "Filths of all hues and odours seem to tell/ What street they sail'd from by their sight and smell". Not the most attractive image of London Town, is it?'

'Interesting enough to write about,' said Bryant. *Or be murdered above,* he thought.

'It was certainly that. One pub backing on to the Fleet, the Red Lion, was the hide-out of Dick Turpin. Another, the Rose Tavern, was frequented by Falstaff. The river was in a ravine crossed with bridges, none more beautiful or extravagantly Venetian than Wren's Fleet Bridge, situated at its mouth.'

'Can you think of any mythical connections?' asked Bryant.

Rachel gave the idea her attention, moving from screen to screen. 'I suppose of all London's lost rivers, the Fleet is most associated with evil. Prostitutes and cut-throats populated its length. Anyone who fell into the filth usually suffocated. In 1862 so much gas collected that the hot weather actually caused the river to blow up. It blasted a hole in the road and knocked down a couple of houses. So I suppose if we were matching them up with the Roman rivers of the Underworld, the Fleet should really correspond to Phlegethon, the river of fire—but perhaps it would be better associated with the Styx. Acheron, the river of woe, would fit the Tyburn, which led to a place of death, the gallows of Tyburn Tree. Victorian passengers could float under Buckingham Palace on the

Tyburn. They sang "God Save the Queen" as they passed beneath.'

Bryant wondered if he had perhaps made a mistake assuming that Jackson Ubeda was pursuing the rivers' mythical connections. One last thought struck him. 'Were any of the lost rivers particularly associated with the Romans?'

'That would have to be the Walbrook. It was the first river to become lost. It ran through the old centre of London, from Old Street and Moorfields to Cannon Street. We know that the Romans used it to sail to a Temple of Mithras, and regarded it as a sacred river. The trouble is, no one really knows where the Walbrook was, because the entire area was wet and marshy, and the riverbanks were poorly defined.'

'What kind of people hit your website?' asked Bryant, not daring to touch any of the keyboards.

'Students, mostly—but anyone with an interest in London history. A few nutters hoping to find treasure trove.'

Bryant's ears pricked up. 'What would they be looking for?'

'Oh, the usual—Roman coins, chains, pottery. To be fair, quite a bit is still uncovered by amateurs from time to time, mostly builders working on the sites of new office blocks. There was a big discovery just a few months ago.'

'Do you have any details?'

Rachel typed in a reference and hit *Return*. A viciously bright news-site unfurled on the screen before her. 'Here you go. Roman chain recovered from a building site near Monument with a large number of its links intact—a very unusual find.'

'Why so?'

'Not many contractors can dig far down in the city because it's a maze of tunnels, pipes and cables. Many new buildings are constructed on steel stilts to avoid the problem of digging out deep foundations. This site was lucky in that they found artefacts rather than ancient architecture.'

'Why is that lucky?'

'If you find building remains, you've got trouble on your hands, because construction keeps to a schedule, and usually you're granted a matter of days to log your discovery before it gets filled in again.'

'That's barbaric.'

'But where do you stop? In this city, the more you dig, the more you find.' She let Bryant read the article. 'The Victorians were keen on loading the lost rivers with mythological Roman connections. Some earl formed a society to navigate a path through the remains of the Fleet, looking for the Vessel of All Counted Sorrows.'

'What was that?'

'It was an Egyptian vessel supposedly constructed to contain all the woes, pains and miseries of the human race. The idea exists in virtually every religion and pagan creed, but takes on particular relevance in Roman mythology because most rivers of the Underworld burned through anything that was placed in them, and this vessel was therefore the only object that could survive such lethal waters. A sort of Pandora's box that protected London as long as it remained underneath the city.'

'Do you think it could have been an actual object? Perhaps a piece of pottery, something like that?'

'Exactly so, Mr Bryant. I imagine it would have

been a sealed clay dish of some kind, symbolically filled, and carved accordingly.'

'What would they have done with it?'

'What they always did.' Rachel smiled. 'Human sacrifice—probably a child, an innocent; casting of gifts on the waters, including the main offering, followed by a long boring ceremony, everyone goes home afterwards and gets drunk.'

'Interesting. Tell me, have you come across a man called Jackson Ubeda?' Bryant dug out the photograph May had given him.

'How funny—that's the guy who came to see us. Said he was related to the earl who founded the society. We let him work out some hypothetical routes on the computer simulation. I think he's still registered with us.' She tapped at the keyboard and ran a match through the site's database. 'Yes, he's a subscriber.'

'Are there any groups or individuals who make it their business to go down into the rivers?'

'Only the Thames Water sewer gangs, but they're checking for leaks and blockages, not historical artefacts. The rivers and the sewers are now interconnected, so it's unsafe to venture in without supervision because of flash floods. Plus there's a series of locked safety grilles that prevent access from one part to another, and many channels are dead ends.'

'Suppose I wanted to get inside one of these tunnels and investigate for myself. What would I do?'

'Find yourself an expert, pay him a lot of money and hope the law doesn't catch you,' said Rachel.

Funny, thought Bryant. *That's exactly how Gareth Greenwood was employed.*

31

THE RIVER FINDS A WAY

The Holmes Road Working Men's Hostel had once been a small Victorian sub-post-office, a fussy urban cottage of ginger brick and curling cream lintels, constructed on a human scale, that welcomed all. Now a pair of standard-issue council doors had been fitted over the front entrance, a wheelchair ramp had replaced the steps, and the ground-floor windows had been mesh-wired. Inside, eye-scorching fluorescent strips and lack of curtains lent the building an almost unbearable air of melancholic dislocation. The borough's approach to rethinking the usage of such buildings rarely extended beyond slapping another coat of paint over frayed interiors.

Arthur Bryant was admitted to a small bare holding bay, and waited while the receptionist checked the register behind a wall of scratched plexiglass.

'If you've come about admittance for longer than a single night, you'll need a referral from your doctor,' she said briskly.

'I'm not a rough sleeper, I'm a Detective Inspector,' Bryant complained. The receptionist eyed his threadbare overcoat disbelievingly. With a sigh of annoyance, Bryant pulled out his ID and slapped it on the window. 'I'm looking for someone called Tate.'

'You're in luck,' she declared, in a booming, institutional timbre that probably proved useful when dealing with the inebriated, but was guaranteed to annoy everyone else. She was the type born for a certain kind of council employment: proprietorial, frozen, rule-bound and battle-scarred, but on some basic level decent enough to care. She flicked the book shut and checked her key board. 'He's back in. Tate usually prefers to sleep rough. He stays out in all weathers. Says rooms make him claustrophobic.'

After examining the accommodation, Bryant could see why. Thin MDF partitions had carved the old sorting rooms into quarters, then eighths. Some dividers segmented windows and parts of the blue and white corridor. Each room was large enough for a single bed and a tiny plywood table. A communal dining room reeked of boiled stews and reheated gravy. There were notices about needles and fires and depression and missing persons, and, oddly, one about ballroom dancing.

'How long has he been with you?' Bryant asked.

'I was only transferred here from Housing six weeks ago,' explained the receptionist. 'He doesn't have much documentation beyond his health record, the usual alcohol-related pulmonary problems. He's had pneumonia a couple of times. The next time will be his last. Admitted without any paperwork— nothing unusual about that, of course—but he does seem local to the borough. Everyone calls him Tate, although it's not his real name. He hoards tins of golden syrup. He's too far gone to remember how he might have been christened.'

'How old is he?'

'Probably in his late fifties. It's hard to tell when they've lived rough for so long.'

'Can I see him?'

'You won't get anything out of him. He doesn't like to talk.' The receptionist buzzed Bryant in and led him to the end of the first-floor corridor. She knocked briskly on the door and slipped her key into the lock before there was an answer. Tate was sitting on the edge of his bed, hands folded in his lap, staring through the condensation-smeared window. 'I'll leave you two alone,' she said, then, raising her voice, added, 'Lunch in ten minutes, Mr Tate.'

Bryant waited until her footsteps had been folded away by the swing-doors, then stood watching the street from the window. The room's occupant had not acknowledged his presence.

'I could watch a London street all day,' Bryant remarked. 'So many different types of people. Much more going on than in the old days.'

'And you think that's a good thing, do you?' said the man on the bed. The voice was surprisingly cultured, but had perhaps lost its edge of late.

'No, just different. More strangers now, coming and going. I used to know my neighbours.'

'You're the copper.' Tate turned and studied him. 'Are you going to keep that coat?'

'This happens to be an old favourite,' said Bryant, pulling the lapels closer.

'I can see that. Am I under arrest?'

'Well, we don't like you sneaking into people's

gardens and watching them, because you upset them, but no, you're not under arrest. What were you doing?'

'Praying. But you have to be careful. Sudden prayers make God jump.' Tate smiled. He had no teeth at all—an unusual sight these days. 'Why are you here?'

'I suppose I wanted to find out a bit about you. My name's Arthur Bryant. I was told you don't talk.'

'I don't talk to her.' He jerked a dirty thumb at the wall.

'Why not?'

'She has nothing to say. It's all square meals and personal hygiene. Not an ounce of poetry in her soul that hasn't been scrubbed away with carbolic.'

'You must have been in this neighbourhood a long time. Everyone seems to know you.'

'You won't catch me out like that. I don't have to answer questions.'

'Oh, it's not really questions, just conversation. I'm interested. Tell me, why would you sleep in the drain, when you have a nice warm bed here?'

'It's safer.'

'Is someone giving you trouble?'

'No, not yet.'

'But you think they will?'

No answer. Tate turned back to the window.

'Well, the weather's changed. The tunnels are flooding. You can't stay down there through the winter.'

'The water will always find a way to go wherever it wants. It can go around me.'

'But it won't.'

'Oh yes, it will.'

'How?'

'I can make it.'

'I see.'

'Why are you here?'

'I told you, I've been hearing things about the area that interest me.' Bryant sat on the bed beside his host. 'These houses, the residents leave a few marks to show they were there, then move on. It's funny when you think about it.'

'They were built for the families of the men who built the railways. Little terraced boxes for the workers.'

'So I understand.'

'That's why there's no decoration, see. No mouldings. No panels or friezes. Workers don't need to see beauty.'

'Why not?'

'Gives them ideas above their station. They won't miss what they've never had.'

As he spoke, Tate lost his nondescript appearance and attitude. For a moment, Bryant was afforded a glimpse of the man inside. He wondered if Tate had once been a teacher. 'Who are you?' he asked gently.

'Poor and old is a terrible combination.' Tate shook his head, barely hearing. 'You become so unimportant. Your past achievements are forgotten. No one believes you. Your life is trodden on by strangers. You've nothing to show anyone who you were.'

'Then tell me.'

Tate glanced back at the window. This time, Bryant saw nervousness in his eyes. 'I'm no one. Let's wash it all away, wash the past away until there are only clean new things left.'

Bryant decided to try another tack. 'You must know the streets around here very well.'

'I know the streets, the houses, and under the streets.'

'There seem to be lots of ghost stories.'

'Because of the river,' Tate agreed. 'Is it any wonder? The roads were laid over the *Cloaca Maxima*, the Fleet sewer, a highway of corpses. Plague and pestilence. On its way to the witch of Camden Town, it flooded and rotted the timbers of the houses.'

'You mean Mother Red Cap.' Bryant remembered the pub of the same name that stood on the site of the infamous witch's house, now pointlessly renamed and spoiled. It had been the reason why Maggie Armitage had based her office, the Coven of St James the Elder, on its first floor.

Tate's voice grew fainter. '1809—the snow was thick, and suddenly thawed in bright sunshine. The torrent of the Fleet was forced between the river's arches, gaining great speed until it burst into the houses of the poor and drowned them. It always drowned the poor.' He rubbed his chin, thinking. 'I had a book on it once. I haven't got it any more. They've no books here, just magazines about football and telly. I miss the books. I've just my own special ones, but they're not for reading. I've nothing to read.'

'Look, if I could get you some books, would you talk to me again?'

For a moment Tate seemed pleased by the prospect. Then his eyes clouded. 'Too late to talk. Look, my useless hands.' He raised trembling red fingers. The thumb of his right hand had been broken, and the bone had knitted poorly.

'I'll bring some books anyway,' said Bryant, rising.

'Please, stay here at the hostel for a few days, so I can find you.'

Tate returned his gaze to the window. 'I can't leave anyway. The rain's not going to stop until the river finds a path again,' he warned. 'Then it will all be too late.'

32

BREATHLESS

At half past one in the morning, Camden Town was almost as busy as it had been that afternoon. Many offices around the lock ran a twenty-four-hour day, light-industrial units refitted with technology, occupied by sound engineers, TV-camera operators, studio personnel, website designers, artists, writers, traffickers using so much electronic equipment that the town was a hotspot on the grid, an area that never cooled down or turned off. Factor in the clubs, bars, pubs, restaurants and all-night stores, the crawling traffic, the trucks blasting trash from the gutters, the teens looking to buy drugs and the tourists just looking, and you had streets that no amount of rain could clear. No witches ruled here now, just neo-goths and charity-muggers, no fishermen beside rushing brooks, just dealers selling grass and pills from the sides of their mouths.

But to step from the gaudy ribbon of the road into the backstreets was to shed a hundred years, among willows fringing wrought-iron gates, dim lights tracing draped windows, angled gables and broken tiles, crooked bollards, empty pavements. The roads were filled with parked vehicles, but otherwise had not changed; they still twisted in unreliable curvature, encouraging the lost to venture just a little further. The speed humps and one-way systems added a new layer of trickery. Nascent lanes led nowhere, amputated stumps of cobbled street were sealed off by railways, canals and housing developments, dead churches and wet green gardens remained in forgotten tranches of land.

Aaron cut a diagonal path across the maze of backstreets. He had been born here, and would have known the way blindfold, guided by the distant thrum of arterial roads. As he slipped through alleys toward Balaklava Street, he thought guiltily about his situation. He knew that what he was doing was wrong, but felt powerless to end what he had begun. He had tried to think of ways of stopping, but now it was too late, and whichever course of action he chose would hurt someone he cared for.

As he passed between high walls topped with broken bottles, it started to rain again. The hottest summer on record had produced a season of statistic-shattering storms. Thunder tumbled in a distant ragnarok of temper as he approached the house. The doused lights suggested that Jake had given up waiting for him and had gone to bed. The sound of his key in the lock was hidden by fresh falls of rain. He ascended the stairs in darkness, shedding his clothes on the landing. The bedroom was silent. At least he had delayed an argument until the morning.

Aaron carefully folded back his side of the duvet and slid into bed. Jake was on the far side, a cold shoulder turned against him. The window shone rivulets of rain on to the walls, as if the room was

crying. Aaron settled against the pillow, listening. He
thought back over the events of the evening, feeling
ashamed of himself. Shifting closer, he pressed his
hand against the small of his partner's back, but there
was no response.

Disturbed by the shifting weight on the mattress,
Jake's right hand thudded against the side of the bed
and his head tipped to face Aaron. Even in the dark,
Aaron could see that there was something wrong
with Jake's face. It seemed to reflect the light from the
streetlamp, as though it was moulded from slick plastic rather than made of flesh.

Aaron leapt back and groped for the light switch.
Jake stared up at him from the bed, his mouth
stretched in a shiny concave ellipse, his hair plastered
to his head as if he had been swimming. As Aaron finally realized what he was seeing, he screamed long
and loud.

Bryant sat on the side of his tall brass bedstead, his
feet swinging above the floor like a child's. Yawning,
he scratched his unruly tonsure back into place as he
listened.

'No, of course I'm glad he called you first. It'll stop
the Met teams from taping off the entire street and
posing in their paper monkey suits. You know what
they're like, one whiff of this and they'll be phoning
in live interviews and getting their pictures in the
Mirror.'

'We need to play this by the book,' warned May.
'It'll go high profile now, and we'll be able to reopen
Ruth Singh's file whether there's a connection or not.
Everyone will be watching us. We can't afford to

make a single procedural mistake. Kershaw and Banbury are on their way. I'll pick you up in ten minutes. I'm assuming you hadn't gone to bed.'

'You assume wrongly,' snapped Bryant. 'Thought I'd have an early night for a change, read over my old case notes.' He was writing a history of their investigations, but his old reports were out of order and handwritten, as well as being unreliable and libellous to a perverse degree. 'The good thing is that Raymond Land will get off our backs now and leave us alone.'

'You'd probably like to know how the poor devil who found his partner's body is doing,' May prompted.

'I'm sure you and Longbright will take care of him,' said Bryant dismissively. 'Now kindly get off the phone. I have no intention of attending the crime scene in my Tintin pyjamas.' Bryant showed little empathy for survivors. Survival was something he expected everyone to do as a matter of course; every life was punctuated with tests.

Less than twenty minutes later, he and May entered the little terraced house. They had hoped to arrive without fuss, but it seemed that the street's other residents were expecting tragedy. Hall lights glowed. Some stood expectantly in their doorways, trying to understand what had happened.

Sergeant Longbright found Aaron in the kitchen with a dressing-gown pulled over his shoulders, his face hidden by his hands. 'I don't know why we always make tea in times of crisis, it seems so stupid,' she said, filling the kettle. 'Do you have any brandy in the house?'

'I can't go up there again,' he told her.

'You don't have to. There can only be one route in

and out of the crime scene, so the stairs are off limits now. Everything must be recorded.'

'What happens next?'

'We have to photograph and log everything as you found it. We'll probably take some items away for analysis. Mr Bryant would like me to get a short statement from you now, though, because there are things you may forget later. The mind has a way of rewriting bad events, taking out details we don't want to recall.' She placed a mug of mahogany-shaded tea on the kitchen table and sat beside him. He wiped an eye with the heel of his hand and regarded her. Longbright's maternal sexiness stood her in good stead during times of stress. She was a warm breast to lean on, an ear to confide in. Aaron felt the need to explain what had happened, and why he felt so bad.

Upstairs, Banbury was measuring distances around the bed and taking digital footage of the body. Jake Avery lay half out of bed, like Chatterton in death, a pale hand brushing the floor. His face was flattened and lined with fierce red creases, his mouth a bright oval rictus.

'He's drunk a fair amount,' Kershaw said, kneeling beside the bed and triggering stills. 'Those lines on his cheeks—the blood's just under the surface. Smells like whisky.'

'Where's the murder weapon?' asked May, looking about.

'Here.' Banbury raised a length of crushed cling-film between the thumb and forefinger of his gloved right hand. 'The boy took it off his face.'

'You mean it was wrapped around his head?' asked May.

'Four or five times. He didn't fight back. Tried to get his fingers through the film and failed. Bedclothes are hardly disturbed. Probably surprised in his sleep, caught at the base of a breath.'

'Asphyxiation.' May shook his head sadly.

'Actually, no. This stuff attracts a terrible amount of static, as you'll know if you've ever tried to wrap something up when you're not in the mood. Judging by the haemorrhaging in his nasal passages, it stuck over his nose and mouth at the same moment. Make someone jump and they'll gasp, drawing in air, so he would have found himself without a breath to take. Then quickly lift the head, wrap once, twice, again and again, he's fighting for oxygen and finding none at all, all his concentration's taken up with the need to breathe, his reactions are slow, he doesn't put up much of a battle. He's been drinking, his pulse is up, bing go the strings of his heart, a coronary thrombosis ten years too early, all over in seconds.'

'How long do you reckon he's been dead?' asked Bryant, who found himself warming to the new forensics lad. He possessed a certain fervour.

'Oh, a couple of hours before the boy found him—I did a quick rectal just before you got here, but I'll get you something more accurate later.'

'What kind of murderer enters his victim's home armed with a roll of clingfilm?' May wondered.

'Weapon at hand,' replied Bryant, hardly pausing to consider the question. 'Unpremeditated.'

'Not so. That would have entailed traipsing through the house to take the roll from the kitchen. Either way, it was planned.'

'You think so? It smacks of improvisation to me. His face was uncovered when you got here?'

'As you see it, Mr Bryant. Seems Mr Avery's partner arrived home late and got into bed without turning on the light, then felt something was wrong. When he put on the bedside lamp he saw the plastic wrap covering the victim's face and tore at it until it came off, as I'm sure you would. I'll try to get some latents off it, but don't hold your breath.'

'Unfortunate choice of phrase, Mr Banbury,' May remonstrated.

'No disrespect intended, sir.'

'Three,' muttered Bryant, studying the body.

'Sir?'

'Three suffocations in three weeks, all in the same small street,' he explained. 'John, what would you say to the natural odds on such a thing occurring?'

There was an eerie glint in his partner's eyes that May had seen before. It occurred whenever Bryant found himself faced with irrefutable proof of a highly unlikely murder.

33

UNDERCURRENTS

'This isn't a police station.' Aaron looked around the unit office at Mornington Crescent, puzzled.

The only personnel to be seen were a pair of hungover workmen in the next room who were seated beside a hole in the floor, eating digestive biscuits. Crippen sat slumped against a filing cabinet, legs apart, licking itself, seemingly in no hurry to be returned to its rightful owner.

'Good God, no,' replied May. 'It's not even a detection unit in the traditional sense. That's why I thought it would be a good place for us to have a talk. You can say what you like here.'

'I've done nothing wrong. I've nothing to be ashamed of.' Aaron was sweating too heavily to be entirely innocent, fidgeting and placing his hands near his mouth in unconscious signs of discomfort. He had been allowed to rest in the living room until dawn, watched over by Bimsley.

'I'm not here to judge you, Aaron. Your partner's murder has raised the status of the investigation. We're fighting to keep the press out; but if they do find a way in, your street will become a major tourist destination. Mr Avery's killer has to be found before that happens. I know you gave DS Longbright a statement, but I want to talk about your movements last night. The ones you didn't mention.'

'I didn't do it, if that's what you're thinking. I'll take a lie-detector test.'

'That's old technology. Subjects can defeat it by simply biting their tongues. It was never very reliable to begin with. These days we use an electroencephalograph that monitors brain-waves.'

'You have one of those?'

'No, of course not. It's far too expensive. Besides, my partner prefers us to use the old psychological methods—non-verbal communication skills, studying your gestures and so on.'

Aaron dropped his hand from his mouth. 'What do you want to know?'

'Quite an age difference between you and Mr Avery. About twenty years?'

'Eighteen. It never made a difference.'

'Happy, then? No rifts, no arguments?'

'I wouldn't say that; nobody would.'

'Tell me about Marshall,' May said casually. 'Did you meet him at the Bondini brothers' workshop, or somewhere else?'

Aaron grew pale, and finally sat on his hands to keep them still. 'I'd seen him around,' he said in a small voice. 'I took a table into the workshop to get its leg fixed, and he was there.' He started to panic. 'You're going to talk to him, aren't you? His parents don't know, they think he's going out with a Greek girl—his father would kill him.'

'When did you first meet?'

'It was just a few months ago, but we didn't—I

mean, we've only gone out together a couple of times.
Jake didn't know anything about it. I would never
have hurt him, he was wonderful to me, and now—'

'I'm sorry, you'll have to excuse me if I don't buy
this "nice chap who made one small mistake" routine. You saw Marshall Keftapolis on over twenty
separate occasions behind your partner's back. Let's
take it from there.'

'It wasn't as often as—'

'I've already talked to him this morning, Aaron.
You met five months ago, and according to Marshall,
you've told him on numerous occasions that you
were going to leave Jake, but he didn't believe you'd
ever get around to doing so because you were dependent on him for money. So let's be a little less disin-
genuous about your innocence.'

The boy sat forward, and lowered his head in his
hands. 'You're making it sound more heartless than it
was.'

'The statement of simple facts has a habit of appearing heartless. I don't doubt you feel bad, you
blame yourself because you lied to him about where
you were going, and you were out with someone else
when he met a nasty end. Yes, I'd be feeling pretty
guilty too. It's why you left the lights off—you didn't
want to wake him up and face his questions. For the
record, I don't believe you did it.'

'Why not?'

'I don't know, perhaps because you took your
clothes off in the dark before going into the room,
and went to the trouble of neatly folding them. You'd
have to be abnormally cold-blooded to do that before
killing someone to whom you were emotionally attached. I suppose you could have folded the clothes

afterwards, but to what end? Your past indiscretions are only interesting if they shed a light on Mr Avery's murder. The best you can do now is think of anyone who might have wanted to hurt him. Had he argued with someone, made any enemies?'

'There were tensions at work; I don't really know the details. And he'd fallen out with Randall Ayson. They had a shouting match about theology in the middle of the street. Ayson's God-Squad, man is born to procreate, the Lord made Adam and Eve, not Adam and Steve, that sort of learned-by rote rubbish. Ayson's condescending because he's got children, but it's common knowledge that he was having an affair behind his wife's back.'

'What do you mean, common knowledge?'

'It was the hot topic at the Wiltons' party. Lauren, the girl who's going out with Mark Garrett. Apparently she and Randall were an item. Your partner was there. He must have picked up on it.'

'Fine, but I doubt Mr Ayson decided to murder Mr Avery simply because he wasn't planning on having children. Anyone else in the street?'

'Well, Garrett, I suppose. He gave Jake some duff property advice.'

'Quite normal. Keep going.'

'Jake had a row with Heather from across the road once.'

'Do you know what it was about?'

'I think it was Stanley Spencer.'

'The artist? Why would they have argued over Stanley Spencer?'

'Jake was researching Spencer's life because his company was planning a documentary. She did PR for a Cork Street gallery before her husband dumped her, had some strong views about art.'

May was beginning to wonder whether his human approach to detective intelligence was less effective than Bryant's lateral habits. He sighed and replaced his pen in his pocket. 'Let's assume for a moment that the assailant was unknown to Mr Avery. You're sure nothing was taken from the house?'

'Positive. You've seen how we live. Jake was into minimalism, couldn't bear ornamentation, not even so much as a magazine lying about. We kept no money at home.'

'You don't think it was unusual for the back door to be unlocked?'

'No. There are gardens on either side of us, and walls at the ends.'

'And you can think of no reason—'

'—why he was murdered? No, of course not, otherwise I'd tell you, wouldn't I?'

They released the distraught Aaron in order to let him inform his partner's relatives.

'I still keep asking myself if it's just an unfortunate series of coincidences,' May admitted. 'All kinds of tragedies occur in the average street. Couldn't this be an extreme example? An old lady dies, a workman suffers an accident, an intruder kills a householder ...'

'There's nothing coincidental about it,' replied Bryant, pouring food for the cat. 'The unusual configurations of London streets mean that there was always a lot of waste ground, and the Blitz bombs created more dead land than ever.'

'What has that got to do with anything?'

'You always think these things are about love and hate, John, but they're really about frustration and poverty and anger, and that has a lot to do with the land. The developers push up property prices, the land is built upon, density increases dramatically, people are thrust into each other's paths, privacy is eroded, tension flares.'

May had heard this particular tune of Bryant's often enough to raise his hand in objection. 'London has a lower population now than it had in the 1950s,' he pointed out.

'But it's become concentrated in city hotspots. Where there are too many people, lives are forced to overlap.'

'This is a pretty affluent street, Arthur. Everyone has a garden, their own space. You're searching for connections where there are none.'

'I'd take your point, old fruit, but for two things. First, Jake was asleep when he was attacked. The bottom half of the bed wasn't even disturbed, which suggests to me that he was taken by surprise. He didn't even have time to react by trying to fend off his attacker and kick himself into an upright position. Second, the attacker *knew* he was in bed, because he came upstairs already armed with the roll of film. Ergo, someone entered the house with the intention of killing its owner. Jake knew something about the deaths of Elliot Copeland and Ruth Singh, and was silenced before he could tell anyone.'

'You don't know that. His colleagues reckon he didn't leave the studio all day. When do you imagine he was the recipient of this blinding epiphany?'

'I don't much care for your tone.' Bryant rooted through his drawer, and began assembling a favourite pipe. 'We know he arranged to meet Kallie Owen last night, then failed to show up. I think he'd been about to tell her something, but was sidetracked by the killer.' He sucked horribly at the pipe stem, checking airflow.

'Why confide in her? Why not tell us?'

'Perhaps his discovery was of particular relevance to her, or this missing partner of hers who was currently last heard from in—' he consulted his notes, 'Santorini?'

'Let's assume for the moment that you're correct, and that this is some kind of domino effect, in which case Elliot Copeland dies to prevent the identity of Ruth Singh's killer from emerging, and Jake Avery dies to keep Elliot's murderer hidden. There's no driving force to the hypothesis—no motive. None of these people had the usual family ties.'

'You forget that following my theory, we only need a motive for the first death, and that could be something terribly mundane. We know that Ruth Singh had been the victim of racism from the tape Kallie gave us, if thirty seconds of guttural filth on a bad line can be taken as racism. We know that, despite Mark Garrett's claim to the contrary, she was visited by him the night before she died. Let's assume she made an enemy, someone who found a way to take her life—'

'—by flooding her bathroom and quickly draining it.'

'Sarcasm doesn't suit you, John.'

'What's wrong with a simple conk on the head? She was an old lady, all anyone would have had to do was push her downstairs. Why go to the trouble of drowning her on dry land?'

'I think we have to set aside the "why" and concentrate on "how" for a while.'

'How is it you always manage to sidestep the logical questions any normal person would ask?'

'I never gave you any reason to assume I was logical. Have you ever known me to plan anything more than two hours in advance, or stay awake all the way through a committee meeting?' Bryant reached back to his bookshelf and began pulling down some dusty, tattered volumes.

'I suppose not,' May sighed. 'If you were logical, you'd have stayed with Alma as your landlady in the old apartment. She washed your socks for forty years. Any sane person would have bid you good riddance, but she's terribly cut up about you dumping her. And I don't think you'll find the answer in any of those filthy old books.'

'Well, of course, that's exactly what you would say,' Bryant bridled, loading them into his briefcase. 'Anyway, what about your granddaughter? I thought you were bringing April in to help us. I thought you were going to have it out with her once and for all. Put your own house in order, I say.'

Stalemate, thought May. 'So what are the books for?' he asked, giving in gracefully.

'Ah, well. Seeing as we divided assignments, I thought I'd try adopting your methods for a change. Any word from Greenwood?'

'Monica called to tell me that Jackson Ubeda and her husband are going off somewhere together tomorrow night, and that he's not expected back until the next morning. I think it was her way of telling me that she'd be alone in the house.'

'Thank God I don't have your trouble with

women. What a moral dilemma. Which duty will you choose, I wonder? To satisfy the unfulfilled wife or to rescue the good name of your rival? The unit can't help you now, you know, not with Raymond having to report our every movement to Marsden and the rest of HMCO liaison.'

'Then I'll inform you of my decision,' said May.

'And I'll do the same if my hunch with these books pays off.'

The axe is about to fall on this place and they're behaving like children, guarding their essays from each other, thought Longbright, watching them from the door. *They're out of step, out of date, and it looks like they're finally running out of time.*

34

THE CONDUIT

Bryant unloaded the books at the end of Tate's bed. 'I'm afraid they're rather esoteric,' he apologized, 'but you may find them interesting.'

The itinerant turned over the first volume and studied the title suspiciously. A gruesome face on the cover of *Dental Evidence in Body Identification. Volume One: Bridgework* stared back at him. 'Thank you,' he said uncertainly.

There was an unbearably terminal aspect to Tate's little room. When he had mentioned the stripped-back bareness of the workers' houses in Balaklava Street, homes that had been built for the poor, he could have been describing this, his own eventual residence. His knotted hands turned the pages with surprising delicacy. On the sill above his bed stood a row of syrup tins containing stunted geraniums. An overpowering smell of stewed beef wafted in from the corridor.

'I wondered if we might talk a little more,' Bryant suggested.

'You want to know something, don't you? There's been another one.'

'You heard.'

'Everyone talks in here. But I saw.'

'What do you mean, you saw?'

'What you told me off for doing.'

'You mean watching?' Bryant sat forward. 'You were watching the house?'

'In one of my positions. Traffic warden uses it. Runs out from his hidey-hole to arrest the cars.'

Bryant knew that rough sleepers developed territorial habits every bit as strong as those with homes. 'Where is that?'

'On the waste ground.'

'What did you see, Mr Tate?'

'Saw the bedroom light go out in number 41.'

'Did you notice who went in?'

'No. You can only see upstairs from there.'

'What about Elliot Copeland? Did you see him on the night of the accident?'

'Yes. The earth swallowed him up.' Tate turned the pages, feigning disinterest in the conversation.

'This is very important,' urged Bryant. 'Did you see anything at all that could identify the culprit?' The moment he spoke, the delicate skein of communication between them was damaged. Tate's eyes clouded as he closed the book. Bryant knew he had to try another approach.

'I thought you might like that volume.' He reached over and tapped the cover of a battered paperback entitled *The Vanished Rivers of London*. 'Fascinating stuff about this area. It even has a picture of your temporary home in the alley. Of course, it wasn't just an alley back then, when the book was written. It was called Streamside Path.'

Tate's eyes flickered.

'Page 201, if you're interested.' Bryant flicked through and allowed the book to fall open at the marked spot. He waited while Tate studied the picture.

'I wonder how many other tunnels there are beneath the terraces around here,' he mused. 'Three or four, at least.'

'Seven,' murmured Tate without thinking. 'All forgotten.'

'Not by you. I presume their waters run into the Regent's Canal.'

'Some. Not all.'

'Why not?'

No answer.

'I just want to know what happened. I can see it's painful to talk about these things. But there are other ways. Can't you give me some guidance, put me on the right track? The river Fleet, I know it's connected, but I don't understand its significance.'

'The river is where it all started. It has the power to change lives.'

'You could show me.'

'You'd tell.'

'I couldn't promise not to if I found evidence pertaining to the investigation,' Bryant pointed out.

'Then we won't go.'

'I can give you anonymity. No one will know it was you who took me. Your identity would remain a secret.'

Tate thought for a moment. 'Can you get more books?'

'Easily.'

'Do you swear?'

'On my honour as a gentleman.'

'Haven't heard anyone say that for a long time.' Tate eased himself from the bed and pulled a hammer from underneath the mattress. 'We'll need this.'

'I don't understand.'

'It was a long hot summer. No rain from June the sixth until three weeks ago. Dried out all the river beds.'

'You mean they became passable? I thought the grilles stopped large objects, including people, from moving along the conduits.'

'Most grilles are rusty. Some are gone. Some are locked.' He pushed his hand into a syrup tin and pulled out a filthy set of long-stemmed keys.

'You can move under the streets?'

'I could. Now it's raining again. The channels have filled back up, but there are still ways.' He left the room with surprising speed, even though old injuries had twisted his body on damaged hinges. The pair of them headed out down the stairs and into the wet street like fugitives.

When they reached the wire fence of the alley at the end of Balaklava Street, Tate slipped through the gap and beckoned to Bryant. He stopped above the grating that Brewer Wilton had lowered himself into. 'Give me a hand.'

Tate groped about in the bushes for his iron T-rod, and together they eased the steel lid off the drain. The water level had risen since Bryant had examined it, and a dull roar of water could be heard in the distance. 'What's that noise?' he asked.

'Gospel Oak sluice emptying into the Regent basin.'

'But Gospel Oak is about half a mile away.'

'Sound carries down there.' Tate dropped to his

knees in the mud and lowered the top half of his body
into the hole. After a minute of searching, he emitted
a grunt of satisfaction, withdrew the hammer and
gave something in the hole a great whack. There
followed a grinding metallic noise, and the rushing
water seemed to ease off.

'What have you done?' asked Bryant.

'Obvious. Can't get down there if it's full. I'm diverting the flow.'

'You can do that?'

'Smooth as a knife. Go down.'

Bryant looked dubiously into the shaft. The cement floor was visible a few inches beneath the water
now, but the rungs to it looked slippery.

'Want to show you something.'

'I'm a bit dicey on my pins.' Reluctantly, the elderly detective eased himself over the side of the
drain, and began to climb down. They stood together
on the draining concrete platform, heads ducked to
avoid the low brick ceiling. The stench of rotting
garbage and faeces settled into Bryant's nostrils and
clothes, but beneath it was another smell, something
he had not expected: the damp bite of green Thames
water. The temperature was lower than at ground
level. His breath plumed before him as he clicked on
May's Valiant.

'Look.' Tate pointed through the olivine gloom at
a pair of large oval holes on either side of the channel.
The junction appeared deeper; water churned in a
putrid eddy of cross-currents. 'The Prince of Wales
Causeway. Six gates to close off before you reach the
basin. Can't leave the gates shut more than a few
minutes because of the pressure. Takes a logical mind
to remember the sequence and survive.'

'The Water Board must know how to do it.'

'So do I.'

'You want us to go down there?'

'Not today, not with the forecast. Takes more than an hour, maybe two. Need waterproofs and a mask. Another day, if you want to know the reason.'

'What reason?' asked Bryant. 'What are you talking about?'

'Reason for all this upset. The water is where it began.'

To Bryant, it seemed the most inhospitable place imaginable. He wondered how the tramp could have slept on the platform without being besieged by nightmares.

'Come on, the rain's getting harder. Tunnel fills up fast. Drains off the Heath, through clay and brick, thousands of gallons in seconds. Get swept away and no one will ever find you again.'

Tate started to climb back up. He pulled himself out of the drain with ease, extending his shattered hand to Bryant. The pair were bonded by a secret now.

Back in the alley, he produced a muddy piece of card from his jacket and held it up. 'You need this.'

On it was printed a faded diagram designed like a Tube map, overlaid with the kind of Helvetica lettering popularized during the War. Instead of underground branch lines, it showed the paths of tributaries, each one variegated and named. Tate was holding the plan to a network of conduits. He tapped a calibrated thick line with his blackened forefinger. 'The Fleet. Each dot is a lock. Each line is a sealed gate.'

Bryant dug out his reading glasses and took a

squint. 'According to this, you can't get as far as the Regent's Canal.'

'No, but you can branch off, all the way up to the York Road Basin. It was fine during the summer, you could walk along it, armed with the right keys. Now you have to divert each of the cross-courses as you go. As you said, the Water Board knows. They got the equipment. But I got all the keys.'

'You've done it?'

'A few of us.'

Bryant squinted through the drizzle that softened Tate's weathered face. 'Who are you?' he asked quietly. Tate's lips thinned, but a moment later the smile had vanished.

'I'm nobody,' he whispered sadly.

35

HUMAN NATURE

'I think our killer is using the underground tunnels,' Bryant explained, obliviously poking pedestrians with the tines of his umbrella as they dodged the puddles in Kentish Town High Street. 'He enters the alley from the back gardens and goes down into the water conduit. It passes right under the road and connects to the backs of all the houses on the east side.'

'Why would anyone go to so much trouble?' May was having difficulty keeping up with his partner this afternoon. A sense of angry urgency invaded Bryant whenever he was faced with the fallout from a preventable death. He and John had spent most of Friday with the shocked residents of Balaklava Street. Now they had left Aaron alone with his guilt in a searched, emptied and fingerprinted house, minus the person who had brought the rooms to life, and the world was expected to turn as usual. In the months following a death, the survivors saw small cruelties wherever they looked. It disturbed Bryant to recognize that the unit should have taken matters more seriously from the outset, and shamed him that they had achieved so little. It was the only time in the investigation when he had displayed any other emotion than a ghoulish enthusiasm. His revenge was to ignore his age and infirmities, to work harder than ever. It was when he needed to be watched most carefully.

'So that no one sees anything unusual in the street, obviously. Look how enclosed and overlooked it is. If you're well known in the area, witnesses are likely to remember you. It's someone Tate and probably all the others know by sight. That's why Tate didn't seem frightened when I talked to him. It's the unknown that scares people, the faceless stranger who attacks for no logical reason, because he's on drugs, or drunk, or just disturbed.' He thrust a crumpled paper bag at May. 'Have a pear drop.'

'You're taking a leap in the dark with this,' warned May. 'There's no reason to make such an assumption. The tramp has a history of mental problems, you said so yourself. He's an unreliable source of information. It might even be him.'

'And what would his motive be? Hang on, I want to get some sausages.' Bryant dragged his partner into the butcher's and tapped the cabinet. 'Are those Gloucester Old Spots fresh? They don't look it.'

'The oldest motive in the world,' May insisted, trying to concentrate. 'They have something he hasn't. Homes, money, security.'

'Then why doesn't he take anything? And why would he insist on showing me his escape route? Give me six Cumberlands and a couple of kidneys—nice fat ones, no rubbish.' He turned back to May while rooting inside his coat for money. 'Tate can't come out and admit what he knows. Perhaps he's afraid for his own life, so he's revealing how the deeds were done, trusting us to figure out the rest of it. But he knows more than he's telling, and that puts him in danger. It's your domino effect: each person with knowledge being systematically removed. Perhaps if Mr Bush had signed the Kyoto Treaty, this might never have happened.'

'Sorry, Arthur, you've lost me.'

'Climate change. The rivers dried out during the long hot summer, making them passable. Now all hell is breaking loose underground, because when it rains, the tunnels briefly turn into white-water rapids. None of the deaths occurred before the bad weather, did they? Perhaps that's because the conduits were too dry to dispose of any incriminating evidence. The killer patiently waited until the rain came back, providing him with a way of dumping anything that would link him to the murders. This is what the rivers were always used for. History repeats itself.'

'Really, Arthur, it all sounds very complicated.' May watched in some unease while the butcher chopped away at a pair of bulbous kidneys, wiping his bloody hands on his apron.

'I have to hang on to this, John; somehow it all comes back to the tributaries of the Fleet. Without the river there would be no houses. Without the houses there would be no murders. The first death is the key: a harmless old lady killed by water, *because* of water, as though the killer was closing a circle, choosing a suitable punishment for her crime. Of course, it's possible we've completely misjudged what's going on. We may have to look at everything in a fresh light.'

The butcher rang up Bryant's purchases. The elderly detective looked at his change in disgust. 'Is that all I get back from a tenner? Daylight robbery. Those pigs' ears look past their best. You shouldn't be selling things that look as if they've died of old age.' He snatched the plastic bag of meat and dragged May with him to the door.

'Another thing. That boyfriend of Kallie's—he's been away for weeks. Suppose he's been conked on the head and dropped down there, the murderer or an accomplice posting his cards from all over Europe? And what about the next-door neighbour, Heather? No one's seen her husband for ages. He's meant to be in Paris—what if he's actually floating about somewhere under King's Cross? And Benjamin Singh, he's supposed to be in Australia, but has anyone actually heard from him? Just how many men are missing from this damned street anyway? Wait, I forgot something.' He turned on his heel and headed back to the surprised butcher. 'Do you have any mutton? I may attempt a casserole.'

'I wish you'd slow down for a moment,' urged May. They were walking back to the unit because Bimsley and Banbury had taken the Rover to drop off evidence. 'Let's stop for refreshment, you can get your breath back.' He steered his partner into a Greek coffee shop.

'Two teas, one with lots of sugar.' Bryant glared at the listless girl playing with her hair behind the counter.

'We don't do tea,' mumbled the girl.

'Don't be ridiculous, it's the national drink, how can you not do tea?'

'Cappuccino, latte or espresso.'

'Those are Italian beverages. You're a Cypriot, surely,' Bryant barked, reluctantly moving to allow a pushchair past. 'You should have mint tea or little cups of Turkish coffee with half an inch of silt in the bottom. No tea! Good Lord, all you have to do is put some fresh leaves under boiled water.'

'Come on, Arthur, ease up a little.' May took his arm and led him to a table, then returned to order lattes.

'You realize if we hadn't started following Greenwood, we would never have made the connection?' said Bryant as his friend returned. 'Everyone knows about the London Tube map; why isn't this other one public knowledge? Who else is in possession of it?' He slapped the underground tunnel plan on the table between them. 'The city functions in much the same way as its streets—every time you think you have something figured out it twists back on you. The answer has to be here in these numbered conduits . . .'

'No, it isn't, Arthur. I've seen you like this before, and to be honest, I think you've got the wrong end of the stick, or possibly the wrong stick entirely. The only answer you'll get is by talking to people. You don't observe, you don't think about human nature.'

'I have you to do that for me.'

May sighed. 'Look at the girl behind the counter, the one you just had a go at. What do you see?'

Bryant squinted over. 'A fat Greek schoolgirl who needs a few lessons in civility.'

'Try again. Her name's Athena and she's about nineteen; she's married with two children, and she has a younger sister. Her father owns the place, and she's working here against her will. Her husband got drunk last night and they had a fight. She's trapped and miserable, and wondering how her life turned out like this.'

'You worked that out from watching her?' asked Bryant, genuinely interested.

'It's not difficult,' said May. 'She's wearing a wedding ring. Look at the photos on the walls behind her: family pictures taken in Cyprus—mother and father, no sons featured. The owner has given his oldest daughter a job because she needs it. Why? Her children are twins. The man who went past with the double pushchair spoke to her by name. He's ginger, from around here. You see his type everywhere. Got into fatherhood too early, and to his dismay finds himself taking care of not one but two small girls—very angry about it. You don't have to be a genius to read the disappointment in his face. Wouldn't work here because it's not a man's job, and besides, the place belongs to her family, which means he would fight with them all the time. She puts in long hours, he puts the kids to bed and goes to the pub. She plays with her hair to cover a bruise. Facial marks like that are rarely self-inflicted. She's trapped between controlling parents and an embittered partner, so she's not really too bothered about whether you get tea, coffee or rat poison.'

'Hmm.' Bryant stirred his cup thoughtfully. 'Perhaps you're right. I should pay more attention to people. Get my nose out of my books once in a while. I do like them, you know—people. It just seems as if I don't.'

'I know,' said May gently. 'You have a good heart, but you don't reveal it very often. As a suspect, Aaron's a non-starter; even you can see that. Tate is the closest we have. I think the first thing we need to do is put a watch on him. No one's been dropped into the sewers, we'd have found drag marks in the gardens or the alleyway, but I agree that it may explain the lack of incriminating evidence. We have no weapons beyond a sheet of clingfilm. You have to admit that's unusual. But you also have to admit that there's another possibility.'

'Which is?'

'You've allowed this whole situation with Greenwood to affect your instincts about Balaklava Street. You love collecting arcane knowledge about underground rivers, so suddenly they have to feature in an entirely separate investigation.'

'The thought had crossed my mind, but *you* have to admit it's a damned coincidence that Balaklava Street is built over a tributary. Have you decided what you're going to do about Sunday night?'

'I thought you and Mangeshkar could keep an eye on Greenwood and Ubeda. Whatever they're planning has to end then, because we start fresh the next morning, whatever happens. Even Raymond agrees that we have a legitimate reason for putting more resources into Balaklava Street now. Meanwhile, post Bimsley at the hostel to make sure Tate doesn't go anywhere. I'll go and see Monica.'

'So I get posted somewhere cold, damp and possibly lethal to a man of my advanced years while you pitch woo to a married woman,' Bryant harrumphed, clattering a sugar lump against his false teeth. 'I suppose I can't blame you. You need affection and reassurance more than I.' Bryant had decided a long time ago that he was far too strange to find anyone who would love him. He had, of course, underestimated the bravery and tenacity of the British female, but now he was convinced that he had left it too late, and had resigned himself to the consolations of work and friendship. 'Still, I think it would be better if we followed Greenwood together. He knows you.'

'I can't be in two places at once. And you're not coming with me to see Monica.'

'So you *are* planning to woo her.'

'Nobody says "woo" any more, Arthur. You're so Victorian.'

'Stop saying that, it's just that there are certain modern habits of which I disapprove. Wet liberals, stealth taxes, the seduction of married women, telephone sales and hamburger outlets spring to mind.'

They remained in the coffee shop as it grew dark, watching the raindrops meandering down the window panes like a million silver comets.

36

BLOWBACK

The passageway was lined with small dun-coloured paintings. May had noticed them on his last visit, but the light had been too low to discern any detail. The wall sconces had no lightbulbs in them. 'We never replace them,' explained Monica.

'But you can't see the pictures.'

'Exactly so. There's a light here somewhere.' She struck a match to a candle and held it aloft. 'Now do you see?'

May found himself looking at several studies, roughs and pencil sketches for Pre-Raphaelite paintings. 'I don't understand,' he murmured, watching as the coppery lines wavered in the candlelight. 'These are beautiful.'

'My husband thinks they're worthless. He has an old-school attitude to Pre-Raphaelites that won't allow him to see beyond the detailed textures to the beauty of intent. So, as a mark of rebuke, to those artists and to me, for having too much materialism, too much sentiment and so little taste, he insists that we leave them hanging here in the basement. The walls are getting damp, and many of the sketches have started to stain. The house isn't alarmed, of course—we refuse to become prisoners in our own home, apparently—so I compromised by removing all the lightbulbs. That way, if we're burgled, the thieves will miss the best pieces in the house. And so another small battle is fought and drawn.'

'Why do you stay with him?' asked May. 'He limits your freedom and makes you unhappy.'

'God knows we certainly like different things. He's Berlin and Bauhaus and brutalism, I'm Turner and Tate Britain. But nothing's that simple, is it? The children are in their nightmare years, veering between innocence and arrogance in a way that makes me fear daily for their lives. Gareth's colleagues virtually dictate how to spend our finances. The paths of our lives seem set in concrete. Do you remember before you had to be grown-up every second of the day, John? How it always felt like morning?' She lowered the candle, and light faded from the gilt frames. Tiny lines appeared on her face, like the craquelure on a painted heroine. 'Now it always feels late in the day. Shadows are gathering, and the best pleasures feel far behind me. Gareth is looking for something he can never have and will never find: respect. I can't help him, so instead I am a hindrance, or an embarrassment. He'll make a fool of himself—or worse, break the law and be disgraced, his expertise ridiculed, his judgement dismissed. And it will kill him, because he has nothing else left.'

Back in her studio, she turned on the radiator and poured tall whiskies. 'He's become indiscreet of late, leaves books and maps lying all over the lounge. But I still have no idea what this ridiculous quest is all about, and nothing I say can change his mind.'

'I can tell you what we know,' said May, 'because I hope tonight will see the end of it. There's something called The Vessel of All Counted Sorrows—an Egyptian alabaster vase like a death urn, intended to represent the woes of the world. It occupies a key place in pre-Christian mythology, but is as likely to exist in a tangible form as the Holy Grail.'

'Gareth is the kind of man who'd prefer to believe in such a thing. He's always been a huge fan of Atlantis. A reasoned intellectual with a fatal idealistic flaw—you see them all the time in our little circle.'

'Ubeda believes the vessel ended up in this country, brought over by the Romans and thrown into one of the rivers, where it became silted up and concreted over, waiting to be rediscovered. The least of your husband's problems is his loss of credibility. Ubeda's past collaborators have shown a tendency to vanish when they've outlived their usefulness; at least, we've had no luck contacting any of them.'

'And he's in this mess because of something that doesn't exist?'

'It's a little more complicated than that. Imagine for a moment that the vessel is real. This isn't some impenetrable search for the true pieces of the cross. You can carbon-date a piece of wood, but you won't prove it came from the crucifixion. Ceramics are hard to copy, because you need clay from the same source as the original. Cast metals are easier to fake. Stone statues are almost all authentic.'

'How is that possible?'

'Forging them is too labour intensive. Sometimes there's a point where a truly elaborate forgery passes into authenticity. But the vessel—ceramics can be dated with thermoluminescence, which measures the natural radiation absorbed by the clay since it was fired. The technique is only useable on very large objects, because it's pretty destructive. But whether the artefact Gareth is trying to find exists or not, it's desirable for the most appealing reasons.'

'What do you mean?'

'It occupies a key position in mythical history, its provenance is intriguingly incomplete, and it possesses just the right amount of romantic appeal. Whenever those factors coincide, human nature takes over and makes such an item appear.'

'You don't think he'd try to palm Ubeda off with a fake?'

'I'm not suggesting that, but the stakes are high. In terms of revenue, the artefact market fits comfortably behind drugs and arms. Looted items from Iraq ended up in the hands of European and American sellers within days of the troops moving in. The problem arises in your husband's eagerness to locate such an item. If by some miracle he achieved his aim tonight, he would be helping to hide a world treasure from sight. Such a valuable item would never surface in public hands.'

'So Gareth will make a fool of himself, whatever the outcome,' said Monica, draining her glass, 'and you can't stop him.'

'I'm afraid we're no longer able to keep track of him after tonight,' May agreed. 'But perhaps we won't have to.'

'Then let's make the most of the evening.' She brushed his arm lightly, but allowed her fingers to linger. May had intended to rebuff her, but was tired of doing the right thing, of always placing duty ahead of his personal feelings. For once, the image of

Bryant's disapproving features did not appear as a rebuke, and he found himself placing his arms around Monica's shoulders, kissing her lightly, seeking out those guilty pleasures they had both sought so hard to avoid.

It was a matter of loyalty—if not to Greenwood or his wife, then to John. His partner had never begged a favour in all the years they had worked together. The least Bryant could do was see it through tonight.

They set off along the Paddington arm of the Grand Union Canal at ten p.m., reaching the point where it joined the Regent's Canal at Little Venice, continuing past the bright enamelled buckets and tarred ropes of the red and blue houseboats. If Bryant had possessed the energy, they would have detoured through Kensal Green Cemetery, just for the pleasure of it, but Greenwood and Ubeda were walking ahead of them, and they could not afford to drop out of range.

May had persuaded Monica to place a tracker in her husband's coat pocket when he left, so that there would be no mistakes. The device belonged to Banbury, and was the size of a five-pence coin, with a battery life of six hours. They hoped it would transmit a signal long enough to last the PCU through to the end of their involvement in Greenwood's affairs. The continuation of the murder inquiry at Balaklava Street took precedence over rescuing the reputation of an academic.

'So many back gardens,' Meera pointed out. 'It's a secret world down here.' They passed the sloping lawns and willow trees of large Victorian villas. The steadily falling rain made the footpaths safer; there was less danger of being caught in the internecine wars of the alcoholics who frequented them. Meera checked the tiny red light on the reader May had given her. 'They're heading toward Regent's Park and the zoo. This isn't their usual patch, is it?'

'No,' Bryant agreed, pausing beneath a dripping green bridge. He leaned on his stick to catch his breath. The spatter of rain on the canal surface echoed on the curved brick ceiling, pulsing distorted reflections. 'Of course, they might be going all the way to Hackney, but I think not. They'll stop at Camden.'

'What makes you say that?'

'It's the only point where any of the western tributaries of the Fleet can empty out. They've been narrowing down their search since this whole thing began. Ubeda is driven, and they're running out of places to explore. Take my arm, would you? This looks slippery.' They continued on over the tilted paving stones and muddied pools of the footpath.

'So we're off the Grand Union now?' asked Meera.

'Oh yes. That was the main waterway between London and the Midlands, built over two hundred years ago, joining the Thames at Brentford. It provided access to the west. Twenty years later, the Regent's Canal was opened to link it to the docks. This canal goes from Paddington to Limehouse, passing right through the zoo. A dozen locks, two tunnels, fairly good paths all the way, and some funny little lock-gate houses that look like old railway stations, decked in flowers. It's not as safe as it used to be, though.'

'Yeah, I've noticed it keeps turning up on charge

sheets as a popular murder site. Bodies fished out of
the water, rapes, drunken stabbings. With these unlit
tunnels you're asking for trouble.'

'A pity,' Bryant agreed. 'There are some rather
pleasing architectural surprises to be discovered
down here, where the canals bend and open into
basins. When I was a nipper I much preferred coming
here to the royal parks. Fewer people, just grass and
trees, the backs of factories and shiny green water.
Now they're busy building "luxury canalside accommodation" beside the council blocks. Gin mills, gar-
ment factories and refrigerated warehouses are all
being carved into pretty little boxes, so that the poor
can peer into the lounges of the rich. Always a bad
idea, I feel.'

'What else is the canal good for now?' It annoyed
Meera that her director wasted so much of his time
considering London's intangible histories. As far as
she was concerned, the city's glorious past was at an
end, and all that anyone could do was make use of
the remains.

'I agree that barges are impractical in today's
world of mass-production, but London keeps growing; they could prove useful again. The cart-lanes
turned into high roads, earth and brick became concrete and steel, but these canals remain as they always
were.'

'They've stopped.' Meera held up the tracker. 'Just
up ahead.'

At the next bend they found themselves in a world
of stippled greens and wet browns, patches of sickly
lamplight falling through the briar bushes from the
streets above the cut. Remaining in the shadows of
the tunnel wall, they watched and waited.

'Are you picking anything up on that thing?'

'Here.' Meera handed him an earpiece.

Bryant listened. 'They're saying something about a cable. *Is there enough cable?*'

He heard Greenwood speak. '*This is too dangerous,* he's telling Ubeda. *It'll bring people running.* I should have worked out what they're up to by now. Think, Arthur, you stupid old fool.' He listened again.

'*Do you see anyone around?*'

'*No, but there's bound to be someone at street level—*'

'*Why is it that academics fall apart when they're required to do something?*'

'*You hired me for advice, Jackson. I have no business being here.*'

'*You get paid when we've achieved our goal— together.*'

'*I didn't think that meant—*' The sound phased and broke into electronic scatter.

Meera crept forward and observed for a minute. She picked wet leaves from her jacket as she returned. 'Come and look. They're so wrapped up in what they're doing, they won't see you.'

Bryant edged closer. He tried to remember May's advice about human nature, and studied the two figures before him. What he quickly recognized was the power one man could exert over another. Ubeda was in control; Greenwood was there reluctantly to do his bidding, hunched with cold in the evening's drizzle, complaining about his instructions because he was frightened.

The path where they stood passed a low baskethandle arch on its inner side, forming a narrow concrete causeway between two bodies of brackish river. The arch was barred, no more than four feet of it showing above water level.

The men were dressed in waterproofs, bent beneath the light of a small lantern, absorbed in their task, unaware of the baroque backdrop formed by the shimmering arch. Bryant could have been looking at some artefact of Atlantean architecture, its mass submerged in icy green darkness. It was not hard to imagine towers and steeples beneath the water's surface. The wall in which the arch's *voussoir* was set ended at an odd height; that was what had alerted Greenwood to the presence of another forgotten Fleet tributary. Bryant recalled the information John had gleaned from Oliver Wilton about the various outlets into the canal being subsumed by the rising water table.

Ubeda and Greenwood lowered themselves chest-deep into the water. The academic was being forced to take the lead, and carried a roll of black wire above his head. They reached the arch's grille, then somehow Greenwood was inside—a narrow panel of bars had been unlocked and pushed back. Ubeda waited outside, shining a torch into the tunnel. He was holding a chunky metal transmitter clear of the water, with a winking red light on the top, and Bryant realized what he was about to do. He had seen—and caused—enough explosions to know what the result might be. He started to warn Meera that any detonation in such a confined space, however small, would channel out the blast in a fiery column, firing any loose debris like ammunition from the muzzle of a rifle. But it was too late.

Greenwood was starting to call back in protest.

He had changed his mind, and was wading out. He took a step toward his benefactor, and for a moment it looked as if Ubeda would not let him back through the bars. But the matter was settled seconds later, when a dull boom echoed from beneath the arch. Meera and Bryant both saw the flash of light, but their confusion delayed their reactions.

The young officer was on her way toward the tunnel when fragments of brick jetted out, funnelled by the pressurized air. Greenwood had gone down with a splash. Ubeda had already pulled himself out of the canal, to fall back against the bushes. Bryant felt a stinging pain in his left ear and realized that something had cut it. As the dust cloud was battered flat by renewed rain, Meera threw herself forward and brought Ubeda down with a kick behind his knees that folded him like a collapsing deckchair, cracking his head against the brickwork. As Bryant arrived beside the half-drowned academic, he realized that Greenwood had sustained a nasty injury. A chunk of brick had torn open the left side of his jaw, and he was losing blood. Meera was stronger than she looked. Forking her arms beneath his, she hoisted the academic out on to the path.

'I'm calling it in.' Bryant dimly heard his own voice through the tintinnabulation of his eardrums. Emergency personnel would have to negotiate the steep banks and railings separating the towpath from the road above. 'We're not near an access path,' he shouted to her. 'We'll have to risk moving him, and take him up to the top.'

Meera was kneeling beside Greenwood, attempting to staunch the flow from his neck. 'I don't want you to help me, Mr Bryant, I'm strong enough to do it alone. Just stay here with Ubeda until I can get back. I kicked him pretty hard. I think he's concussed.' She gripped Greenwood's body and dragged him off as a spray of blood soaked her shirt and jacket. Bryant was left beside Ubeda.

'I'm an old man, but I have the strength of the law behind me, so I wouldn't advise making a run for it,' Bryant told him shakily, trying to regain his breath and calm his hammering heart. He checked for the gun Ubeda was known to possess, and was relieved to find nothing. 'I know what you're looking for. I want to know where you got the explosive material.'

'You can get anything in this city.' The entrepreneur's eyes never left Bryant's face. 'Anything at all.' He had the audacity to smile as he climbed shakily to his feet. Bryant suddenly saw the situation as it would have presented itself to an outsider: a rather frail, elderly man with the canal at his back, faced with a determined and possibly lunatic predator. He began to grow uncomfortable. True, the law was on his side and the water was shallow, but these days such odds were too long for Bryant's liking.

'Stay exactly where you are,' he warned.

'If you know what I'm looking for, surely you want to see it as well.' Ubeda began climbing over the shattered bricks toward the blasted entrance to the tunnel. Bryant stumbled behind him, his left ear singing, as Ubeda dropped back into the oily water and began wading under the arch.

'Come out of there, it's unsafe,' Bryant called ineffectually, but now he could see nothing, only hear the splash of water and the soft chinking of loose bricks. Once he heard a single shout of anger and frustration, and knew in that instant that Ubeda's goal had not been achieved.

When the collector returned, his arrogance had been swamped by the recognition of defeat. He climbed out of the canal and dropped on to the grassy embankment, closing his eyes.

'Did you really expect to find the vessel after all these centuries?' asked Bryant.

'You don't understand,' Ubeda told him. 'My great-grandfather knew of its whereabouts. Everything indicated that it had been washed to the end of a tributary. They were scaling off the rivers, putting in walls and grilles. He said that was where I would find it.'

'An alabaster pot older than Christ? You think it survived intact? How would that be possible?'

Ubeda opened his eyes and raised himself on one arm. 'No, of course not. Do you think I'm a complete idiot? Anubis carried the sorrows from one vessel to another. Why else do you think the society existed for so many years?'

Bryant recalled the broken Anubis statues in Ubeda's attic. 'I don't understand what you mean,' he admitted.

'Then you never will.' Ubeda rose in pain and limped away toward the shadow of the next canal arch, daring Bryant to stop him.

By the time Meera arrived with reinforcements, the waters beneath the arcade had smoothed to green glass, and Bryant stood alone at the water's edge.

37

HOME FIRE

DC Bimsley was frozen to the bone.

He stamped his boots on the pavement to bring feeling back to his feet, and tried wriggling his toes inside his cold wet socks, but nothing worked. Even his nipples had gone numb. Chilled rainwater bounced off his shaved head and dripped through the tiny gap between his neck and his collar. On the other side of the river, above a pub in Vauxhall, his pals were at a party hosted by Russian flight attendants, who would be introducing them to girls with cool grey eyes and unpronounceable names. They would be getting themselves into an advanced state of refreshment, slamming vodka mixes and copping off while he paced the street like a common constable.

Behind him, the blaring light of the hostel seemed as inviting as a country hotel in midwinter. He couldn't see the point of keeping guard on such a night. In the past two hours, a handful of melancholic men had drifted to the scratched glass of the reception window to collect an overnight pass for one of the overspill hostels in Camden. Two of them, having qualified as 'being in a condition of dire need', had been admitted to the overnight dormitory. Depressing as his own situation was, it could not equal the plight of these helpless and possibly unhelpable men. He wondered if Bryant was punishing him for some transgression by giving him such a menial task, and tried to recall whether he had filled in all his paperwork for last week.

In order to get a quick heat-fix from the convector over the entrance, he kept popping in to say 'All right?' to the bored little man at the reception desk; but no amount of foot stamping or arm flapping brought an offer of tea. He tried another tack. 'Busy tonight?'

'Not too bad,' managed the clerk.

'You been here long?' asked Bimsley, desperate to prolong his time under the heater.

'I used to be on nights up the Whiston Road Refugee Centre in Hackney. All Cambodians and Vietnamese, used to living in big families back home and putting all their money in one big pot. Then they come here and the first thing that happens is their kids take off. The families get split up, can't pay the rent and get kicked out.'

'It must make your job harder, trying to keep track of them all.'

'Everyone's all over the place, how can you keep track? Kurds in Finsbury, Albanians in King's Cross, Jamaicans in Harlesden, Colombians down the Elephant and Castle, Ethiopians in Highbury and Tufnell Park—the paperwork's a nightmare, I can tell you.'

'Forgive me for asking, mate, but why work here at all if you don't like it?'

'My old man was a right old racist, see, and that was when there were just Caribbeans here—neat little schoolkids, husbands on the buses, wives down the Baptist church on Sundays. He never understood that people are just looking for a place to call home. I suppose if I can learn to make sense of the changes, I'll never get to be like him.'

Bimsley had to admit the approach was a fair one. He realized he was propping open the door to let in the rain, and reluctantly bowed back out.

On the street he drifted back into a fugue state, watching the building without seeing. A wavering light still flickered in Tate's bedroom: Bimsley supposed that the old man was smoking against the rules, staring at the rain patterns reflected on the ceiling, or perhaps reading by torchlight after curfew, for it was now nearly midnight.

Had he considered the evidence with more care, he would have recalled the sprinklers set in the ceiling of every bedroom, provided for the specific purpose of preventing accidents caused by a confluence of alcohol and flame. Had he not been so numbed by the rain, he would also have remembered Bryant's order to check around the building every fifteen minutes for the first hour after the hostel's front door was locked at eleven p.m.

The flame in Tate's room was too large to be from a cigarette. It bounced and flickered, stretching to the walls. No alarm sounded. When Bimsley was finally signalled by the frantic receptionist, who had spotted the fire on his blurry, ancient CCTV monitor, the conflagration was in firm possession of the plasterboard walls with their so-called fireproof coating.

After the cold of the night, Bimsley at first failed to feel the roasting heat on the staircase; but as he progressed the tar-like smoke grew thicker, the fire stronger, until he knew he would be forced back. The former post-office had been cheaply converted into narrow units that failed to ignite fully but trapped scalding pockets of gas. A bizarrely clad troupe of men shoved past: pyjamas and greatcoats, one in a neon-yellow candlewick bedspread, another in a dressing-gown and balaclava. Someone was on all fours, looking for a bag that probably held all his possessions. If the situation had not been so desperate, Bimsley would have been ashamed to witness strangers in such painful private moments. Instead all was chaos, and he saw that there was no shame for any human being in fighting to stay alive.

The flames stuck to treated wood and inflammable wall coverings until they combusted. Bimsley smelt it at once: Tate's room, and indeed the entire corridor, had been splashed with white spirit. A plastic gallon drum was buckling and melding to the sisal hall carpet. The electrics popped as the circuits burned out. Oily smoke rolled across the floor in a poisonous tide.

Seven men from the second floor were able to make their way to the fire escape; but there were eight rooms, eight occupants. Bimsley kicked the doors wide and shouted out, but the fumes filled his lungs and drove him back, eyes streaming, chest on fire.

The detective constable acquitted himself bravely, and was taken to University College Hospital suffering from smoke inhalation and minor burns. The clerk and the fire brigade counted heads. The hose-drenched rooms were empty now.

The blackened eighth occupant, the only man not to leave the building alive, was covered and removed before bystanders could gain an understanding of what had happened.

38

ELEMENTARY IDENTITIES

'You're probably wondering why there are no cable-network vans parked in Balaklava Street,' said Raymond Land with sinister cheerfulness, 'no breaking news items on *London Tonight*, no journalists doorstepping the few residents who are still in the land of the living. Two reasons: most of the investigative reporters in the capital are busy trying to find links between footballers and underage call girls, and have so far failed to connect what appears to be a series of random deaths in a north London backstreet; and DCS Stanley Marsden, whom you may recall has the unenviable task of being your HMCO liaison officer, believes that such tragedies are the result of underpolicing by the People's Republic of Camden, and that by leaving them to accumulate to epidemic proportions, he will be provided with ammunition for having certain thorn-in-the-side councillors removed and posted to even less salubrious areas.'

'Why can't he talk normally?' whispered Bryant, who was doodling in an exercise book like a bored schoolboy. 'Your chastened cuckold's going to be all right, by the way. He'll be in hospital for a while, but his secret's safe. The shame will leave a bigger scar than the flying bricks.'

Longbright shot him a silencing look. Land spent his days justifying the unit's expenditure in long, boring documents, and lived for the chance to belittle anyone who treated paperwork with disdain. No one was more disdainful than Bryant, who had once provided a report written in ink that rendered itself invisible when placed in the higher temperature of Land's office.

'I can't hear a word you're saying, I've gone deaf,' said Bryant loudly. 'I've been injured in the course of duty.'

'Yes, I heard you got blown up again,' snapped Land. 'I trust you're not going to make a habit of it. Do you want to see Doctor Peltz?'

'No I don't, thank you. He gets cramp writing out my prescriptions as it is. But I do think it would help speed things up if we had more resources at our disposal.'

'You're in no position to request a larger budget. Whatever else happens in this case, it will only ever be an irritating pimple on the nose of the face that is London's crime problem. Right now the ground forces are out there trying to cope with the serious gunsters. Do you, in your rarefied little world up here, have *any* notion of the shit that's been happening around you in the last three years? Do you have any idea how many armed gangs the Met are coping with right now? I have a partial list here for your edification, Mr Bryant. Our boys are currently tackling the Lock City Crew and the Much Love Crew in Harlesden—six deaths and around a hundred non-fatal shootings so far this year—the Holy Smokes,

Tooti Nung, Bhatts and Kanaks over in Southall, the Drummond Street Boys are looking to expand in Camden, the Snakeheads, 14K and Wo Shing Wo are chopping each other up in Soho, you've got Spanglers and Fireblades in Tottenham, Brick Lane Massive, A-Team up in Islington, Stepney and Hackney Posses, Bengal Tigers, Kingsland Crew, Ghetto Boys, East Boys, Firehouse Posse and Cartel Crew in Brixton, maybe two dozen other named—that is, official—gangs. For every ethnic group that's 99 per cent decent and just wants a quiet life, we have 1 per cent that's pure bleeding evil. Kurds and Turks in Green Lanes smuggling heroin, Jamaicans doing the same in Ladbroke Grove, King's Cross Albanians running 80 per cent of the city's prostitutes, the Hunts nicking posh cars in Canning Town, the Brindels and Arifs shooting each other up in Bermondsey, Peckham Boys facing off against their own junior arm in Lewisham, and you can't just let 'em sort each other out because innocent people get caught in the crossfire. So let's keep your situation in perspective, shall we? I'm right in thinking, am I not, that you've made no advance in the single case you are supposed to be sorting out before Monday?'

'You only just agreed that there is a case,' May complained, chastened.

'That's because no one had bothered to point out the connection between their deaths.'

'What connection?' asked Bryant.

'Four instances of suffocation, of course,' Land all but shouted. 'A common repeat method. Stone me, it's not rocket science.'

'Hardly a repeat method.' Bryant waved the idea aside. 'I mean, all the deaths have involved blockage of the lungs, but that's not unusual. Life-traumas have to affect either the lungs, brain or heart. A drowning, a burial, an asphyxiation and now arson, it's more a matter—Oh, Raymond, Raymond, you're a genius!' Bryant's eyes widened excitedly. 'Why didn't I think of that?'

'Think of what?' asked Land, mystified.

'Not now, there's a chap—come back later once we've had a chance to go over this.' Bryant waved him from the room. 'I'm sorry we're not getting into machine-gun battles with your posses, but perhaps we can make an advancement here after all. Go on, off you go.'

'I will not be shooed out of my own unit,' warned Land lamely.

'Don't be ridiculous, it's not your unit, any more than Number Ten Downing Street belongs to the Prime Minister. I swear to you this will be sorted out in the next twenty-four hours, in time for your new Monday caseload. Now do us all a favour and bugger off.'

'You're really going too far, Arthur.' Land trudged away as Bryant booted the door shut.

'I'm getting senile, John, my synaptic responses aren't what they used to be. I should have spotted this earlier.'

'What?'

'It's blindingly obvious now. The four methods of death correspond to the four elements. Ruth Singh—water. Elliot Copeland—earth. Jake Avery—air. Tate—fire.'

'Now wait a minute, Arthur, don't go running off—'

'Are we dealing with something pagan and elemental? London has always had strong connections with the four elements, you know. Look at the Ministry of Defence on Horseguards Avenue, framed by the elements: two stone naked ladies, symbols of earth and water. There were going to be two more statues, but fire and air were lost in spending cutbacks. More alarmingly, does that mean it's now at an end? If the killer has successfully concluded his business, how will we ever discover the truth? Successful murderers know when to stop, John. Suppose he's achieved his aim without us ever getting on the right track? We need some confirmation from old miseryguts. We have to go and see Finch.'

'The only good thing about still having to work with you, Arthur,' said Oswald Finch, carefully folding away something that looked like a body part in tin foil, but was in fact a liver-and-onion sandwich, 'is that you're now so fantastically old, you no longer have the energy to play disgusting practical jokes on me.' Finch had been the butt of Bryant's amusing cruelties for nearly half a century, and had thought—wrongly, as it turned out—that semi-retirement would protect him. Only last month, a whoopee cushion attached to a cadaver drawer had nearly given him a heart attack.

'Oh, I wouldn't bet on it,' grinned Bryant. He usually only smiled when hearing of someone else's misfortune. Consequently, most of his acquaintances had learned to dread the glimpse of his ill-fitting false teeth. 'Look at you, though. Not in bad nick for an old fart. Exactly how old are you now?'

He watched as the ancient pathologist, so pale and serious that permanent misery-lines had formed on either side of his mouth, eased himself from the counter to search the cadaver drawers. He still had the spiky hair and raw bony hands of his youth. Even in his twenties the sight of Finch, with his long death's-head face, his creaking knees and lab coats that reeked of chemicals, caused all but the most optimistic people to avoid him. He still worked part-time at the Central Mortuary in Codrington Street, but was available to certain small, specialized branches of the Met because younger pathologists were considered more valuable employees, and therefore not a resource to be spared to such an esoteric, pointless unit as the PCU. And he wasn't thrilled about being dragged over to the makeshift mortuary at Mornington Crescent on a Sunday morning.

'I'm eighty-four,' he said. 'Or eighty-three. There were conflicting reports from my parents.'

'Last time you told me there was coffee on your birth certificate,' said Bryant. 'You don't have to lie about your age any more, Oswald, they can't fire you now. You're so far past retirement age nobody even remembers you're still alive. Do you have a body for me? Fire victim, filed under Tate but we've no idea of his real name. Probably died of smoke inhalation.'

'You might let me be the judge of that. I thought you were going to send over Kershaw. I liked him. Don't tell me you've driven him from the unit already.'

'Incredible as it may seem, he's still with us. I'm just keeping him busy. He's still getting used to the idea of having to work a seven-day week.'

Finch grunted as he struggled with the drawer,

then tugged back a slick grey sheet covering the corpse. 'We're testing this out—bloody clever stuff. Made of the same material they use to cover satellites. Stops the skin fragmenting in cases of extreme epidermal damage.'

The body was charred as black as barbecue embers. Very little skin remained intact, and his eye sockets were empty. Only his feet had been spared the flames; his ankles were bizarrely still sheathed in trousers, his socks and shoes intact.

'He would have been in better condition if the developers had insulated their floors properly. It's the same old story: corners cut and lives lost. It's all very well to spray the walls with fireproof resin, but not much good if you're going to leave cavities under the carpets without any batt insulation. Protective foam or loose fill would have worked just as well. The residents sneak in booze, you see, usually high-proof spirits because they're smaller to hide, then after a few drinks—' He slapped his hand against the steel side of the drawer, '—whoosh—they knock over the bottle and it soaks between the floorboards. Not enough to start a fire from a falling match, you understand, but over time ... sounds as though this was arson, though. The lovely Longbright informs me that there was white-spirit residue all over the place consistent with someone splashing it from a bottle. Not my field of expertise, of course, I'm better off with the dead. Where's my poking stick?' He searched around for the car antenna he used for demonstrations. 'Look at this.' He wiggled the antenna through the tramp's gaping jaw and carefully retracted it. 'See on the end there?'

'I haven't got my glasses,' Bryant admitted. 'What is it?'

'Soot. Burning is a common form of accidental death, rare as a method of suicide because it's far too slow and painful, virtually unheard-of as a means of homicide, despite what you see on the telly. My second question is always, was the victim alive or dead when the fire started? Soot in the air passages suggests he was alive. I ran a blood test, and the presence of carbon monoxide and cyanide from the armchair fabric proves it, not to mention the fact that his blood is fire-engine red, which indicates the presence of poison. So we know he wasn't fatally injured before the fire.'

'What about those?' Bryant pointed to what appeared to be knife wounds on the corpse's upper arms.

'Actually, they're heat ruptures. Third-degree burns, partial destruction of the skin using the old Glaister six-degree methodology. Feet left intact because he fell head-first toward the door with his shoes against the building's outer wall, which didn't burn. Hyperaemia, that's the clustering of leukocytes—white blood cells sent to heal damage—around the ruptures, which suggests to me that he was dead drunk when the blaze started, and blistered while he was still breathing, poor bugger.'

'Why are his arms up in a boxing pose?' asked Bryant. 'He looks like Henry Cooper.'

'Heat stiffening,' Finch explained, snapping the plastic sheet back in place. 'The muscles tend to coagulate on the flexor surface of the limbs.'

'Did you get a chance to check gut contents?'

'Of course.' Finch looked at him as if he was

mad. 'I know how to do my job. He'd hardly eaten in days, but the stomach lining had plenty of alcohol damage. His liver was little more than a meaty lace curtain. You could stick your fingers through it. I presume your lad can set the time of the fire pretty accurately.'

'So what's the cause of death?'

'Well, technically poisoning, but you can say fire.' Finch swept the cloth back over the body like a magician covering an assistant.

'Four deaths, four elements.' *This is where the trail stops cold,* thought Bryant. *I promised Raymond we'd wrap this up, but what the hell do I do now?*

'Kettle's nearly boiled,' said Finch. 'I'm making Madagascan Vanilla Pod.'

'Do you have any PG Tips?'

'No, I gave up dairy the year Chris Bonnington climbed Everest. You should too, a man of your age.'

'I am not a man of my age,' replied Bryant indignantly. 'I'm more the age of someone much younger.'

'You think that,' Finch morosely dangled his teabag over the mug, 'but a look at your insides would tell a different story.'

'Wait a minute. You said confirming whether the victim was dead or alive is always your second question. What's the first?'

'Well, am I sure the body is who it's supposed to be, obviously. Death removes so many human characteristics that identification can be hard even for a close relative, and in this case we have no relations, close or otherwise, only your frankly inadequate description and that of the hostel clerk. Running a height-and-weight match was easy enough—I didn't have to allow for fat burning or being drawn off because you don't find much excess baggage on homeless men—and that was consistent enough.'

Bryant glanced at his old sparring partner with suspicion. 'But what? You were heading for a "but" there, weren't you?'

'Well, it was the lack of positive identifiers,' Finch complained. He suddenly looked uncomfortable, almost embarrassed. 'We made the mistake with your false teeth after the unit blew up, didn't we?'

Bryant harrumphed. 'So what did you look for?'

'I checked for signs consistent with long-term crippling on the left side of the body, severe bone-wear in the hip-joint, damage to the femur, then I checked the radius and ulna. Nothing unusual, perfectly normal limbs, no ligature damage apparent to the naked eye. Scar tissue doesn't burn so easily, so I checked all over. Either your fellow was faking his disabilities—and why on earth would he do that? Didn't you say he limped when trying to get away from you?'

'Or what?'

'Or you have the wrong man.'

'The body definitely came from his room.'

Finch sighed with annoyance. 'Then he switched rooms with someone else. Use your head. Maybe he even switched clothes and left the building. It means he's not as daft as you thought. He was on to you, and now he's got away.'

39

GOING UNDER

Kallie reread what she had written, then highlighted a sentence and deleted it. After three further deletions, there was virtually nothing left of the email, at which point she knew it would not be sent.

She had no way of knowing whether Paul was still checking his hotmail account. Perhaps he had moved on, heading further south to the sun, only to become lost among the travellers who passed lifetimes searching for themselves in shadowless landscapes. She was already starting to forget certain things about him. If he decided to return, she would consider her plan of action, but nothing would ever be the same between them.

At least the house was becoming more presentable. Fresh paint and paper had brightened the rooms, and with the fee from a new modelling contract she would be able to afford a new kitchen in the basement. An electrician had provided plans for a runway of halogen bulbs that would bring much-needed light into the lower-ground floor.

The basement bathroom still needed work, but something stopped her from tackling the job. Dampness lived on in its corners like the shadows of a persistent illness. On some mornings, she could see her breath in the room's cold spots. The spiders had returned, despite all her efforts to dislodge them, and a patch of parquet remained permanently slick with icy sweat. Until she could bring herself to tackle the problems, she would continue to stay out of the room as much as possible.

The doorbell made her jump. As Kallie opened the front door, Heather pushed past her excitedly. 'He's back!' she called. 'Look in your garden, I saw him a moment ago.'

'Who? The old man?' For once, Kallie was almost glad to see her neighbour. At least she provided a distraction from her own problems.

'Can you believe it? He's right where he always stands, inside that bush—you should really cut it down.' She peered from the back landing window, wiping the glass. 'Damn, I can't see him, but he was there. I was trimming shallots over the sink and looked up. Goes to show the police are telling us lies.'

'What do you mean?' Kallie asked, searching for signs that Tate had returned to the garden.

'I immediately rang the Peculiar Crimes Unit and spoke to Sergeant Longbright. She told me the old tramp had died in a fire at his hostel. But if he's dead he must have a twin—although I do think he's wearing different clothes now. What could have happened?'

Kallie was taken aback, less by the news than by Heather's attitude. With little else to focus her energies on, she had lately become the eyes and ears of the street, watching and listening with a hysterical intensity that disturbed Kallie.

'Either the police know and are lying to us for some reason, or he got out of the building somehow,' said

Heather. 'This means we can't rely on them for help, don't you see? I'm sure that disgusting, sinister old man is behind it all. You could be in danger, and the police aren't willing to do anything about it. They'll see you murdered in your bed first, like poor Jake.'

'We could all be in danger, Heather.'

'He's in your garden, don't you understand? It's you he wants. Why don't they do something more to protect us?'

'How can they unless they know what they're dealing with?' asked Kallie. 'They haven't a clue. It's like when you report a burglary; you never expect to get your stuff back. I was just about to make some tea. Stay and have one.'

'I can't stop long.' Heather reluctantly left the window.

'Does he never come into your garden?'

'Oh, I've seen him there once or twice, but he seems far more interested in you.'

'That's comforting.'

'I'm sorry, I don't mean to frighten you. I mean, this is having an effect on all of us. Randall Ayson's wife is threatening to leave him, did you hear? Everyone says he's been having an affair, and he's supposed to be a born-again Christian. Which means that the only people down this street who are still in stable relationships are Omar and Fatima, despite the fact that she can't have kids and he's desperate to be a father, and that horrible property developer, Mark Garrett, and his girlfriend, who of course will never get a wedding ring out of him, and the Wiltons, although I wouldn't be surprised if Oliver wasn't playing away. Brewer's been telling his father he wants to be a policeman, but Oliver wants him to become a lawyer.' She paused for a breath. 'Have you heard anything more from Paul?'

'Nothing. He seems to have vanished off the face of the earth.'

'Men! What is it that requires them to turn into teenagers for the whole of their thirties? Nobody ages gracefully any more. Whatever happened to pipes?'

'Mr Bryant smokes one.'

'Well, there's a limit. He's short enough to be my grandfather. I honestly believe that if women could learn to read an A-Z in a moving vehicle we'd have no need of men at all. Have you thought of moving out?'

The question, tacked into part of Heather's random thought process, caught Kallie by surprise.

'No, of course not. What do you mean?'

'Only that with all the trouble in the street, and Paul taking off, you might prefer something in a smarter, safer area. I mean, the attacker is clearly someone who lives in the neighbourhood, and he's still at large, isn't he? So there's no telling who might be at risk.'

'You're the one who thought this would be a good idea in the first place.'

'Yes, but that was before everything started to go wrong.'

'And before George left you,' Kallie prompted. 'Why haven't *you* considered moving?'

'Oh, I probably will once the divorce is finalized. I have a wonderful lawyer—very cute, Jewish, married at the moment but I'm working on it.'

'Heather, you are terrible.'

'Which reminds me, George is coming round this afternoon.' Heather glanced at her watch. 'I need to get back home to practise my living-in-poverty routine.'

Although Kallie had never met George, she had formed a mental image of him, so she was surprised to discover how much older than Heather he was when his black Mercedes drew up in front of their house a couple of hours later. An elegant suit could not disguise the fact that he was out of condition, sporting the kind of sclerotic complexion she associated with hill-walkers and coronary thrombosis. She tried to dismiss the image of him creeping around a Paris apartment in his dressing-gown, and concentrated on clearing the last of the paint tins from her cupboards instead.

As she worked, she thought of Heather's parting remark—'still at large'—and tried to avoid looking toward the basement bathroom.

The Sunday-morning downpour did little to dissuade the tourists from packing out the markets in Camden Town, but the area around Mornington Crescent Tube station remained becalmed. Rain pattered on to the hornbeams and hawthorns in Oakley Square, and the rose bushes were bowing their heads in contemplation of finer weather. With just twenty-four hours to go before Raymond Land's deadline, the staff at the PCU were to be found at their desks, despondently clearing paperwork.

'I don't think Mr Bryant likes me,' said Giles Kershaw. 'I've tried to be as helpful as possible.'

'Oh, I shouldn't worry about it,' May consoled the young forensic officer. 'He's like that with everyone: hateful until you get to know him, then merely difficult. He'll get used to you. We never had an independent forensic expert before. Oswald Finch always handled everything, animate and inanimate. Arthur used to say he was in charge of General Debris and Criminal Fallout. He didn't mean to bypass you. What have you got there?'

Kershaw carefully unzipped the clear plastic bag on his bench. 'Dan Banbury's sorting out some anomalies in the crime-scene log, so he passed me Tate's belongings. Nothing in the room survived, but from the look of it there wasn't much beyond a few syrup tins. I nipped over to the hostel for a quick rummage, and found the lockers on the ground floor intact. I called to get permission to open them, but some health-and-safety jobsworth refused to give me the go-ahead without Dan present, so I got one of the firemen to accidentally drop his crowbar on it.'

'Oh, I think Arthur is soon going to like you,' smiled May. 'His sense of civic responsibility is tempered with a similar impatience.'

'Then I think he might be pleased with this,' Kershaw pulled out a set of small cloth-bound books. 'Tate's sole possessions, according to the clerk. Very particular about them, his "special" books, he had an arrangement to leave them permanently in his locker—said he was worried that the water would get at them. He liked to check that they were safe every time he stayed over.'

'Have you looked at them yet?'

'I've only done an external examination. I should tell Dan—after all, he's the crime-scene manager.'

'Don't worry, we don't stand on formalities around here. May I?'

The first three blue cloth-bound volumes matched, and made up a somewhat random history of English painting. The edition had been published in 1978.

'The printing is cheap,' May told Kershaw. 'Poor-quality paper, and half of the colour plates are out of register.'

At the back of each volume he found a photograph of the author, presumably in his late thirties, prematurely haggard in the way of so many young men who were children during wartime. The fourth book was a volume on the life and works of Stanley Spencer, published in 1987. 'I need to show these to Arthur,' he explained. 'One of his regular contacts is an art teacher. I'll bring them back.'

'Think this stuff might be useful?'

'It just makes me wonder; we assumed Tate got his nickname from the syrup tins. What if he didn't? What if it was something to do with the Tate Gallery?'

'So what?' Kershaw packed away the rest of the material. 'Forgive me, I'm still getting to grips with how you chaps work. You all seem to avoid the obvious routes. I mean, most killers are known to their victims. Shouldn't you be out there interviewing friends and relatives, asking for witnesses?'

'The interviews and witness appeals have been covered by Mangeshkar and Bimsley,' May explained. 'I think we're far beyond pedestrian procedures now. You and Banbury have turned up nothing useful at any of the sites.'

'Yes, sorry about that. I was sure we'd get something from Jake Avery. I mean, a man murdered in his own bedroom. According to Dan, it's the room that generates more static than any other in a house because it's occupied for half of every twenty-four-hour period, lots of different fibre-attracting surfaces and fabrics. But that's part of the problem: there's a surfeit of material from different sources. The wardrobe's in the bedroom, so every item of clothing in the building has passed through it. I'm not saying that somewhere in amongst all that fibre residue there isn't an alien skin flake, but we haven't found it yet. Edmund Locard, the French forensic scientist, said that every contact leaves a trace. That may be, but reading them is the problem. We've got partial bootprints on the downstairs floor that don't match any footwear found in the house, and that's about it. We did a vacuum sweep from the carpet at the edge of the bed, but there was nothing of any size there. I'm trying to get a fibre selection from the bedroom on to a light microscope—no chance of getting body particles from Avery's face near an SEM, as the only one in the area is in for repairs and there's a horrendous waiting list. I've done the doors and window-ledges, and drawn a blank. What bothers me most, I think, is that Balaklava Street has become a blighted spot, what with murders, fires, missing bodies and drownings all within the space of a month, while you and Mr Bryant drift off down the investigation's most obscure side-alleys at the slightest provocation.'

'Is that how it looks to you?' May asked.

'It's just that—well, people outside the unit keep asking me questions. They make fun of me. They don't see what we're hoping to achieve.'

'You'll get used to that,' May promised. 'Outsiders never understand how we work. They're too busy following guidelines and checking results tables. Balaklava Street is far from being an especially blighted spot. There are now over a dozen Murder Miles in London.'

'How does one qualify for status as a Murder Mile?'

'You need six murders in the same road over a six-month period. Hackney, Kentish Town, Peckham and

Brixton have qualified many times over. Arthur remembers Hackney as a town of wide empty streets and neat family houses bordered by marshlands. Now people throw rubbish from the balconies of tower blocks into crack alleys, and overdosed corpses lie in their apartments undiscovered until the council comes to redecorate. But ...' May tapped his pen on the streetmap before him. 'The events in Balaklava Street have a rarer quality: they're premeditated. We think that whatever happened there began as an accident, then became a plan, and is now in a state of improvisation. When plans become extemporized, people make mistakes. But we can't afford to wait for an error when lives are at risk.'

'So what are you going to do?'

'Arthur and I have been investigating this from separate angles. I think the only way we'll find the answer now is to combine our strengths.'

'You'll have to be quick. Land's bringing in something new tomorrow, and reckons he's taking every other file out of the building. That means he'll turn your findings over to the Met, and you'll never get the case back.'

'Believe me, I'm aware of that.' May threw the last of the witness statements into a box and sealed it. 'It's not all that's at stake. Arthur's going through one of his periodic lapses of self-confidence. He says if he can't sort this out in time, he doesn't deserve to remain at the unit. This will be his final case.'

40

BUILDING ON BONES

'Come in, come in, mind the violins.'

A short fiftyish woman with a pageboy haircut and heavy breasts squeezed into a dusty black sweater beckoned Arthur Bryant into the narrow hall, every foot of which was lined with musical instruments. 'My son repairs them. Since his workshop was sold and turned into apartments he's had to carry on the business here. I'll put the kettle on. It's less crowded in the kitchen. That's my territory.'

Bryant removed his trilby and looked for somewhere to hang it. He caught a glimpse of a frenetically wallpapered lounge filled with violas, cellos, catgut, rolls of plyboard and blocks of yellow resin.

Mrs Quinten pulled out a chair and cleared a space at the bleached oak table. This may have been her territory, but she had chosen to clutter it as much as every other part of the house. Over a dozen Victorian milk jugs filled with dried flowers added dust to the already asthma-inducing air. 'We have goat's milk. I hope that's all right.'

'Absolutely fine,' said Bryant, already warming to his host. 'My God, you keep an untidy house. You're nearly as bad as me. I bet you know where everything is.'

'Of course—please, call me Jackie—what's the point of having a home where you don't use every inch of space? You're simply depriving others of room to live. I grow so many vegetables in my little garden that I'm able to take bagfuls down to the Holmes Road hostel during the summer. I understand they had a fire.'

'Yes, and I suppose that's what I'm here about, in a way. I'm sorry—' He pulled a crumpled sheet of music from beneath his buttocks and searched for somewhere to put it.

'That's all right, we use the backs for shopping lists. Penniless artists often used to paint on the back of sheet music, did you know? There's no reason why you should, of course. That's the problem with running the local historical society—one is always telling people things they have absolutely no interest in hearing. The modern world has severed itself from its history, Mr Bryant. Only the wealthy can afford the luxury of remembering the past, and we are far from wealthy. What can I tell you about? I'm afraid we only cover the immediate area. Somers Town, St Pancras, Camden and King's Cross have their own historical societies, but we're all struggling. We're short of members, and no one has enough free time to do the research.'

Bryant scratched the side of his nose and thought. 'Well, it's a bit of a long shot. There have been some strange occurrences in the surrounding streets. I'm required to examine every feasible possibility, and find myself trying to understand.' He accepted a mug of orange tea and drank a trusting measure. 'Searching for someone with motive and opportunity hardly seems to apply in this instance. Instead, I've been wondering if the solution lies in the actual ground itself.'

'I'm not sure I follow you,' Mrs Quinten admitted, seating herself opposite.

'The area is a victim of its past. People have made their homes here for centuries, have lived and bred and fought and died here, around the river beds, in damp and squalor, in marshlands and on hills of bones. You can concrete over the land, but you can't change its character without moving everyone out and replacing them all.'

'But that's precisely what is happening, Mr Bryant. In the last two decades, these streets have been filled with virtually every nationality on earth. The city's character is rapidly changing, thanks to the advent of mass transit and economic migration.'

'But migrants bring comparatively little of their hereditary culture with them,' argued Bryant. 'Recent experiments have shown the growing power of nurture over nature. The first law of behavioural genetics states that all human traits are inheritable, but a large proportion of those traits are unaccounted for by genes or families. Children spend less time with their parents, so they're changed more by their peers. The city quickly imposes its own will. If you raised one identical twin in Istanbul and the other in London, you might doubt they were ever related by the time they were twenty.'

'I'm sorry, Mr Bryant, you really are losing me.'

'A murderer, Mrs Quinten!' Bryant blurted. 'I can't make myself any plainer.' Coming from Bryant, it sounded like an apology. 'Three residents and one transient have died, while another is in hiding. An old Indian lady, a builder, a television producer, a homeless alcoholic. They have absolutely nothing in common with one another except their location. It leads me to assume that they were attacked not for who they were, but simply because they were here at all. I asked myself what was so special about this place, beyond the fact that it seems to suffer from a surfeit of water, then wondered if that was it. Water rising from below, falling from the sky, soaking into the walls of houses. But if that is the connection, what on earth does it mean? Which leads me to ask if you have anything in your historical records that reveals a precedent for such violent behaviour in the area. Has it happened before, perhaps the last time the streets flooded?'

'Ah, I'm with you now,' said Mrs Quinten finally. 'Feel free to delve into the biscuit barrel while I go and look.'

She returned with an immense folder of newspaper cuttings, which she dropped on to the kitchen table in a cloud of fine dust.

'Are you allergic? I hope not. This one has been on top of the wardrobe for years.' She folded back the front cover, wiping it with her sleeve. 'I think you'll find that the same three roads around here have flooded every thirty years or so.'

'When was the last time?' Bryant unfolded his glasses and pinned back the clippings.

'1975. Before that, 1942. Covering over the Fleet didn't stop it from flooding. The council can't do anything about it. They thought that drains added at the time of the new London ring-main would help, but there's a gentleman in Balaklava Street who works for the Water Board, and he reckons it's due to happen again.'

'Oliver Wilton,' said Bryant. 'You know him?'

'Yes, he belongs to our society. Gave a talk last year about the problem. He's an expert on the subject. Very passionate about it. He has maps showing the exact patterns of flooding.' She turned a page and pointed to an article taken from the *Camden New Journal*. 'Here you are. Bayham Street, Archibald Road, Balaklava Street. Bayham Street was one of the poorest roads in the whole of London. Charles Dickens lodged there when he came up from Chatham. It was so wet that the weeds came up through the paving stones and split them clean in half.'

'When was this?'

'Around 1822. At one end of the street was the Red Cap tea garden, named after the local witch. A lot of people thought the place was haunted by her and her familiars. Old photographs show how grim and unlit the side streets were, and naturally there were many fights and murders in such a poverty-stricken area. Bayham Street is better than it was, but there are still muggings, car thefts, drug-dealing, and the odd murder, as I'm sure you know. Archibald Road went during the War, firebombed out of existence—all that's there now is a car showroom and an estate agent's office. There were sightings of ghosts there before the War, but it was a time when everyone seemed to see phantoms, almost as if they were having premonitions of the terrible times ahead. And there had been sensational cases widely reported, like the haunting of Borley Rectory, so strange sightings in local neighbourhoods made good press copy. Look.' She tapped a nicotine-coloured photograph showing a brick flying through the air. 'The Rectory hoax would fool no one today. Attention-seekers staged these ridiculous stunts, hysterical parlour maids saw ladies in white, old gentlemen swore they saw Cavaliers walk through walls. People can be so silly in times of social panic; how quickly they all start to agree with one another. Perhaps we should look at more recent events. This might interest you.' She carefully emptied an envelope of cuttings and unfolded them. 'A railway worker murdered his wife and children in Inkerman Street, no reason ever given—he died in a mental institution.'

'Arrested in October 1975,' said Bryant. 'The time of the last flood. What about the previous occasion?'

'I don't think we have anything on that date, but there's something from much earlier.' She pulled a large volume bound in crimson leather, one of six, from the kitchen bookcase. 'Walford's *Old and New London,* probably the best set of reference books ever published on London. Here we are: "Ghastly murder at the Castle Tavern in 1815". The route had long been popular with highwaymen travelling out of town through Hampstead. Dick Turpin had regularly held up the coaches using it. It would seem that this particular horseman threatened the tavern's entire clientele, then began shooting them dead when they refused to hand over their money and jewellery. The interesting part comes afterwards, for he appears to have drowned during his escape. He attempted to cross the Fleet, but the river rose suddenly and cut him off in mid stream. The horse stumbled, throwing him into the fast-moving water. His body was never recovered.'

'Mrs Quinten, I can't start believing that the ghost

of a drowned highwayman is bumping off twenty-first-century residents, however much I'd like to—my partner would kill me.'

'Then I don't see how I can help you.'

'Thanks anyway.' He attempted a smile. 'It was a long shot, but I feel happier for having covered it.' He was closing the volume when his eye drifted to the page that followed. 'Life and Times of Dr William Stukeley, the Celebrated Antiquary.' He read down the column a little, reaching the Latin inscription that had been set above the antiquary's front door.

> *Me dulcis saturet quies,*
> *Obscuro positus loco,*
> *Leni perfruar otio,*
> *Chyndonax Druida.*

'Chyndonax—I've seen that word before in relation to Druid ceremonies.' Bryant wondered if he still had the unit's spare mobile, and was amazed to find it intact in his jacket pocket, even though there were sherbet lemons stuck to it.

'Maggie? I hope I'm calling at a convenient time. You're not summoning up dead jockeys for racing tips again?'

The white witch often conducted séances at around this hour on a Sunday.

'Oh, you're watching the wrestling. Listen, you're good with Druids, aren't you? Dr William Stukeley, resident of Kentish Town near Emmanuel Hospital for the Reception of the Blind— *Chyndonax Druida,* he had the words engraved over his porch because they were important to him ... good woman, I *knew* you'd know.'

He listened for a minute and rang off.

'Well?' asked Mrs Quinten, intrigued.

'I'm afraid it won't mean much to you. It isn't what I expected at all. Thank you for your time, and for the tea, although I'm not sure about those heart-burn-inducing biscuits. Perhaps we could meet again. It's pleasing to find a kindred spirit. My card.'

Mrs Quinten looked at it, perplexed. 'This is a ticket for the rotor at Battersea funfair, priced 1/6d. It expired in 1967.'

'I'm sorry, it's an old coat. Try this one.' He hadn't made the effort to be charming for quite a while, and was out of practice.

'Thank you,' said Mrs Quinten, taking the PCU's number. 'I hope we meet again.'

41

ABANDONED SOULS

Monica Greenwood and John May stood before the statues of conjoined children with penile noses and tried to look shocked, but the effort was too much. 'I enjoy sensation-art,' said Monica, 'but when the sensation wears off you're left with very little to admire except technique.'

May knew he should have cancelled their Sunday-afternoon arrangement to visit the gallery together, but had fallen under her spell. Even though he had promised to return to the PCU within an hour, Bryant was unmollified.

Monica shifted around to examine the statue from another angle. 'I loved the new British artists at first. Even after Rachel Whiteread had concreted negative space for the fifth time, I still felt there was something fresh happening. But then it just became about money, and left little of abiding interest. I suppose that's the point; every sensation dies. But why must it?'

'I never had you pegged for a Royal Academy reactionary,' teased May.

'I'm not. I've no interest in the chocolate-box ceilings of Tiepolo, but I'd rather stare at them for a fortnight than one of Damien Hirst's spin paintings. Do you want me to leave my husband?'

'I hardly think it's a fit subject for discussion while he's sitting at home with a bandaged head,' May pointed out.

'That's a pretty feeble excuse. His ego took most of the battering. He'll never change. He's only worried about his colleagues finding out.'

'Well, I feel guilty. I should have been there to protect him instead of leaving the job to Arthur.'

'What difference would it really have made? Now you have a charge on which to hold Ubeda, assuming he ever surfaces again, and Gareth has been frightened away from illegal activities until the next time someone appeals to his vanity.'

Monica blew a lock of hair away from her face. The gallery was overheated and bright, hardly the best place for a romantic meeting. 'I consider myself a modern woman, but just occasionally I'd like a man to make the decisions, John. I spent my entire marriage making up Gareth's mind for him. Now someone else can have the job. Doing the right thing for everyone eventually makes other people hate you. I want to be free to make a fool of myself.' She took his hand in hers and held it tightly. 'You know I would leave him for you.'

'Monica, I—'

'Don't say something you might regret, John. I know you. You have no guile. You're honest and enlightened, which makes you very good at your job, and rather desirable. Tell me why you brought me here. If I know you, it's something to do with your work. Let's keep the conversation on safer ground.'

They walked back to the centre of the immense turbine hall of Bankside's former power station, now the home of the Tate Modern, where an elegant resin sculpture curled and unwound through the agoraphobia-inducing space. May pulled open his backpack and removed the art books. 'There was a fire in a hostel. These volumes belong to the man who may have started it. If it turns out that he did, we thought they might offer some kind of insight into his motive.'

'It's not much to go on, is it?' Monica found a bench near the entrance and seated herself with the books on her lap.

'Arthur wants to call in his loopy art-historian friend Peregrine Summerfield, but I thought I'd try you first. What do you know about Stanley Spencer?'

'Not much. He was named after a balloonist. He fought in the First World War and was a War artist in the Second. Lived in Cookham, beside the river, became fascinated by the concept of resurrection. His paintings are odd, naive and eerie. Some are downright disturbing. He had a bit of a split personality, painting in two distinct modes, his realist pictures and his so-called heavenly-vision paintings. His style was very dynamic—you can see from these illustrations— but there's a great sense of harmony in the compositions, even though the figures disturb. That's about the extent of my knowledge.'

'It seems an odd sort of book for a homeless man to lug about.'

'Perhaps not; it could be rather comforting to carry a visual depiction of the Resurrection with you. I've never seen these before.' She opened the first of the matching cloth-bound volumes. 'Printed back in a time when ordinary men and women might wish to read about English art. Dreadful cheap reproduction, but rather valuable, I'd imagine.'

'Oh, why?'

'You don't find too many records of these paintings and sculptures. A lot of stuff's vanished now. It wasn't valued much at the time.'

May watched as she traced the pictures with her fingers, as if reading messages hidden in the ink. 'Anything else?'

'They're by minor artists, certainly, but what makes this set interesting is that all the art has a common connection.'

'Really? I couldn't see one.'

'No reason why you would, darling. They haven't been seen for fifty years. I think you'll find that these pictures were all lost or looted during the Second World War. I've certainly never seen them gathered together in volumes like this. Some of them are very peculiar. Naive paintings so often are. An insight into the abandoned soul; amateur artists can develop highly personal visions as a response to their inability to communicate. Pity the second volume is damaged.'

'Show me.'

Monica allowed the book to fall open at the centre, and he saw that a number of pages had been removed with a knife.

'Check the index,' he instructed her.

'Hm. The missing pages contained the works of an artist called Gilbert Kingdom.'

'Ever heard of him?'

'Doesn't ring any bells, but I can give you a few

college websites to search. They might be able to help you.' She took a notepad from her bag and jotted them down. 'Use my password. You go and solve your crime, I'll stay with my husband until he's mended, and then perhaps we'll talk again.'

42

SECRET HISTORIES

'Ah, you're back. *Chyndonax Druida,*' said Bryant excitedly. 'It was carved on the door of William Stukeley's house in Kentish Town.' He waited for a response, but there came none. 'Look, I know it's demanding, but please make an effort to follow this. It's really important.'

'All right, then explain.'

'It's a reference to an urn inscribed in France that was believed to hold the ashes of the Arch Druid of that name, one of the grand masters of Stonehenge.'

'How do you know these things?' asked May in some exasperation.

'I looked it up in this.' Bryant raised a moulting paperback entitled *The Mammoth Book of Druid Lore.* 'The Victorians believed that the urn itself had a greater purpose. Lord Carnarvon tried to buy it from the French, but of course they wouldn't sell. There was an immense fascination with Egyptian artefacts at the time. As you know, Carnarvon financed Howard Carter, the discoverer of the tomb of the Boy Prince Tutankhamun, and subsequently died, some believed as part of the "curse". His supporters thought that the vase was modelled over a much earlier container that had been smuggled out of Egypt.'

'Don't tell me, let me guess,' groaned May. 'They thought it was the original vessel containing all the counted sorrows of mankind.'

'Exactly, well done. So you see, it does exist, and now we have proof that the urn is linked to Kentish Town. Ask me what happened to it.'

'I'll bite, although I'm sure I'll regret it. What happened?'

'It was stolen from the Louvre two years after the unsuccessful purchase bid,' said Bryant with an air of satisfaction. 'The French government suspected one of Carnarvon's pals of taking revenge for his death, but they had no proof. So it could conceivably have wound up in this vicinity, hence Ubeda's need to enlist a local expert like Greenwood in his search.'

'None of which helps us in the slightest when it comes to solving matters of murder.' May felt old and tired. Bryant was starting to draw the lifeblood from him again, he could feel it.

'You may say that, but I have a feeling that if we find the urn, we find our murderer.'

'Why?' May all but shouted. 'Why must the two be connected? They were entirely separate investigations! We have no reason—no reason at all—to assume anything of the kind. Do you realize there's not a single element of this investigation that's built on empirical data? Do you have *any idea* how annoying you are?'

Bryant's watery blue eyes widened with boyish surprise. 'I don't mean to be.'

'I know you don't, Arthur. I'm not sleeping well,

that's all. I should go home. Let's face it, we've missed the deadline. We've failed.'

'I'll drive you.'

'No offence, but your driving would really put me over the edge. I'll get a bus.'

'You might want to stay for a while,' said Janice Longbright, entering the room without knocking. 'There's a lady here to see you, Arthur. A Mrs Quinten. She says she has the information you requested.'

'Then show her in.' Bryant made a half-hearted attempt to smooth down his unruly ring of white hair. 'How am I?'

He turned to May for approval, like a schoolboy submitting to a neatness check. May shrugged. It was a long time since his partner had considered his appearance before the arrival of a woman. He smiled to himself. 'You'll pass.'

'What's so funny?'

'Nothing. Here's your lady now.'

Jackie Quinten looked about her with obvious pleasure. 'This is nothing like I imagined. Not like a police station at all,' she beamed. 'How lovely. It looks like somebody lives here.'

'We do,' said Bryant. 'I'm thinking of opening up the fireplace.'

'I miss real fires, don't you? Worth the effort, I feel.' She planted her ample rump in the chair beside Bryant's. Nobody ever dared to do that; it was May's chair. 'There's a lady in our street whose husband is a cartographic restorer attached to the British Library. I went round to borrow their belt sander, and while I was waiting for her to repack her collapsible attic ladder I thought about what you said, about the history of houses and the sort of people who lived in them,

and I asked her if she'd ever heard local stories about
strange events occurring in or around the flood years,
specifically involving death or injury. She remembered a story about an eccentric old man who lived,
she thought, in Balaklava Street. At that time the
street was pretty rough—the police went around in
pairs. The families of the men who had built the railways had prospered and outgrown their terraces, and
as they moved out, poorer families moved in. Those
families sublet their rooms, and the overcrowding
and unemployment brought trouble—you know how
it is.'

May reseated himself, beaming. It looked like
Bryant had finally met a soulmate.

'Anyway, some local kids got it into their heads
that the old man was hiding a fortune somewhere,
and beat him up trying to find its whereabouts.
Unfortunately they kicked him unconscious and left
him in the street while they searched his house, just at
a time when the heavy rains were causing the roads to
flood. The old man had fallen into a dip in the road
where the cobbles had sunk, and as the water rose
over the blocked drains, he drowned. The neighbourhood constables knew the identities of the boys—
everyone did—but communities kept close then, and
no one was ever brought to trial. Many of the houses
in Camden, Somers Town and St Pancras have such
odd histories attached to them. Most of the stories
are forgotten now, of course.'

She opened her bicycle pannier and carefully un-
rolled a plastic-coated sheet of rough vellum, laying it
before Bryant. 'Janet's husband has a detailed map of
the area, made just before the War. He'll kill me if he
discovers she's lent it out again, so I won't be able to

leave it with you, but we thought there was something on it you might like to see.'

As there was no more room behind the desk, May was forced to study the map upside-down, which vaguely displeased him.

'As you'll notice, it's rather fanciful. I imagine it was designed as a wall-hanging, a gift to a neighbour, rather than an accurate ordnance of the area. This, in particular, is intriguing.' She traced the ink-line of the streets with her forefinger, arriving at Balaklava Street. 'Supposedly, the houses on the north side of the street had been constructed on the site of a much earlier dwelling, an old monastery that had collapsed when the Fleet had broken its banks; and even before the monastery, a similar fate had befallen an earlier house. This building belonged to a sect of Druids, and became known locally as the House Curs'd By All Water. Look, it's marked here.'

Bryant examined the map. The scrolled calligraphy spread so widely across the street that there was no way of knowing which house now occupied the site.

'Another property was known as The House of Conflagration, nobody remembers why. That's marked too.'

Bryant fully expected to see the appellation scrawled across the site of the hostel, and was disappointed to find it written halfway along Balaklava Street. This time, the site could be more accurately discerned. He withdrew a magnifier from his top drawer and examined the markings. 'Four from the left, three from the right. The buildings haven't changed, have they?'

'Not to my knowledge.'

'Then I know this house.'

'Which is it?' asked May.

'Number 43. The House of Conflagration belongs to Tamsin and Oliver Wilton. I think we should get Bimsley around there right now.'

'Why?'

'The fire at the hostel failed to take Tate's life. We don't have the arson tests back yet, but let's suppose for a moment that Tate is behind the whole thing. He knew he was being watched, could have switched clothes and set the hostel alight, escaping in the confusion. But this wouldn't have been part of his original plan.'

'Then what's his plan?'

'The street is flooding again. When this has happened in the past, strange crimes have occurred. What if he's taken it into his head to repeat the past? Suppose the House Curs'd By All Water is where Ruth Singh died. This House of Conflagration would have nothing to do with the hostel, but it could well place the Wiltons in danger. Tate may well have burned down one building. Suppose he's about to do it again?'

'I don't understand why he would do such a thing. But you're right, we can't afford to take any chances.' May called in Longbright and briefed her. 'Make a reduced copy of this, would you?' He handed her the map. 'Then I want you to take Mangeshkar and Bimsley with you back to Balaklava Street.'

Bimsley arrived before the others. The rain was heavier than ever now. Water flooded across the cobbles in a swathe, frothing over the congested drains. The front walls of the houses were sodden from their roofs to their bedroom windows, soaking the shoulders of the terrace. Bimsley jumped the steps and hammered on the Wiltons' door knocker, but no one stirred inside. He tipped back his baseball cap and looked up at the dim windows. 'There's no response,' he told Longbright. 'Can you try their mobiles?'

Bimsley closed his phone and stepped back. He looked about the street. Further down, someone was standing in the bushes on the waste ground, watching him. It was hard to see in the rain, but it looked like Tate. As they saw each other, the onlooker turned and limped off.

'You're not getting away this time,' said Bimsley, breaking into a run.

43

OIL AND WATER

'Blimey, a rare sighting of the lesser-fancied detective, *Homunculus Senex Investigatorus*,' said Peregrine Summerfield, scratching his face through his wild ginger beard. 'Come in before the neighbours see you. Excuse the pyjamas, I prefer to paint in them because of the mess.' He waved Bryant in with a flick of his paintbrush, dabbing the wall turquoise. Bryant noticed that there was vermilion paint on the ceiling. 'How the devil did you find me?'

'Lilian told me you were living up here now,' Bryant explained. 'I bumped into her a few weeks ago.'

'I hope you were driving a bulldozer. She's been a proper cow since she walked out. I only own one painting, a small and rather sickly Wols that looks like a regurgitated prawn biriani, but Bauhaus stock is higher than ever and now she's demanding it in the divorce settlement.'

'I had no idea you liked German abstract art. I don't suppose there are any clean cups.' Bryant wandered into the kitchen and ran a kettle under the tap. Every piece of crockery on the draining board was covered with brushes and half-dried blobs of acrylic paint.

'I use plastic ones now, saves on the washing up. Well, you can look upon me and despair. How the once mighty art lecturer has fallen, Ozymandias in Stoke Newington. I haven't seen you since that business of the vandalized Pre-Raphaelite at the National. You only bloody call on me when you want something.' Summerfield wiped a brush out on his striped pyjama shirt. 'What is it this time?'

'I need some information on an artist. At least you've started painting again.'

'Well, after Countess Dracula left I packed up the classes and stopped going out for a while, until my pupils came around one day and accused me of giving up on them. What could I do? I couldn't mope about for ever. Besides, there's good light in here. I can sit around all day in my underpants flicking paint at the walls if I want to. It feels like a proper home. I still teach art two days a week, but I'm selling my paintings down the Bayswater Road at weekends. Frightful rubbish, sunsets and puppies for tourists with no taste, but I'm making a living wage for once. Who are you after?'

'Did you ever hear of an artist called Gilbert Kingdom?' asked Bryant.

Summerfield fondled his beard ruminatively. 'Not for a very long time,' he said finally.

'So you do know of him?'

'Of course. A great enigma, something of a *bête noir*. He was a disciple of Stanley Spencer, perhaps a more formidable talent.'

'Then why have I never heard of him?'

'Because he never fulfilled his potential. But he's

known to most fine-art historians worth their salt. Kingdom suffered the fate of so many geniuses. Showed great promise as a student at the Slade— Spencer went there, of course—then he underwent some kind of epiphany in much the same way as Spencer had done. Kingdom took a more pagan approach to understanding the world, dividing it into elemental spirits of fire and water. He wasn't interested in knocking out gilt-framed portraits for punters, he was preoccupied with linking pagan rituals directly to the land. All the talent in the world can't save a man born out of fashion. Eventually he went barking mad and died in poverty. There are hardly any books on him.'

'I have one.' Bryant removed the volume from a scuffed leather briefcase. 'Unfortunately, the section on his work has been removed.'

'Ah, I've got that book,' said Summerfield with obvious pleasure. 'I think it's pretty much the only place where I've ever seen his work reprinted. Let me see if I can find it for you.'

Bryant drank his tea and listened while the art master rooted about in his lounge.

'I'm afraid the cover's torn off, but it's the same edition.' His rough, paint-stained fingers ploughed through the volume until he came to the pages missing from Tate's copy. He passed it to Bryant.

'All we have is a tantalizing glimpse of the man's brilliance, two paintings now both in California, a few studies and sketches. Just as Spencer painted Cookham, Kingdom painted London. He broke the city down into four distinct colour palettes, densities and timescales.'

'How did he do that?'

'Well, there's London of the Great Fire, and later, during the industrial revolution, a city of steely flame, a man-made inferno of pumping pistons and belching boilers. Then there's the city of swirling unhealthy fogs, mists and windswept hills, a place of mystery, disease and danger. Then the city of water, crossed by a great meandering river and a hundred tributaries, a landscape of waterwheels and mills, of rain and floods. And finally, the city of rich clay earth, wherein one could find the bones of plague victims, the soul and soil in which its residents take root like the Hydra's teeth.'

'The four elements, in fact.'

'Exactly so. Such thinking was unfashionable at a time when postwar modernism was gaining so much ground. He failed to find a patron, and was eventually kicked to death in the gutter by children, somewhere around your neck of the woods.'

Bryant examined the paintings, the half-finished outpourings of an extraordinary mind, ragged deities commanding the earth and sky while cowering acolytes toiled in tiny brick houses. The colours and detailing were extraordinary. Bryant was reminded of Victorian faerie paintings, reproduced on an epic canvas.

'And this is all he painted?'

'Ah, there's the paradox. Those whose abilities set them ahead of their time are often rewarded posthumously, but failure hides them from sight. The more they forge ahead beyond the spirit of the age, the more the world is intent on burying them. It was said that Kingdom created other pieces, but all of them were destroyed. Nobody knows for sure.'

'Who would do such a terrible thing as destroying a work of art?'

'Dear naive fellow, every decade has its self-appointed censors. The only mercy is that time forgets them and remembers the artist. In the history of the world, no censor has ever been looked back on with respect. There were those who objected to Kingdom's choice of subject matter. For some, his style was too close to that associated with fascist art. Nazism was on the rise, the times were uncertain, and no one wanted to see depictions of a future free from Christianity. At the Slade, it was said that Kingdom was the one artist capable of depicting the missing episodes of England's pagan past.'

'Do you think he could have destroyed his own work?'

'Difficult question. One doesn't want to believe such things, of course, but what other explanation could there be? He died a pauper, homeless and friendless, unloved and unremembered. Not for him the eager wake of adoring students. There's so little to go on, you see. He didn't die at a youthful age like Firbank or Beardsley. They both produced fair bodies of work in their short young lives.'

'How old was Kingdom when these boys attacked him?'

'I believe he was in his forties, not quite so young in those days as it is now. He drank, he starved, and looked much older. Here.' Summerfield turned the page and pointed out a monochrome photograph depicting a gaunt, sickly man in a ragged tweed jacket. The figure standing beside him was clean-shaven and crop-headed, but as Bryant had suspected, was clearly Tate as a young man. 'And that's his son,' confirmed Summerfield.

'What do you know of this boy?' asked Bryant.

'His name was Emmanuel Kingdom. He was said to be devastated by the old man's death, swore to take revenge on those who killed his father—but that was probably just a romantic notion circulated by art teachers. Of course, such a boy had no way of doing so, and I imagine the obsession eventually sent him along the same path as his father.'

'Do you have any idea what happened to him?'

'I believe he worked for a time as a guard at the Tate Gallery, in order to be near one of his father's paintings. Must have devastated him when they flogged it to the Yanks. Never heard anything about him after that.'

'I think I know where he is.'

'You do?' Summerfield fairly inflated with excitement. 'If we could locate him, he may be able to throw light on his father's life. Do you know how important this could be? Information is money, Arthur.'

'I have to find him more quickly than you can imagine,' Bryant agreed. 'But for an entirely different reason. I fear he's connected with terrible events.'

'At any rate, it's good to see you again,' smiled Summerfield. 'Did you ever catch the vandal who ruined the picture in the National Gallery?'

'Yes, I think so,' Bryant replied distractedly, pulling on his coat.

'I hope they managed to repair the painting. The Waterhouse.'

Bryant was caught with his arm in one sleeve. 'Remind me?'

'The painting was by Waterhouse, wasn't it? *The Favourites of the Emperor Honorius*, if memory serves. One forgets he'd churned out all of those ghastly witchcraft paintings like *The Sorceress* and

The Magic Circle. He's got an occult following, would you believe.'

'Waterhouse,' Bryant repeated, dumbstruck. 'My goodness, thank you, Peregrine.' It was only after he had gone that Summerfield found the elderly detective's trilby, stuck over a brush-pot on the hall table.

44

TEMPEST RISING

The stack of postcards had stopped growing.

Kallie shuffled through them again, counting to seven. The last card Paul had sent was from Croatia. What the hell was he doing in Croatia? In the darkest part of these rainy nights, after even the streetlamps had died, she began to feel that he was no longer part of her world.

Just a few days ago she had imagined him lying in a clay-walled house, his head bloodily bandaged, trying to explain to kindly but uncomprehending fishermen that his passport had been stolen. Now she realized the absurdity of the fantasy. Even ancient souks housed Internet cafés. There were few places in Europe where English was not understood by someone. If anything bad had happened to Paul, he would have found a way to get in touch with her. The postcard was upbeat, distant in tone, like a child fulfilling a duty to write home.

After a few hours' respite, the rain had returned with a vengeance to north London. It fell with a tropical intensity, bouncing and spraying, pouring and dripping from every roof, gutter, porch and awning. The drains were overwhelmed, and the middle section of the street was flooding in earnest. She thought of getting out, catching a train to her aunt's, where she might escape the worst of the weather. But something kept her at the house. It had become her home, and she was determined to stay. She sat at the kitchen table with the colour swatches for the bathroom and tried to concentrate on the job, but the rain proved too distracting. Knowing that it would be better to concentrate on some mindless practicality, she descended to the lower-ground floor and picked up the sledgehammer from where she had left it.

She had decided to remove part of the bathroom chimney breast to provide some space for towel-shelves. There was little money left to hire anyone else, so she would carry out the work herself. However, after slamming the breast with seven or eight hammer blows, she realized that she could not summon enough power in her arms for the job. She had barely managed to put more than a few crescent-shaped dents in the brickwork. There was no electrical socket in the bathroom, but she had run a cable through from the kitchen for a radio, and the inane babble of the DJ drowned out the rush of running water that sounded as if it was passing right through the basement. The noise had continued unabated for so long that she barely noticed it now.

A sickly grey damp patch had appeared just above floor level, and was spreading so quickly up the adjoining wall that she could almost see its growth. Oddly, the plaster felt dry to the touch, as if designed to absorb moisture. Perhaps it would be necessary to live with the intact chimney for now; it could be removed at a later date. She hated the bath because both taps had a tendency to stick, either jamming open or shut. The plumber wasn't able to come for another week.

Kallie decided to remove the row of tiles behind the washbasin. But after working at the wall for nearly half an hour, she abandoned her chisel and switched to a knife to begin cutting away the old paintwork that overlaid the surrounding plaster. It lifted easily, and work progressed with greater speed. She was sweating hard, even though the bathroom was freezing. The room defied any attempt to be heated. Didn't they say that the temperature always dropped when spirits were present? She felt surrounded by ghosts: the doleful presence of Ruth Singh; the shadowy figures of Elliot and Jake; even Paul, his features blurred and already half-forgotten, lost to the new loyalties of strange lands.

She watched from the steamed-over kitchen window while waiting for the kettle to boil. The street was so close to Piccadilly Circus, self-proclaimed hub of the universe, but she could have been in the heart of the English countryside. The drone of traffic usually made itself felt in low bass-notes you sensed in your bones rather than heard, but today the rain cascaded through the densely foliated branches of the ceanothus and enveloped the house in a clatter that sounded like gravel pouring down a chute. It was as though sluice gates had opened to flood the city, turning London into an inundated world of Atlantean phantoms.

Kallie returned to the bathroom and noticed that the stain on the wall had spread during the few minutes she had been out of the room. Now it extended fully halfway up the wall in a suppurating mushroom cloud, and was wet to the touch.

She was about to resume work with renewed vigour when the lights went out.

'I really thought I had him,' said Bimsley. 'I might have done if I hadn't gone arse over tit on the kerb. It's these shoes. I've done my coccyx in, and the back of my jacket's soaked.' The detective constable wiped his eyes and pulled his baseball cap closer to his head. 'I can't believe this weather,' he complained. 'Global warming. We're getting pissed on night and day just so mums can drop their kids off in SUVs. You all right?'

'I've been drier,' Meera agreed, squinting up at her colleague.

'It's going to be dark soon. Sunday evening, we should be home. I want some soup. Tate's not going to turn up here again. Whatever he's up to, he knows we're on to him. Something's tipped him off.'

'How could it?'

'Suppose he went back to the hostel for his books and found them gone. It wouldn't take a genius to figure out who took them. He's scarpered.'

Meera checked her wrist. 'We're not off duty for another hour.'

'My watch has steamed over. Besides, the Old Man reckons nobody goes home until we've got him.' People often thought of Bryant as the Old Man, even though he was only three years older than his partner.

'We could do another door-to-door.'

'That'd go down well, wouldn't it? Any more

interviews and it'll constitute harassment,' warned Bimsley. 'Civvies either complain that they can never see police on the streets, or moan about being picked on.'

'Don't start, Colin, you're starting to sound like the Peckham South boys. Let's just get through the shift.'

Bimsley stamped and splashed. 'He's not going to show tonight.'

'Why not?'

'The rain. It's not going down the drains any more, which means his precious underground tunnels must be flooded, which means Tate can't use them to get around.' Bimsley narrowed his eyes, trying to see through the caul of mist. 'Something's really wrong here. I can feel it. There's a disturbance in the force.' He mimed wielding a light sabre. 'I mean, what's he going to gain by faking his own death? He already had a way of disappearing. Why didn't he use it when he still had the chance?'

'In south London you get three deaths in the same street, nobody tries to link them together. He's just a tramp, he's not a murderer.'

'He killed one of his own, Meera. I've seen people like him before. There's a solid wall between his type and us, people with homes. Why would he let one of his own kind die? There's something missing that the Old Man hasn't put his finger on, and he's into extra time. I should worry, I'm off home as soon as I get the signal. Dry out, order a curry, open a beer, bung on the telly, thank you and good night.'

'I thought we were a team, Colin. You wouldn't leave poor old Bryant and May out here on their own, would you?' asked Meera.

'What's it worth?'

'I might join you for the curry.'

In the distance, thunder scraped and tumbled with the obliterating force of the rising storm.

'Can't you put the de-mister on?' asked May. 'I can't see a thing.'

'I could, but it'll burn out the contacts on my brake lights. If you turn the radio on, the interior light comes on.'

'There's something very strange about the wiring of your car.' May fidgeted in his seat. 'I'm sure these are stuffed with horsehair. You should get yourself a nice little runaround.'

'It wouldn't be much good in a high-speed pursuit, would it?' snapped Bryant.

Dear God, let's never have another of those, thought May, remembering the last time. 'This is a Mini Cooper.'

'Not under the bonnet, it's not.'

'It's nearly dark. Doesn't that strike you as odd?'

'No,' said Bryant, digging in his paper bag for a cola cube. 'It happens every night.'

'I mean there are no street lights on. No interior lights in any of the houses, either. Look, over there, you can see them in Inkerman Road. Maybe the water's got into a sub-station. I'd better call it in.'

'Where's Longbright?'

'Janice should still be in number 43, with the Wiltons. I can't see Meera or Colin. I told them to stay within sight.' May reached over to the back seat for a baseball cap.

'Must you wear that awful thing?' Bryant complained. 'It's intended for someone a quarter of your age.'

'I don't know why you have this High Tory attitude to fashion.' May straightened the peak in his mirror. 'You're not exactly Calvin Klein.'

'I've had my trilby since the War.'

'I'm surprised it hasn't fallen over your ears, considering the way you're shrinking. Where is it, anyway?'

'I think I left it at Peregrine's, along with my stick and my gloves.'

'I'm going to tie them to your jacket one day. Keep your mobile handy in case anything's wrong. You do have that, don't you?'

'Naturally.' Bryant dug into his coat and was amazed to find his own Nokia there; he had begun to suspect it had fallen under the exposed floorboards at the unit.

'Is it on? Of course not.' May turned it on and threw it back. 'I won't be a minute.' He climbed out into the downpour.

Kallie found a torch and some candles under the sink. Illuminated by pale spheres of radiance, the house appeared to be returning to its Victorian origins. There was something graceful about being able to carry the light from one room to another, bringing each space into focus as she passed through.

The twilit garden was now brighter than the interior of the house. The glow of the city was reflected on low racing clouds. As she stood framed by the window, she saw that Tate was standing inside the bush once more. She recognized his crippled shape immediately. Shining the torch through the window, she picked up his startled eyes in the light, and panned the beam over his body.

He was holding a carving knife in his right hand.

She flicked off the torch and made her way to the back door, checking that it was bolted top and bottom. The opaque-glass panel above the handle was wide enough for an intruder to smash and put his hand through. She dragged a chair from the kitchen and wedged it against the handle, then ran back to the window, staying low. Tate had moved closer, and was brazenly loping up the garden toward the house. A squall of rain hit the window with the force of a thrown shingle. She had forgotten to set her cordless phone back on its stand, and began searching the kitchen for it.

When she looked back into the wavering darkness, Tate had vanished once more.

45

ALL THE HOUSES

Kallie had no intention of running away.

Let the men in the street do that; it was the women who stayed and fought. This was her home, somewhere she finally belonged, and she would stay to protect it. The more logical you were, the less there was to be afraid of. She took stock of her surroundings.

It appeared that only the lights were out. The phone was still working. Forcing herself to breathe slowly and deeply, she listened for sounds beyond the river under the bathroom and the falling rain. This time, pride kept her from going for help. Tate was distracted and crippled. She was more than a match for him. She could not pretend to understand what might drive a man to act this way, but so many residents of the metropolis had become lost inside themselves that it was no longer a disease afflicting isolated communities; lunacy had spread to the city.

She kept a check from the windows; no sign of him—what kind of mad game was he playing?

Water was seeping in under the back door. Kallie rolled up a bath towel and laid it across the step. Something made her turn in her flight back through the basement hall to the bottom of the stairs; she caught the chiaroscuro of her reflection in the bathroom mirror, illuminated by a single tall candle. *How different I look,* she thought. *A grown woman I barely know.* The candle flickered, and in that instant she saw something else. A young man with bare white shoulders peering back at her through the brickwork.

John May walked back along the darkened street, trying to avoid the sputtering channels from inundated drainpipes. He counted down the houses as he passed them: number 37, the Ethiopians hardly anyone saw; number 39, where the Ayson family was riven by suspicions of infidelity; number 41, where Jake Avery had been suffocated in his sleep; number 43, where Longbright was now on guard with Tamsin and Oliver Wilton, their son impatiently roaming the upstairs rooms of the house, disturbed by the downpour; number 45, the medical students who slept through their days. The swamped waste ground where Elliot Copeland's body had been found buried in city soil, where Tate had once watched from barricades of plywood and cardboard. The builders' yard where Aaron had been tempted to betray his partner. So much energy and anger in one small street.

No sign of Bimsley or Mangeshkar, but he knew they couldn't be far away. He crossed the road and was about to start back when he spotted their matching black baseball caps. They were rounding the corner toward the alley behind the houses, where the dipped gravel path had become a tributary once more.

'Hey, where are you going?' he called.

'It's where Tate normally hangs out, sir. Thought we'd check it.'

May shone his torch on to the dark tree-lined corridor. 'There's nothing you can do back there. I want you to call on every house in this street and check that nothing is wrong. Take a side each. I don't know how, but he's tricking us.'

The two officers separated. May turned off his torch, and dropped back against the dark wall of the alley. *Let's hope he heard that,* he thought. *I'm going to be here when he makes his move.*

Kallie took a step forward and raised her candle, but the boy did not move. Locks of shining blond hair hung at either side of his face like shavings of varnished wood. She realized that she was looking back at a painting. She had been working too closely in artificial light to spot it earlier. What she had taken for water marks were muted colours.

From this distance she could clearly make out the top of the boy's body, set against twists of drowned green branches. He was floating in water, his arms drifting away from his torso, the world submerged beneath him, the victim of some apocalyptic deluge.

As she drew nearer, she studied the wall more carefully. He was imprisoned behind the thick layer of emulsion with which the wall had been covered. Taking up the scraper, she pushed its tip into the soft ochre paintwork. Three distinct layers lifted off together, and there, staring at her with unnerving clarity, was a single large eye.

Now something else made sense for the first time. In the original layout of the house, the bathroom had been considerably larger than any other room. Walls had since been removed, ceilings altered, chimneys closed; the bathroom had been repainted and demoted in importance until it had been diminished. Six large hardboard panels covered the alcoves on either side of the chimney breast. They had been painted over several times, so that the screws holding them had vanished.

In the toolbox beside the bath she found a screwdriver. Cracking the paint from the screwheads was a task of no more than a few seconds, but the threads were rusted and refused to turn. After tearing up the first two in frustrated haste, she switched to the chisel and worked at the join between boards and brick.

Tying a dishcloth around the head of a crowbar, she inserted it behind the first hardboard panel, bending back the board until it split. The mural behind it ran the entire length of the wall, presumably wrapping itself around the chimney breast. The section she could see was a view downward from a window depicting an extraordinary procession through the streets of London: sorrow, judgement, punishment, death, resurrection. An immense distortion of buildings and people that incorporated such details as gold braid and coat buttons, yet included the curvature of the earth. The top half of one winged figure disappeared behind the next panel.

Kallie began to realize that this panel would prove impossible to remove without damaging the artwork, so she followed it to the next wall, wondering if the frieze could possibly continue all the way around the room. Choosing a random spot, she gently peeled away the dampest patch of paintwork to reveal the screaming head of a young black woman.

Dragging the stepladder from the cupboard under the stairs, Kallie climbed up and shone her torch at the ceiling, scratching lightly at it to reveal what appeared to be a bursting storm cloud seen from directly underneath: fat, glistening drops of rain plunging in perspective toward the viewer. *It's the entire room,* she thought. *I have never seen anything like this in my life.*

The noise of rushing water beneath the house had grown in intensity. She tried to move the bath away from the far wall. The flexible pipes attached to its taps looked as if they would allow it to be moved as far as the centre of the room, but it was far too heavy to budge more than a few inches. Squeezing herself between the bath and the wall, she carefully scraped away another section of paint. This time the image was indecipherable: gingerish strands of weeds, flowers or possibly flames.

The emulsion flaked away from the hard varnished surface of the extraordinary mural. Feeling something at her feet, Kallie shone the torch down and saw that the spiders were back, thousands of them, tiny and brown, forced up by the rising torrent below. She stamped her boots, scattering them across the floor in rippling waves, and turned her attention back to the wall.

The red strands were soon explained: they were the floating tresses of a drowned woman, floating pale and serene beneath the green submerged city.

The doorbell rang, startling her, then rang again. She felt reluctant to leave the painting, as though it might fade away without her gaze upon it, but descended the ladder and made her way upstairs. The silhouette on the glass suggested a tall, broad-shouldered man, clearly not Tate. As she unlocked the door, he stepped inside without waiting for permission to enter. There was a palpable sense of aggression in his attitude. His face was turned away from the pale light of the street.

'What did you think you were going to do?' asked Randall Ayson.

'Where did your husband go?' Longbright asked, looking around.

'I don't know. This rain.' Tamsin Wilton barely concentrated on the question. The ferocious deluge had distracted everyone. 'I don't see why you have to be here.'

I'm not so sure myself, thought the detective sergeant. 'Mr Bryant has reason to believe that you could be at risk, that someone might try to, well, set fire to your house.'

'*Fire*? I can't imagine anything catching fire tonight. There's no power. The electricity company warned us this might happen. Look out there. It's like the end of the world. Brewer!' She shouted up from the foot of the stairs. 'Stop running about like that!'

Longbright returned to the lounge window and cleared a patch, trying to see Bryant's Mini Cooper. He appeared to be alone inside. At the far end of the road she could make out Meera standing in a porch, probably conducting another door-to-door check. Something strange was happening out there, and it annoyed her not to be a part of it.

* * *

Bryant poked about in the glovebox and found a chamois leather to clear the windscreen, but water was trickling in through the corners of the passenger windows. He wanted to be with May, but did not trust himself on the sluicing cobbles without his stick, so he sat and fidgeted, frustrated and fed up. Searching about for some useful purpose, he came upon the underground river map that Tate had pressed into his hand. The paper had wrinkled in the damp, so he used one of Tate's art books to lay it flat and press out the creases. As he did so, a tingling premonition caressed the back of his neck; it was a feeling he had experienced many times before.

The map, the art book. Pulling his briefcase across from the back seat, he searched for the A4 photocopy Longbright had made from Jackie Quinten's original. He needed more light. He switched on the radio to illuminate the interior, and manoeuvred the drawing over Tate's map. It was surfacing now, the idea; a coalescence of everything he had heard and seen in recent weeks. Using the House of Conflagration as a co-ordinate, he slowly rotated the map, then checked the details with the magnifying glass he kept for reading the A-Z. The artwork was fanciful and out of scale, but the outline of the street roughly corresponded to the card, allowing him to pinpoint the properties on either side in conjunction with the Fleet tributary.

Now he noticed what he had not seen before on the drawing: two other co-ordinates, not words but pictograms placed over sites, one a lumpen creature emerging from the soil, the other a sinister cherub with its bare rump turned toward the viewer, expelling wind. What he had dismissed as decorative patterning beneath the illustrations was tiny calligraphy.

'Blasted eyesight,' said Bryant aloud, holding the picture closer. 'House of Foul Earth, House of Poison'd Air.' He looked at the other two dwellings, the House of Conflagration and the House Curs'd By All Water, and knew that he not only had his four elements, but had located four sites in the street. He was still trying to pinpoint the positions with certainty when the interior light shorted out. The dashboard was streaming with water. Folding the map and the drawing together in his overcoat pocket, he clambered out into the thunderstorm.

Randall Ayson stood before Kallie with rain dripping from his fists. 'I want you to tell me exactly what you told my wife.' It smelled as if he had been drinking rum.

'I don't know what you're talking about.' Kallie backed out of his reach.

'Don't lie to me, woman. You told her I was having an affair. You've screwed up my marriage.'

'I did no such thing. You've got your wires crossed, Mr Ayson. And I didn't invite you in.' She wanted to push him back toward the door, but thought he might strike out at her.

He took a step closer. Behind him, rain fell from the porch in a silver sheet. 'She told me that you rang her up to make trouble, and all you've done is hurt everyone involved. I'm sorry you've got domestic problems of your own, but my marriage is my own damned business.'

'I have not spoken to your wife, not on the telephone or in person, do you understand?' She spoke calmly and clearly, anxious to move him back to the door. 'I promise you, I have no knowledge or interest in your personal affairs.'

He took another step forward into the darkness of the hall. 'It's one thing when a woman's unhappy, but it's pretty damned pathetic when she wants other people to be unhappy with her.'

'I want you to get out of here right now,' she shouted, shifting between him and the opened front door.

'Not before you go over there and tell her you were lying. I'm not leaving without your promise.'

'And I keep telling you, I haven't spoken to her!' She pushed at his chest, but he raised his hands to bat her away.

'Do you need any help?' asked Janice Longbright from the doorway.

'John, wait a moment.'

Arthur Bryant hopped around the flooding gutter and grabbed his partner's arm to stop himself from falling over. 'It's all making sense now. There are four houses. Or rather, there were. It's what I always said about London homes, we rent them and buy them without knowing who lived there before, or who'll live there after us. We're merely curators. It's not about who they are, Elliot, Jake, Ruth, it's about where they chose to live. Four houses, four residents, four elements, three deaths, so I thought there would have to be a fourth—my tidy mind at work, you see, always having to align the facts neatly. But the death in the hostel wasn't part of it. I was doing what you always accuse me of doing, making up behavioural patterns to fit the facts. He'd always known about the houses, there's no question of that, because he'd watched his father working on them when he was a nipper.'

'You're talking about Tate?'

'Of course, he was photographed with his father. Tate's determination to save the houses tipped over into obsession, then madness. He started to tell me when I interviewed him at the hostel, but I didn't get the full story.'

'I still haven't got it now,' May admitted, perplexed.

'It's fine,' said Kallie, raising her hands defensively as Randall stepped back into the rain. 'Mr Ayson was just going.'

'We're calling on everyone to make sure they're OK,' Longbright explained. 'What with the power being out.'

'I've seen him again,' Kallie told her. 'Tate—he was in the garden and he had a knife. Just a few minutes ago. Then he disappeared. I was trying to call you but the lights went—'

'Leave it with us.' Longbright leaned back into the street and waved for Mangeshkar and Bimsley. 'They'll check your garden. They can't get any wetter than they already are.' She held the door open for Randall. 'I think your wife is looking for you, Mr Ayson. You'd better get back there.'

'Thanks,' said Kallie as she admitted the officers. 'He was really angry.'

'Don't worry, I can take care of him.' Longbright smiled reassuringly. The detective constables trooped downstairs and removed the chair from the back door, stepping into the storm-battered garden.

'You've noticed she gives us all the crap jobs,' Meera complained, climbing the steps to the lawn and shining her torch into the bushes. 'He's like a bloody ghost, this bloke. I don't see why we can't just—wait a minute . . . I don't believe this.' She beckoned to Bimsley with a grin. 'He's only got a kitchen stool in here.' She shone the torch over the black lacquered seat wedged into the muddy ground beneath the bush. 'Must have reckoned he was in for a long wait. Doesn't make sense.'

'Waiting for her to come home?'

'Normally he'd see a light on. Not today, though. Why didn't he come for her when she saw him? What kind of murderer travels around with a kitchen stool?' Meera knew better than to move it, but the angled position puzzled her. 'He wasn't even facing the house. He was watching the place next door.'

Her torch picked up fresh splinters of wood from the verdigris-covered fence. A hacksaw line marked a panel cut from the staves. She gave it a kick and it fell in. 'Looks like he grew tired of shinning over walls and decided to cut himself an escape route,' she called back. 'Come on.'

'I don't like you being here alone,' said Longbright, covering the mobile to talk to Kallie. 'Why don't you go to a neighbour until the lights come back on? Or I'm sure I can get one to come here.'

'I don't want to be any trouble, really,' Kallie protested. 'I'm fine.'

'Hang on a sec—Mr Bryant, where are you? I can hardly hear you—' She turned back to Kallie. 'Don't be daft, it'll only take a minute to get someone, and I'd feel a lot happier.' She stepped away from the door, talking into the phone. 'Slow down, I can't understand what you're saying . . . No, they're still looking for him . . . What—?' She stepped back out into the rain, trying to improve the phasing signal.

Looking down the inundated street, she saw the detectives in the distance, half-obscured as they moved away through the downpour. 'It's no good, I can't hear a word you're saying. Hang on—'

She set off along the street, leaving Kallie alone once more.

46

IMMERSION

'The sergeant was quite insistent,' Heather explained. 'I said you were welcome to come over and stay with me, but she wanted me to come here and look after you. What do you think is going on outside? She wouldn't tell me.'

Kallie cupped her hands at the back window and tried to see into the garden, but it was dark now, and the officers seemed to have disappeared. 'I got scared. Tate was in the garden and it looked like he had a knife. They're searching for him now. Do you think we're safe?'

'I don't know.' Heather had been on her way out, and was irritated by the sergeant's request to babysit her neighbour. It was bad enough having to dress and do her hair by candlelight, without this. Everyone was so protective of Kallie, as if she would never be able to cope by herself, yet she had managed well enough since Paul had disappeared. 'There's water coming in under your back door.' She pointed at the sodden towels leaking in the gloom of the hall.

'There's nothing I can do until this lets up.' Kallie chewed at a fingernail, unsettled by the peculiar atmosphere of the evening, the distant shouts and footfalls, the beams of torchlight in the rain.

'I can't stay long, Kallie. I'm having dinner with an old friend.'

'I told the sergeant not to bother you,' Kallie apologized. 'It's been a really strange—my God, I didn't tell you.'

'Tell me what?'

'Follow me, you won't believe this. Bring the other torch.' She grabbed Heather's hand and pulled her in the direction of the bathroom.

'What is it?' Heather laughed uneasily.

'Look.' Kallie walked into the room and closed the door behind them. The noise of rushing water was louder than ever. It sounded as if they were sitting on a lock-gate. She reached over and pointed the end of Heather's torch up toward the wall. 'It's some kind of huge quasi-religious mural. The inundation of the world—it's frightening but utterly beautiful.'

'Oh my God.' Heather's jaw had fallen open.

'I didn't have time to take the lower panels off, and it would be a pity to damage it. Look, though, this one's loose. Give me a hand.' She began to pull at the corner hardboard panel.

'No,' screamed Heather. 'You'll ruin it!'

But Kallie had already managed to shift the board around on its single remaining screw to reveal more drowned figures, all with their left arms outstretched, pointing down at the floor of the room.

'They're pointing to the river underneath,' said Heather tonelessly.

'It's got to be valuable, hasn't it? The ceiling's covered as well. The thing is a complete piece. I've no idea what I'll find up there.'

Heather's face looked waxy and sick in the fierce light beam. 'A fish-eye view,' she said. 'You'll find a distorted view of the street, and the town, and the horizon of the world. The planet consumed by a prophesied deluge. And at the centre you'll find the other three houses. The House of Foul Airs. The House of Poisoned Earth. The House of Conflagration.'

'Are you all right?'

'Why did you have to find it now?' asked Heather, reaching behind her and locking the bathroom door.

Bryant had stopped in the middle of the street, images swirling in his head. Rain on the floor below the window. Randall Ayson's row with his wife—accusations of infidelity on both sides. The old-fashioned raincoat left on the Wiltons' bed. Kallie said that Jake Avery had struck some kind of a deal with Paul the night they went drinking together. The borrowed map ... the noise of falling water was inside his head, like being beneath a waterfall, like tinnitus, tearing his thoughts into scraps of nonsense. London, the 'city of springs and streams', the turbulent Fleet, the soughing Falcon, the excitable Westbourne, the sluggish Tyburn, all sweeping to the Thames ...

'What's the matter?' May asked. 'You're standing there as if you've been struck by lightning. Let's get you out of this before you catch pneumonia.'

'I think my phone's ringing,' said Bryant distantly.

'Oh, come here.' May patted his partner's overcoat. 'Why must you have so many pockets? And what are you doing with the unit's mobile as well as your own? I prefer absentmindedness to kleptomania.' He dug Bryant's Nokia out, detached several boiled sweets and flipped it open. 'Janice? Where are you?'

'I'm out the back now. We're following Tate's trail through the rear gardens. I don't think he intended to be a threat to Kallie. Nobody brings a stool along to their hiding place, as well as a knife. I think he was waiting there because he wanted to watch over the house and protect her. Or rather, he was watching the houses—his stool was turned away.'

'Tate's protecting the Water Room,' said Bryant, closing the phone. 'It's why he never left the street, always living at the end on the waste ground, always hiding in the gardens. But who would he think it needed protecting from? What's inside it? No one else knows the location, because we got it from—I'm an idiot . . .'

'What are you talking about?'

'I don't listen. Something Jackie Quinten said about her friend's map,' Bryant muttered. 'I didn't think anything of it at the time. She couldn't leave the map with me, because, as she put it, "He'll kill me if he discovers she's lent it out *again*." I wasn't the first person in the neighbourhood to ask about the map.'

'Call her up.'

'I didn't keep the number. She's just in the next street. It'll only take a minute to go round there.'

Jackie Quinten was surprised to find two soaked elderly men on her doorstep. 'Would you like to come in?' she offered.

'We can't stop,' said Bryant, attempting an unsodden smile. 'Your friend Janet's husband—who else did he lend his map to?'

'Did I mention that? It was some while ago—the lady at number 6, Heather Allen. The one whose husband left her.'

'You know about that?'

'He was a local businessman, so there was quite a bit of gossip about the divorce. He divorced her for someone younger.'

'When was this?'

'Oh, a couple of years ago, at least.'

'You've been most helpful.' Bryant tipped his hat, getting water everywhere. The pair set off from the doorstep.

'Are you sure you don't want to come in and at least dry your trousers?' called Mrs Quinten.

Heather hammered the cold tap of the bath with the heel of her hand. 'You have to do this,' she explained. 'The washers are corroded. If it hadn't been for the taps, none of this would have happened. She was old, she had no grip in her hands.'

Kallie tried to understand what was going on, but the pain in her temple sang and soared if she tried to move her head. She had been hit with something from the tool box, possibly the hammer. The tiny brown spiders were pricking across her legs, so presumably she was lying on her side. Her hip felt sore and cold against the parquet. She could taste blood in her mouth.

'She couldn't turn the tap off, you see. She was frightened it was going to overflow, so she knocked on the wall. When I first moved in I told her, if you ever need me in a hurry, just bang on the wall. So when I heard the knock, I grabbed the raincoat Mark Garrett had left at my place the day before and came over to help.'

Kallie could see Heather's back bent over the bath. She couldn't sort out the different sounds in her head: the water underneath, the flowing tap, the liquid buzz in her ears. Heather rose and pushed up her sleeves.

'She was so old and frail, like a little doll, and she had no idea that she owned the Water House. No idea! Of course, the walls had been painted over years before. The property belonged to her brother, and he wouldn't sell it as long as she was alive. Suddenly it seemed so simple. Now it's all got complicated. Come on, you.'

She pulled Kallie to her feet, then tipped the top half of her body over the bath. Setting a comfortable temperature was not an act of thoughtfulness; she did not want Kallie to be shocked awake by a sudden plunge into cold water.

This is pleasant, thought Kallie. *Just what I need to take away the pain.* The warmth enveloped her right arm, then the top of her head and one side of her face. She was slowly tipping, being gently lowered. The buzzing suddenly stopped, and all she could hear was the dull sonar of immersion. Water filled her nose and made her cough, and then began to flood her mouth. The sensation was not disagreeable. *I'm going to join the people on the walls,* she thought. *I'll get to see what they see. I'll look out at the world with them from deep beneath the river.*

She felt her head being turned further into the water, so clear and untroubled, the curving white arc of the bath below so close that her face was touching the cool ceramic base. A soft red cloud drifted slowly before her eyes. *That's just my blood,* she thought, *from the cut on my head, nothing to be alarmed about.*

The water wasn't deep enough. The hot tap was too slow, and now it had stuck. Heather turned on the cold with her left hand, keeping Kallie's neck gripped firmly in her right. It was taking too long. She should have been struggling by now. Why was she so relaxed? It wasn't a normal reaction. Her throat should have closed, she should have been sputtering and fighting for life. It was the worst thing that could happen. She needed the reaction; without it, Kallie wouldn't gasp and suck water down into her lungs.

They're helping me, thought Kallie, *the men and women on the walls. They're all underwater, and look how calmly they're behaving. The waters rose and drowned them all, but in death they can see everything. They're pointing to the river below the house. They want to be released of their tied-up lives, filled with rules and manners and pious Christian lessons. They want to be washed away, back into an ancient pagan world, to be free to swim to the wide grey sea. And that's all I want now, to be taken with them. My life above has ended. All I have to do is breathe gently and follow them.*

'Why won't you fight?' screamed Heather. But even as she tried to tighten her grip on the neck of the limp, heavy body, she could feel it pulling away from her, back toward the wet floor. She had dreamed of the mural for so long, but now the exposed white faces were unnerving her, judging her. *Another few seconds at the most, surely that's all it can take,* she told herself. *Then this whole nightmare will be over.* Ignoring the blue underwater-wide eyes that stared down on her, she pushed the head in her hands down hard once more.

Even at this crucial moment, Kallie was aware of the growing sound of water all around her. One of the candles on the floor guttered and fell over, its flame hissing out. Water was gushing from between the bricks in the chimney breast, where she had been striking them with the sledgehammer. One brick began to rattle, thin sheets of water spraying around its edges, until it was extruded from the wall and blasted to the floor.

The rest of the chimney breast came down easily. Heather was horrified to see that the wall of water extended halfway up the breach. Moments later, the icy torrent hit them both, throwing them against the far wall as the pressure loosened more bricks. All around them, the acolytes of the water room looked down, happy to accept their fate, to be condemned and redeemed beneath the absolving waters of the world.

47

INTO THE UNDERWORLD

'No answer,' said May, peering through the brass letterbox. 'There's someone home, though.'

'How do you know?' Bryant tried to hunch in beneath the shallow porch.

'There are lit candles all over the place. You wouldn't go out and leave them burning, would you?' He turned his ear to the letterbox and listened. 'I can hear water.'

'Yes, it's pouring down the back of my neck right now,' Bryant complained impatiently.

'No, splashing water, downstairs. My God, what is that noise?'

'The river's breached the basement. That does it—we have to break the door down.'

May looked at the front door in some alarm. 'I don't know whether I can.'

'The wood's older than our combined ages, it'll have a spring-weight in the wall and a single Yale lock holding it shut. Get out of the way.' Bryant pushed his partner aside and raised his shoe. He would have fallen backwards down the steps if May hadn't caught him.

'Oh, for God's sake, let me. This is a woman's job.' Longbright appeared behind them. On the third kick of her steel-tipped boot, the lock popped open. They squeezed into the hall and headed for the stairs, flashing torches to the floor below, and saw water pouring from beneath the door of the bathroom.

Heather tried to hold herself upright and reach the door as the glaucous Fleet-water swirled and shoved around the room. The level was no higher than her knees, but the floor was now too slippery to gain a foothold.

The sound of the front door slamming back sounded above her. As she watched Kallie slide from her grasp and become submerged in the breached river, she felt no distress in knowing that her friend would drown. Where better to fill your lungs than here, watched by the watery corpses of those who had faced a similar fate? She stared up at the calmly floating figures revealed on the walls, the pale bodies of drowned acolytes welcoming their ancient gods, and felt suddenly glad to be leaving behind her own distress. The weight rising from her came as an immense relief. Someone else could take over the responsibility now.

Heather barely noticed the female police sergeant who dragged Kallie free. She didn't even complain when May threw a bath towel around her shoulders. The burden of the Water House, and its terrible possession of her, had begun to wash from her heart, leaving her pure and free again, an innocent child. She smiled tightly, looking from one old face to the other, knowing that she would tell them nothing, for there was no longer anything left to tell. They would never know what she had been through, and without her testimony there was no proof.

She was safe at last.

Longbright laid Kallie's body on the stairs and squeezed filthy water from her chest, breathing air into her lungs. 'She's fine,' the detective sergeant called up the stairs. 'She's swallowed quite a bit, though. She'll need shots.'

'John, stay here with Janice. Try and get the women dried off and warmed up while they wait for an ambulance. I'll meet you later.' Bryant rose and gripped the bannisters, climbing unsteadily over Kallie's body.

'Where do you think you're going?' asked May.

'Tate's opened the conduit between the canal and the house. That's why the water is in direct contact with the basement wall, because the river Fleet runs behind it whenever the channel—the Prince of Wales Causeway—is used. He's changed the path of the water. I'm going after him.' Bryant didn't look overly keen on the idea.

'Don't be ridiculous,' said May. 'You're not up to it. I'll go with Bimsley.' He turned to climb the stairs, but Bryant scurried on ahead.

'Come back! You are absolutely not going down a sewer at your age, with your legs. The very idea!'

'You need me. You can't predict my mind. You know it never follows logical routes. You'll be too sensible.'

'Then I'll just have to compensate for you not being there by thinking rubbish,' warned May.

'You don't know where he is, but I have a good idea. Besides, I had the presence of mind to wear my

waterproof long johns, which is more than you're doing. I always said if anything happened to us we'd go
down together. If we don't get Tate tonight, we'll
have nothing. Look at the state of that woman downstairs, look at her eyes—they'll get a doctor to say
she's unfit to stand trial. Is that what you want? For
once in my life I'm not at all cold, and I'm coming
with you.'

Accepting that winning an argument with Bryant
was as likely as finding a tobacconist's shop at the top
of Everest, May gave in gracefully, and chased his
partner up the stairs. They met Bimsley in the street.

'What about getting Oliver Wilton to help?' asked
May as they headed toward the alley. 'He knows how
the system is routed.'

'Only from above ground,' said Bryant. 'He's a
technician. It's not the same as seeing the world from
underneath the street. Besides, the unit couldn't be responsible for his safety. We know Tate's down there
because he's just re-routed the water flow. The system
can be reconfigured by manipulating valves, but once
the channels start to fill the power of the river becomes too great to reach them, and we're having the
heaviest rainfall in thirty years. But I'm betting there's
an overflow route, one that can be opened by high
water pressure.'

'What do you mean?'

'An escape route; this level of flooding probably
switches the largest channels. The bigger the conduit,
the greater the volume of water passing through it,
the more pressure it will exert. It's a track-switching
system that only gets fully tested to its maximum level
every few decades. Tate used a junction-rod to clear
a dry path for himself through the tunnels,' Bryant

explained. 'He made the necessary changes, then waited for the water level to rise to the point when it would re-route to a high-volume shaft. I think one of its side effects was to put pressure on the basement wall of number 5. He explained the process to me; he even gave me a map, but we couldn't follow it because of the rain. He wanted me to understand.'

'Then why didn't he simply tell you what was going on?' May asked.

'I don't think he's capable of explaining the full story to anyone, of why he was there and what has happened to him. How long has he been living on the street? Do you have any idea what that does to a person?'

The alley was under several inches of water at one end, but the raised area around the grating was virtually dry. The lid had been removed and cast aside. Bryant pointed to the iron rod sticking out of the turntable at the bottom of the shaft. 'You see?' he crowed. 'He's kept this path free for himself, and now he's gone down to follow the re-routed channel. We're going to lose him if we're not careful.'

'Could you explain what's going on, sir?' asked Bimsley, fighting to stay balanced in the shifting mud.

'Later,' Bryant promised. 'Help me down.'

'Are you sure it's safe?' Bimsley asked.

'At the moment it's still passable. The volume can rise at an incredible speed in times of heavy rainfall, but it also runs away fast. There are emergency drains which open to reduce pressure. I'm more worried about what will happen if it stops raining.'

'Why?'

'The levels will fall and switch from the overflow

conduit back to this route. Which means these smaller corridors will become inundated once more.'

'How long have we got?' asked May.

'That depends. The channel will take Tate directly to the St Pancras Basin, but if the rain eases up, the tunnels could switch back in just a few minutes.'

'Then we should go overland.'

'We have no way of tracking him from above, and to do so would be to miss the entire point. I think he wants us to follow him down there. We need the final piece to this.'

'Then I'll tell Janice and Meera to follow above ground, and keep us apprised of the weather conditions.'

'How will we know where Tate's gone?' asked Bimsley, reluctantly lowering himself into the steaming drain.

Bryant smiled and held up his river map. 'He left us a guide. Let's get going.'

The first two tunnels were dry and easy to negotiate, but by the time they reached the third, it had been joined by another channel from a different tributary, this one bringing in floating islands of animal fat from a riveted lead pipe. The stench of rotted meat and sewage caused Bimsley to throw up his lunch over a blocked drain.

'The construction of these tunnels is remarkable,' Bryant enthused. 'Look at this metalwork, you don't find craftsmanship like that any more. And the decoration—why would anyone bother to put a neoclassical bay-leaf-garland motif around an arch that no one will ever see? That's Victorian pride for you.'

'Jesus, there's bloody great big rats down here.' Bimsley hopped on to one foot and banged his skull on the ceiling, shattering calcified stalactites as a bedraggled squeaking creature with matted fur shot past him.

'Don't be such a baby,' said Bryant, turning the map around. 'John, we need to concentrate all our lights, please.'

They forked left at a pair of yellow-brick arches coated in slender black tree roots.

'We must be under Prince of Wales Road, heading toward the Regent's Canal by now. Look, there are plaques.' May pointed to the conduit's brass name-plate bolted into the wall, a subterranean echo of the street names on the roads above.

Bryant's torch-beam fell on what appeared to be a bundle of rags. 'Tate's jacket. He wants us to follow him.'

'For the life of me I don't understand why,' said May.

'Oh, he's been waiting for this since the rains began.'

'Does Mr Bryant know something we don't?' asked Bimsley, confused.

'Mr Bryant *always* knows something we don't,' May admitted. 'We're going to need inoculations after this.'

'Perhaps, but we'll have learned something new.' Bryant shone the torch over the tunnel arch. A wider channel ran crossways, like the junction of an arterial road. Shallow, cleaner water was flowing fast through it. 'I don't weigh very much. Think we can get across that?'

'Hang on to me. Bimsley, you're the heaviest, lad—you lead.'

The trio clutched each other's hands and waded

out, but Bryant was nearly pulled off his feet. May and the detective constable yanked him to the other side like parents controlling a recalcitrant child.

'Look at this.' May pointed to the wall beside them. 'One of your fail-safe conduits.' He slapped his hand on the riveted steel panel, layered with grease and grooved at its base to shift around a matching steel arc, like the flood gate in an underground station. Behind a grille at the top, water was rushing away into darkness. 'If the water rises too high, it'll come over and re-flood this tunnel, creating a run-off.'

'Some of these tunnels look dry,' Bimsley pointed out.

'I don't think we've reached the part of the system designed for peak flooding yet,' said Bryant. 'We'll know it when we see it.'

From here the floor sloped downwards, and they found themselves going deeper. 'According to this, there's an emergency escape drain above us, but I don't see it.' May waved his torch about.

'There,' said Bimsley, illuminating a narrow round shaft far above them. 'It looks like the ladder has rusted away and fallen in.'

'That's reassuring.'

Following the map to the St Pancras Basin, they turned into a narrower ramped tunnel with slender iron platforms on either side. 'This is part of the system newly exposed by the flood switches,' said Bryant. 'Look at the walls.' They showed clear signs of long-term immersion. Strangely, the stone floor beneath their feet was less slippery, and the air smelled healthier. 'Nothing's had time to stagnate here. It's probably been kept full just coping with the natural run-off of freshwater from Hampstead Heath and the other high areas above the city. It isn't wide enough to cope with severe flooding, but it's fine for everyday use. Wonderful workmanship; not a stone out of place. Beautiful bevelling.'

Bimsley's radio crackled, making him jump. 'The rain's easing up,' warned Longbright. 'You'd better start heading for the nearest exit.'

'We must be nearly there.' Bryant waded on ahead. 'The light is less dense.'

He was right. A faint sickly glow changed the colour of the walls before them, but as they approached, they found themselves entering a network of claustrophobic culverts, each one barred at the end.

'We'll have to turn around,' May warned. 'This one's a dead end too.'

'Interesting,' said Bryant, seemingly unconcerned that they might be swept away at any minute. 'I'm assuming that Tate is down here looking for something that has been unexposed for some thirty years, and I would have thought that this was the most likely place for him to be. The tunnels fill to their highest level, then empty, washing everything out this way.'

'There's no sign of him.'

'He must have left some kind of trail. Keep looking around.'

'Bimsley, how long since it stopped raining?'

'Twelve minutes, sir.'

'The levels will be falling. We should try to find an exit. Call Longbright and find out where the nearest drain shaft is, would you?'

Bimsley tried his phone, but failed to locate a signal. 'No response. We're in pretty deep ground.'

'So we're on our own. I wouldn't fancy our chances of climbing those slopes back up. We'll have to go on,' said May.

'*Very* interesting,' said Bryant approvingly. 'The Fleet was choked off by the expanding metropolis, but its waters still ran, albeit at a fraction of their former power. And at the highest flood levels, the water would fight to find a way around the obstacles. The system is beautifully simple when you think about it. The engineers knew the floods were cyclical over decades, so they allowed for the Fleet to return by a series of self-controlled gates that can only be opened by a specific volume of water. Under such conditions, the river cuts a path all the way through the local district conduits to form a single united flow heading to Camden Town and Clerkenwell, following the old route just as it used to, before emptying out into the Thames.'

'Yes, Arthur, and as soon as the level drops and the weight recedes it will switch back, leaving us, all too literally, I fear, *dans la merde*. So can we push on?'

'Let me see the map again.' Bryant held it beneath his torch.

'I can hear something,' warned Bimsley, putting his ear as close as he dared to the wall. 'It doesn't sound good.'

They shone their torches back to see the first of the great steel plates grinding across on its arc as the Fleet redirected itself back to local channels. The group pushed on and down as the water started to deepen. 'It's probably refilling from the highest gate first,' warned May. 'I doubt any one gate could handle the full amount of water, so the switch-back will be staggered with locks, but the effect will still be like flushing a cistern. The water has to maintain a momentum in order to reach the river. We really have to find a way out of here.'

'You can hear it coming,' called Bimsley, an air of panic creeping into his voice.

'The sound is probably magnified,' said Bryant cheerfully. 'It's echoing down the entire length of the shaft. According to the map there's a drainage shaft down here on the left.'

They found themselves in another dead end filled with the detritus of the past thirty years. As they pushed through the rubbish, the bloated corpse of a cat swirled by.

'Sorry,' Bryant apologized, squinting at the plan. 'Now a right turn—it's hard to read the scale of this thing. It should be right here in front of us.'

'There's your shaft,' said May, reaching a halt. 'Somehow I don't think we're going to make it out of here.'

'Why do you say that?' asked Bryant.

May shone his torch up to the roof, illuminating the chimney to the surface, more than thirty feet above their heads. 'The ladder is missing. There's no way of reaching the drain without it. And we can't go back.'

Bimsley pinched his frozen nose and tried to think. 'There were three corridors at the last junction. We know that two are dead ends, so let's go back to the first one.'

'Admirable idea, Bimsley.' Bryant struck out through knee-deep scum. 'The water's much warmer than I thought it would be. I think it's coming from a heated source—dishwashers and washing machines, perhaps. There's a distinctly soapy smell now.'

'Arthur, I think we should concentrate on the problem at hand.' May towed his partner back until they reached the junction. They turned into the only remaining tunnel as the rumble of water rose to a roar behind them. They had gone less than a hundred yards when the corridor narrowed sharply and twisted off.

'Fingers crossed,' called May, wading ahead. 'If this doesn't lead out, we won't be going home tonight.'

He was almost frightened to raise the torch.

'Well?' called Bryant.

Bimsley followed the beam across the now thigh-deep water. The tunnel appeared to open out to a much larger space beyond, but there was no way of reaching it: a matrix of scabbed iron bars blocked the way ahead. May slammed his fist against the metal as he realized the impossibility of moving it.

'There's a grille across the outlet,' he called back. 'Can you open it?'

'I suppose there might be a handle, but it's not on this side.'

'Then that's that.' Bryant arrived beside them. 'This is my fault. I made you come down here.'

The tunnel began to vibrate with the subway-train rush of water arriving from the upper Fleet tunnel.

May shone his torch back toward the source of the noise. They watched in horror as a great wave of water, its virescent crest touching the roof of the tunnel, swept down toward them.

48

ST PANCRAS BASIN BLUES

Bryant was the first to fall backwards because he had been pressed against the grille. Bimsley and May followed him as the bars behind them slammed up into the stone ceiling, flushing flat into the brickwork. As the water hit, the trio found themselves washed across the end of the tunnel and over a great latticework grating as the river flushed itself away into the ground.

'What a wonderful piece of draughtsmanship,' enthused Bryant, rolling to his feet, half-drowned. 'A simple cantilever.'

'Is everybody all right?' asked May.

'I think I swallowed something disgusting,' coughed Bimsley.

They slowly rose and looked about. Their torches had been lost in the river's diverted path, but now there was light from another source. They found themselves in an immense arched cathedral of smoothly varnished brown tiles.

'My God, it looks like a mirror image of the King's Cross and St Pancras railway arches,' Bryant exclaimed, pulling a plastic Sainsbury's bag from his leg and wiping himself down with it. 'I suppose it would have been built at the same time.' The vaulted peak of the hall was lost in Stygian gloom. 'St Pancras Basin.'

Pigeons living in the high iron rafters dropped down through the hall, their wings fluttering like the ruffled pages of old books.

'Doesn't this section get filled as the system switches back?' asked Bimsley.

'No, it's very clever—the bars around the edges of the floor act as a gigantic drain, so it stays dry. No wonder they picked this spot to build the Channel Tunnel terminal—half the underground work is already done for them. Ah, Mr Tate, or should I say Mr Kingdom—you are Gilbert Kingdom's son, aren't you? Perhaps you can explain why it was so important to lead us here.'

The others turned to find their quarry seated on a pile of sacks, eating a tuna sandwich from a Tupperware tub. He appeared to be expecting them.

'I wanted to show you this,' he said simply, raising his hand and indicating the basin.

Bryant realized now that what he had thought was a deserted underground hall was in fact populated. Wrapped in blankets and brown cardboard, the residents blended invisibly with the shadowed walls, but the noise of the re-channelled water had stirred them, and people were sitting up, standing, stretching, stamping the circulation back into their limbs.

'Bloody hell,' said Bimsley. 'Where did they come from?'

'Good question,' Bryant replied. 'More to the point, I think, is where they go from here.'

'The basin is used by anyone seeking refuge—people who have no homes, no identities, no lives,' said Kingdom. 'During the War, deserters hid in the St Pancras Basin. I first came here with my father thirty years ago. It was safe and dry. This time, when the rains arrived, the walls began dripping dirty water. Bad chemicals washing in from above. The basin's run-off drains are blocked with rubble from the terminal construction overhead. They've become stagnant. People are getting sick. Pneumonia, stomach bugs and worse.'

'Why not take the risk and head above ground?' asked Bryant.

'The police—the other police, the ones in uniforms—are waiting for us above. Everyone said you were a good man, and would help. I wanted to ask you when we met at the hostel, but then the man in the next room—'

'—set fire to the place,' said Bryant, 'and you knew we would blame you. Are you surprised? There was inflammable spirit everywhere.'

'He started throwing it all around the floor. A crazy man who thought he was being persecuted, thought the police were out to get him. He looked out of the window and saw your constable coming in. What could I do? I seized the chance to get away. No one else could help these people.'

He watched them for a moment, thinking. 'I remember the last time the tunnel flooded and opened a clear path straight through to the basin. I knew you were investigating the street that passed right above the river channel. The basin exit was being watched, so there was no other way for you to get here. I needed you to follow me.'

'Look, I'm frozen and wet, I've been poisoned

with half the toilet waste of north London, I've probably swallowed parts of a rancid cat, and I still don't understand what any of this has to do with the case,' complained Bimsley. 'Am I completely stupid?'

'No, Colin, not completely.' Bryant looked at the crippled son of the Water House's creator. 'I think you'll find it's about the difference between a house and a home,' he said finally.

49

MR BRYANT EXPLAINS IT ALL FOR YOU

Longbright insisted on driving her complaining superiors to UCH for a set of inoculations, releasing them on the condition that they went straight home to bed. They didn't, of course; none of them did. The offices above Mornington Crescent were quiet now. Only one room was illuminated. It had just turned midnight, heading toward the Monday morning of the unit's fresh start, and the heating had gone off. Kallie was with them, wrapped in a moth-eaten fun-fur that had belonged to Longbright's mother.

'If you're going to light that thing, open a window,' warned May.

'I can't, the rain has swollen the wood.' Bryant sucked at his pipe, releasing a plume of aromatic smoke. He produced his flask and poured a measure of crimson syrup into a glass. 'Would anyone like a cherry brandy?'

'No wonder your teeth fell out.' May served beers to the group. 'I take it Heather Allen's guilt didn't surprise you.'

'Well, of course not. Even when it's the person you least suspect, you still sort of suspect them because they're the least suspicious. Female killers are rare, but when one comes along she can be more calculating and dangerous than any man. Heather Allen has been a very angry woman for a long time. I suppose she had a lot to be angry about. I take it you understand everything now.'

'No,' admitted May. 'I'm with Bimsley on that one.'

'Then I shall endeavour to explain, now that Kallie here has provided some of the missing pieces. I'll rather enjoy making my case report this time, because the answer came from tracing the confluence of three sources, rather like following tributaries back to a river. The gaps can be filled in with a little guesswork, but I'll wager you won't find the truth far different.' He smiled, displaying his incongruous dentures.

'To untangle this, we have to go back more than thirty years, to Gilbert Kingdom, an unappreciated artist who manages to sell just two paintings in a lifetime. The nation has survived a terrible depression, only to be plunged into another World War; now that a painfully rationed peace has been won, people find they have no taste for art, especially the kind of peculiar mythologies Kingdom likes to paint. You see, Kingdom believes that the salvation of the world lies in Christians renouncing their faith in order to become Pagans. He's a man born out of his time. Luckily he and his son are photographed for the book in Peregrine Summerfield's possession, otherwise we would never have identified him. So, the artist's wife has run off, leaving him with a young boy to support. When the terrace is repaired after the bombing raids, a property developer moves in to renovate several of the houses, and Kingdom—perhaps because they've been friends during the War—persuades the developer to let him paint murals. He plans four, directly based upon the physiology and mythology of the area, which still has strong connections with its past.'

'You think he saw the map?' asked Longbright, emptying her beer into a pint mug.

'He certainly knows of it, or discovers the area's history in local books. He realizes that the sites fit with his personal obsessions. A House of Conflagration— a monastery that defied the Catholic Church in its thinking and was burned down for its heresies. A House of Foul Earth—a burial site for plague victims. A House of Poisoned Air—on a hill too close to a tanning mill, where people become sick. A House Cursed by Water—which sounds like a property that floods every few years, don't you think? Gilbert Kingdom looks at the street, and chooses four houses on the approximate sites of their original histories, because each house fortuitously represents one of the four elements.'

'So it gives him a grand artistic theme,' said May. 'A personal endeavour.'

'Precisely. They are to be his crowning achievement, and, more importantly, will raise the value of the properties at a relatively small expense to the developer. It seems to be a wonderful plan; art and commerce combined. He will provide for his son, he will create permanent monuments to his beliefs, and he will reap rewards deserving of a great artist. But like so many wonderful plans, there's a flaw.'

'The neighbourhood fails to go up in value,' Longbright pointed out.

'Unfortunately its connections with its past are

strong—too strong. It remains a place of lawlessness
and trouble. Nobody wants to live there, let alone
pay extra for having built-in artworks of an un-
Christian nature. The government is busy trying to
rebuild the country—no one has time for art! The developer is bankrupted, and the artist, who has been
living rent-free in one of the properties and has taken
four long years to finish the work, is thrown out into
the street with his son, where he dies a pathetic, ignominious death at the hands of local ruffians. Life imi-
tates art, and drowning proves a fitting end.'

'The boy is taken into care—' added May.

'Exactly. He's in and out of foster homes, but he
never forgets what happened to his father. He holds
down a job at the Tate Gallery for a while, just to be
near one of Gilbert's two paintings, then loses his position after causing a fuss when the paintings are sold.
He has no money, and therefore no voice in the
world. He is seen by all, but becomes invisible.'

'What a sad life.' Kallie pulled the coat tighter
around herself, settling into her seat as Bryant rose
and stalked the room, relishing his chance to marshal
the facts.

'Now we move on. Time passes. The area
changes. The yuppies arrive. Among them is Heather
Allen, the original material girl. She thinks she's going
to get everything she wants from life, but life lets her
down. First her husband's business collapses, then
he leaves her for someone younger. Terrified by the
thought of her failure, and concerned with outward
appearances, she covers up the fact that she is now
broke and alone. She does this by denying her divorce, and pretending against hope that everything is
fine. I think you'll find that the man who came to her

house—the one Kallie saw from her window—wasn't her husband at all. He's probably an old family friend from whom she's trying to borrow money, or her finance manager coming for a not-so-friendly chat. Heather Allen has a good brain, but even she can't put her life right. She's eaten up with bitterness over the way things have turned out, but she'll make the best of it.'

'She told me all she had left was the house, which she really hated,' said Kallie.

'Because it reminds her of her failed marriage.' Bryant stabbed a forefinger in Kallie's direction. 'So she decides to sell it for as much as she can get. To do this, she first needs to decorate—but there's hardly any money. So she uses the local bodger, Elliot Copeland, who comes in and starts stripping the basement. And that's when he finds the wall.' He paused before the misted window, looking down into the night street.

'This is the moment when Heather makes the mistake that will destroy her life. She knows how to look the part—she's a woman of surfaces. She knows a little about a lot of things, but not much about art, even though she's worked in a gallery and has helped to curate an exhibition of Stanley Spencer's work. Wrinkling her petite nose, she tells him to tear off the disgusting plaster and repaint, and poor drunk Elliot is happy to oblige his client. Bad timing, as it turns out, because just as the mural is destroyed, Heather finds the book belonging to Kingdom's son. How does she find it? Well, of course, it's been left out for her by the street's guardian, Kingdom's powerless, protective, penniless boy—Tate—who wants recognition for his father and is going about it all the wrong way. Flicking through the book that has been posted through her letterbox, she sees four illustrations, mythic, epic subjects supposedly painted by an artist of great merit, now sadly presumed lost. And, of course, she recognizes her own house, number 6 Balaklava Street, the Air House, which she has just finished renovating, thereby nullifying its value. Tate doesn't allow her to keep the book, of course—he breaks in and takes it back, because it's all he has left. What can Heather do? The only money she has is tied up in the property. It's not a home to her, just bricks and mortar. She's destroyed her only escape route, and has only herself to blame. But with a little smart thinking she can work out which are the other three houses. Could it be that their basements are still intact, and—please God—that their new occupants have no knowledge of the fortune hidden within their walls? Tate expects her to save his father's work. Instead, he accidentally creates a monster.'

'There's a bit of guesswork going on here,' said Longbright, draining her beer.

'I think you'll find I'm right when you confront her with this, Janice.' Bryant hated interruptions. 'Where was I? So, Heather borrows a map from a member of the local historical society. She asks around, even makes an effort to talk to the neighbours. And what does she find out? That the Fire House, number 43, belonging to newcomers Tamsin and Oliver Wilton, was gutted in the sixties. That the Earth House, number 41, now in the hands of another newcomer, Jake Avery, was similarly renovated a few years later. Which just leaves number 5, the Water House.

'But this, she discovers, is the key to all four

houses. It is the reason why Kingdom chose elements and elementals as the channel for his beliefs, because it is built right on top of the river Fleet. It is the original site of the House Curs'd By All Water, and he can exorcise it or, more likely, celebrate the fact in his art. According to the book, this house contains the most elaborate mural of them all, the one upon which Kingdom lavished the most time, the one that caused his patron to finally lose faith. And it belongs to an old lady who has lived there since 1949, so she is the house's only owner since the mural has been completed.

'Heather is a worrier, an aggressor, but also a natural planner. She suddenly becomes Ruth Singh's new best friend. She can't do enough for her—fetches her shopping, cuts her toenails, fixes her hair, but is careful not to let anyone else know. While she's doing chores, she discreetly checks out the basement. Imagine her excitement when she discovers that the mural is still there, completely intact. Ruth has painted over it several times—but it's undamaged. It will be the wonder of London, on a par with Leighton House or Debenham Hall. London is filled with extraordinary properties that become national treasures. She'll have wealth and respect, everything she had expected from her marriage. The old dear can't have much longer to last—how difficult can it be for Heather to worm her way into the will?'

'Quite difficult, as it turns out,' said May, 'because Ruth has a brother.'

'True, he doesn't bother much with her, but he's still a blood relative. Heather's not about to give in easily, though. Soon she's been invited to meet Benjamin Singh, who confides in her that he wishes to move to Australia, which would mean he'd sell the house when he inherits it. But not to her—he takes an instant dislike to this grabby, hysterical woman asking personal questions about his family's property, acting like she's Ruth's best friend. And the old lady seems as strong as an ox. She may live to be a hundred. So Heather tries a little debilitation.'

'You mean she leaves the racist messages.' May topped up everyone's drinks. 'Dan may be able to prove it's her voice on the tape.'

'Still, the old lady is unfazed,' Bryant continued. 'Then fate takes a highly appropriate hand, in the form of a stuck tap. Heather has told Ruth, "If you're ever in difficulty, just bang on the wall and I'll come running." Ruth goes to take a bath, but can't turn the tap off. Frightened, she hammers on the wall, and Heather, ever cautious about her appearance, puts on the coat Garrett has left at her place. What was it doing there? The likeliest answer is that he had come round to give her property advice.

'So, Ruth Singh, in her dressing-gown, lets Heather in—where she is seen by Jake Avery—and Heather goes down to the bathroom to give the tap a clout. When she sees the running water, everything suddenly becomes clear. She's been given a sign. "Why don't I wait here while you have your bath?" she suggests. "Then I can turn the tap on if you need more hot water."

'She waits, and talks, and waits, until the old lady is drowsy. Then, with a grimace of disgust, she reaches into the soapy water, picks up Ruth's ankles and pulls. She's as light as a feather and barely makes a sound, her heart stopping in an instant, although she gets a small contusion from the tap. But instead of leaving her in the bath and making the whole thing look like an accident, Heather is forced to drain out the water, because the police will realize that Ruth couldn't have turned the tap off by herself. What if she's not dead? How can you tell these things? Ruth is naked in the drained bath, her head beneath the taps, so Heather turns on the cold water and forces open her mouth, just to make sure.

'But now something odd happens. The rains have begun, and under the street Tate is testing his conduits, opening valves and sluices. As if summoned by the Water House itself, diverted river water thunders under the bathroom. It is sucked up through fine cracks in the brickwork, blossoming in damp patches. It comes up the overflow of the bath and out of the water pipes in a blast of green scum, to be ingested by Ruth Singh. But at least there's no doubt now that she's dead.'

'So Finch was right in his summation,' said May. 'Credit where it's due.'

Bryant harrumphed and chewed his pipe stem. 'Heather has seized her opportunity, but won't be able to buy the property because she has no money. She'll worry about that later. Meanwhile, she dries and dresses the old lady to throw the police off the scent, not realizing that her throat is still full of water. It's like taking care of a doll. Then she climbs over the back wall into her own house.

'But she's seen by someone: Tate, who is emerging from the drain in the alley. Luckily he's just a crazy old tramp. No one will ever pay attention to him. She's quick to point that out to Kallie.'

Bryant stood behind Kallie's chair in what he fancied was a dramatic posture. Outside, a police siren seesawed into the night.

'Which brings us to your timely arrival, Kallie. You're her old schoolfriend: innocent, susceptible, liked by everyone, and clearly in awe of Heather. It's a more roundabout route, but one which should work just as well. Heather will persuade you to buy the house. Afterwards, it will be a simple matter to put you off the place, make you desperate to sell it. Heather will have sold her own property by then, and will be able to offer a reasonable price.

'And this time it all goes according to plan. You and Paul move in, and duly grow disillusioned. There are strange noises, and even stranger occurrences as the river rises and falls. Now Heather starts to get nervous. What if the rain doesn't stop? The forecast is bad. The area is prone to flooding; what if the basement is soaked and the art is ruined? She must act quickly. The best way to do this is to get rid of Paul, who already has itchy feet and is looking for an excuse to escape his responsibilities. Heather drips poison in his ears, telling him that you deliberately tried to get pregnant in order to keep him, and the tactic pays off. Paul leaves in order to "get his head together"—and not before time, because Jake Avery has been seen talking to him in the local pub. Jake, who saw Heather on the doorstep of number 5 the night before Ruth Singh died. Without Paul you're alone and more vulnerable than ever. Heather manipulates you shamelessly.

'She also realizes that the consequences of her one big mistake are still with her, because she sees drunk old Elliot Copeland the builder—the only other person apart from Tate who saw the mural in the Air

House, talking to Jake at the Wiltons' party. For all she knows, Jake could have told Paul when they went out drinking together. Men talk too much when they've had a few, and even now Elliot might be telling everyone how he's noticed something strange about the houses in the street.

'Heather has to do something. If she leaves things as they are, the truth about the Water House will surface. She's a woman prone to subterfuge—she already took Garrett's old coat to the Wiltons' party rather than her own—it's always a good idea to spread blame and confusion around, as she knows when she later phones Kayla Ayson, posing as you, to suggest that her husband is having an affair. Meanwhile, there are two dangers in her mind. Anyone?'

Kallie raised a hand. 'She's frightened I'll discover the wall for myself.'

'Absolutely. You're doing up the property, although it's more of a struggle with Paul gone. Two, suppose Elliot mentions the wall in Heather's house, the one she made him destroy? She can't prevent the first, but she can sure as hell fix the latter. She's done it once before; she can do it again. She waits and watches for an opportunity, and weirdly, just as the stuck tap represented a chance, so does Elliot's work on the waste ground opposite. She throws you off the scent by claiming to see someone else from the window—or perhaps she has really seen Tate lurking in the bushes—and sends you on a pointless errand to buy booze, before heading over in the obscuring rain to see if there's anything she can do. And there, perilously close to the half-cut Elliot, is his truck. She looks in the cab, spots the button that empties the flatbed, and allows the bricks to tip forward. Then she runs home, and is careful to be seen at the window by you as you return.'

'That's why there was a puddle of water on the carpet,' May realized.

'Heather's out of danger. Everyone knew Elliot was a drunk. The rain will obliterate the crime scene. All she has to do now is wait for the Water House to fall into her lap.'

'It's true I was very depressed,' said Kallie. 'Maybe I did start to think about moving on, and could have been persuaded to sell to Heather. I should have seen the signs. God, when I think about our conversations together, the number of mistakes she made. She even referred to her cat as "a legacy from George" and I didn't pick up on it. How did I fail to notice?'

'Everyone makes mistakes when they're improvising,' said Bryant.

'Maybe Jake did say something to Paul about making money from the house, but they got drunk together, and the next morning he'd forgotten their conversation.' Kallie accepted another beer from Longbright. 'I'll never take him back now. Sorry, Mr Bryant, please go on.'

'Well—I think it's safe to assume that, by this time, Heather Allen is no longer thinking rationally. The scheme obsesses her. And that's when the domino effect really kicks in. Jake Avery comes calling to tell her about something Elliot told him. He's suspicious of Heather, but can't decide what to do. He'll sleep on it before going to the police. She starts to panic now. She's so close to her goal, but all her efforts will go to waste if Jake talks. I'm guessing this part, but I think we'll find out it's true: Heather has seen Aaron and Marshall together. She goes to the workshop and talks to Marshall, and here she finds out something to her advantage. Jake's always having a go at Aaron about little things, like leaving the back door open. Extemporizing wildly, she uses Tate's fence-panels to climb into Jake's back garden, entering his house. Passing through the kitchen, she sees the roll of cling-film—why, when there's a rack full of knives? Maybe she's squeamish—she's managed to avoid any real bloodshed, after all. She finds Jake asleep and reeking of booze. Smothering him takes virtually no effort at all on her part.'

Bryant dropped down into the seat behind his desk. 'This should be the end of the chain. No one else knows the truth, and no one will ever know. Whether by coincidence or malicious design, she has murdered three people in accordance with three of the four elements. It's fate's grand scheme. Even the land is working with her. She feels invincible. Nothing else can possibly go wrong.

'Which is exactly when the other weak spot in her plan is breached. Kallie here discovers the mural. To Heather, it seems as if the river is rising up to protect the house and defeat her. How appropriate, then, that she should bring events full circle and drown Kallie, turning her into one of the mural's subjects. But of course, Tate is watching both houses—Kallie's and, more importantly, Heather's. He's determined to protect Kallie and save his father's work. But each time he comes running to help her, we chase him away. Still, he returns. At least now his hard work has finally paid off, and the mural—albeit a little frayed and wet around the edges—will be restored and preserved for posterity.'

'She should have killed Tate,' said Longbright. 'That could have protected her.'

'Well, you have reason to feel very pleased with yourself, Arthur,' declared May.

'I would only feel that if we had been able to save the lives of her victims,' Bryant admitted. 'But there is still something left to do tonight.' He rose and began pulling on Longbright's spare overcoat, which was far too large for him. 'Janice, you can take Kallie home, can't you?'

'Where are you going?' asked May.

'I have to return to St Pancras Basin, and you're coming with me. Don't worry, this time we won't be getting wet, and at least we can put something right.'

50

DIASPORA

They used the river map to locate the entrance, a dank drainage shaft behind a bathroom-accessory warehouse at the back of King's Cross. But gaining access proved impossible, because the iron hatch covering the shaft had been sealed under new tarmac. Night construction workers covered the area, so the detectives drove to the only other location they had listed, in nearby York Way.

This proved an altogether easier affair, consisting of a concrete stairway straight down into the basin. Unfortunately, the exit was in the centre of a secure construction compound, to which the detectives could only gain access by showing their police authorization.

'The construction company must know about this,' said Bryant as they descended the undamaged drain ladder. 'It's right on their site.'

'Perhaps they haven't been granted access yet. You know how long this sort of insurance documentation takes to approve.'

The great cavern of the basin lay before them. As John May crossed the dripping tiled hall, a distant susurration of alarm suggested that its inhabitants had heard the arrival of a stranger. 'You know we could get into serious trouble,' whispered May.

'When you're old, you can afford to take risks,' Bryant whispered back. 'It seems perverse to become more safety-conscious just when you have less to lose.'

They stopped before a row of slumped bodies. A young East European in a hooded sweatshirt and jeans rested on his haunches, keeping guard for the others.

'Does anyone here speak English?' May asked him.

'David Beckham,' smiled the youth. 'Posh Spice. Lovely Jubbly.'

'I blame tourism,' sighed Bryant. 'Those are the three phrases Egyptian boys use when trying to sell themselves as guides at the pyramids. I don't suppose he knows any more English than that.'

The boy was put out. 'I am Amir. I watch television, I speak English good, more words than many English people. I see English television. *Absolutely Fabulous*.'

'Which means you don't know how to get through passport control, but you know who Joanna Lumley is,' moaned Bryant. 'What a world.'

'What he say?' the boy asked May.

'He's being rude, take no notice. How many of you?' May pointed at the others.

'Maybe fourteen now.'

'Are there any children?'

'No, the children have gone with their mothers. Only men left. The youngest man is ten years.'

'Arthur, I need a word with you.' May pulled him to one side. 'We have to tell the immigration authorities. They'll take care of the boy. I don't suppose they're carrying any papers or passports. They're economic migrants, not political refugees. Apart from anything else, they could be harbouring diseases.'

'Please, John, you're sounding like one of the more hysterical tabloids. Look at them. If we turn them over, they'll be sent back or thrown into detention centres. We'll have betrayed them. What have they had to go through, what have they risked just to get here, living in a sewer?'

'How *did* you get here?' May asked the men sitting up in their makeshift beds, watching the conversation in defeated silence.

'Some by truck, some in private boats,' Amir explained. 'Police watch Dover but there are fishermen in Folkestone. We come here to meet another man who says he will help us, but he does not come.'

'They're tearing down all the arches and tunnels around King's Cross, building the Eurostar terminal, and accidentally opened up the access to the St Pancras Basin from above,' Bryant explained. 'Obviously someone tipped off the police, so now they're watching all the streets, and these people can't use the way they came in.'

'What about the drain behind Balaklava Street?'

'It would have been too steep to climb back up all the way from here, and now it's flooded again. You can use the local drainage network between the three streets in Kentish Town, or leave the basin via York Way. But there's no way of bringing over a dozen people up on to a fenced-off construction site guarded by a copper. Soon the company will start demolishing the tunnels and sinking concrete shafts. It's probably only the rain that's been delaying them. These are people who need our help.'

'We could lose everything over this,' May warned.

'But we could get them out.'

'I don't suppose it would be difficult. We'd just

have to call the security officer to another location for a few minutes. That's not the question, Arthur. It's whether we have a moral obligation to do so. We work for the State. Suppose we let them go free, and the first thing they do is rob someone? How would you justify that?'

'I wouldn't,' Bryant agreed. 'But if you hang around in King's Cross long enough you're going to get mugged anyway, and besides, they'd be stupid to stay here where the police are watching out for them. They'd have to split up and head off into other parts of the country.'

May looked nervously at the expectant group. 'You're sure there's no other way?'

'Of course there are other ways, but they'd result in more human misery. If you want a moral obligation, consider that our imperative to protect life should override all regulations set in place by passing politicians. Everyone needs a place they can call home. It should be as fundamental a right as freedom of speech.'

'You cannot act against the law, Arthur.'

'You can when the law is an ass. Time will prove us right. *Qui vivra verra.*'

'Do you honestly believe that?' asked May.

'I have to believe it.'

May sighed. 'Then let's do it.'

They used a couple of Indian lads from the Drummond Street gang who sometimes acted as informants for the unit. Creating the diversion was easy enough, but the detectives had to be sure that the site security guard could be cajoled into lending a hand in what appeared to be a gang confrontation. Amir insisted that they could get everyone out within five minutes, but would need extra time to disperse from the torn-up backstreets of the Cross.

May watched as they gathered up plastic-wrapped bundles of belongings containing their only possessions—photographs, religious artefacts, a few items of clothing—and milled around the fractured iron staircase at the far end of the basin. The need to hold out hope made them trusting; for all they knew, unscrupulous traffickers could have been rounding them up for mass execution. Amir spoke to each man as he passed, explaining something about the detectives. Several came over and grabbed their hands, murmuring thanks. May shot his partner a disapproving look.

One old man was wrapped in yards of chequered scarfing. He looked like an Arabic version of Bryant. Shuffling to a stop before them, he held out a Sainsbury's shopping bag in his arms.

'He says you are kind men,' Amir translated. 'He wishes to give you a gift.'

The old man grinned back, revealing thin pink gums. The boy by his side could have been a son or a grandson; denied a healthy diet, he had already lost the immunity of youth. Bryant could only accept the bag and bow his head in thanks. He watched as they filed to the ladder, patiently awaiting their turn to reach the surface, and saw why such people accepted their fate: they were too weary to do anything else.

'Wait,' Bryant called, summoning Amir. He held out a small blue card. 'I almost forgot. Tell your friends to call this number when they reach Birmingham.' The card read: *Division of St James the Elder: Birmingham*

Coven—Prop. Betty Wagstaff. 'She's the daughter of a very old friend. She can get you medical help if you need it.'

The detectives watched as the last of the immigrants climbed toward the patch of liverish light that was the sky above King's Cross.

'Twenty minutes,' said May, checking his watch. 'That should be long enough for them to get a head start. If this ever gets back—'

'Oh, don't make such a fuss about helping people. You should be glad it's not you going out there. It could have been, you know. You're a quarter foreign, after all.'

'My grandfather was Welsh, Arthur, not East European.'

'That's worse. They wanted home rule once. They could have invaded us. They might have put checkpoints along Hadrian's Wall.'

Bryant sniffed and peered into the Sainsbury's bag. 'Pass the torch, would you?' He shone it inside, then carefully pulled the plastic away to reveal a chipped white vase, six inches high and covered with patches of dried mud.

'What is that?' asked May suspiciously. 'It looks . . .'

They studied the heads of Horus and Anubis painted in black and gold around the top of the vase. 'Egyptian? He must have found it in the channel when the water was drained.' Bryant bent closer. On one side, rows of blue-black Nubian slaves were depicted crying into the Nile. On the other, the same slaves were pouring the river into a vase of the same design, as though the pictogram might be infinitely repeated back into the past.

May's eyes narrowed. 'Tell me that's not what

Ubeda and Greenwood nearly lost their lives trying to find. Tell me it's not the Vessel of All Counted Sorrows.'

Bryant ran his fingers over the figures, peering at them intently. 'No, it's not,' he said finally. 'Even though there's a figure of Anubis. You need Anubis to carry the sorrows from one vessel to another.' He turned the vase over and studied the base in the torchlight. 'Liberty's. A mass-produced replica. I told you the Victorians were big on Egyptiana. I think if we took this to Rachel Ling, she'd tell us about the ritual involving the casting of such a vessel into the waters of the Fleet to protect and regenerate the City of London. Of symbolic value only, but a fitting souvenir of this whole business. I shall give it to Greenwood when his head's better. Neither he nor Ubeda would ever have found it, because they didn't know that the Fleet switched to another course in times of high flooding, something an ordinary Water Board employee like Wilton could have told them. Poor old Gareth: the curse of intellect without practical application. Let's go and find some decent breatheable air.'

'That's King's Cross above us,' May pointed out, 'not Hyde Park.'

'Perhaps, but for once it will smell as sweet.'

As Bryant climbed on to the ladder, his foot missed a step and the vase slipped out of his hands. He tried to catch it, but was too slow, and could only watch in dismay as it fell, shattering to pieces on the wet stone floor below.

May reached down among the ceramic shards and held something aloft in his hand. 'Actually, I think this may have been what Ubeda was searching for after all.'

The intricately carved emerald Anubis was the size of a duck's egg, and would subsequently prove to be three thousand years old.

Bryant started laughing so hard that he nearly fell off the ladder. 'Jackson Ubeda's grandfather placed it inside the vessel as part of the ritual, and in their zeal the acolytes forgot to take it back out. I would love to have seen the look on his face after he tossed it into the river and then realized what he had done. I wonder how many years the family has been searching for it.'

'What are we going to do with it?' asked May.

'Return it to the Cairo Museum, I think,' said Bryant. 'The British did quite enough pilfering for one dynasty. The irony is that now Ubeda has gone into hiding, he'll never know that his familial duty has been performed.'

'Although I imagine he would have kept the thing for himself, don't you? Perhaps it took all of this to return it to the right hands.'

The Anubis was indeed returned, but it stayed—for three glorious days—on the shelf above Bryant's desk in Mornington Crescent, where he could admire it at close quarters. It kept him in such a good mood that Raymond Land thought he had turned over a new leaf; a notion Bryant happily disabused him of once the jewel was returned to Egypt.

51

GEZELLIG

'Alma told me I'd find you up here,' said May, seating himself beside his partner on the bench at the top of Primrose Hill. Bryant was muffled up in the patched brown scarf and squashed trilby he had worn for over fifty years. The frost on the grass looked as artificial as Christmas-card snow. The distant city was soft and blue in the autumnal morning haze, the shade of ceanothus blossoms. It hummed softly, powered by batteries of working men and women.

'I thought you'd join me. Here.' He handed May a polystyrene cup filled with tea. 'I was saving you a jam doughnut, but I ate it.'

May raised the lid and took a tentative sip. 'I can't believe you're making your landlady move house, just to come and look after you.'

'I thought that was what you wanted me to do. Everyone was going on about how upset she was. John, her great pleasure in life has always been to cater to my every whim. The lease on her house in Battersea is running out, and there's enough room in the new place. Perhaps it's a bit bigger than I thought. It makes sense for her to move where she can keep an eye on me. I've been very nice to her, I bought her a new iron.'

The converted workshop behind Chalk Farm Tube station had proven too much for him to keep clean, and although Bryant would have been the last person to admit that he hated the idea of living alone, he did, and Alma was one of the few women left in the world who would put up with him.

'I meant to tell you, Raymond Land is talking of expanding the unit after our success in Balaklava Street. He wants us to take on cases for the whole of the south of England, with another unit set up in Manchester to handle the north. He's really upbeat about the idea.'

'Typical. The one case we're forbidden from pursuing provides a partially fruitful outcome, and suddenly he wants to franchise the policing equivalent of Starbucks.'

'Just think of it, Arthur. With a decent infrastructure in place we could finally retire.' The second he spoke, May realized it was the wrong thing to say.

'Does he really think we were successful?' Bryant gave a disdainful grunt. 'What about Ruth Singh, and the others who died on Balaklava Street? With all the resources at our disposal, we still couldn't save them. How is that possible?'

'We saved Kallie Owen's life,' said May. 'And we restored two masterpieces to grateful nations.'

'I suppose those beautiful tiles in St Pancras Basin will be drilled out to carry computer cables. On cold nights I wonder about our homeless men. I checked with Betty; nobody has yet called the Birmingham coven. Do you think we did the right thing?'

May thrust his hands into his pockets and

admired the view. 'I know you, Arthur. You like the idea of them taking their chances, being masters of their fate, rather than being stranded at the mercy of bloody-minded immigration officers.'

Heather Allen was awaiting trial for murder, but although the detectives had uncovered motive and opportunity, their evidence hinged on the word of an unreliable witness, who was himself still under suspicion of arson. Perhaps the immigrants could have vouched for Tate, but they had disappeared. It was as Bryant had predicted: everyone of real importance had promptly vanished into the urban labyrinth.

'Did you hear that Kallie's boyfriend finally came back? Picked up a nice tan, apparently. She chucked him out on the street—for the time being, at least.'

'He wanted his independence.' May smiled. 'Our first duty is to protect those at risk. Homeless people arrive every day in the capital, and instead of making them welcome, we shut our doors in their faces. Where will they go, now that the St Pancras Basin is being dug out?' He settled on the bench and studied the bitter blue sky. Unlike his partner, May had always been attracted to light and space.

'I like my cases with fewer loose ends,' Bryant complained. 'I want to know what Ubeda's up to right now, whether he's hatching some new way of filching relics in Egypt. And I want a full signed confession from Heather Allen, preferably acknowledging that I was totally correct in my assumptions. There are no open-and-shut jobs any more. Too many extenuating circumstances to take into consideration. It's a crowded and complicated world.'

'I know what you mean, Arthur. Did I ever tell you why I first became interested in crime?'

'If you did, I've forgotten.'

'I was a sickly child and spent a lot of time in bed, so my parents used to give me Agatha Christie books to read. I became addicted to unusual crimes. At the end of each book, someone would always stand up and announce, "It's very simple, Major Carruthers rewound the vicar's clock and replaced Lady Home-Counties' mackintosh in the belfry *before* hiding the boathook under a tin of caramelized peaches in the fête's jam tent." Christie thought she was writing about ordinary people, but the lives of her characters were filled with these arcane rituals, and they had servants, for God's sake. To me, a poor kid growing up in south London, they all seemed impossibly exotic, and the world was a simple place full of solvable crimes.'

Bryant nodded in recognition of the memory. 'I grew up reading about Fu Manchu, Raffles and the Black Sapper. They were even worse, all Limehouse opium dens, fifth columnists, stolen diamond tiaras and "the grateful thanks of a nation". Of course, we're virtually the only members of the British police force to have actually read a novel, which places us at a disadvantage. If you're in public service, it never pays to reveal a sense of imagination.'

May drained his cup and set it down. 'I suppose that's a good enough reason for staying with the unit. Where else are we going to find cases that aren't just about drunken brawls outside pubs or crackheads stealing from each other? God knows I covered enough of those during the two years we were separated and returned to regular duty. How I hated it.' The unit had once been disbanded on the orders of Margaret Thatcher until it could provide ways of turning a profit. Nobody wanted to remember those times. 'What have we got on today?'

'Ah yes, Raymond's caseload. A couple of Iranian guys found an anaconda in a Bankside fried-chicken outlet—looks like a war between business rivals; a priest set fire to a number of cars at the Elephant and Castle, because Satanists have been causing trouble in a fetish nightclub that's opened in the precinct of his church—Longbright's sorting out that one; the King's Cross Prostitutes' Collective is complaining that the new one-way system is ruining their trade, and they're threatening to reveal a client list that includes several MPs—could we look into it? There's that thing with the deaf circus midget. And of course, your grand-daughter April is starting as our researcher at the unit tomorrow.'

'Perhaps we should take her for a pie at the Nun and Broken Compass. What deaf circus midget?'

'He was a pimp for some Russian dancers who were caught doping greyhounds with tainted cough mixture at Catford Stadium. They hung him inside the bell of St Mary's church until the noise ruptured his eardrums. He's demanding compensation from the bell-ringers, who were bribed to leave the belfry door unlocked.'

'Oh. Business as usual, then.'

'Funny how we've always attracted peculiar cases. Do you remember that fighter pilot during the War who couldn't be placed at a murder site because he'd been found tied to the back of a cow in Regent's Park?'

'My goodness, I'd forgotten about him. Hell of an alibi.'

'*Hell* of an alibi.'

'Yes.' May accepted a length of liquorice from Bryant and chewed it ruminatively. 'I suppose it hasn't been *all* bad.'

'When we were in the St Pancras Basin, I saw something scratched on to the wall of an arch. It showed up in my torchlight. Do you know what *Gezellig* means? It's a Dutch word, one of those words that has no exact equivalent in the English language. It means "the comfort of being with friends". They made their *bonheur* there, their happiness, even in such a depressing place. Everyone has to find peace somewhere. They have to find home.'

'*Gezellig*. I like that. That's like us.'

The pair remained side by side, sitting in silence as the golden sunlight of the morning grew around them.

52

NO PLACE LIKE HOME

Heather sat in the bare white interview room with her bag open at her feet and her compact mirror in her hand, carefully repainting the edges of her lips. It was essential, in every circumstance, to maintain one's poise and keep a smart appearance. There was no reason to stop looking one's best, simply because one had been arrested for multiple murder. No blanket over the head upon emerging from the station, thank you, nothing less than grace under pressure and calm before the cameras.

The room was so absurdly bright; she felt sure that the flaws in her make-up showed. Institutional furniture and hard-faced officers talking to each other about last night's television, as if she wasn't even there. The entire experience was designed to alienate and isolate. But it didn't, because she had never felt at home anywhere—not with her parents, not with her husband, certainly not at Balaklava Street. A numb void opened in her heart the moment her expectations were not met.

Boring, stupid police, guards and doctors. They would only ever see a selfish criminal, when they should have been looking for a disappointed child, promised so much and given so little—not that she expected or demanded sympathy. They would never understand how few options she had been given, and she would never let them see inside, no matter what they did to her. The truth of the matter was that the taking of life had hardly disturbed her at all. It wasn't as if she had attacked someone with a knife in a moment of passion; there had been no moments of passion at all, only the nagging ache of failure, and blinding, debilitating panic.

She studied the bare white walls without emotion. From now on her life would consist of being in communal government rooms like this, but it didn't matter. She had no care for where she lived, because now she lived inside her head.

'You could do with some paintings on these walls,' she stated imperiously to no one in particular. 'You might brighten the place up a little, make it more lived in.'

It was only when no answer came that she realized she would never again find home.

'What has he been painting?' asked Alma Sorrowbridge, peering over Sergeant Longbright's shoulder. The pair of them had decided to tackle the daunting task of clearing up Bryant's study while he was out, and had discovered the half-finished canvas set on an easel beneath a south-facing window in his cavernous new apartment.

'It appears to be an allegorical depiction of the end of the world,' Longbright suggested, stepping back to decipher the chaotic muddle of purples and greens. 'What do you think?'

Alma sniffed with vague disapproval before wielding her J-cloth on his work surface. 'That big naked lady in the middle is a very odd shape.'

'I think he painted her from memory,' said Longbright, tilting her head.

'Then he must be getting Alzheimer's,' Alma told her, spitting on the cloth and settling down to a good scrub.

'John's putting him on a refresher course. They're double-dating tonight. Monica Greenwood and Jackie Quinten.'

'The only toy boys in town with bus passes. Mr Bryant has never been very successful with the ladies. His idea of a chat-up line used to be asking a girl if she'd like to see where he had his operation.'

'What did he show them?'

'The Royal Free Hospital.'

Their laughter could be heard in the street, where the lamps glowed into life, lighting all paths to home.

ABOUT THE AUTHOR

CHRISTOPHER FOWLER is the acclaimed author of twelve previous novels, including the Bryant & May novels *Full Dark House* and *Seventy-Seven Clocks*. He lives in London, where he is at work on his next novel featuring Arthur Bryant and John May, *Ten Second Staircase*. Visit him on the web at www.christopherfowler.co.uk.

"Invulnerable, genial, and crafty," raved the *Los Angeles Times* of the superb—and utterly unique—sleuthing duo of Bryant and May. Now the odd couple of London's Peculiar Crimes Unit returns in a tantalizing new mystery guaranteed to keep you reading late into the night.

Read on for a special early look into Christopher Fowler's **Ten Second Staircase**, coming soon in hardcover from Bantam Books. And don't miss any of the Bryant and May mysteries— look for them at your favorite booksellers!

Ten Second Staircase

A Bryant & May Mystery

CHRISTOPHER FOWLER

On sale summer 2006

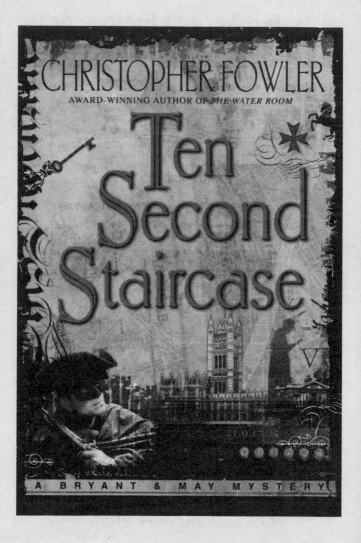

CHRISTOPHER FOWLER

AWARD-WINNING AUTHOR OF *THE WATER ROOM*

Ten Second Staircase

A BRYANT & MAY MYSTERY

Ten Second Staircase

On sale summer 2006

SMALL PROVOCATIONS

'I hope you're not going to be rude and upset everyone again.'

Detective Sergeant Janice Longbright examined her boss for signs of disarray. She scraped some egg from his creased green tie with a crimson nail, then grudgingly granted her approval.

Arthur Bryant took a deep breath and folded his notes back into his jacket. 'I see nothing wrong with speaking my mind. After all, it is a special occasion.' He fixed his DS with a beady, unforgiving eye. 'I rarely get invited to make speeches. People always think I'm going to be insulting. I've never upset anyone before.'

'Perhaps I could remind you of the Mayor's banquet at Mansion House? You told the assembly he had herpes.'

'I said he had a hairpiece. It was a misquote.'

'Well, just remember how overwrought you can get at these events. Did you remember to take your blue pills?' Longbright suspected he had forgotten them because the tablet box was still poking out of his top pocket. 'The doctor warned you it would be easy to muddle them up—'

'I don't need a nurse, thank you. I'll take them afterwards. I haven't quite drifted into senility yet.' Unlike most men, Bryant did not look smarter in a suit. His outfit was several decades out of date and too long in the leg. His shirt collar was far wider than his neck, and the white nimbus of his hair floated up around his prominent ears as though he had been conducting experiments in electricity. Overall, he looked like a soon-to-be-pulped Tussaud's waxwork.

Peering out though a gap in the curtains at the sea of gold-trimmed navy blazers, Sergeant Longbright saw that the auditorium was now entirely filled with pupils. 'It's a very well-heeled audience, Arthur,' she reported back. 'Boys only, that can't be very healthy. All between the ages of fifteen and seventeen. I don't imagine they'll be much interested in crime prevention. You'll have to find a way of reaching them.'

'Teenagers are suspicious of anyone over twenty,' Bryant admitted, brushing tobacco strands from his lapel, 'so how will they feel about me? I thought there were going to be more adults here. Teenagers can smell lies, you know. Their warning flags unfurl at the slightest provocation. A hint of condescension and they bob up like meerkats. Contrary to popular belief, they're more naturally astute than so-called grown-ups. The whole of one's adult life is a gradual process of dulling the sense, Janice. Look how young we all were when we started at the PCU, little more than children ourselves. But we were firing on all synapses, awake to the world.'

Longbright brushed his shoulders with maternal propriety. 'Raymond Land says the sensitive are incapable of action. He reckons we need more thick-skinned recruits.'

'Which is why our acting chief would be better employed in parking control, or some public service which you could train a moderately attentive bottle-nosed dolphin to perform.' Bryant had little patience with those who frowned on his abstract methods. Critics offered him nothing. They made the most senior detective of London's Peculiar Crimes Unit as irritable as a wasp in a bottle and as stubborn as a doorstop.

'The school magazine is out there waiting to take your picture. They've seen you on TV, don't forget. You're a bit of a celebrity these days. Show me how you look.' Longbright jerked his tie a little straighter and pulled his sleeves to length. 'Good enough, I suppose, I need photographic evidence of you in a suit, even though it's thirty years old. Make sure you stick to Raymond's brief and talk about the specifics of crime prevention. Don't forget the CAPO initiative—we have to reach them while they're in the highest risk category.' Seventeen-year-olds were more likely to become victims of street crime than any other population segment. Their complex pattern of allegiance to different urban tribes was more confusing than French court etiquette—territorial invasion, lack of respect, the wrong clothes, the wrong ethnicity, attitudes exaggerated by hormones, chemistry, geography and simple bad timing.

'My notes are a little more abstract than Raymond might wish,' Bryant warned.

Longbright threw him a hopeless look. 'I thought he vetted your script.'

'I meant to run it by him last night, but I'd

promised to drive Alma to her sister's in Tooting. She fell off her doorstep while she was red-leading it, and needed a bread poultice for her knee.'

'Surely the head of the department ranks above your landlady.'

'Not in terms of intelligence, I assure you.'

'You should have shown Raymond what you're planning to say, Arthur. You know how concerned he is about the media attention we've been receiving.'

The PCU had recently been the subject of a television documentary, and not all of the press articles following in its wake had been complimentary.

'I couldn't stick to Raymond's guidelines on the history of crime-fighting because I don't want to talk down to my audience. They're supposed to be smart kids, the top five percent of the education system. I don't want them to get fidgety.'

'Just fix them with the angry stare of yours. Go on—everyone's waiting for you.'

The elderly detective took an unsteady step forward, then balked. He could feel a cold wall of expectancy emanating from the crowded auditorium. The hum of audience conversation parried his determination, stranding him at the edge of the stage.

'What's the matter now?' demanded Longbright, exasperated.

'No one in our family was good with the young,' Bryant wavered. 'When I was little, my father tried to light a cigarette while holding me and a pint of bitter, and burned the top of my head. All of our childhood problems were sorted out with a clout round the ear. It's a wonder I can name the kings of England.'

'Don't view them as youngsters, Arthur, they're at the age when they think they know everything, so talk to them as if they do. The head teacher has already introduced you. They'll start slow handclapping if you don't get out there.' It occurred to her that because Bryant had attended a lowly state school in Whitechapel, he might actually be intimidated by appearing before an exclusive group of private pupils from upper-middle-class homes.

Bryant dragged out his dogeared notes and smoothed them nervously. 'I thought at least John could have been here to support me.'

'You know he had a hospital appointment, now stop making a fuss.' She placed a broad hand in the small of his back and firmly propelled him onto the stage.

Bryant stepped unsteadily into the spotlight, encouraged by a line of welcoming teachers. Having recently achieved a level of public fame for his capture of the Water Room killer, he knew it was time for him to enjoy his moment of recognition, but today he felt exposed and vulnerable.

The detective wiped his watery blue eyes and surveyed the hall of pale varnished oak from the podium. Absurdly youthful faces lifted to study him, and he saw the great age gulf that lay between lectern and audience. How could he ever expect to reach them? He remembered the war; they would have trouble remembering the nineteen-eighties. The sea of blue and gold, the expensive haircuts, the low susurrus of well-educated voices, teachers standing at the end of every third row like benign prison guards. It was surprisingly intimidating.

Most of the students had broken off their conversation to acknowledge his arrival, but some were still chatting. He fired a rattling cough in the microphone, a magnified explosion that echoed into a squeal of feedback. Now they ceased talking and looked up in a single battalion, assessing him.

He could feel the surf of confidence radiating from these bored young men, and knew he would have to work for their attention. The boys of St Crispins were not here to offer him respect; he was in the employ, and they would choose to listen, or ignore him. For one terrifying second, the power of the young was made palpable. Bryant was an outsider, an interloper. He rustled his notes and began to speak.

'My name is Arthur Bryant,' he told them unsteadily, 'and together with my partner John May, I run a small detective division known as the Peculiar Crimes Unit.' He settled his gaze in the centre of the audience, focussing on the most insolent and jaded faces. 'Time moves fast. When the unit was first founded, much detection work was still based on Victorian principles. Anything else was untried and experimental. We were one of several divisions created in a new spirit of innovation. Because we're mainly academics, we don't use traditional law enforcement methods. We are not a part of the Met; they are hard-working, sensible men and women who handle the daily fallout of poverty and hardship. The PCU doesn't deal with life's failures. The criminals we hunt have already proven successful.' His attention locked on a group of four boys who seemed on the verge of tuning out his lecture. He found himself departing from the script in order to speak directly to them. He raised his voice.

'Let's take an example. Say one of you lads in the middle there gets burgled at home. The police handle cases in order of priority, just like doctors. They send a beat constable or a mobile uniformed officer around to ask you for details of the break-in and a list of what's missing. They are not trained as investigative detectives, so you have to wait for a specialist to take fingerprints, which they'll try to match with those of a registered felon. If no one is discovered, your loss is merely noted and set against the chance of the future recovery of your goods—a possibility that shrinks with each passing hour. The system only works for its best exemplars. But at the Peculiar Crimes Unit, we adopt a radically different approach.' As he still seemed to have their attention, Bryant decided to forge ahead with his explication.

'We ask ourselves a fundamental question: What is a crime? How far does its moral dimension extend? Is it simply an act that works against the common good? If you are starving and steal from a rich man's larder, should you be punished less than if you were not hungry? All crime is driven by some kind of need. Once, those needs were simple—food, shelter, warmth, the basic assurances of survival. But as soon as our needs are taken care of, new crimes appear within society. As we become more sophisticated, so do the reasons for our misdeeds. Now that we are warm and fed, we covet something more complex: power. Spending power, power over others, the power to be noticed. And sometimes that power can be achieved by violating the accepted laws of the land. So criminal sophistication requires sophisticated methods of detection. That's where specialist units like the Peculiar Crimes Unit come in. Think of internet fraud, and you'll find it is being matched by equally subtle methods of detection that require as much knowledge as the criminal's. I'm sure you boys know far more about the internet than your parents, but does that place you at less of a risk?'

He's off to a decent start, thought Longbright from the wings. *A bit all over the place, but no doubt he'll draw it all together and make his point.*

'Fraud, robbery, assault and murder are all cause-and-effect crimes requiring carefully targeted treatment. But all modern lawlessness carries the seeds of a strange paradox within it, for just as ancient crimes appear in cunning new versions, others appear entirely unmotivated. One thinks of vandalism. Some will have you believe it was invented in the postwar period, but not so. Acts of vandalism have been recorded in every sophisticated civilization; the defacing of statues was quite common in ancient Rome. Now, though, we are reaching a new peak of motiveless transgression. Criminality has once more assumed the kind of dark edge that existed in London during the eighteenth century. London was always the home of mob rule. The public voiced their opinions about whether it was right for a man to hang just as much as the judge. The joyous assembly would jeer or cheer a prisoner's final speech at Tyburn's triple tree. They would choose to condemn a wrongdoer or venerate him. Pamphlets filled with prints and poems would be produced in a criminal's honour. He would achieve lasting fame as a noble champion, his exploits retold as brave deeds, and there was nothing that governments could do to prevent it. Criminals became celebrities because they were seen to be fighting the old order, kicking back at an oppressive system.' Bryant eyed his audience like a pirate frightening cabin boys with tales of dancing skeletons. 'Often, thieves' necks would fail to break when they were dropped from the Tyburn gallows, and the crowd would cut down a half-hanged man to set him free, because they felt he had paid for his crimes. They rioted against the practice of passing bodies over to the anatomists, and pelted bungling hangmen with bricks. If a murderer conducted himself nobly as he ascended the gallows stairs, he would become more respected than his accusers. But time has robbed us of these gracious renegades. Last week, less than a quarter of a mile from here, in Smithfield, a schoolboy was stabbed through the heart for his mobile phone. An elderly man on a tube platform in Holborn was kicked to death for bumping into someone. These criminals are not to be venerated.'

A murmur of recollection rippled through the auditorium.

'Statistics show that the nature of English crime is reverting to its oldest habits. In a country where so many desire status and wealth, petty annoyances can spark disproportionately violent behaviour. We become frustrated because we feel powerless, invisible, unheard. We crave celebrity, but that's not easy to come by, so we settle for notoriety. Envy and bitterness drive a new breed of lawbreakers, replacing the old motives of poverty and the need for escape. But how do you solve crimes which no longer have traditional motives?'

He's warming the audience up nicely, and he's still got their attention, decided Longbright, feeling for a chair at the side of the stage. *Let's hope he remembers to talk about Raymond's initiatives and can get all the way through without saying anything offensive.* She knew how volatile her boss could be, but now was the time for Bryant to exercise restraint. For once, the fortunes of the Peculiar Crimes Unit were on the rise. Indeed, they had been ever since a remarkable murder in a quiet north London street had placed them all in the public eye. Arthur's partner, John May, had appeared on a late-night programme discussing the importance of the case with several bad-tempered social commentators, a number of articles in *The Guardian* and *The Times* had examined the case in detail, government funding for the coming year had miraculously appeared, and mercifully no one outside the unit knew the reality of the case's conclusion; if they did, Longbright doubted that any of them would have survived with their careers intact. Arthur Bryant's decision to break the law in order to close the investigation had been so contentious that Longbright had turned down the BBC's offer to feature her in their film, in case she accidentally let slip the truth.

Basking in the glow of the publicity, Bryant had been asked to deliver a lecture to St. Crispin's Boys School, the exclusive private academy founded by a devout Christian group in 1653 in St John Street, Clerkenwell, and had shyly accepted.

Longbright turned her attention back to the stage. 'What we have here is a fundamental alteration in the definition of morality,' Bryant argued. 'What does it now mean to have a moral conscience? Do we need to develop different values from those of our parents? Most of you think you can distinguish right from wrong, but morality requires information to feed it, so you build your own internal moral system from the intelligence you receive, probably the hardest thing anyone ever has to do, judging by the number of times the system fails.

'In London's rural suburbs, not far from here, middle-class Thames Valley towns like Weybridge and Henley are awash with a new kind of malicious cruelty. Here the system appears to be failing. The criminals are not suffering inner-city deprivation, nor are they gang members protecting their turf through internecine wars based on divisions in ethnicity. They are wealthy white males facing futures filled with opportunities. So why are they turning to unprovoked violence and murder? Part of a generation has somehow become unmoored from its foundations, and no one knows how to draw it back from the harmful shallows. You all face complex pressures, problems that gentlemen of my advanced age are scarcely able to imagine. From the day you were born, someone has been targetting you as a potential market. Your attention has become fragmented. You are offered no solitude, no peace, no time for reflection. You are forced to create your own methods of escape. Some choose alcohol and narcotics, other form social cliques that combat the status quo. All of you in this hall are in danger. Many people of my age would suggest that you desire to break the law not because you've had a hard time growing up, but because you haven't. You've been spoiled with everything you ever wanted, but you still want more.'

He's forgotten the script, Longbright worried, *and he's stabbing his finger at them. At this rate he'll have them throwing things at him.* Some of the pupils were fidgeting in annoyance. They were clearly uncomfortable with the hectoring tenor of Bryant's sermon. The old detective hadn't given a lecture in years, and had forgotten the importance of keeping the audience on his side. *Keep it light in tone but heavy on factual data,* Land had warned, *be positive but don't say any-thing controversial. Remember, their parents are fee-paying voters with a lot of clout.*

Bryant's raised voice brought her back to attention. 'Well, I don't believe that,' he was saying. 'Children today have a far more complicated time growing up that I ever did. At the Peculiar Crimes Unit, we have the time and capability to see beyond stock answers and standard procedures. We claw our way to the roots of the crime, and by understanding its cause, we hope to provide solutions.'

As the audience half-heartedly pattered their hands, Longbright rose and made her way from the stage, back to the stand at the rear of the hall, where she accepted a polystyrene cup of coffee. Only the question-and-answer session was left now. Longbright had tried to talk her superior out of holding one, bearing in mind his capacity for argument, but half a dozen teenagers had already raised their hands. There was a palpable attitude of aggression and defiance in the pupils' body language.

'You say it's a question of morals,' said a pale, elongated boy with expensively layered blonde hair.

'Stand up and give your surname,' barked the teacher at the end of the row.

The boy unfolded himself from his seat with difficulty and faced the audience. 'Sorry, Sir. Gosling.' He turned to Bryant. 'Are you saying we're the ones who commit crimes because we lack a moral code?'

'Of course not,' Bryant replied. 'I'm just saying that it's understandable you're confused. You know that sneakers are made in Korea for starvation wages, so you buy a pair from a company promising to make their product locally for a fair price. Then you discover that the company you chose destroyed ancient farmland to build their factory. How do you feel about your purchase now? You've been lied to, so why shouldn't you commit a victimless crime and steal them? You're given horrible role models, your divorced parents are having sex with people you hate and have given up caring what you do, you're expected to take an interest in the lifestyles of singers who'll make more money than you will ever see, so its no wonder you start taking drugs and behaving like animals.'

The hall erupted. Longbright covered her face with her hands. Bryant had never been much of a diplomat.

A small lad with a pustular complexion rose sharply. 'Parfitt. You just don't like the fact that we're young, and still have a chance to change the world your contemporaries wrecked for us.'

A heavyset boy with shiny red checks, cropped black hair and bat ears jumped angrily to attention. 'That's right, we're the ones—'

'Surname!' barked his master, leaning angrily forward.

'Jezzard—you always blame the young, but we're the ones who'll have to correct the mistakes of the older generation.'

'My dear boy, don't you see that you no longer possess the means for changing the world?' replied Bryant, adopting a tone of infuriating airiness. 'You've been disempowered, old chap. It's all over. The things you desire have become entirely unattainable, and you take revenge for that by being furious with your seniors all the time.'

Another boy, slender and dark, with feral eyes and

narrow teeth, launched to his feet. 'You're accusing us when you know nothing about us, Mr Bryant—nothing!'

'*Name!*' squealed the teacher on the row.

'Billings. It's not us who's the problem, it's you. Everyone knows the police are corrupt racists—'

Now several more pupils stood up together, all speaking at once. Their teachers continued to demand that they identify themselves, but were ignored. Sides were swiftly being taken. Bryant had managed to divide the hall into factions. He threw up his hands in protest as the pupils barracked him.

'You condescend to us because you don't have a clue—'

'You victimize those who can't protect themselves—'

'Why is it that young people never want to take responsibility for their actions?' protested Bryant, as students popped up from their chairs in every section of the hall.

'Just because you messed up your own society—'

'Why should we be blamed for your greed when—'

'We're just starting out,' shouted Parfitt, 'and you're trying to make us sound as cynical as you!'

'I am not cynical, I simply know better,' Bryant insisted, trying to be heard, 'and I can tell from experience exactly how many of you will fall by the wayside and die before you progress to adulthood, because the cyclical nature of your short lives is as immutable as that of a dragonfly.'

There were so many things wrong with this last sentence that the Detective Sergeant could not bear to reflect on it, and could only watch the response helplessly. The lanky boy, Gosling, was the first to kick back his chair and leave. His friends swiftly followed suit. The distant authority of the teachers collapsed into panicked attempts at censorship as chairs fell across the centre of the audience, causing a clangorous ripple that quickly spread throughout the hall.

Longbright had been worried that Raymond Land might get to hear of the debacle. Now she was more concerned about getting Bryant out alive.

IT'S NO MYSTERY...

Bantam Dell has the finest collection of sleuths around, from professional P.I.s to unwilling amateurs

SEAN DOOLITTLE

BURN $6.99/$10.99

RAIN DOGS $6.99/$9.99

CHRISTOPHER FOWLER

FULL DARK HOUSE
$6.99/$10.99

SEVENTY-SEVEN CLOCKS
$6.99/$10.99

THE WATER ROOM
$6.99/$9.99

RON FAUST

DEAD MEN RISE UP NEVER
$6.99/$10.99

SEA OF BONES
$6.99/$10.99

THE BLOOD RED SEA
$6.99/$10.99

VICKI LANE

SIGNS IN THE BLOOD
$6.99/$10.99

ART'S BLOOD
$6.99/$9.99

PAUL LEVINE

SOLOMON VS. LORD
$5.99/$7.99

THE DEEP BLUE ALIBI
$6.99/$9.99

VICTOR GISCHLER

GUN MONKEYS $6.99/$10.99

THE PISTOL POETS $6.99/$10.99

SUICIDE SQUEEZE $6.99/$9.99

SHOTGUN OPERA $6.99/$9.99

Ask for these titles wherever books are sold, or visit us online at *www.bantamdell.com* for ordering information.

BD MC2 4/06